SWEET |

Hortense is a cynic. Love is great and all that, but it's money that makes the world go round. Maxie is in love with Hortense. She won't give him the time of day, but he knows if he can just put together a big real estate deal, she'll be his—at least for awhile. One night, Maxie introduces Hortense to Hugh, his best friend, who also falls in love with her. Hugh is a realist, willing to take Hortense on her own terms. This is the story of three lives that collide one December in New York City—Hortense, the dance instructor who knows how to look out for number one; Maxie, the mama's boy who just wants his shot at happiness; and Hugh, who wrecks it for all of them.

LIFE AND DEATH OF A TOUGH GUY

Joey Kasow is a skinny Jewish kid growing up in the 1920's in Hell's Kitchen. Tormented by the Irish thugs in the neighborhood, he eventually gains their begrudging respect and is allowed to join their gang, the Badgers. Joey grows up tough. He knows he's got to take whatever is dished out to him to stay in the gang. He learns how to inflict pain—he learns how to kill. And gradually he works his way up the ladder to become the Spotter's enforcer. He is now Joey Case. But Joey can't escape his past, falling in love with innocent young Sadie Madofsky, his refuge from the brutal world around him. All Joey wants is to get ahead—but the Spotter has other plans for him.

BENJAMIN APPEL BIBLIOGRAPHY

FICTION

Brain Guy [reprinted as The Enforcer] (1934)

Four Roads to Death [reprinted as Gold and Flesh] (1935)

Runaround (1937)

The Power House (1939)

The Dark Stain (1943)

But Not Yet Slain (1947)

Fortress in the Rice (1951)

Plunder (1952)

Hell's Kitchen [stories; reprinted as Alley Kids] (1952)

Dock Walloper [stories] (1953)

Sweet Money Girl (1954)

Life and Death of a Tough Guy [reprinted as Teenage Mobster] (1955)

Alley Kids [stories; orig pub as Hell's Kitchen] (1956)

Teenage Mobster [orig pub as Life and Death of a Tough Guy] (1957)

The Raw Edge (1958)

The Funhouse [reprinted as The Death Master] (1959)

A Big Man, a Fast Man (1961)

A Time of Fortune (1963)

The Enforcer [orig pub as Brain Guy] (1972)

Gold and Flesh [orig pub as Four Roads to Death] (1972)

The Death Master [orig pub as The Funhouse] (1974)

The Devil and W. Kaspar (1977)

Heart of Ice [adapted; fairy tale] (1977)

Hell's Kitchen [novel] (1977)

POETRY

Mixed Vintage (1929)

NON-FICTION

The People Talk (1940; reprinted 1972, 1982 as The People Talk: American Voices from the Great Depression)

We Were There in the Klondike Gold Rush (1956)

We Were There at the Battle for Bataan (1957)

We Were There With Cortez and Montezuma (1959)

The Illustrated Book About South America Including Mexico and Central America (1960)

Shepherd of the Sun: The Story of the Incas (1961)

With Many Voices: Europe Talks About America (1963)

Hitler: From Power to Ruin (1964)

Ben-Gurion's Israel (1965)

Man and Magic: Magical Practices in All Ages Throughout the World (1966)

Why the Russians are the Way They Are (1966)

Why the Chinese are the Way They Are (1968)

The Age of Dictators (1968)

The Fantastic Mirror: Science Fiction Across the Ages (1969)

Why the Japanese are the Way They Are (1973)

Ben Shahn: Prophet With a Brush [article] (1974)

Across the Zodiac: The Story of a Wrecked Record [ed by Percy Greg; abridged & afterword by Appel] (1978)

SWEET MONEY GIRL
LIFE AND DEATH OF A TOUGH GUY

TWO NOVELS BY
BENJAMIN APPEL

STARK
HOUSE

Stark House Press • Eureka California

SWEET MONEY GIRL / LIFE AND DEATH OF A TOUGH GUY

Published by Stark House Press
2200 O Street
Eureka, CA 95501
griffinskye3@sbcglobal.net
www.starkhousepress.com

ISBN: 1-933586-26-5
ISBN-13: 978-1-933586-26-7

Text set in Figural. Heads set in Phoenix American.
Cover design and layout by Mark Shepard, home.comcast.net/~shepdesign
Proofreading by Rick Ollerman

The publisher wishes to thank Carla Appel for all her help on this project.

First Stark House Press Edition: April 2009
0 9 8 7 6 5 4 3 2 1

INTRODUCTION
BY CARLA APPEL

If only I had paid attention to my father when he discussed his writing. If only I had listened, instead of tuning it out, taking it for granted, assuming it would go on indefinitely as background conversation around the dinner table. When you're 13 or 14 as I was when he wrote these two novels, you don't pay attention. You're too busy growing up and you don't suspect that 53 years later you will be quizzed on the information you disregarded.

I did finally start to pay attention, when it was too late to ask him questions, reading all his novels when I was an adult, so I can make some guesses about what he had in mind while writing *Life and Death of a Tough Guy* and *Sweet Money Girl*. Both deal with small-time people trying to make it big in New York, my father's city and frequent backdrop. In both he manages to make you sympathize, against your better judgment, with the lowlifes who are his main characters. In both novels the lofty themes of loyalty and betrayal are played out in gritty settings and thuggish action.

But any other half-way alert reader could make the same observations. What I am able to add comes from having had Benjamin Appel for a father. For example, a small piece of family history: my father's brother Dave's experience catching rides on freight cars, hoboing across America as a young man, is incorporated in a brief episode in *Life and Death*. More importantly, the whole opening section of *Life and Death*, the childhood of the chief thug Joey, comes straight from my father's childhood in Hell's Kitchen, even to the name of the earliest gang, the 1-4-Alls. Although he was never arrested, never killed anyone, and never stole anything other than apples from pushcarts in Paddy's Market, he knew people who did. The point at which the action of the book veers off from autobiography into fiction is hard to spot. In fact, upon reading my father's novels, friends have asked me how the parent I describe to them, loving, caring, worrying and fretting over me, could have written these books? How does my characterization of him square with the cynical, murderous, conniving people he wrote about as convincingly as if he were one? To which I can only reply, he had a good imagination.

My father was a politically aware man. Out of his concern for social justice come these descriptions of the effects of a greedy society on its underclass, the circumstances that can turn ordinary people into crooks. He was always smuggling some larger idea into his world of tough guys, gangsters, and dames. In

Life and Death, in addition to the fast and brutal action, you get the trajectory of organized crime in New York; in *Sweet Money Girl*, a sense of history in the changing, post World War II city.

It is difficult to put my father's writing into a box. Other than similar geographical settings, *Sweet Money Girl* is a very different sort of novel from *Life and Death*. It is the only one of his 15 in which the core is a hard-boiled love story, the chief hustler a woman. It is the only one in which each chapter is narrated from the point of view of one of the three main characters, a device my father's old friend Kenneth Fearing used in *The Big Clock* and many other novels. He may also have had in mind the Japanese film "Rashomon," in which the same events are presented as they are understood by different people, in sequence. "Rashomon" was one of his favorite films. He often referred to it as an example of the subjectivity of truth.

Sweet Money Girl is the only one of his novels into which my father injects his opinions on a topic seemingly unrelated to the main thrust of the story, in this case his disdain for contentless abstract art and mindless art critics. In 1954 "modern" art was a hot topic, especially in Roosevelt, New Jersey, the small town which was like an unofficial artist's colony, where we lived for many years and where my father was fast friends with several fellow Rooseveltians who happened to be painters of the realistic school.

He occasionally used names of friends and relatives, slightly altered, for minor characters; I note a mobster named "Ed Roscamino" in *Life and Death*, in actuality a friend who lent him his car and a spare room in his house as a studio. *Sweet Money Girl* is full of names familiar to me, chief among them "Sophia Marsh," one of the dance hall teachers/call girls. This is my mother's name, Sophie Marshak, thinly disguised. Did my mom laugh at finding herself portrayed on paper as a quasi-prostitute? Well, she was already familiar with my father's outrageous sense of humor. Other Roosevelt friends appear briefly as a doctor, a window cleaner, and a race horse, this last one of his best friends, the artist David Stone Martin, who in real life designed the cover for the first edition of *Life and Death*.

Maybe it is just as well I didn't read his novels when I was a kid. I would have been shocked, unable to get past the hard-edged characters and frightening situations. As an adult I can appreciate the reality behind the unsavory surface. And now when I reread his books I sense the irreverent, informal, wisecracking personality behind them. I can hear his voice.

APRIL 19, 2008
WASHINGTON, D.C.

SWEET MONEY GIRL

BY BENJAMIN APPEL

To Rowie, Jack, and Sylvia
and all the dance-hall
boys and girls

I: THE WITNESSES

HUGH

The truth? Who knows what the truth is? I used to think Maxie was crazy wanting to marry a girl like Hortense. But now I'm not so sure. Hortense was the kind of girl who only came alive in the night, when all the neons are shining, and all the pretty moths are fluttering. She had the big eyes, the passionate mouth, the dream-girl shape with which the advertising-agency guys tease the subway riders. As for Maxie, he was Joe Subway himself. Those two looked as if they didn't belong in the same room with each other.

But when I think of them now, I get an image of one of those lovers' hearts scratched with a stick into the West Side sidewalks when the concrete's wet, and long since hardened. Nothing can rub them out—lovers' hearts scratched in haste, with their enclosed pairs of initials. Sidewalk poems, they endure. So it was with Maxie. The enduring hope in him might have changed the moth into a wife. Who knows?

Well, let me begin. Maxie, Hortense, and me.... Yes, me. I was no observer on the side lines. It was a three-way street that Hortense, Maxie, and I traveled that year after the war....

The year was 1946. I was twenty-seven, back from war, and my one ambition was to live in the big city. "Hightstown's just forty-nine miles from New York," my father tried to argue with me. He wanted me in the family business. There was the lumberyard in Hightstown that my grandfather had founded and the new aluminum-foil factory near Trenton in which my family owned almost one third of the stock. My only brother, John, was a dentist in Trenton, so my father was really anxious. "I'll give you your own car, Hugh," my father said. "The way you drive, you can get to New York in an hour."

But it wasn't a question of mileage. My home town is a farmers' town, with one movie and two banks, surrounded by potato fields, apple orchards, and a huge population of chickens. When the late movie gets out, Main Street isn't too different from Main Street, say, in Kansas. "Thanks," I said, "but I'd like to get my degree first before I settle down."

"What degree?" my father said sarcastically. "And in what?"

I had to laugh. My father had a point. Before the war I had completed three years at two colleges and—to continue the statistical approach—I'd played around with at least five futures. As a freshman at Rutgers, I'd thought of becoming a doctor or a dentist like my older brother, John, but halfway through I was writing for the newspaper and thinking of journalism. The next year I transferred to Michigan and for a while I kind of fancied myself as an overseas correspondent and then as a State Department attaché or an executive for some corporation in South America or the Middle East. I could see myself spotlighted against the exotic backgrounds of the world, with women to match.... If I seem cynical about my prewar fantasies, it isn't because the war changed me so drastically. In my case, the war simply speeded up a process of self-revelation that had already begun in college, the realization that there were two of me. As in every man.

There was the former waist gunner of a B-24 Liberator, who believed in taking what he could today, for tomorrow might be *Der Tag*. And there was the Hightstown kid, still dewy-eyed about life, who with the war over could still get excited at the idea of living in New York City. In a way, it was like going to college again for the first—and last—time. "I want a degree, I said to my father.

I registered at the N.Y.U. School of Commerce. Then I had lunch with Maxie. Maxie Dehn had been the only New Yorker in our crew, Sergeant Maxie Dehn, ball gunner. He was much older than any of us, thirty-two or thirty-three even then, and of course we had all called him Pop. Unlike the rest of us, he'd gone to war with a solid bank account. He had worked for years for a real-estate firm in Manhattan. It was all very convenient for us. We borrowed his money for our dates, and ungratefully we kidded him about his own taste in women. It had struck us as humorous that a New Yorker should rate so low as a ladies' man. Even in newly liberated Rome, where the girls were bright as ribbons and about as easy to tie up, Maxie'd been seen with what our navigator, Ping, had described as "the fatlegs with mustaches."

"My father won't give me a cent," I told Maxie at lunch. "Thank God for the GI Bill of Rights."

"Where you going to live?" Maxie asked me.

"Where can I find a cheap room? You're a real-estate man."

"Hugh, remember what I used to say?" he reminded me. "How if any of you guys got to New York you could stay with me?"

"For a short visit that would've been fine. Thanks, Pop."

"Forget this Pop stuff. Look, Hugh. Why don't you move in with me?"

"I can't do that, Maxie. Thanks."

"Why not? There's only Mamma and me, and we've got plenty of room."

"I couldn't impose on you."

"Impose what?" he said. "You sound like a guy from the sticks. Impose."

If anyone looked like a lifelong and bona fide resident of the sticks, it was Maxie Dehn, who had been born and bred in Manhattan. He didn't look like a New Yorker or what out-of-towners expect New Yorkers to look like, although he talked like one. He had a small neat blonde face, almost too neat. His blonde hair was thinning and he had slicked it down with some kind of hair preserver. It shone, his hair, and it contributed to his over-all appearance, which was that of a piece of colorless glass. "You move in with us," he insisted.

I couldn't argue with him. Maybe I didn't try too hard.

Mamma or Mrs. Dehn owned the house where they lived, a five-story brownstone on West 47th Street between Eighth and Ninth avenues. It was another tenement street, but to me it was fascinating. You could eat Spanish food on Maxie's street or you could eat Greek food. Up near the corner of Eighth Avenue there was a little place whose plate glass let the whole world know that this was "Prof. Mazzochetti, Originator of the Spaghetti System." Many Italians and Irish lived in the tenements. There were also a few old-time German families like the Dehns, who remembered the days when this West Side neighborhood had been known as Hell's Kitchen. To the Puerto Ricans, coming in off the flying crates with their banjos, Hell's Kitchen wasn't even a name. All day long the traffic of the city rolled west toward the Hudson River and the Lincoln Tunnel under the river, and in the still night when there was no traffic you could hear the boat whistles. I would listen to them and think how fine it was that the war was over and I didn't need my father's help, and how wonderful it was to be living in the heart of New York. My room was on a shaft, the single window dark and gloomy even in the daytime, but I didn't feel shut in. For all about me were millions of people, all kinds of people. Just a few steps away there was Eighth Avenue, with its tough bars and bar girls, Times Square and Broadway and the Broadway crowds, and to the east, Fifth and Madison and Park Avenues, with expensive and beautiful girls in taxis, their faces seen behind the glass, glassed in like hothouse flowers, returning to haunt my room in the shaft.

The second night after I'd moved in with the Dehns, Maxie asked me into his room. He shut the door and, grinning foolishly, showed me the photograph of a smiling girl with dark smooth hair and dark eyes, a very pretty girl. "That's Hortense, and if things work out, you'll be my best man," he said all in one breath.

"You should break news like that gradual," I said to him, amazed. "Very gradual, Maxie."

Still grinning that big foolish grin, he said, "Keep your voice down, will you, Hugh? Mamma'll hear us."

"Don't tell me she's against this lovely creature?"

"Don't give me the old Pierson sarcasm," he said seriously. He looked at me, his eyes pale and blue and worried, and I looked at him. Maxie and a pinup— it was unbelievable.

"Your mother's against her?" I said slowly. "Why?"

"Because Hortense's a dancer. She teaches dancing, I mean. But you'd think she was in one of those buy-a-ticket joints over on Broadway."

"Where does she teach?"

"The George Lawrence School. You've seen their ads, Hugh?"

Who hadn't? Ads always featuring a Hollywood-type couple. They were popular, and you, too, could be popular if you became a pupil at the George

Lawrence School of the Dance. I walked to Maxie's dresser, where Hortense's photograph was tilted against the mirror. I looked at her smiling pretty face and I thought of Maxie's fat Italian sweethearts. "So you decided to become popular, Maxie?"

It was the wrong thing to say, for it killed all his confidences for that evening.

Later on in the week, when Maxie left the house for his dancing instruction, it was Mamma Dehn's turn. We had both been reading in the kitchen. She put down her German-language *Zeitung* and nodded approvingly at my thick book on business management. "You read books, Hugh," she said with a sigh. Education was a sacred cow in the Dehn household, where Maxie had only finished high school while Mamma Dehn's own schooling in the old country hadn't gone much beyond the three R's. "It is fine, it is good to read books," she said in her husky accent, which made her English sound like a German that somehow I could understand. With Mamma Dehn I always felt like a linguist.

"I read for my classes, Mrs. Dehn."

"Why do you not remember to call me Mamma, like Maxie?"

"I will," I promised.

"Ach, you have the future, but Maxie—he goes out without the hat! A cold he wants, and for who, for what? For a no-good dancer!"

I was astonished at her sudden outburst. Her entire appearance had changed, too. Mamma Dehn was a small dumpy woman with graying blonde hair combed back tightly from her forehead—the scrubbed German type. Usually she looked as if she'd dipped herself and her personality into the same foamy white detergent in which she washed her dishes. But now her eyes had dulled, her thin lips gnawing against each other. She seemed soiled, even unclean. "A no-good dancer," she muttered. "A street woman, you will please excuse the expression," she added hastily. "I have seen her, belief me!"

Astonished as I was, I realized that the two Dehns must have agreed not to discuss Hortense in my presence. At supper tonight they had presented a front that might have been labeled: All Is Sweetness and Light in This Home. We had talked about the mild September weather and Maxie's brother, Pete, and his sister, Johanna, and their families, about my classes at N.Y.U. and Maxie's position with the Jacob Groteclose real-estate firm, where he worked.

"I have seen her!" Mamma Dehn repeated mournfully. "I know what I say. I have seen her."

"Did Maxie bring her here?"

She threw up her spotless hands, and with a kind of horror stared about her spotless kitchen. The kitchen was Mamma's pride and joy, the main room in the apartment, or railroad flat, to use Maxie's expression. It overlooked the back yard, the bedrooms strung behind it like so many boxcars, the front room or parlor on the street. The kitchen was the room where the family lived as well as ate. The linoleum floor shone, the dishes sparkled in the cupboard, the refrigerator and gas range were always a dazzling snowy white. On the walls, as a final testimonial, there were framed German mottos: *Arbeit Macht Das Leben Suss,* Work Makes Life Sweet, and *Sternenmusik and Glaube,* Music of the Stars and Faith; the letters had been hand-stitched and embroidered by Mamma Dehn herself.

"Here?" she whispered in horror. "Here in my house? How can you ask such a thing, God forbid!"

"I'm sorry," I said stupidly, not knowing what else to say.

"Sorry, sorry, everybody is sorry. But to break a mother's heart...." Her voice trailed off, her head lowered.

"I'm sorry."

Her eyes lifted to mine. They were pale and blue like Maxie's. Wet and moist now. She wasn't crying, but I was afraid she would be in another second. "I went to see this woman," she said.

"You did?"

"Maxie didn't tell you? You his best friend from the war?"

"No, he didn't tell me."

"Ach, he still has shame!" she exclaimed. "Hugh, I will tell you, I must! When he begins with this woman I don't say nothing. He is home from the war, yes? War, war. Yes, the war! I do not like it but I say nothing, but when he speaks to marry this woman—to throw away his life for such a woman!" She shook her head violently, as if Hortense's photograph in Maxie's room had come to life and stepped into her kitchen. "I go to her, to the fancy George Lawrence. Leave my son alone, I beg from her. So what does she do, this woman, this no-good dancer? She has the nerve to ask me questions. Such questions, like everything is her business. Am I his mother? she asks me. Am I his mother! Who then is Maxie's mother? And where do we liff, and are we rich people? Everything is her business, so I tell her to mind her own good-for-nothing business and to leave my son alone!"

I didn't know what to say, so I listened.

"For one month, one whole month, you will not believe this, Maxie, my own son, he does not speak to me. This from my own son I have received in my old age!" She stared at me as if I were somehow to blame. "Promise me!" she demanded suddenly.

"Promise what?"

"Promise to tell me if Maxie speaks of marrying this woman."

I was Maxie's friend, not Mamma's. "Mrs. Dehn," I said quickly, "I sympathize with you, but I don't want to hear any more."

"No? Why not? You are his friend, I am his mother."

"I don't want to mix into this, Mrs. Dehn."

Her staring eyes made me feel uncomfortable. Then she sighed. "All right, all right. But you can still call me Mamma. Ach, to throw away his life for such a woman...."

Mamma Dehn had a mother's hunch. Her son was ready to throw his life away, if by life is meant all the respectable things and habits valued so highly by the Mamma Dehns of this world. And although I didn't know it then, I, too, was ready to scrap the respectable future I was working toward, no matter how vaguely, by attending classes at the N.Y.U. School of Commerce.

I was more tactful when Maxie again spoke to me about Hortense. It was an unbelievable story I had from him. Unbelievable, I thought. Then I remembered what my brother John had once told me about a friend of his. This man not only had run off with another man's wife, but had helped himself to his partner's money. I remembered my brother shaking his head and saying, "I can't believe it about George. It's unbelievable! I thought I knew George inside out."

And Maxie? It seemed I hadn't known him so well, either. We had fought together in Italy, been frightened together in the huge air over enemy territory. We'd both been wounded in heavy flak on our twenty-seventh mission, slept and eaten together, swapped our life stories, or so I had thought. I had borrowed his money, but what was locked up inside his heart, this most secret of coins, had never been suspected by me, or I wouldn't have thought: Unbelievable.

Briefly, this is Maxie's story: In May, he had enrolled at the George Lawrence School. His teacher, he admitted, was a cute blonde, but when he saw Hortense in one of the school's ballrooms, he immediately had changed teachers. Since the blonde had already collected the commission on his fifty-hour course, Maxie promptly paid $355.50 for an additional fifty hours, so Hortense would get her commission, too. As I've said, Maxie had plenty of money. His salary at Jacob Groteclose was $95 a week. He'd worked there about a dozen years before the war. It was his first job after graduating from high school and he had saved most of his salary. He could take Hortense out in style, and he did. The combination of her looks and expensive night spots must have started poor Maxie off for the wild blue yonder. He felt like a big shot, and he began to talk like a big shot. In the beginning, he'd only claimed that he was a partner in his firm. This was a modest piece of bragging, because old Jacob Groteclose, a millionaire bachelor without any known relatives, had actually promised to leave his business to his employees. The firm was something of a family institution; Maxie's own father, for instance, had collected rents for Jacob Groteclose until his death some seven or eight years ago. It wasn't hard for Maxie to claim he was a partner, and so by easy steps, at different night spots, he had climbed the golden ladder of success; until one dizzy night he had bragged—and who was there to call him a liar?—that his family was one of the older real-estate families in New York, like the Rhinelanders and the Astors, and that his name was really Maxwell Dehn, Jr.

"And she believed you?" I had asked.

"When you spend money like water," he answered, a sad look on his face, "they'll believe anything. The money has to come from somewhere, doesn't it? Why shouldn't it come from where you say it comes from?"

When he had asked Hortense to marry him, she'd said yes. That was when he'd broken the news to Mamma. Mamma had seemed a little stunned, Maxie admitted, but he'd never expected her to hit the warpath. A few days later she had breezed into the studio, and when she left, Hortense knew that the family estate of Maxwell Dehn, Jr. was off Eighth Avenue and up two flights. Hortense wouldn't go out with him any more. She had even demanded that he transfer to another teacher, but he wouldn't agree to that. At George Lawrence, as elsewhere, the customer was always right, so Hortense continued as Maxie's teacher. Twice a week he had an hour with her, and gradually he had patched up things between them. He had signed up for a third fifty-hour course, and their relationship went into a new phase. She began to borrow money from him, loans of ten or twenty dollars, and sometimes when Hortense was going out with a crowd of teachers, she would ask Maxie along. But there were no more dates, and Hortense was dating other men. "I don't blame her," Maxie said to me. "Once I put over this big deal I'm promoting she'll step out with me again. Maybe she'll even marry me. That's what I hope, anyway."

"Maxie, don't get sore, but why do you have to marry her?"

"She's good for me," he said. "I want to marry her."

"But why?"

"Hugh, you sound dumb like my family. Don't you know girls like Hortense're different from some li'l dame out in Brooklyn?"

"Different? How?"

"Out in Brooklyn, if they play around, they play around on the q.t. But girls like Hortense, Broadway girls like that—it's out in the open. They're like a feller before he settles down."

"I see what you mean, Maxie. But she only seems interested in money, Hortense."

"So what?" He had smiled calmly and looked at me as if I were a child. "Money makes the world go round. When I promote this deal, I'll have enough for both of us."

But he wouldn't say another word about the deal that would make him rich and satisfy Hortense. And as I walked by myself of an evening along Broadway, I wondered if Maxie's big deal was real or just another hopped-up dream like his Maxwell Dehn, Jr., the scion of a family as important as the Rhinelanders and the Astors. It was a big dream town. A million dollars was waiting around every corner. The neons were dazzling, and the end of the rainbow was surely in the next pot of gaudy light. The big deal! With the blues music singing out of the music stores and the Broadway faces streaming by, I thought that in those huge and anonymous crowds there must be other Maxies in love with other Hortenses. She was good for him, he'd said. That remark of his intrigued me. Good for him? In bed, of course. But still, why did he have to marry her?

Nobody could have had a more respectable background than Maxie Dehn. "We were a good German family," Mamma used to say proudly whenever the conversation got around to Hell's Kitchen. She hated the old Hell's Kitchen days, when there had been a saloon on every corner, hoodlums in every block, the cops patrolling their beats in pairs. When Mamma looked back on that time, it was like some pioneer remembering the rough wilderness days. Except that in Mamma's wilderness, the Irish had been the Indians and the good German families the settlers. The garment lofts now stood on the sites of the vanished red-brick tenements, and to all the people of the new time, the garment workers, the pleasure-seekers overflowing from Broadway, the commuters in the endless busses, Hell's Kitchen was not even a memory, but a time clock, a parking lot, a narrow strip of Manhattan situated between the Hudson River and the neon river that was Broadway. Only graying women like Mamma remembered, saying proudly, "We were a good German family."

Maxie, the youngest of her three children, had gone to work after high school for a good German firm, Jacob Groteclose, Real Estate and Insurance. Its offices were on the fourth floor of the Groteclose Building on 42nd Street. When I first visited Maxie there, I felt as if I were thumbing through the old photograph albums we have at home, only here the photographs were alive. Maxie had introduced me to Jacob Groteclose, a white-haired man in his seventies who wore a thick gold watch chain across his vest and smiled at me as if he were my uncle. There were five elderly rent collectors besides Maxie, the baby of the place. The two typists were in their late fifties. All of them, with the exception of Maxie, had worked for old Jacob, as they called him among themselves, when the offices were on Ninth Avenue, in the years before the First World War. The furnishings, too, seemed to be lifted intact out of another era, the gaslit city I had read about in O. Henry. Old-fashioned roll-top desks and waist-high yellow oak partitioning; a huge iron box of a safe with scrolled gilt letters and a teller's cage inside the entrance where tenants could pay their rents. On the walls were photos of Groteclose properties, choice corners and the like, torn down long ago for the skyscrapers of the garment industry. Old Jacob, as I've mentioned, was a millionaire, a bachelor, and when I had seen his office, I didn't find it surprising that he intended leaving his money to charity—to the Lutheran Church, to city hospitals like Bellevue and Manhattan—and the firm itself to his employees, the six rent collectors, and two typists. All would be given shares on his death. It was an office out of the storybooks, and it only seemed incredible when I stepped out of the Groteclose Building to the honky-tonk of 42nd Street below, with its movies lit up with neon even in the daytime, with the hurrying modern city only stopping a quick minute to gulp down a quicker hot dog. I had to laugh. And all the hurrying people I saw, salesmen out for the last nickel and stenos who knew all the answers, seemed to be laughing with me. God, I thought. Crazy wasn't the word to describe Jacob Groteclose's rent collector, Maxie Dehn, in love with a cheap gold digger like Hortense. Crazy was too weak a word, much too weak.

By this time, of course, I'd become intensely curious about Hortense and was looking forward to meeting her. I said so to Maxie. "Why not?" he replied. "She ought to be giving me a break one of these days."

One mild evening after supper Maxie and I went walking on Eighth Avenue and then over to Broadway. The blue neon of Planters Peanuts, the red, white, and blue of Pepsi-Cola were now familiar sights to me. From the Camel sign on top of the Hotel Claridge, a gigantic Mr. New York was blowing immense smoke rings into the night. Maxie tapped my elbow, and, grinning at me, he pointed at the Bond sign with its waterfalls flanked at each end by a four-story-high naked man and naked woman, each of them draped in white light. "Every hick has to know that," Maxie said, grinning.

"Know what?"

"See the strings around the middle of the dame up there on the sign?"

"Yes."

"You find the third string, the third wire."

I counted the strands. The third wire crossed over her triangle. Maxie, watching my face, laughed. "That's the spirit of Broadway!"

I laughed. "Thanks for letting me in on the know." Maxie's grin was an eye-opener. It was a crooked grin, and a little obscene, like that of an old man telling a dirty story. It revealed something about Maxie I hadn't suspected, and for some reason I thought of his fat girl friends overseas. We walked on past the movies and the pineapple-drink places, the drugstores and the restaurants. A legless concertina player, seated on a three-wheeled platform, pushed himself along with two canes as he played his concertina. A sidewalk peddler of toy metal dogs chanted, "Yes, folks, they're itchy. Wind 'em up and look at 'em scratch!" In the noisy and glittering night I felt as if I had come closer than ever before to something dark and secret in Maxie. I thought of what he'd said about Hortense's being good for him... and suddenly, without turning around, I had a flash of the woman in the Bond sign, huge as a goddess above the midget humans on the sidewalks, and among them men obsessed with the third wire. Men like Maxie....

We approached the Times Building and stopped as if by a wall, the wall being the city south of Times Square. A city without lights or people, seemingly, the dark lofts of the cloak and suit industry on Seventh Avenue. "You have enough sight-seeing?" Maxie asked me with a sigh, and before I could answer, he said, "Want to see where Hortense works, Hugh?"

"Yes," I said.

We cut east to Fifth Avenue and walked north. It seemed dark and quiet here, too, after the dazzling arcade of light that was Broadway. We didn't say much. Maxie took me to an office building between 51st and 52nd Streets and silently waved his hand at a small display window fronting on the avenue. Inside the window, I read the invitation of the George Lawrence School of the Dance.

WHY WON'T YOU BE OUR GUEST?
IT IS FUN TO DANCE WELL. STUDIOS ON
THE 11TH FLOOR. NO BIG INVESTMENT
IN GOLF CLUBS OR THEATRE TICKETS.

Three or four other display windows lined the entrance into the lobby. In the first one, a male doll, very handsome and elegant, was dancing with a beautiful blonde female doll wearing a violet evening gown; the card in the window read: "The George Lawrence Samba." In the second, another pair of dolls was fox-trotting in some hotel like the Waldorf-Astoria—"The George Lawrence Fox Trot." There were also "The George Lawrence Waltz," whose scene might have been old Vienna, and "The George Lawrence Tango," where the scene had shifted to Cuba or Florida, with the dolls tangoing under broad green leaves.

"Hortense looks like that one," Maxie said, pointing the same pointing finger he'd used to show me the third wire at the dark-haired doll in the tango display window. She was wearing a flaring white tropical evening gown and her doll's face was painted with a splendid smile.

"Pleased to meet you, Hortense," I said, extending my hand.

"Never mind the old Pierson sarcasm," Maxie muttered.

"Excuse me, Maxie. I didn't mean any harm."

"You'll meet Hortense soon," he promised, and laughed uncertainly. "Aw, what's the good of talking? Wait'll you see her, Hugh. She's beautiful, and I mean beautiful. When I'm with her I forget everything." He laughed with so pure a happiness I envied him a little. I thought of the girls in my classes at N.Y.U. and I contrasted them with the dolls in the display windows.

"All I need's a little money. This deal," he said, muttering as if to himself.

I stared at him. "You've been so close-mouthed on that deal," I said, hesitating. "Maxie, want to know the truth? Sometimes I've thought that deal of yours is just some kind of gag."

"A gag?" Maxie looked at me with surprise. Then he smiled almost condescendingly. "I'd hate to tell a guy on the GI Bill the money in this deal! This is a Fifth Avenue deal, Hugh. Fifth Avenue!"

Before my eyes he seemed to puff up, and I had a notion of how Fifth Avenue appeared to him that second. The millionaire row I'd read about as a kid, its traffic lights changing from emeralds into rubies.

We left the George Lawrence display windows, and we hadn't gone a hundred feet before Maxie exclaimed, "I'm walking like a duck!" Staring down at his feet, he said, "Like a Charlie Chaplin!"

I waited for an explanation.

He punched my shoulder as he used to do overseas when he felt good. "That's what Hortense said to me when I first met her. 'Never walk like a duck, Mr. Dehn. Your feet should never go sideward.'" He laughed at my expression. "You must think I'm nuts."

"Maxie, what made you decide to take up dancing, anyway?" I asked him.

"Want to know?"

"Of course."

"I just got sick of the bags I was seeing." He punched my shoulder, chuckling. "So what do I do? I blow my mouth off! Maxwell Dehn, Junior! Maxwell's right! What're we hoofing it for, buddy? No more cabs in this town?" He lifted his hand as if signaling a taxi and then he snorted indignantly. "Cab, nothing! My limousine. The Caddy limousine! Why be cheap? The Rolls Royce!"

I stared at Maxie, clowning as he'd never done when he had been the Pop of our crew.

"Mr. Pierson, I want you to meet James, my chauffeur." His voice deepened, becoming the voice of all the English butlers he had ever seen in the movies. "Pleased to meet you, Mr. Pierson. Where to, Mr. Dehn?"

"The psycho ward."

"The Stork Club, James," Maxie said, ignoring me. "And, James, at eleven we'll pick up Miss Hortense."

"How about taking the needle out, Maxie, old kid?"

"What for?" he challenged me good-humoredly.

To that I had no easy retort. We walked on to Rockefeller Center. In the shadow, the golden metal giant with the three golden rings of the globe on his shoulders seemed like all the enchanted figures of my childhood fairy books. We entered the promenade, the walls of this city within the city rising steeply on all sides, stone, all stone, but down the center of the promenade there were flower beds and sea girls riding fish that spouted water from their mouths. At this dreamy hour with our moods so light, the metal out of which the fish and their riders were cast seemed no more solid than the water of the seven oceans that flowed unseen between the three golden rings on the shoulders of the golden man who had fetched the world itself to Fifth Avenue.

Maxie paused in front of one of the store windows on the promenade. It was full of fine leather suitcases. "My old man could've been rich," he said quietly, as if he had been brooding about this a long time. "He could've bought real estate like old Jacob, cleaned up, but what'd my old man do? Buys the house we live in. That was my old man for you."

"Well," I said. "Well."

"Even Fifth Avenue real estate was cheap once."

"I read somewhere that Rockefeller Center used to be a meadow."

"Go to the head of the class," he said almost bitterly. I couldn't keep up with Maxie's moods that night. I whistled and stared up at the leaning walls of the city built by Rockefeller. Walls dotted with light like inhuman mechanical eyes, seeing everything. I tried to imagine the lost meadows with their ancient cows, but they had gone forever, inconceivable, a myth, leaving behind a few expensive suitcases in a shining window.

Maxie moved to the next window. Here there were pink corals, tropical fish-es, and an illuminated map of Bermuda: "Where Every Moment Is a Happy Memory." "That's what they all want," he remarked as if to himself.

I guessed he was thinking of Hortense again, but I said nothing. We came to the end of the promenade, and down in the sunken ice rink two die-hard skaters were still circling around and around with the set faces of prisoners doing exercises. "Can you skate?" I asked Maxie, just to make conversation.

"They're jerks and so am I. What do you say we hit the sack?"

Across the street, on the blank wall of Radio City Music Hall, the Corps de Ballet and the Rockettes watched us go. The legs of the Rockettes were lifted high, perfect legs that seemed manufactured somewhere to a set of specifications. "The World's Greatest Precision Dancers" —that's who they were. That, and all the dream girls of the fabulous city....

Those ending September days were almost springlike. We would awake at eight o'clock, with Mamma calling to Maxie. When we breakfasted in the morning, a spring wind rattled the kitchen windows. Below, in the back yard, the faded red paint of the sheds gleamed bright as the red in circus posters and the sky was like a blue tent. Invisible acrobats with unseen and magic holds leaped from the swinging shirt sleeves on the clotheslines over to the flapping pajama trousers. All sorts of revelations, not only about Maxie, but about myself, seemed poised on the soft air.

When we went downstairs, Maxie bound for his office and I for my classes, there always seemed to be a warm west wind blowing from the Hudson. A river wind blowing away the war years, the old years, the stale years, with yesterday's newspapers. On the sidewalks the kids going to school across the way from Mamma Dehn's house tried to outrace and outshout that wind. The sun picked out their young faces. The sun shone on the plate-glass store fronts, and the green turtles painted on the plate glass of the Turtle Distributing Company almost seemed alive. On that warm west wind, my heart and mind flew. I felt as if West 47th were a street in a city new to me, never before seen by me, where the people were different, where I myself was different. The Puerto Rican *comidas* and Molfeta's Greek cafeteria weren't half as real as the shores of Puerto Rico and Greece, strangely near in that blowing wind on West 47th Street. Beauty was stirring in all the world, and as I thought of Maxie and Hortense, I wondered if I too would find a girl in this city who would be to me what Hortense was to Maxie....

The night of Maxie's date with Hortense, we again walked to the dancing dolls on Fifth Avenue. Hortense had informed Maxie that she would meet us downstairs after her last lesson, a few minutes after ten. We waited. Then after the elevators carried down the last of the George Lawrence pupils, the teachers began to slip out into the quiet night, the dolls in the display windows becoming life-sized men and women.

A slender bareheaded girl in a black coat walked over to us, and even before

Maxie introduced us, I was thinking: So this is Hortense! She was pretty, all right, I thought, as if despite her photograph on Maxie's dresser, I somehow had continued skeptical.

"Hortense," Maxie said. "Meet Hugh Pierson, my old buddy."

The slender girl smiled a hello and immediately deserted us for a group of teachers gossiping on the curb. "Maxie," she called a few seconds later, "we're going to Tom's. You can come and bring your friend if you want."

Maxie didn't reply, his face stubborn. We tagged behind Hortense and her teacher friends into a side-street tavern. After all, we had as much right as any other cash customer to squeeze standing room at the bar. They ordered high-balls. We ordered beers. They spoke shop and sex. We listened.

"Maxie—" I said.

"Keep it to yourself," he interrupted me. "I explained how she is," he added apologetically.

"She's pretty," I said diplomatically. "Very pretty."

Suddenly he was smiling, all his defensive irritability gone. Smiling! And for the first time in my life I really understood what they meant when they talked about a man being wrapped around the little finger of a woman. During the war, I myself had gone overboard for a woman, for two different women, but compared to Maxie, I'd been a free agent.

I glanced down the bar at Hortense, who was separated from us by three or four teachers; a tall man, a French-looking girl, and a big lush blonde. Hort-ense was pretty, but no prettier than the French bit of fluff or the blonde. Three sexy babes, I thought, different sizes, different shapes, but with some-thing similar about their looks, like girls in a chorus or in a department store. Then Hortense, who had been busy chattering, stopped to light a cigarette. I stared at her. She no longer looked like the other girls. It was as if she had another face. I noticed for the first time that under the red of her lipstick, her mouth was like a schoolgirl's, and her forehead was wide and clean. Most girls, especially pretty sexy girls, seem to have no foreheads. For a split second, this second face was the real face, and then as she puffed on her cigarette, getting back into the bar talk, it seemed to disintegrate, to disappear into the smoke. The schoolgirl mouth turned Broadway, her lips became as sly and scornful as her words, her dark eyes shining with everything she knew about her body and everybody else's body. I was jolted. It was like seeing two girls fuse into one, and as they fused, I felt the unmistakable electric shock of sex. Her sex and mine.

It was no use telling myself that any man would have felt what I was feel-ing, and that I couldn't blame myself for wanting her. It was no use telling myself that the build-up on Hortense from Maxie and Mamma Dehn had been terrific and that maybe I'd fallen for the build-up, or that Maxie was my best friend. The words meant nothing, all the words. For whatever the reasons, this slender girl with the smooth dark hair and dark brown eyes had become the girl I'd been looking for, that we are always looking for, the girl who haunts the lonely bedrooms of the city, the red-lipped apparition without a name. For weeks I had come across her in glimpses. She had shown herself, a golden face inside a cab, a body wrapped in a wind-blown coat on a windy corner, her eyes sometimes blue, sometimes gray, sometimes hazel, meeting mine for a second in a crowd and then lost, always lost. Girl without a name, I'd caught up with her at last. Her name—Hortense.

Maxie

Maybe I'm a jerk. But when it comes to Hortense, I've got a seventh sense. The wolf eye that Hugh gave Hortense was something I never expected. Not from Hugh Pierson. From the average guy, what can you expect? But Hugh was high-class. He was educated and smart, besides being my buddy. Aw, what's the use of talking?

Right away I thought I better stop stalling on the Doyle deal. I'd been stalling because it was on the shady side. That's why I hadn't told Hugh a single thing about it, because if there's one guy I hated to lower myself before, that guy was Hugh Pierson. The bonus Doyle was all set to pay me wouldn't've taken a penny from the firm. But just the same, it was shady, because we didn't do business that way—under the table. You see, I managed the Shaw sisters' real estate for the firm, and if I said sell, the Shaw sisters would've sold Doyle the parcel he wanted. That part was all right. It was the bonus part that wasn't. But who was I kidding? For Hortense to marry me I had to have a big piece of money.

I felt so mixed up, thinking how Doyle and his bonus and Hugh Pierson'd all got into one screwy package, that I switched from beer to whiskey. Hugh switched, too, when I switched. We must've had two or three shots. Then most of those George Lawrence teachers went off somewhere else and what was left sat down at a table. There were six of us, so we had to squeeze in, three on a side, Hortense between me and Dexter Rolfe, who from the name alone you could guess what kind of a heel he was. One of those redheaded heels with a little red mustache. He'd been born a heel and would die a heel. He didn't want Hugh and me around. He'd already made some nasty remarks, but who the hell cared? I was used to prize heels. With Hortense I'd got used to about everything. On the other side of the table there was Hugh making believe when he threw a look at Hortense that he was just being social, and this dizzy blonde Milly in the middle, and Ted Mansfield. Milly, she had on a tight black dress like you could expect from a dizzy blonde. She must've put away six or seven at the bar, for when she laughed, she laughed with real concentration, putting her heart into it, and about everything else, since she wasn't wearing a brassiere. When she wasn't laughing she was stroking Ted Mansfield's hands or face. This Ted, he was a little guy. The top of his head wasn't much above her shoulder. He was supposed to have been a jockey before he'd become a dance teacher. About him, Hortense used to say, "It's his years of racing why he likes to ride the big blondes." That's Hortense for you. Always full of gags.

By now things were going lively at our table. Hugh was busy talking to Hortense. He said he'd heard a great deal about her from me. Dexter butted in and said the only place to get reliable information about Hortense was the police blotter. Milly stopped petting this ex-jockey, Ted Mansfield, and she said that ever since she'd been married to Dexter, all she'd ever heard was that corny joke about the police blotter. I forgot to mention that those two were married. Not that it made much difference to them. That's the kind of friends Hortense has. That's why she's the way she is. All of them running around like cats in a back yard and anybody's guess who ends up with who. And while they're running, they're wisecracking, because all of them want to be Bob Hopes.

I settled down to my whiskey, but it didn't help much. Here I was eating my heart out because of this redheaded heel Dexter, so now Hugh had to get into the act. Telling her about the war and how he'd first met me. She was kidding him, calling him Air Force, but she was listening. They made a good-looking pair, all right, both of them dark and sharp. Hugh, with his black hair and brown eyes and hawk nose, could've been an Eyetie, only the Eyeties'd known he wasn't one of them. He really looked like some of those RAF pilots. Classy. Like he'd gone to Oxford. She was smiling at him and I felt like crying because her smile was so damn cute and all.

"So you teach dancing," he says to her, like he was just being social, but who the hell was he kidding? "How do you like it?"

"It's a rat race. All day long, one pair of left feet after another. Like Maxie, here." She blew me a fake kiss. But fake or not, it gave me a thrill, because it was the first time tonight she'd noticed I was alive. I thought to myself, So the Doyle deal's on the shady side, and so what?

We had some more drinks and Dexter started panning the Air Force. He said they had the best public relations in the whole damn war. That was why all the suckers thought the Air Force'd won the war singlehanded. Hugh got mad and said he wasn't interested in a barroom opinion. Dexter laughed at him not to be so high-hat, the war was over. He said Hugh could take off his lousy wings, or did he think he was too good for this cheap crowd? Ted Mansfield stooged along with Dexter and said it was a very cheap crowd, that Dexter and Milly were nothing but a couple of nymphos. They were ganging up on Hugh. That's how that crowd get their fun.

"Milly and me never have an argument," Dexter says. "Everything's on the level. Maybe we're cheap, maybe we're nymphos. But everything's on the level, Air Force."

"Aboveboard," Ted says.

"Like tonight," Hortense had to chime in, too. "Milly and Ted were going out. Dexter wanted to come along and it was O.K. with them. Nothing like a happy marriage is what I say."

I yelled for them to cut it out, but when that bunch of Bob Hopes are started, the only thing to stop them is the police wagon. Hugh tried to wisecrack back, but they paid no attention to him or to me. They only let up when Milly excused herself to go to the powder room. That gave me a chance to treat to drinks. Then Ted treated. Then Hortense, a round I paid for. The smoke was so thick you could hardly see, and I guess we were all pretty lit up.

"All George Lawrence got is dumb luck," Dexter says for no reason at all except that he's the kind of heel who always has to snipe at somebody. "He can't dance, he has no personality or brains. Only luck."

"You've got to have luck," Hortense says. "And be sure the L for luck don't turn out the L for lousy."

She looked wobbly to me, and I wished she wouldn't drink so much. It was a habit, like the wisecracking was a habit. I had a hunch that if we ever got married she'd slow down. Thinking of marrying Hortense made me think of the Doyle deal, and I didn't want to think of that. I didn't want to think. Period.

Dexter was now full of sweet words for George Lawrence. He'd gone into reverse on all he'd been saying. That was the kind of a heel he was. "The man's a born salesman. You've got to give G.L. credit."

"You give him credit," Hortense says, "and I'll give him the old Bronx cheer."

"Hugh," Dexter says, "I'll give you the low-down on this G.L. character." He was Hugh's friend all of a sudden, the big explainer. "G.L. deserves plenty of credit for selling an idea. He goes ahead and tells the world one dance step is the key to all. The Secret Step, he calls it. Rumba, fox trot, samba, they're all based on the Secret Step. He slaps his name down on every dance there is. The George Lawrence Samba. The George Lawrence Thissa and Thatta. The boys on Madison Avenue go to work and G.L. becomes rich and famous. I could've done the same. Anybody could've done the same!"

Hortense laughed at him. "Anybody, only they didn't. You and your ideas!"

"I'd rather have talked to you private about what you call my ideas," Dexter says to her. "But since we're all friends, you in or out?"

She banged the table with both hands and let out a hoot. "Friends! Please, Dex, not friends! Call me a tramp, a floozy, anything, but when you call me friend, you've got to say it with a smile."

Dexter grinned at her. "You lousy actress. Hugh, to get back to G.L.—"

"Let's stay away from G.L. for a change." Hortense groaned like she was sick.

"That's what I told this fat horse of a schoolteacher I sold a lifetime course to!" Dexter shouted, and laughed like it was a big joke. "Let's get away from G.L."

"Dex," Milly begged him. "Not again, honey. We all know that story about the schoolteacher you sold the lifetime course to."

"Hugh don't know it!" that redheaded heel practically screamed at her. "Hugh, I made seven hundred and fifty bucks commission! What do you think of that, Hugh? Isn't that salesmanship? Salesmanship with a big S!"

"The big S for you know what," Hortense kidded him.

Dexter laughed so loud you could've heard him in Brooklyn. "The good old double S, honey. That's just what I gave this schoolteacher, Eleanor Flack."

This redheaded heel Dexter was feeling so good because the biggest course they sold down at George Lawrence was the lifetime or thousand-hour course, price $4,995. It was called the lifetime course because the buyer got three free hours of dancing every month for the rest of his life. The schoolteacher he'd sold it to was a pupil of his by the name of Eleanor Flack. She'd been taking a hundred-hour course when her old man up and died, leaving her a flock of bonds. First Dexter only convinced her to sign up for a five-hundred-hour course. But before she did, he got greedy and shot for the works, the lifetime course with its top commission. I'd heard Dexter spin this story a couple times myself. Milly and Hortense and Ted, who saw Dexter more than I did, must've heard it until it was coming out of their ears. But it never failed. Whenever that redheaded heel got a little drunk, you heard it again.

"The good old double S!" he says, and laughs like a hyena. He reached across the table, grabbed Hugh's hand. "Eleanor!" he says, making believe Hugh was this schoolteacher, Eleanor Flack. Hugh had to wrench his hand loose. "Eleanor! Eleanor!" Dexter raved. "Eleanor, you're in a position to make a personal investment. Eleanor."

Milly and Ted tried to go to sleep on him while Hortense threw the monkey wrenches. Hugh was listening, smoking. And me? I was listening too. I didn't want to think. Period.

"A five-hundred-hour course comes to twenty-six hundred dollars, Eleanor! Two five-hundred-hour courses come to fifty-two hundred dollars! A thousand-hour course is only four thousand, nine hundred and ninety-five dollars! It's cheaper, Eleanor! It's just simple arithmetic, Eleanor!"

"Simple larceny," Hortense says, and she blew a smoke ring into his eyes.

"Don't do that!" he yelled. But nothing could discourage the heel. He had to give us all the details. How he'd kept after Eleanor with the lifetime course, and what a bargain it was. Three free hours a month for as long as she lived, and how one hour cost eight dollars and change. So the three free hours was the equivalent of an income of more than twenty-four dollars a month for as long as she lived. Hortense blew another smoke ring into his eyes, she made dirty remarks, but it was no use. He went on yapping how schoolteachers weren't easy to sell. You had to give them the highbrow treatment, how a girl of brains could do anything providing she didn't let her career ruin her personal life. How a woman owed it to herself to realize her possibilities and not bury everything womanly for the sake of her career.

"Know what else I had to do?" he asked everybody. Nobody wanted to know, but he gave it to us anyway. "I promised that sucker that if she made this investment, I'd help her realize her possibilities. I promised to go with her to Saks Fifth Avenue and have the consultant there select her basic dresses and suits. She was so thrilled, she wrote it all down in a little notebook like you'd expect a schoolteacher. Saks Fifth Avenue and Helena Rubinstein's on Fifth

Avenue for an analysis of her hair. See, I told the sucker she had a beautiful red tint in her hair that should be brought out. And when we went to Helena Rubinstein's she had to buy the Silken Look Kit. It's salesmanship and nothing else."

"You signed her up only because she had her hopes on you," Hortense tried to tell him.

"I didn't want her flesh!" the heel laughed. "I only wanted her money. Did you ever see that meatball, Hortense?"

"How fat was she, anyway, honey?" Milly asked, showing some life.

"One-eighty, at least. But from the day I wrote in her Course Book her jitterbug had verve, I had her sold!"

Hortense poked her elbow into my ribs. "Throw the jitterbug at 'em to shake 'em up. Then a li'l rumba to prove they own an ass like everybody else. Then a li'l tango, a li'l romance, to tie up the pieces."

She didn't have to poke me. I knew the formula, but if she wanted to kid me, she could go right ahead. I didn't give a damn what she thought or what Hugh thought or what any of them thought. I loved her and I was going to marry her. That was enough for me. She thought she was so smart, Hortense, like she was some kind of a sex machine. She wasn't. I'd only been with her twice at her apartment, and those two times.... Aw, what's the use of talking? I'm no poet or anything like that. But I can say this much. She was no sex machine. She reminded me of my brother, Pete, who was wild from the time he was a kid, but when he got married he settled down. That was Hortense. She'd settle down too, if I could prove to her I was no fourflusher and had a big piece of money in the bank. I thought I'd phone Doyle the first thing in the morning. Shady deal or not. If my old man would've known he'd've turned over in his grave. And so what? Everything was a deal. And girls like Hortense you don't get for nothing.

Why we all moved back to the bar I don't remember, for by now I was good and drunk. I remember Milly griping away how she only wanted to go dancing at the Arcadia. Maybe the bar, it was some kind of a compromise. Anyway, we had a drink there and then some strangers invited themselves into the party. You know how it is at bars with strangers. First they're nowhere and then they're your long-lost brothers. These were a pair of lulus. Both of them wearing tweed jackets and the one called Selden had on a black shirt and an orange necktie, and the one called John an orange shirt and a black necktie. At least, that's how it seemed to me when I looked at them in the mirror. They'd pushed themselves in on the left side of Hortense. Dexter and me and Hugh were on the other side. And Milly and Ted were down at the tail end of the bar by themselves. It was easier looking at Hortense in the mirror, I was that drunk. When I turned my neck I felt like I was floating. Hortense didn't look so good herself, her face white as a sheet in the mirror, the faces of the two strangers on one side, and the faces of Dexter and me and Hugh on the other.

Surrounded, like. She could've been a ghost, I thought, and she would've been surrounded. But I had no kicks coming, I thought. Funny, when you're real drunk sometimes, how you know the score. At that bar, with Hortense surrounded by all kinds of guys who wanted her, I thought she could walk over me from morning to night and I'd still have no right to kick. She'd done more for me than I could ever do for her, so how could I kick?

This Selden and John were treating to drinks now. When I listened to them they gave me a big headache. For they'd started yacking about art, which is what you can expect from guys in solid-color shirts and neckties. I looked at Hortense in the mirror. She was white, her eyes two holes in her head. I felt like telling her to take it easy on the drinking, and that I loved her and if she only married me things wouldn't be so bad. But I said nothing. I'd been along on other drinking parties with Hortense and her booze-hound pals, and when I'd said take it easy, she'd jumped on me with some mean crack like: Look who's talking, Mr. Dehn, Junior. So I said nothing. Dexter and Hugh were arguing with this Selden and John and the noise about art was something fierce. What Dexter knew about art you could pour in a pint bottle, but that heel could argue about anything. As for Hugh, he knew a lot about such things as art and music. Many a time overseas I'd gone to sleep on him while he and some of the other highbrows in our crew batted around Beethoven or somebody like that.

"Aw, shut up!" Hortense says to all of them. They were my sentiments too and I could've kissed her. "What in hell am I doing here, anyway?" she asked, shaking her head.

"Having fun," her new pal Selden says, or maybe it was her new pal John.

"Let me take you home, Hortense," I says to her, although I knew it was a mistake. "You've done enough drinking, baby, for one night."

"Maxie, hell with you," she says.

Milly the mumbler mumbled about dancing at the Arcadia and Ted said what they should do was go home and sleep. But this Selden and John weren't satisfied. "We all ought to have one more drink. Hortense," they says, "will you have a drink with us?"

"Hortense?" she says, foggy. "Who's Hortense?"

"Hey, actress!" Dexter hollered at her, but he didn't faze her.

"I've got no name," she says real sad. "Got nothing, got nobody. Only wished I had somebody. Somebody who cared."

"I care," this Selden or John says.

Me, I couldn't tell whether Hortense was acting or not. That's the kind of a jerk I am sometimes. "Don't listen to these guys, Hortense," I says. "Stop drinking, baby."

Dexter says, "Maxie's right. A couple of phony artists!"

That was Dexter all over. After he'd sponged a lot of free drinks he was ready to do a little knifing.

"Why does everybody call a man a phony just because he happens to be an artist?" this Selden says.

"Is that what you are, you bastard!" Hortense says, and she laughed like a goof. "Married one myself!"

"You married an artist?" this Selden wanted to know.

"I married a phony, a phony actor. And I was a phony actress!"

"Do you act now?"

"Do you paint now, and if you do what do you paint and who gives a damn?" she says, talking a mile a minute.

This Selden had to take her serious, or maybe he just wanted another excuse to keep on yacking about art. "If you know Picasso's work, Hortense..." he says.

"Sure," she says. "Picasso, the guy mixed up with City Hall who made a killing in those paint-supply contracts. Sure, you're Picasso and I'm Eleanor Flack, or do you mean to stand there and admit you haven't heard of Eleanor Flack?"

"Crap!" Dexter hollered. "I'm not listening to any crap like that."

But Hortense was wound up good now. I'd seen her pull other stunts in bars when she was drunk. Hugh was grinning but it wasn't funny to me.

"You wouldn't believe it, but I used to weigh one hundred and eighty pounds before I became an actress!" Hortense says, and she pushed her chin down into her neck to look fat.

"Crap!" Dexter hollered.

"Let's go to the Arcadia," Milly mumbled.

"Let's go home," Ted says.

The bartender hurried over and Hugh smiled at him. "It's O.K. She's doing a take-off on an actress."

"They can do any kind of a take-off they want except religion," the bartender says. "Not even on a rabbi in this bar."

"I'm a rabbi's daughter," Hortense goofed at him. "Rabbi Flack's daughter herself."

"Is that right?" the bartender says, and he cracked the bar with the flat of his hand. "See this bar, lady? See this bar? Some of 'em think it's a public platform to make their speeches. You can make a speech or do a take-off. But religion's out, lady."

"You're a philosopher," Hugh says to the bartender. "So this bar's a public platform? But to you it's more like a workbench where you make the drinks. And when you're not making drinks you're policing the drinkers. That makes this bar an alley where you pound your beat, right?"

"Who is this guy?" the bartender says. "Who is this guy?"

"A philosopher, like he called you," I say.

"Crap," Dexter hollered at everybody.

Hortense heard enough. She walked up and down, her stomach pushed out. "Eleanor Flack, who can't be a rabbi's daughter. Poor Eleanor Flack. Poor Eleanor."

"For God's sake," Dexter begged her.

She looked at him. "Aren't you the Saks Fifth Avenue man?" She fingered the material of her blouse. "Ten dollars a yard I paid for this, but who cares? Is money everything? Goddamn right it is. Please, God," she says, as if praying. "Please God, no girl's waist should be more than twenty-four inches, hips no more than thirty-six. 'Eleanor,' he said to me, 'you've got to stop eating all those chocolates and get ready to make a personal investment.'"

"Let's keep it down," the bartender says.

"I'd eat half a box out of frustration," Hortense explained, her eyes rolling and her face all twisted. "What do those psychiatrists call 'em, this Dr. Picasso, for instance? Oh, yes. Frustration chocolates! Could you blame me when my waist was thirty-six inches, and my hips a perfect sixty-six? That's what I say. Never under sixty-six in the bank even if the bank is up the creek."

"You're drunk!" Dexter says to her,

"Keep it down!" the bartender warned him. "And cut it out!"

"Don't mind him." Hortense smiled at the bartender. "He's the one got me to diet and go to Helena Rubinstein's, where they brought out the hidden gold in my hair." She patted her hair. "Every girl has some hidden gold in her hair, did you know that, mister?"

"Looks a li'l dark, your hair." The bartender had to laugh.

"Look harder and you'll see the gold in it!"

Dexter bent over double like he was doing a floor-touching exercise. "How about me?" he says upside down, his head between his legs while he patted his rear-end with both hands. "How about me? Can't you see the gold?"

We all had to laugh.

"None of that!" the bartender says. "I said cut it out!"

"Don't mind that loudmouth," Hortense says to the bartender. "He's O.K. and deserves a little credit when you consider that a lifetime course comes high and the law of averages isn't what it used to be. What the hell's happened to the law of averages, anyway?"

"Lady, you're right," the bartender says. "Absolutely and positively right."

"You bet," she says. "Somebody has to be right."

"Maybe." The bartender smiled. "All you folks ought to go home. Not that I'm rushing you, mind you."

And that was how that party ended. Like other parties I'd been to with Hortense and her pals. We left the bar and she and this Selden and John went off in a cab. Milly and Ted disappeared and Dexter beat it off somewhere, with me holding the bag and Hugh for a witness.

Hugh said how about some coffee and I said O.K. We went into a place all white tile, with guys drinking coffee and eating hamburgers, everybody half asleep, or bug-eyed like they were thinking of killing somebody.

"You must think I'm the biggest jerk in town," I says to Hugh when we sat down at a table with our coffees.

"I don't think that, Maxie," he says.

"Don't snow me, Hugh. It's too damn late."

He stirred up his coffee, not looking at me. A hackie at the counter opened his face for a western egg sandwich. Then it got quiet again like all those places are late at night. I felt worse than drunk. I felt dead tired and blue, and my head sick. I don't know what I felt. And at the same time I knew I had no kicks coming, not even if Hortense played the whole field. Just the same, it hurt to see her chasing off with a couple guys she met in a bar. It hurt like hell.

I looked at Hugh stirring his coffee, too high-class or polite or something to come out with how he thought I was the world's number one jerkeroo. For a second I felt like giving him the low-down on how it was with me and women and what Hortense'd done for me. But I was too ashamed. Maybe if I hadn't watched him with Hortense, I might have. A guy can't hold it in all his life, a thing like that. It's like a sickness or a poison.

"Bet you could go for her yourself," I says to Hugh.

He smiled as if I'd cracked a big joke. He made me feel a little dopey. So he had shined up to Hortense tonight, and so what? A high-class guy was human like anybody else. "Hugh, what I'm getting at is this: She's a knockout and she knows it, so she plays around. But once she's married, she'll be different."

He shook his head. "Maybe, Maxie."

"No maybe about it, Hugh. I know her! All I need's some money, and I can get the money. This deal I've mentioned—remember?"

"Sure, I remember. The mystery deal."

"The mystery was because it's shady. Crooked, you might say. That's why I've kept mum on it. But tonight I got to talk to somebody. I got to get it off my chest. You've been up to the office, Hugh. You've seen the kind of office. A hundred percent honest, no kickbacks with us. Aw, I feel so goddamn low and cheap about it."

But how low and cheap it was, I couldn't have got across unless I took half the night. I would've had to begin back in the prohibition time when I first went to work for old Jacob after high school, when the bootleggers and cordial-shop operators had a fistful of money for anybody helping them get the kind of lease they wanted, when the cloak-and-suiters who rented whole floors in the loft buildings we managed were also ready and willing to pay for little favors. The do-me-a-favor boys. But with us at Jacob Groteclose, there were no favors. Nothing under the table. How could I get across somebody like my old man? "Max," my old man used to say when I first went to work, "you are a young boy and the easy money is so nice and so easy. Here in this office we go to lunch if we are asked. At Christmas we keep the presents they give us, but the presents must be under five dollars. That is the kind of office we are." I would've had to tell Hugh how when my old man died, Jacob Groteclose'd said I could use my old man's desk, and the feeling I had when I sat in the same chair at the same desk where my old man'd worked for over twenty years. And when Christmas came and the office had its big blowout down at Luchow's Restaurant on 14th Street, it didn't seem funny when old Jacob thanked us for being good men and good Christians. Down there at Luchow's with the high-class oil paintings on the walls, and the musicians playing soft music, and the German waiters who've been there, some of them, thirty or forty years, we all felt proud to be what we were, a hundred percent honest and straight with old Jacob. And when old Jacob made his little speech like he did every Christmas, promising that when he passed on he'd leave the firm to us, because he knew we'd carry on in the Jacob Groteclose tradition of honesty and service, it seemed just the way things should be. After the first few drinks, the stories'd begin, all kinds of stories, stories about the old days, about landlords and tenants, and with always a story or two about my old man. And I'd feel it was a big privilege working for old Jacob like my old man, to know the men he'd known, Gerber and Schonwald and Eckstein and Platt, and Perpente, who although he had an Eyetie name was a *Deutsch* like the rest of us, and when Perpente, who'd been my old man's best friend, gave me a box of Uppmann Havana cigars just like he used to give my old man, it was hard keeping the tears from my eyes. At Luchow's, the do-me-a-favor boys didn't exist, and when Eckstein did his imitation of them, like he did every Christmas, we all howled. Eckstein would imitate a big-time bootlegger we all knew who had wanted to give Christmas presents to all of us, and when he learned they had to be under five dollars, he had thrown a fit. Eckstein would imitate that bootlegger's lingo perfect: "Up there at that Dutchman Groteclose, they're just a bunch of poor igerant bastids. They're igerant because the Dutch bastids're honest. Like they think they own alla Forty-secon' Street all by their li'l lonesome. Them kinda igerant bastids think they're Mr. Forty-secon' Street himself. In person...."

No, it would've taken half the night to get over to Hugh how low and cheap the Doyle deal was. But he'd been up the office and he was smart, and he got it quick enough.

"Mr. Forty-Second Street, that's the nickname for all of us." I stopped talking and looked at him for a second. "Here's where Doyle comes in, Hugh. Joseph Henry Doyle, the big lawyer and politician. He wants to buy this property I manage—the Shaw sisters'. I manage all their property. Collect the rents, order repairs, alterations. I've got the whole say. Well, what Doyle wants're six tenements on West Sixty-third Street off Broadway. It's a hundred-and-forty-five-foot frontage. First, Doyle tried to buy direct from the Shaw sisters themselves, but they sent him over to the office, where old Jacob turned him over to me because the Shaws're mine. Doyle treats me to lunch and I told him the truth. I told him the Shaw sisters hated to sell any of their property. They're old maids and rich. They don't need his money. Besides, one of them, Virginia Shaw, was born over on West Sixty-third in one of her houses and she was soft that way. Doyle, he listened, a real wise guy, and then he says, 'Soften them up for me. I want that property.' The next thing I know I get a case of twenty-year-old Scotch. I sent it back. Doyle phoned me and we have another fancy lunch. This time he has an offer that isn't bad. Three-fifty. And in the mail I get an unlimited charge account at Lord and Taylor. I sent that back. To make a long story short, Hugh, the Shaw sisters turned down Doyle's offer. He upped it to three-eighty."

Hugh held up his hand like a traffic cop. "Hold on, Maxie. Do those figures stand for what I think? Three hundred and eighty thousand?"

"That's right, kid. Real money."

Hugh whistled. "Why is Doyle so anxious for that particular property, Maxie?"

"You ever hear of television?"

"Of course. But that's for the future, isn't it, Maxie?"

"What future? It's the year 1946. Television's on its way. Doyle's got a hot tip, or maybe he's the front man for movie or radio money. When he got after the Shaw property, I spoke to our friends at our bank. Television, they said, when I described the location of the Shaw property. You see, the whole West Side north of Times Square has been going into entertainment. South of Times Square it's cloak and suits. North, it'll be television. Well, when I saw Doyle again, I came right out with it. 'Your offer'll have to be better,' I let him know. He thought I was trying to put the squeeze on him. He says, 'Now I know why you wouldn't take my little presents.' 'Mr. Doyle,' I says, 'we don't take presents at our office.' But he only laughs and says, 'Every man has his price if the price is right.' 'Wrong again,' I says. He thinks a minute, smiling, and then he says, 'This is my last offer, Maxie. I'll come up to four hundred, and I'll give you a bonus.' Well, I kept saying no to him, and to make it short, the last time I saw him he'd upped his offer to four-twenty with a ten-per-cent bonus for me."

I had to smile at the way Hugh was looking at me. Like he couldn't believe his own ears. I couldn't blame him. In this joint, with guys dumping the free catsup on their hamburgers, 10 percent of $420,000 must've sounded like all the money in the world. Then he must've seen I wasn't kidding him, for he looked at me with the look. That look I'd seen in business before. It's the look when somebody meets somebody who they don't think's in the chips especially. Then it turns out that the guy in the impressed fifty-buck suit is only round-shouldered from the money he's carrying.

"I said no to that, too, Hugh," I says to him.

"Because it might leak?" he answered. "I get it. If it ever leaked, you'd be through. Out of the firm, the partnership."

He thought it was only the promise of the partnership that was keeping me on the level. Well, I couldn't blame him. His old man had never worked for old Jacob and he'd never been at one of our Christmas dinners at Luchow's.

"I can get the Shaw sisters to sell at four-twenty, Hugh. Know what I'm doing? I'm phoning Doyle in the morning and find out if that bonus of his still holds."

"What!" He lets out a yip like a dog whose tail's stepped on.

"That's right. It's low, it's cheap, it's all wrong, but what's a guy going to do?"

"I don't think you should do it, Maxie," he says, his face serious, you might say solemn. He reminded me of a chaplain saying the last prayer for a guy whose missions were all over.

"It's the only way I can get Hortense to marry me."

"She'd go through that so fast—" Hugh stopped himself as if he expected me to be mad or something. When he saw I was only listening, he went on. "Maxie, she's not worth it!"

I was listening to him and I wasn't listening because I knew what I knew. She'd been the first big break in my life. Money was nothing compared to it. She was the break where it counted, in my personal life, in my sex life. So when Hugh began to argue there were other girls, I said, "For me there's only Hortense."

Maybe it was the tone of my voice, but he quit arguing. He looked at me without saying another word. He was like a guy feeling his way in the dark. Why only Hortense? He didn't say it. His eyes said it. His eyes were something to see, like a pair of searchlights. He was a smart cookie, Hugh Pierson, and almost I felt like telling him why for me there was only Hortense. Almost, but then I was too ashamed and all.

HORTENSE

This is exactly how it was. You can draw your own conclusions, and if you're like nine out of ten, you'll draw them black.

Came the dawn.

As soon as I heard the alarm clock, I reached to shut the damn thing off. I had it on the floor alongside the bed, where I always make sure to put it the night before.

An alarm clock, the midget size, is one of the handiest things a girl with a job can take along on a date, and I'm not kidding. What's the sense of risking a good job for any man, I say.

It was twelve noon and I was due at the studio at one.

I turned sideways to see who I was with. The back of a brown curly head was what I saw. There'd been two of them, two artists, I remembered, and this must be one of them, unless the other one was in bed, too. I took another look. No, only one, but which one I couldn't have told you, nor did I give a damn.

One at a time's my motto. The trouble was there'd been too many times lately. Sometimes I used to think I was becoming a nympho. Not the real kind like Milly, who had to have a man every night or chew nails, but some off-beat kind, who wasn't especially wild about the male principle, as I once heard an English actor call it, but slept with them or it pretty regularly. Dipso more than nympho, in my own case. I'd get so crawly drunk I'd go to bed with almost anybody. And last night I wanted to prove to Dexter that his propositions were nothing special in my life. Some of these bastards think that money can buy anything, and they're so right, damn them. By going in with Dexter, I could make a clear hundred and fifty bucks a week as against sixty bucks, plus commissions, at the studio. Don't ask me why I didn't take his proposition. It made sense. I might as well get paid for the time I was putting in in bed. Dexter had promised me seventy-five clear a night. And two nights a week as a call girl was what I thought I could give. Not bad.

I lay there, too tired to get up, listening to the tick-tick-tick of the alarm clock. Another day at the George Lawrence School of the Dahntz was staring me in the face. I thought of the pep meeting at one o'clock. We always had some kind of pep or uplift between one and two, and then at two the dance marathon'd start all over again, a cripple due every hour on the hour until the last bell at ten. It was a dismal prospect.

I dragged myself out of bed, and where do you think I was? This orgy had ended up in a room full of pictures. They covered the walls. They were stacked in the corners. An unfinished picture hung on an easel. Maybe it was finished. I don't know. They all seemed unfinished to me. Modern art, you know. I looked at a masterpiece. It had a bunch of yellow ice-cream cones spotted with red and purple, and some dark brown squares floating around. There was another painted with every shade of blue, and lined with heavy black lines like a sheet of music. Advanced art, dearie, so advanced you had to run like hell to keep up with it. Some of the serious types at the studio were always talking about modern art. The idea is to have no idea the herd can see in five minutes. There were fifteen or twenty pictures in the room, but in the whole collection there wasn't one real human face or shape, one landscape with real trees, one ocean with real waves. I'll take a barbershop calendar any time.

I went into the bathroom. Two masterpieces that someday would be worth millions were in the tub. I took them out. The ring of dirt around the enamel was a real creation. But I'd lived in so many furnished rooms that I wasn't bothered. When there's no shower and you don't want to clean the dirty tub, the technique is simple. You take out the stopper, turn on the hot and cold water, and when it's running lukewarm, you step into the tub and squat. It's not much of a shower, but you can get washed and cleaned.

When I was through, I went over to the mirror. I'd avoided it, coming in, but sooner or later a girl has to face her face. I examined the victim. My eyes were red in the corners, but not too pouchy. The hangover shadow wasn't too bad. Considering everything, I looked only medium lousy. Next, I dressed, which wasn't as easy as it sounds. My bra was on a chair, my blouse on the floor, my shoes seemed to have walked off somewhere. I hunted under the bed and under the dresser. No shoes. I felt like waking up the genius, but one peek at that zombie and I knew he wouldn't be any help.

I found my shoes in the wastepaper basket together with an empty whiskey bottle. I read the label to see how I'd finished the evening. It was a cheap 60-percent-neutral-spirits whiskey. Just what a girl could expect in a room without a shower.

I put on my blouse. The row of buttons were all there, which was something. Some of these grain-alky bastards have never learned buttons are meant to unbutton. If any'd been missing, I had some emergency pins in my bag, and at the studio I always kept a spare dress in my locker in reserve. I went into the bathroom again for the final touches. I smeared on the lipstick. My lips felt hot and dry, as if with fever. Whisky fever, I call it. I didn't look bad, but neither did I look good in that genius's mirror. My skin was dead, lined with fine little lines that would fade away after a few hours. So far they always had, but if I kept up this pace, what would I look like in a few years? That's what I asked myself. I could imagine myself as I'd be, the lines in my face permanent, my eyes larger once my cheeks started to hollow out, my nose getting that bony look like on those skinny little sexy dames you see in the Broadway bars, their hair dyed yellow, and on the downgrade and no more upgrade in this life. You've seen them yourself. Broadway sparrows picking up the leavings.

I felt miserable. I was twenty-six and not getting any younger. A man who's twenty-six can imagine himself thirty without falling into a dead faint, but for a girl, twenty-six means that time is running out. I still had the looks and the shape, but in the big town a girl has to have luck to come out ahead of the rat race. I had two more years, maybe three, at most four, to find a guy with money! Money, money, money! The catch was there were too many girls dreaming of diamonds and minks. Show girls, models, dance teachers like me, not to mention the stenos with an eye on the boss. Luck! You had to have luck or even the law of averages wouldn't work out. In two, three years, I ought to hit a winner. But when I thought of how I'd been eighteen once with a whole lifetime ahead of me and nothing happening, just nothing, and here I was twenty-six—God, nothing can beat time! Good old Father Time, and wouldn't that bastard have to be a man, too.

I broke away from that damn mirror. If a girl's a day over twenty she should-n't do her thinking in front of a mirror. Leave that to the sweet sixteens, I say.

My coat was hanging on what resembled a plaster horse or maybe it was really a symbol of the morning after. I liked that idea—the morning after. It made me forget the mirror. That's what a sense of humor can do for you. Then I thought: Swell, Hortense, you've got not only the looks and the shape, but a sense of humor, and when you're thirty you can heave it out of the window with everything else.

I put on my coat, dropped my trusty alarm clock into my bag, searching around in the bottom for the gum I always carried. I treated myself to a slice and tossed the paper wrapper on the floor. A childish trick, but I felt like it. I was on my way out when the thought hit me: Why not help yourself to a sou-venir? Among so many masterpieces, one more or less wouldn't be missed.

I picked a small picture with some nice color slapped on in streaks like the design for a Hattie Carnegie exclusive. It was a perfect-sized painting, fitting just right inside a New York Times I retrieved from the floor. So long, Selden, I thought as I breezed out, or was it so long, John?

Who do you think was waiting for me on Fifth Avenue in front of my build-ing? Nobody but Maxie Dehn, big as life and just about as dumb. "Hortense," he said, agitated. "I have to talk to you a second."

They always have to talk to you a second. "Honey," I said, "I love you but I'm late now."

"I have to talk to you."

"I know, honey, but do you want me to lose my job?"

"What do you want a job for?"

The rumba look was in his eyes and I could guess what was coming. Lately, every time he showed up for an hour's dancing, all he could talk about was his big deal. But I'd fallen for his line once, and once is once too many. "Why do I want a job?" I said. "Well, there's my old mother and my old grandmother, and the Siamese twins—"

"Hortense, will you marry me if I put this deal over?"

"Maxie, for God's sake, peddle it someplace else!" I said, losing my temper.
"You don't believe me."

"For God's sake, Maxie, what do you think I am?"

He grabbed my hand and the rumba look in his eyes spread all over his Dutch face like he was seeing the ten best-looking girls in New York dancing around in peach-colored tights. "Hortense, you don't believe me, but I can make forty thousand on this deal. Honest to God!"

Maybe it was the look on his face or the look of Fifth Avenue in the middle of the day, the sun shining, the crowds the stenos mixed in with the minks, but I almost believed him. Maybe because he'd named a definite figure, which he'd never done before when talking about his deal. "Forty thousand! I don't believe it," I said.

"I don't blame you, Hortense, but it's so."

This almost believing is a dangerous business. In a second I was practically believing him. "Maxie," I said, "this isn't another Maxwell deal?"

"This is the real thing," he said. "Honest to God!"

I felt dizzy, I felt as if it were raining money. "You make it," I said. "Just make it," and I kissed him on the cheek. Any man who wants to make forty thousand dollars deserves all the encouragement he can get.

I wasn't breathing when I went into the lobby. Forty thousand, I thought. It couldn't be true, but why shouldn't it be? Why should I be the only one to get cheated all the time? Why shouldn't the law of averages work out for me?

I wasn't breathing when I stepped out of the elevator on the eleventh floor. Shirley Rollins, the receptionist, called me over to her desk. "You're late," she said, "but you don't have to rush out of your slip, honey."

"What's happened?"

"G.L.'s got the butcher boys downstairs in the fish tank. The teachers're hanging around."

We speak a special little language at the George Lawrence School of the Dahntz. G.L., of course, is the mastermind himself. Butcher boys, male or female, are our supervisors, one supervisor for every nine or ten teachers. By the fish tank, Shirley meant the business offices down on the tenth floor, where G.L. and his executives do their big thinking, not only for us up on the eleventh, but for the 209 studios all over the country.

"I could kiss you, Shirley," I said.

"None of your poison kisses, honey. Tell me, what's the dirt these days in the teachers' lounge? Who's making time with who?"

I laughed. "Shirley, honey, honest. What's the difference?"

"What do you feel so good for? You making some time yourself?"

But nothing could get under my skin that day, not even a dose like Shirley. She didn't like me, but it wasn't personal. Shirley had no use for any girl who was young and pretty. If you were young and pretty, you were like a different breed of animal to Shirley Rollins. She was about thirty-five herself and fading like a funeral-parlor lily. She was one of those candy-stick blondes that never last long, with perfectly lovely and gorgeous breasts that were nothing but an optical illusion. I didn't envy her her job. All day she sat at her desk in the reception room, which that year was a duplicate of a Westchester County living room. Chintz curtains, a fireplace with pine logs, and freshly cut flowers brought in from the gardens outside the door, but don't slip down the elevator shaft by mistake. It was like sitting inside a department-store window. I almost felt sorry for Shirley. She was stuck. "Shirley," I said, "let's call off the war."

She smiled, too, a smile sprayed with acid. "What in hell's the matter with you, anyway? You act like you've found a million bucks."

"That's right, but cut it in half."

"What've you got there?" She pointed at the New York Times under my arm.

I'd forgotten the work of art I'd heisted. "The Times, honey." On her desk there was a tabloid open on a halfpage photo of a half-dressed dame.

"Since when do you read the Times?"

"I'm an intellectual, Shirley, didn't you know that?"

"Nuts," she said. "What've you got inside that paper you found on the subway?"

"A painting you wouldn't understand, honey. Very intellectual. Who's the dame in your paper?"

"Let's see that painting."

I held it up for Shirley. She looked at it and said, "What in hell's it supposed to be?"

"It's a naked dame," I kidded her. "Modern art, so she's kind of disguised."

"Yeah? What's she supposed to be doing?"

"She's being divorced or murdered or something, like that dame in your paper, and the picture's called: 'Men Are All Bastards.'"

"You ought to know," Shirley said, and she grinned. "How many bastards've there been in your life?"

"You're going to get me mad someday, honey," I said. I walked off, but Shirley wasn't satisfied.

"Have you got your alarm clock in that bag, honey?"

I turned around. "Sure thing. With an extra pair of falsies you can borrow."

She couldn't say a word and I was almost sorry for hitting her below the belt, or was it below the neckline? I went down the corridor. There was no sense trying to call off the war with Shirley. It wasn't her war or mine, but she couldn't understand that. All she knew was that time was passing her by. A shiver ran down my spine, for time wasn't exactly slow motion for me any more either. If I believed in praying I would've prayed right then and there for Maxie's deal to go through. I would've prayed to God or to luck, or to the law of averages. Or maybe it's time you had to pray to.

Nobody was in the teachers' lounge. They were all with their butcher boys.

I hung up my coat in the lockers in the rear and cached the picture. I changed into my spare dress and looked at myself in the mirror. That's what the lounge is, mirrors—a great big room with two wall-length mirrors on both sides, with green leather wall seats under them. My dress was dark gray and it fitted me perfectly. I began to feel better. I thought of how big forty thousand was and all my blues went. I thought I looked like a forty-thousand-dollar dame in that mirror. I liked my big brown eyes, and my dark hair swept away from my forehead, and the shape of my mouth, the upper lip short and curved, the lower lip full. I didn't need falsies, I didn't need anything. I had it all. I could have been a starlet. At least, a cigarette girl in a top-drawer night club. Glamorous, yes, sir. That's why they flocked to George Lawrence, where we gave off glamour like heat from a radiator.

That's why the wall-length mirrors. Even when a girl wasn't booked, she had to be conscious of her appearance. The refrigerator in the teachers' lounge with its containers of milk and chocolates supplied free by G.L., the public pay-telephone booth, the quota board or misery board, as we call it, to remind you if you're behind in your renewals—they're all part of the furnishings. But the big thing in the teachers' lounge is the mirrors. Because the big thing at the George Lawrence School of the Dahntz is Appearance with a capital A. Down on the tenth floor they've got it organized into a science. Teachers can look like college kids and wear blouse-skirt ensembles, or like debs in tea dresses, or like smart but beautiful executive types in tailored suits. But we can't wear evening dresses because evening dresses, although glamorous, are also, shut your eyes, sexy. And we can't wear comfortable dancing shoes like the men teachers because we have to look feminine, which means our shoes have to start a gleam in the cold eye of a cripple. Isn't that sexy? No, say the masterminds on the tenth floor. A man first looks at a girl's feet, they say on the tenth floor. What the tenth floor should do is send an investigator to the reception room and let him see for himself where the eyes of the cripples go when they spot Shirley and her bosom.

I hurried out of the lounge to join my group and I began to play a little game with myself, I felt that good. I pretended this was my last day at the George Lawrence School of the Dahntz. Maxie had made his pile and I was quitting. Everything about the school struck me as a big joke. The corridor walls painted green—green was the favorite color of the tenth-floor masterminds that year—made me smile. I scuffed my heels into the green carpeting and I laughed. Green was so relaxing, I thought, especially the green of folding money.

I passed by the private soundproof studios in the corridor. Their doors were also green, a dark green, each with a little peephole because too many wives and husbands had complained, "I'd just like to know what goes on when you're alone with your teacher, or is teacher, excuse me, the wrong word?" What went on in the private studios was salesmanship. Prospectives were interviewed and sold dancing courses and old pupils signed up for more hours. And between one and two, except when there was a general meeting in the main ballroom, the teachers met in them with their butcher boys.

My group was in Studio 6. They were all there. Diana in a skirt-blouse ensemble up on the desk, Milly in a tea dress sharing the only chair with Claudia, Bernarda and Ilus in the S.R.O. contingent, Thelma and Sophia sitting on the floor and smoking as if at a party, glamour girls one and all. Milly waved at me. "I want to talk to you later, honey."

"See my lawyer," I said.

"Still drunk? That's what you get from taking on two guys in one sitting, and two artists, at that."

It was obvious how she'd been entertaining the company. "Where's Hortense?" they must have asked, and Milly'd given them her two-at-a time routine. I wrapped both of my arms around my head and in an imitation man's voice I yelled, "S.O.S. Save me from Milly, signed Ted. S.O.S. Save me from Milly, signed her poor husband."

They all laughed. I sat down on the floor next to Thelma. She was all ready with a questionnaire to fill out about last night. "Honey," I said to her, "it's a long haul to ten o'clock, so let me alone." She started talking to Sophia on what was wrong with the theatre. I felt like saying, Only the theatre? But I kept my big mouth shut. My motto's never get into an argument with the serious types. They talk too much. Thelma Sanchez, born Griswold, was taking a master's degree in psychology at Columbia. Sophia Marsh was studying at the Art Students League on 57th Street. Both those girls were teaching dancing only until they'd completed their schooling. They had a future, and could they bend your ear about it! They were the exact opposites of girls like Milly and Claudia, who didn't have any more future than a butterfly with one wing off, and who didn't give a damn, dancing after hours at the Arcadia or Palladium or Havana-Madrid and knocking around all over town.

Serious types, butterflies, and Macy saleswomen—that about describes it. The Macy saleswomen were the ambitious girls who were always putting the pressure on their pupils, selling hours like crazy, so they could make a good record and become a supervisor or even a branch manager in Newark or Philly or L.A. We had some in our group, girls like Bernarda Sann and Diana White. "I've got a cripple from Scarsdale," Diana was saying, "who signed up for twenty-five hours, but I can't squeeze another hour out of him. Give me Brooklyn any day." I thought I could sell hours with the best of the Macy saleswomen when I was in the mood. But who wanted to be in the mood? I was just a half-breed anyway. Half Macy and half butterfly, Hortense the alarm-clock kid. Yet not so long ago I'd been a serious type myself. That was before I'd come to the studio, when I'd still hoped to be an actress. Sitting there, listening to all the buzz, I thought to myself if Maxie cinched the forty thousand, why couldn't I give it a whirl again?

"Hortense," Thelma said, "what are you smiling like that for?"

"This is my last day at George Lawrence, honey."

"She's going to be an artist's model from now on," Milly laughed at me.

Before I could say anything, Lila Rand, our own little butcher boy, blew in, yelling for Diana to get off the desk. Lila dumped her folders and reports and then she looked at us with a pair of eyes cold as a policewoman's heart. "G.L.'s planning himself a vacation." As she spoke, her eyes were punching away at Thelma, Ilus, and Sophia, the three girls in our group behind on their sales quotas. Sure enough, after some more general remarks, she went for them. "Twelve solid weeks to sell a thousand hours in renewals! So we have to have three deadheads! Thelma, what kind of stuff do they teach you at Columbia?"

"My quota period isn't up yet, Lila," Thelma said.

Lila Rand snatched up a report from the desk and shook it at Thelma. "You've got three or four more weeks to go and nothing like that last-minute finish," Lila said. "Of course, of course!" She studied the report in her hand. "You've got two beginners, Thelma. A twenty-five hour and a fifty-hour, taking one hour a week each. Can't you push them up to two? All these beginners are hot early in the course, don't you know that, Professor? Push them up to two and they're riper than bananas to renew."

"Lila, I'll try," Thelma promised her.

"You'll try!" Lila sneered. "What are you waiting for, Professor? For the feeling they're Clark Gable to wear off? I've watched you dancing, Thelma. You act like your cripples have b.o. and every other kind of stinko, and you're supposed to be the hot Spanish type. Snuggle up to them, *Espanol!* That's the kind of psychology pays off, Professor! Take this fifty hour of yours, this Mr. Mausberg. Why doesn't he renew?"

"He hasn't the money," Thelma said swiftly. "He's only a file clerk. Where can he get the money for another course, I'd like to know, Lila?"

"Where he gets it isn't your business!" Lila shouted. "Let him steal it. Let him hock his furniture. Where he gets it! Why don't you bring him the money if you're so sorry for him? God Almighty, if that's what they teach you at Columbia, they ought to close the joint down!"

"What do you want Thelma to do?" I butted in. "Renew that cripple and support him the rest of her life?"

There was a shocked silence. Even Lila was silent. I was shocked myself. No teacher ever talked back to a butcher boy. But it wasn't me giving her the lip. It was the forty thousand. The guy who said money talks never was so right.

"I'll report you!" Lila shouted at me when she was normal again. "I'll report you, Hortense Walton, you goddamn—"

What else she might've said or done I don't know, but just as she was recovering her voice, the warning bell, the five-of-two bell, rang. She threw me a dirty look, and grabbing her paperwork from the desk, she shot through the door. We all tore after her. "You're on Lila's list," Thelma said, as we rushed down the corridor into the teachers' lounge for the Course Books of our two o'clocks.

"Why'd you have to stick your nose in?" Milly said. "You rummy!"

"This is my last day in this rat race," I said.

"You're a wack!" Milly said. "But there's a limit. Kids, you hear what this wackeroo says?"

There was the usual mob scene at the files and nobody was much interested, not with the two o'clocks waiting in the reception room. Milly broadcast what a hero I was, but nobody cared. I dug out my own two o'clock's Course Book and just then somebody goosed me. I turned around. All the faces of the men anywhere near me lifted toward the ceiling like they were praying. "You, you crumb Dexter!" I yelled, and then I laughed. He must've thought I was really touched in the head. He didn't know that the curtain was going down on his call girl proposition even before it'd gone up.

I hurried out of the lounge with the swifties, behind us the thundering herd. I thought of how I'd said this was my last day. If only it'd been true! All around me, the groaners were groaning as usual, the moaners moaning. Everything was as usual, except for me. Some man teacher was saying, "If only the old cripple I've got doesn't ask me to hold her tight." Somebody else cheered him up with, "If you don't hold those old crocks tight they'll fall apart." A girl ahead of me let out a shriek and said, "I'm still behind on my sales quota," which left her wide open for the standard gag, "That's because you don't put your behind behind it, honey." Everything was as usual except for me.

"White teeth!" I said as we reached the reception room where the two o'clocks were waiting. If I hadn't said it somebody else would have. It was standard, too.

We all smiled, flashing that happy and carefree smile recommended by the Teachers' Guidebook, and which the pupils naturally expected from handsome men and glamour girls.

"Mr. Graham," Thelma the Sanchez was saying near me. "How are you on this wonderful autumn day? I know we'll have a marvelous lesson!"

"Mr. Plunger," Milly was saying. "Shall we do a little rumba?"

My own two o'clock was near the fireplace. There were six pine logs in the fireplace, and the story going around the studio was that G.L. had selected them personally; he spent a couple of hours doing it, and when Mrs. G.L. had asked him why he wasted his valuable time like that, G.L. had picked up the Teachers' Guidebook and found the sentence he wanted, which was: "The little detail helps you retail." I remembered that story as I went over to my two o'clock, but it didn't seem funny any more.

"Mr. Ralph!" I smiled at my cripple. "I'm glad to see you."

"Maybe you are and maybe you aren't," he said with a grin. He was one of the suspicious types. He owned a ladies' shoe store, which he left once a week to become a movie star. We swapped a few witty remarks and went into the jitterbug ballroom. As usual, it looked like a mass demonstration on how to

commit a crime of passion. Twenty or thirty couples were knocking themselves out as the canned music banged out the wha-wha-wha. Some of those
jitterbugs looked as if they'd get down to it after finishing a marathon race—
they were doing Step No. 3 in the George Lawrence Jitterbug, the Sophomore
Pursuit; others after a wrestling match with Step No. 5, the Whacky Whoo;
still others after imitating two sidewalk pigeons in the mating season with
Step No. 6, the Dustoff. I gritted my teeth and got ready. We jitterbugged until
the half-hour bell, when we walked to the rumba ballroom. Jitterbug and
rumba. My two o'clock was one of these combination schmoes. I looked at his
happy flushed face. He was relaxed, loosened up, jitterbugged into Sunset
Boulevard, the pride of Hollywood, and the ladies' shoe store was still thirty
minutes away. Now was the time to renew him. The hell with it, I thought.
Wasn't this my last day at the school? It wasn't, but thinking it was gave me a
thrill. I guess I'm one of those born with a soft spot in the brain.

In the rumba ballroom, too, everything was as usual, with the hips in full
control. Hips swaying, revolving, shaking like cocktail shakers. "Let's go," my
happy boy said. "Let's rumba, Hortense. What do you say we rumba?"

"Eyes strained, hips unrestrained—that's a rumba hound," I said.

"Did you just make that up, Hortense?"

"No, it's standard around here."

"Standard?" he said, puzzled. "Let's rumba, Hortense. All I want to do is
rumba, and no sales talk!"

We walked over to the ballroom chairs, but I didn't put down his Course
Book. I showed it to him. His name was handwritten under the school's
emblem, which was a golden dancing girl like those Greek statues at the museum. She was running across a green shield with a big golden L in the middle,
running fast like some joker'd given her the hotfoot.

"What's that?" he asked me.

"That's your Course Book, Mr. Ralph."

"Hortense, don't sell me—"

"Since you've reminded me, Mr. Ralph—"

He laughed. "Yeah, I reminded you."

"We ought to plan a more detailed course, Mr. Ralph."

"Nope," he said. "I'm broke, Hortense."

"You're halfway through your course, a fifty-hour course, Mr. Ralph. Now
you didn't get to own a shoe store in fifty hours," I said, warming up. If he had
been a lawyer I would've said, You didn't get to practice law in fifty hours. We
had a thousand little comebacks like that listed in the Teachers' Guidebook,
which is, among other things, the most up-to-date collection of moldy old
clichés ever assembled between two covers. "Mr. Ralph, your jitterbug is fair,
but your rumba needs a lot of improving."

"Let's improve it, Hortense," he laughed. "I'm not here for a lesson in speech-
making, or am I?"

He thought he was pretty wise, like some of the suckers do. "You're right," I told this victim. "You're here for a lesson in the rumba." The rumba music was pouring out of the can and I could see he was aching to throw himself in, hips first. We walked to the ballroom floor and for about five minutes I let him enjoy himself. Then I said, "Keep your body straight, Mr. Ralph. The dance floor should move under you."

"Like this?" he said.

"No, like this. You should move like a door, all in one piece, Mr. Ralph."

"Like this?"

"That's a little better. But sway those hips slightly. Slightly, Mr. Ralph, I said."

"Like this?"

"No. You're sailing them out to Fifth Avenue."

"Hortense!" he squawked.

"Mr. Ralph, I can't help it. You've got to think of your styling."

"You're being too critical, Hortense, because you want to make a sale. Sell, sell, sell!"

"Nobody's forcing you to buy anything, Mr. Ralph. You can use your own judgment. But do you want me to praise your rumba when I shouldn't?"

We rumbaed until the five-of bell stopped the dancing. *Bonggg* it sounded. By *onggg* we were all saying good-bye to our two o'clocks. Good-bye, good-bye, dear left feet, dear cripple, good-bye, for in the reception room were all the dear little three o'clocks. I unloaded my two o'clock and thought what a feeling it'd be to hear those bells for the last time. To hear the *onggg* fading to *nggg* for the very last time. On the subject of those bells, I'm not all there. Why, I even have dreams about them. In one dream, the bells were bonging but I knew they weren't really bells but the voice of somebody, somebody you couldn't see, and when I woke up I thought that the somebody was the one who ran the whole studio from G.L. down to Tilson, the porter. *Bonggg* and *onggg* and *nggg*. All day long, on the hour and on the half-hour, the dear suckers waiting in the Westchester County living room with the six pine logs and Shirley's gorgeous falsies, the teachers caught by the bells as much as the pupils, and that went for me, too, Miss Wise Guy in person, in the flesh, especially the flesh that I tanked up with booze every other night and then dumped on some bed somewhere. I was the biggest sucker of all because I thought I was such a wise guy.

As I rushed into the reception room to pick up my three o'clock, I thought I'd been caught but good, almost two years working for those bells, caught like any other sucker, and if not for Maxie Dehn, where would I be? For there's only one way to stop being a sucker, and that is to catch one. To catch yourself a sucker with forty little G's to his name.

"Dr. Boyden," I said to my three o'clock. "I've missed you very much. How are you on this wonderful day?"

He smiled but his smile didn't help his looks any. He was one of those men with an eyeglass face. He'd signed up for fifty hours to please his wife, who was about twenty years younger than he was. He had plenty of dough, Dr. Boyden, but anybody behind the eight ball of a December-May marriage could only be a sucker. But of course he didn't know it and I didn't tell him. Even if he learned to dance like G.L. in his prime or like Fred Astaire, it wouldn't have done him any good with Mrs. Boyden.

We went into the fox-trot ballroom, and as we fox-trotted, I noticed him frowning. I waited for him to explain what was bothering him. They always do, sooner or later. It was either the lousy wife or the lousy girl friend or the lousy business or the lousy job. "Hortense," he said, "there's a tune in my head I can't get rid of. I'm always humming it. Just this morning one of my patients, Mrs. Fiske, asked me what it was."

"She did?" I said, only half listening, for I was again playing that game—Last Day at the Studio. A game like that is like the drug habit—you're in cloudland before you know it.

"I couldn't admit what it was. It's an aria from 'Aida,' I told Mrs. Fiske. You understand, Hortense. My practice is high-class. What else could I say?"

"What was it?"

A foolish smile spread all over his face. It reminded me of Maxie downstairs. "It's that 'Nino Yacovino' tune," he said.

I sang him a line of it: "'Nino Yacovino has a gleam in his eye till the cute senoritas will sigh.'"

"Please," he begged me, blushing. We danced for a few minutes and then he said, "Hortense, have I any real ability as a dancer?"

They're always keen to know if they have any real ability. I could've answered him by quoting from the Teachers' Guidebook. Under the heading "Sympathy," there was: "Think back to the time when you couldn't even hold a girl properly in dance position, let alone do such a nice fox trot." Etc. But today, this one day, I didn't feel like hand-picking a nice little sympathy for Dr. Boyden. He was really a nice man.

"You're improving," I said, trying the straight unadulterated truth.

It worried him, for he said again, "Have I any real ability, Hortense?"

What can you do with a sucker? I couldn't give him what he really wanted, which was to be as young as his wife. He wanted magic. All the suckers did. What else, with the ballroom, all five of them, painted the softest of greens like Central Park in the springtime, and the music sweet and low? Naturally, they didn't want the truth, none of them, and the Teachers' Guidebook was right, as usual. Around the 200-page mark there was exactly what the patient, who in Dr. Boyden's case happened to be a doctor, craved: "It is not enough to concentrate on a pupil's dancing present or to remind a pupil of his unsatisfactory dancing past. Every pupil is entitled to a dancing future." This gem was under the heading "Psychological Pointers for Your Pupil."

"You're making splendid progress," I said, feeding Dr. B. the syrup he was crying for. "I know you will be one of our best dancers someday."

A dancing future was what he wanted, and I gave it to him via the George Lawrence Fox Trot, with each step exactly eleven inches long. Measure it, folks. Not eleven and a half or ten and a half, but exactly eleven inches, with Dr. B. gliding on the balls of his feet, and with me up on my toes. He began to feel better, humming this "Nino Yacovino," and I encouraged him. "Co-ordination between the mind and the feet improve if you hum while you dance," I said to Dr. B.

I was glad when the five-of-three bell stopped the dancing. I was beginning to go dead. Some girls can work off a big night by dancing, but me, I need sleep.

"Am I improving?" Dr. B. asked me hopefully.

"You're improving," I said, and I smiled as the Teachers' Guidebook recommended at parting: "A smile costs you nothing but to your pupil it may mean everything." "Dr. Boyden, I know you will become one of the best pupils I've ever had."

I wasn't booked between four and five, so it was the teachers' lounge for me. Milly, who wasn't booked either, tried to corner me about Dexter, but I sidestepped her. "I've got a date with the milk company," I said, heading for the refrigerator. I felt tired and sleepy. The forty thousand Maxie had waved under my nose just about vanished into thin air. When you're exhausted like that, it's hard to believe in anything.

"Since when do you drink milk?" Milly shouted after me. "What you doing? Building yourself up because you're on Lila's list?" She followed me over to the milk-and-chocolate crowd. That goddamn big blonde just had too much energy. "You look like hell, honey," she kept pestering me. "Terrible, honey. Awful."

I couldn't get rid of her. I would've needed the help of a couple of lady wrestlers. I took my container of milk and walked over to where Claudia and a couple other girls were talking, Milly tagging along. Claudia and her pals put big fake red smiles on their mouths when we came over.

"Who's getting knifed, Claudia?" I said.

"Sh!" she whispered. "G.L.'s just stepped inside. Sh!"

I sat down next to Claudia, Milly next to me, and we all watched G.L. make his entrance. "Is everybody happy?" He smiled right and left, and in return we gave him our biggest smiles. It was like a neon sign flashing on when you consider that there were about twenty of us in the lounge.

This was one of G.L.'s conservative days. He was wearing a double-breasted blue suit, a white shirt and a black necktie, and he could've been a banker with his bald head and thin long face with its bushy blond eyebrows and little blue eyes. On his not so conservative days, G.L. would sport a Riviera jacket and Monte Carlo trousers carefully selected not to match and a necktie with which you could've started a fire. There was a story about him that when he was revising the Teachers' Guidebook, he always dressed conservative, but when he was editing the monthly magazine we have, "The Lawrence Dansant," with its glamour photographs of teachers and snappy keyhole style, he would be dressed sporty. A book could be written about G.L. Busy as he was, he always had the time to come upstairs for a surprise visit. We were his very own little boys and girls, and he was Papa, always reminding us that we were the envy of the teachers in all the other studios. Dear, dear Papa. But he certainly was generous to us. The milk and chocolates were just a trifle. Girls who kept up with their quotas were given dresses, and the men received monogrammed shirts. When we were sick he paid our doctor bills and sent us flowers. We were just one big happy family. Still, life with Papa had its headaches. Because Papa was wacked up on what he called *élan*, which may mean one thing in France, but up at the Fifth Avenue studio it meant perfection, with a big P.

He marched in, smiling at us. Then he sniffed. "The air is bad in here," he said. He was also wacked up on the subject of fresh air. "Open some windows! We don't want any colds, do we?"

A couple of the boys broke an ankle to obey. G. L. breathed in the fresh air. He looked kind of tense. Down on the tenth floor they put in an hour a day just whipping each other—that's my theory. When G.L. left, we all relaxed.

"Sooner he goes on his vacation, better I'll like it," Milly said. She nudged me with her elbow. "You coming in with Dex?"

"Don't rush me, kid," I said, wriggling my feet out of my shoes.

"Nobody's rushing you, but we have to know. We're starting in in a couple weeks. Dex wants to talk to you."

"Honey, Dex'll have to talk to my private secretary. Now let me sleep! I'm dead." I shut my eyes to get rid of the sight of her face. She had a face like a doll's, all yellow hair and big blue eyes, until you looked more closely and saw that something was wrong with the eyes, the same thing that was wrong with her mouth.

She let me alone, getting into the conversation with Claudia and the others. Claudia was saying a Martini would come in real handy now. Milly said her favorite was rye on the rocks, which reminded her of the guy who'd taught her about rye on the rocks. Claudia said she could stand almost any guy who knew his liquor. I thought Claudia was a natural for Dexter. She wasn't kidding about standing any guy. And she was pretty, a redhead with a milk-and-cream complexion that her life as a part-time dipso hadn't ruined yet. Still, according to Dex and Milly, they hadn't approached Claudia. She could take my place, I thought. The hell with them all.

I leaned back against the leather seat and let my muscles go limp. I could hear the lounge comics performing as usual at the refrigerator, at the misery board, and even at the public phone booth. Some card was explaining an invention to ferment cow's milk, while at the misery board the wisecracks were on the blue side. In the phone booth some man was saying, "This isn't a dancing school, sir. This is the Bellevue Mental Clinic, sir." A girl yelled, "I'll kill you, Jimmy, if that's Herbie." I listened to the racket and I hoped Maxie's deal would work out so I could say the hell with it. I was fed up with the George Lawrence School of the Dahntz, this lonely hearts club set to music. This little dreamland painted nice and green where every pair of left feet, with a face that not even a mother could love, unless she was stone blind, could dream himself, herself, themselves—watch your tenses—delirious. To hell with it, I thought. And to hell with Dexter, the future call girl impresario. I just had to get a break sometime. A break to make up for my ex, Ronny, and the cat-and-dog year we'd been married. Ronny was a bastard, but my marriage with him was soft violins compared to the four or five months with The Bastard, in caps. Sitting there in the lounge—thinking, praying, hoping, God knows what I was doing—I still hated to think his name even. The Bastard....

I couldn't stand my thoughts any more. I opened my eyes like you do when you try to forget a nightmare. Claudia was talking, so I concentrated on her, her red hair, her small delicate features. She had a sweet face, like so many of these dipsos. And why not? She'd quit the rat race for good, quit believing in breaks, in luck, in the law of averages, quit hoping for someone to care for her, quit everything but her one true-blue friend, the bottle.

"I knew a man," Claudia was saying. They were all reminded of some man or other. As usual. Milly called Tommy Nivens over for a story. Tommy crossed the lounge. He had wine-colored suedes on his feet and his cardigan jacket was an expensive one. His blond hair was long and smooth and it looked as if he spent a couple hours every day arranging it. I was sick of Tommy, sick of homos, sick of dipsos and nymphos. I was sick of the serious types and the Macy saleswomen. I was sick of the whole damn studio and everybody in it.

Milly started in on her story about the man in the jukebox business whose wife hated jukeboxes, so once when they were in bed, he began to croon, and his wife began to cry he was never to croon like a jukebox when he was with her. It was a dopey pointless story but it got a laugh because it was supposed to be true, and maybe it was. Milly told another, about the man who had to have all the lights on like he worked for the electric company. Maybe this one was true, too. The victory girls that had worked the fleet had nothing on Milly.

I lit a cigarette and waited for the five-of bell to ring. Five to six was chow-time. We'd scramble downstairs for sandwiches and coffee. Or for a couple quick ones, if we were drinking. Then we'd rush back to beat the five-of-six bell. Five of, I thought. Five of, five of, five of. I made myself stop on those damn bells. What I needed was some fresh air. And not the G.L. brand blowing through a window, but a whole streetful of fresh air. I thought of Fifth Avenue at five o'clock, the city hurrying home to dinner, but not us, the avenue getting darker, the limousines riding by, the cocktails and dinner hour, the theatre, the lights, but we'd be rushing into the elevators, the bells going *bonggg* and *onggg* and *nggg,* and even when the last bell bonged at ten, the first bell for tomorrow was being tuned up. Tuned up by whom? By The Bastard....

I inhaled my cigarette deep into my lungs because I felt afraid. Of what, I don't know. I thought that all I wanted was somebody halfway decent to care for me, and I prayed to God to let Maxie make those forty G's. It'd been a long time since I'd prayed to God. It made me feel kind of peculiar, like I was trying to get in somewhere where I didn't belong.

II: GUILTY, NOT GUILTY

HUGH

I tried to keep away from Hortense. That's the truth. I did try. For two weeks every time I had an impulse to phone her, I would think of Maxie sitting over a cup of cold brown coffee and talking his heart out to me. Maxie, who was prepared to risk his partnership, his entire future for Hortense....

If there were no other girls for him, there were for me.

That Saturday night we both had parties, and as we showered and shaved, I had no thought, not a single thought—I swear it—of crashing Maxie's party. But when we reached the corner, the Saturday-night headlights on Eighth Avenue moving in a yellow chain, I had *the thought*—suddenly and overwhelmingly. I held onto Maxie, ashamed of myself, but wondering how I could ask him. Maxie's party, I knew, would be a real party for him, not like that frustrating night in the bar when Hortense had gone off with those two artists. Maxie was escorting Hortense to this party, and he'd be taking her home, maybe sleeping with her tonight. That was how much progress he'd made, or to be cynical, how much progress Maxie was making with Doyle.

"If things are quiet at my party," I heard myself saying, "do you think anybody would mind if I came up, Maxie?" I was ashamed of myself. That's the truth. My own party would be fun. It was down in Greenwich Village on 11th Street, where a girl I'd become friendly with at N.Y.U. shared a place with two other girls. Her name was Rita Hanauer and she was developing quite an interest in me. Rita was a slant-eyed blonde, the kind of girl I had expected to meet in New York, pretty and sophisticated, who between one cocktail and the next could start a conversation on politics or the new music or the ten Egyptian rooms at the Metropolitan Museum of Art.

It seemed a year before Maxie answered me, but he hadn't hesitated for even a second. He laughed. "Come up if you want, Hugh. They'll be too drunk to notice."

"What is it? Another drinking party, Maxie?"

"They always drink, that crowd," he said. "The guy's in the phone book. Tommy Nivens. Like I've told you, he's one of these faggots with money." He punched me softly in the shoulder, almost condescendingly. *"Auf Wiedersehen,"* he said, and walked off.

I stared after him. He was a new man these days. His negotiations with Doyle were going smoothly. He was Maxwell Dehn, Jr., again, and there wasn't one single reason for me to crash his party. No reason—that was true. Only emotion.

Twice in the last few years I had felt this kind of emotion. In 1943 in Charlestown, where our bomber group had been in training, I'd met a girl called Alice Ennsley, and in Rome, the last year of the war, there was an English girl, Beatrice Day. Twice I had wanted a woman so much that nothing else mattered. Call it love if you want. Certainly love had been a part of what I felt for Alice. She was a sweet little blonde who carried her body like a flower pinned inside her dress. I would have married her. Four or five of us future heroes had wanted to marry her, but she'd married a shy slender pilot from Wisconsin. Beatrice I almost hated. She was the worst liar I'd ever come across, with a streak of selfishness that had constantly amazed me, but I would have married her, too. I wanted her that badly. It had been an eye-opener, my affair with her. For an egotist like me, it was shattering to realize how helpless I could be. When Beatrice'd thrown me over for an Air Force major, I couldn't sleep for weeks. I'd written her a long letter every day, and she'd answered just as regularly, using my letters for her stationery, writing a nasty line or two on the bottom. I would glance at my hotly written words and then at her cool flippant replies, and curse her for a bitch. She was a bitch. But what I felt for her, I guess, could have been called love, too.

I walked down Eighth Avenue. Hortense.... She was made of the same illogic as Alice and Beatrice. It was stupid, I thought, whipping up my conscience. And Maxie? He was crazy to hope in the face of the facts when the facts about Hortense were so plain. She was no wife for any man, and why shouldn't I sleep with her if I felt like it? Like those two artists a few weeks ago. Hortense, I thought, and the feeling I had for her wrapped me close. No woman's arms can be so soft.

Before me was a new city. The neons of the Eighth Avenue bars gleamed bright like jeweled metalwork fastened onto the dark tenement brick. Inside the smoky plate-glass windows of the bars, the evening's first drunks were buying drinks for laughing girls who in some strange way knew about Hortense and me, smoky figures in another world who wished me well. The taxis beeped, the cloudy sky was tinted pink, and make-believe dialogues raced off drunkenly inside my mind:

Hortense: How've you been, Air Force?

Me: Pretty good, and how have you been?

Hortense: O.K., I'm glad to see you, Air Force.

Me: Why don't you call me Hugh?...

At Rita's party, I avoided any personal conversation with her, joining the drinking contingent. At a quarter of twelve I kissed Rita good night. She was puzzled, hurt, but she managed a sophisticated hostess smile. I felt like a heel, but the twinge of conscience didn't last, and when I stood at the door of Tommy Nivens' apartment up on Riverside Drive and heard the drunken laughter inside, I thought I hadn't left Rita's party after all.

A thin blond handsome man let me in. He nodded vaguely at the information that I was a friend of Maxie Dehn's. I explained that Maxie had come with Hortense. The thin blond man laughed and fluttered his fine blond hands, and in general seemed to be imitating a swan, so that I was quite sure he was what I thought he was. "You're Tommy Nivens?" I said to him.

"Yes, yes, of course," fluttering. "And you're interested in Hortense, aren't you? And who isn't? Come in, come in, won't you? Throw your coat into the bedroom."

The bedroom was dark, but not so dark that I couldn't see the shapes of two couples without faces on the floor in the far corner. Hastily I tossed my top-coat onto the mountain of clothing on the bed and went into the living room. Here, too, as in the bedroom, they seemed to be allergic to light. The only light came from a blue and green Chinese vase with a huge fringed yellow shade. Eight or nine couples were dancing, and as they circled, the faces of the girls moved from shadow into light into shadow, all the lovely faces of the girls. For that was how they seemed to me. I recognized the blonde teacher Milly Rolfe, the wife of Dexter, but Hortense and Maxie weren't among the dancers. I went looking for them. The dining room had been converted into a bar, the only room in the apartment where all the lights were on. Ten or twelve men and girls were drinking, smoking, and noisily telling stories. "Hello, Dexter," I said to the redheaded teacher I had met that night with Hortense.

He examined me with drunken narrowed eyes as if I'd come up through the floor, while the woman with him, who was also a redhead, a coppery redhead, grabbed both of my arms. "No butcher boys allowed tonight!" she shouted at me, breathing a ripe and mellow whiskey bouquet into my face.

"We met a few weeks ago," I said to Dexter. "I'm a friend of Maxie Dehn's."

"Maxie Dehn," he repeated after me.

"Didn't he get here yet?"

Dexter squinted at me for a second and then he laughed. "How about a drink, pal-o?"

"Thanks! Didn't they get here yet?"

"They're in the bedroom. Ten bucks buys you a ride!"

"Oh," I said.

"Oh!" he imitated me, winking at the redheaded girl. "What'd you say your name was, pal-o?"

"Hugh Pierson."

"Hugh Pierson, I want you to meet Claudia. Claudia Fifth."

I said nothing. Dexter patted me lightly on the chest. "Don't you think it's an odd name—Fifth? Say so! Don't you think it's an odd name? Four fifths of a quart!" He howled with joy.

"Next time I won't miss my cue," I said sourly.

The girl Claudia grinned. "You need a drink, Hugh."

I said, "If he begins on Eleanor Flack and how he sold her a lifetime course, I'll need more than a drink."

Claudia laughed. Dexter looped one arm about her shoulder and the other about mine. He said, "Take this Mrs. Van Raalte cripple of mine. There's a character. Rich but tight. Except when it comes to her dachshund, Baron. Nothin's too good for this pedigreed mutt Baron. Today at the studio she's all upset. Baron bit the butler. 'Dexter,' she complains to me, 'Mortimer may be a good butler, but he simply doesn't understand Baron.' 'How'd it happen?' I ask her, looking sympathetic. 'Poor little Baron, he wouldn't bite anybody.'"

I said, "Let's have a drink."

Dexter said, "I butter up Mrs. Van Raalte and she explains Baron biting the butler like this: 'Dexter, I asked Mortimer to put on Baron's coat before we took our usual morning walk. It's rather heavy, you know, fur-lined. All of Pedro Perer's creations for the well-dressed pet are on the pretentious side, I think.'"

Claudia sighed. "Hurry up, Dex."

"When the butler reached for Baron's coat, Baron growled. 'The dear thing was warning Mortimer,' Mrs. Van Raalte says. 'Baron has been very possessive about his coat ever since he hid those steak bones in it. Why, the psychiatrist said that the dear dog associated his coat with his dinner and naturally was afraid it'd be stolen from him. A perfectly normal neurosis.' "

"Time for a drink!" Claudia said.

"Two drinks," I said.

I stopped counting after the second drink. I concentrated on the liquor and I was rewarded. The room tilted interestingly, and seemed full of redheads. Later, I don't know how much later, I was back in the living room. They weren't dancing now, for a show was going on in the dance space in the center. Tommy Nivens, the thin blond man who had let me into the house, was reciting. "Another day in the George Lawrence Empire. Scene, the fox-trot ballroom. Characters, a wolfess aged forty-two and yours truly." He rolled his eyes like a woman's. "Tommy, hold me tight, will you, honey?" he whispered in the role of the wolfess. Then the woman's eyes changed into the sly and sad and abandoned eyes of a homo. He clapped his hands quickly like an announcer. "Every day, coast to coast, they want to be held tight. Can anybody tell me what their husbands are so busy holding every night from coast to coast?"

As if in a dream, I remembered that Hortense and Maxie, for all I knew, were still in the bedroom. They were having a party of their own, I considered vaguely, and I should've stayed at Rita's. Not that it mattered, I thought. Nothing really mattered. It was a comforting thought.

A girl in a white evening dress danced out toward Tommy Nivens. She threw her hands over her head, laughed wildly, and began to do the bumps. Tommy coyly covered his eyes with his hands and asked, "What does the Guidebook say about this?" He peeked between his fingers, and as he peeked, he danced about the bumpmaker, gliding about her as if skating on ice. The bumps came faster and faster. "Oh, where is my Guidebook?" he cried in mock horror. "Where is my very own Teachers' Guidebook?" Dancing, he snatched at an imaginary book, thumbed through imaginary pages. The girl flung herself to the floor. Her dress slid up over her thighs as she tossed about. "I have it," Tommy Nivens said to the crowd, and gripping the imaginary book he read, "A pupil must understand that rhythm is an indispensable asset if the pupil has an asset, and what pupil hasn't?"

The crowd laughed and applauded, but I felt sour about the whole performance. Drunk as I was, and come here tonight for my own doubtful purposes, I could still reserve a moral judgment.

The girl in white stood up, smiling at the applause. Somebody shouted, "How about the maharaja act, Tommy?"

"Hortense!" the girl in white said, as if inspired. "Where's Hortense? I'll get Hortense."

Tommy Nivens said, "Will you, honey?"

The crowd waited and I waited too. My head ached and the cigarette smoke of all these strangers bit into my nostrils. I was sobering a little, wondering about the "maharaja act," and wondering about myself. With the edge of my drinking wearing off, I thought that what I should do was go home.

It was a tired Hortense who finally appeared, a Hortense without Maxie. She had obviously straightened up, her hair brushed and neat, new lipstick on her lips. The crowd called to her, advised her, kidded her, while I asked myself what there was about this dark slender girl in the black cocktail dress that had caused me to walk out on Rita and her party. She seemed about to fall apart, as probably Maxie had. There were shadows under her eyes, her shoulders drooped.

Tommy Nivens bowed, and in the character of announcer he said, "Scene, the teachers' lounge. Miss Hortense Walton, relaxing between cripples. Hortense is seventeen years old and pure as the driven snow."

Hortense closed her eyes, rocking her body and humming a lullaby, a simper of innocence on her face. Tommy Nivens danced toward her. "Hortense!" he cried excitedly. "We've got a maharaja in the school! Hurry!" Hortense's eyes opened. She, too, began to dance. She danced as if it were her very first big dance and she were really seventeen. She danced with an inner beauty, her face radiant and sweet like that of a young girl to whom the world itself is a ball. The tired Hortense of a few minutes ago was gone, gone with the Hortense I remembered, the barfly Hortense and Maxie's double-crossing sweetheart. This girl dancing, without music, was the girl I had come to see. There was a mystery about her, I felt. Her acting, her impersonations concealed something secret. Corn? Inner Beauty and Secret and Mystery! Of course! But the only difference between corn and the real thing is the beat of your pulse. As I stood there in that crowd, in that living room, I felt as if only now was I waking up. More corn? Maybe, and who cared? I was in love, and only a minute ago I had been staring coldly at the girl in the black cocktail dress.

"If you're nice to a maharaja, he'll introduce you to a raja," Tommy was singsonging, his blond homosexual face lifted toward the ceiling, like some weak angel's. He clapped his hands, his head loose on his neck, his eyes wicked, singsonging, "Raja, baja, waja."

A few in the crowd laughed, but most of us were quiet, expectant.

"The maharaja has brought his wife to the studio," Tommy Nivens said in the character of announcer. "His wife wishes to learn to dance, but no man can teach her! It is their custom!"

He began to dance about the dancing Hortense, singsonging, "No man can teach her, raja, baja, waja. Her teacher has to be a girl, raja, baja, waja. Pure, untouched, and undefiled!" he sang madly. "It's one of their customs, raja, baja, waja. East is east and west is west, and if you're nice to a raja, he'll introduce you to a paja, a waja, a maharaja." His body circled Hortense faster and faster. Dancing closer, he put both of his hands on her cheeks. "Pure, untouched, and undefiled," he sang, as if mimicking the famous "bewitched, bothered, and bewildered" line out of "Pal Joey." Neither of them had stopped dancing for a second. "You'll pass, Hortense, unless there's an autopsy, raja, baja, waja," Tommy singsonged, patting her hips.

As if he'd pressed some button, Hortense's hips swayed wickedly, although her face was still like a young girl's.

"Come on, virge!" Tommy Nivens cried. He clapped his hands over his head and sang, "Vaja, baja, waja. Props!" he called to the crowd. "Props!"

A silken scarf fluttered out to him. Tommy caught it, knotted it around his hips. As he did so, his body seemed to reshape itself to the silk. Not only was he dancing like a girl; he now looked like a girl, his eyes widening, his lips jutting. Tommy's dancing slowed, his arms described sharp angles like an Oriental dancer's. "The maharaja's wife!" he cooed shyly.

Hortense, very hippy now, fox-trotted over toward Tommy with the energy of a bebop kid. "Mrs. Maharaja," she said. "I'm Miss Pure, Untouched, and Undefiled!"

Dancing, Tommy singsonged, "Paja, paja, paja."

"You've never danced American style?"

"Naja, naja, naja," answered Mrs. Maharaja, shaking her head no.

"Not even with your husband, Mrs. Maharaja?"

"Not even with my husband, the Maharaja, waja, paja."

Hortense stroked the silken scarf wrapped about Mrs. Maharaja's hips. "What a beautiful sari!"

Mrs. Maharaja stood perfectly still, his body weaving like a snake's, his eyes rolling toward the ceiling.

"It's made of gold thread, Mrs. Maharaja!" Hortense said.

"Raja, baja, waja."

"Let's dance, Mrs. Maharaja. Let's rumba." She stared straight at the crowd, clicked her fingers. "One rumba coming up!" she shouted like a waitress.

The crowd roared, the drunks whistled, and somebody started a rumba record going on the player. In this informal intermission I asked the faces about me if Hortense and Tommy had rehearsed this show. The faces said no, they improvised.

Tommy had covered his eyes with his hands, singsonging in a pathetic voice, "I do not wish to be taught the rumba, rumja, bumja, wumja."

Hortense rumbaed in front of him. "Why not, Mrs. Maharaja?"

"It's too suggestive, saja, saja, saja."

"Everybody rumbas in America," Hortense cried, and she pulled Tommy's hands from his eyes.

"Do unmarried girls like you rumba publicly?"

"Let's rumba, Mrs. Maharaja."

"I hesitate."

"Nobody ever hesitates in America," Hortense chanted as she rumbaed. "Remember the rhythm isn't only in your feet, it's in your teeth."

"Maja, maja, maja," Tommy singsonged as he rumbaed.

"Mrs. Maharaja, let's dance together, now."

Tommy stopped rumbaing. He pressed his arms tightly against his sides and stared at Hortense flashing around him. Shaking his head sadly, he singsonged, "Naja, naja, naja."

"What's the matter now, Mrs. Maharaja?"

"I've never been held by anybody in a dance, daja, daja, daja."

"I'm not anybody, Mrs. Maharaja. A girl doesn't count when she dances with another girl."

"Naja, naja, naja."

"What's two girls, anyway, Mrs. Maharaja?"

Tommy grinned, and as the announcer he said, "We'd hate to tell you, virge!"

"Give me your hand, Mrs. Maharaja."

"Naja, naja, naja."

"It's all right to give me your hand, Mrs. Maharaja. What's a hand, anyway?"

Suddenly they were both rumbaing like two rumba fiends. It was the finale. The show was over. There was applause and the thirsty adjourned to the dining room. I trailed Hortense and four or five others, giggling critics of the show and hangers-on, into the dining room. After I had a stiff drink in my hand, I edged into the circle about Hortense. When I had the chance, I smiled and introduced myself, congratulating her on her acting. Dexter, who apparently had skipped the show, grinned drunkenly at me. "You ought to look in on Maxie. Somebody ought to look in on Maxie!" Hortense lifted a highball glass to her lips. I thought I had never seen so white a throat. I felt like telling her about her white throat. Instead I asked if Maxie needed any help. She smiled and said Maxie was sleeping like a baby. More men and girls trooped into the dining room, waving at Hortense. Ice cubes tinkled in glasses. The party had climbed like a plane as far as it was going to, and now was coming down in a field of whiskey. You could hardly breathe in that jammed dining room. I turned to Hortense and said that I'd like to talk to her where there was less noise. Dexter kissed her. She told him to go away and to take me with him. I forced a grin on my lips as if to prove I was enjoying every minute of this and asked Hortense why she didn't want to talk to me.

"Pal-o," Dexter said, "shall I tell you?"

"Tell him," Hortense laughed.

"You haven't any character pal-o. The little lady always looks for some sign of character in a man."

"Like the dollar sign," Hortense said.

"Don't you ever let up on the performance?" I said to her. "Or are all of you dance teachers frustrated actors too?"

Instead of getting angry, she smiled and held out her empty glass to me. I pushed my way in at the bar, fixed a new drink for Hortense, laced my own with a couple of inches. Then I went over to her. "Hortense, if you want this drink, you'll have to hike for it."

She nodded and escaped Dexter's arm about her waist. In the living room, a last moony couple was dancing near the windows. On the couch a jokesmith was knocking out stories, and in the big soft chairs the twosomes were whispering. We sat down on some brocaded pillows, our backs against the wall. "Where does Tommy get all his money?" I asked her. It wasn't a very sensational beginning, but I'd forgotten all my witty openers.

"His folks're rich. They send him all the money he wants to stay the hell out of there."

"The hell out of where?"

"Cleveland."

"That's no town," I said, as if I didn't come from Hightstown, New Jersey, myself.

"Cleveland?" she said, and laughed. "Tommy calls himself a New York beachcomber."

"He's quite an actor."

"You said that before, honey. We're all actors at the George Lawrence School of the Dahntz. And don't ask me if I was really an actress before I became a teacher. Never acted in my life."

"No? I remember you as Eleanor Flack. You were great, colossal!"

"Don't remind me," she laughed.

"That night you said you'd been married to an actor."

"What're you? A private eye?"

"I'm the most curious guy you ever met. Especially about you, Hortense. So you're going to marry Maxie?"

She stared at me, her eyes suddenly sharp. "Any objections?"

"Who said I had any objections?"

"You don't have to say it. I know your type! Maxie's given me an ear on the subject of Pierson. Old family from out in New Jersey. Rented George Washington a bed when he passed through. Listen, Pierson, if your friend Maxie were to make twice the forty thousand he expects to make, I'd still be doing him a favor marrying him."

"What do you mean?"

"You're a private eye, aren't you? I've made my speech and I'm through. Now get me a refill, Pierson."

What had she meant? I wondered as I went into the dining room. What favor? I thought of some of Maxie's statements: "For me there's only Hortense." "She's good for me." I thought of Maxie sleeping it off in the bedroom and I had to smile. If Mamma Dehn could see her darling boy!

Suddenly the very regularity of Maxie's life seemed significant to me. As if it were some kind of yardstick with which I could measure his infatuation with Hortense. Every morning began in the same way, with Mamma calling in her eight-o'clock voice, "Maxie, wake up!" Always she would be waiting in the kitchen, fully dressed, as if about to go out. At my first breakfast Mamma'd smilingly explained that there would be orange juice one day and stewed fruit the next. Tuesdays, Thursdays, and Saturdays were orange-juice days; Mondays, Wednesdays, Fridays, stewed-fruit days; on Sundays, grapefruit with a maraschino cherry. Maxie always had one egg, two slices of toast, and one and a half cups of coffee. One and a half cups—like some kind of New Year's resolution. German discipline or something, I had thought. At eight-thirty Maxie would kiss Mamma good-bye, at eighty-thirty-one, he'd open the vestibule door downstairs. Once or twice Maxie had remarked to me that he didn't have to consult his wrist watch. "I'm back in the old grind with the war over," Maxie had said, as if it needed saying.

I thought now as I wove among the drunkards in Tommy Nivens' dining room that the war for Sergeant Maxie Dehn, the Pop of our crew, had been only a fleeting minute of fear and heroism and death. He was back in the same grind, the long years with Jacob Groteclose, the lifetime with Mamma. I reached for a bottle of rye, and as I did so I thought, a fleeting minute, yes. But for Maxie Dehn it had also been a breakaway: a breakaway to the girl in the living room. For her sake, he had become another man, equally careless of what Mamma Dehn thought, or of his future with the Groteclose firm.

When I returned with the drinks I said to Hortense, "Here's a favor for you."

"A favor?"

"You're doing Maxie a favor marrying him. I'm doing you a favor."

"Honey," she said, "I think you're a sneak."

"I like private eye better." I sat down next to her.

She lifted her glass. "Here's a toast for you, Pierson. If you turn the other cheek in this life, all you get is a kick in it."

We drank to that one and she said, "You must think forty thousand is a hell of a lot of money."

"What's a lousy forty thousand?" I grinned.

"You're right. You see before you a girl who used to run around with an empty bag in the U.S. Treasury. Why, I once had a pupil from Park Avenue who gave me a hundred-dollar tip after each lesson."

"Really? You know I believe anything, Hortense."

"You don't believe me?"

"I believe you. Why not?"

"The trouble with Park Avenue was he came to the studio for the exercise. His doctor advised him to exercise. He was just a golfer at heart, only he didn't like golf."

I laughed.

Deadpan, she ignored me. "He was a millionaire. He called all his chauffeurs Jones. When I knew him, his chauffeur was a Polack with one of those long Polack names. But he was Jones, too. This Polack Jones was after me. That was the closest I ever got to Park Avenue."

"How many hundred-dollar tips did he give you?"

"You don't believe me, sneaky. Well, maybe they were only seventy-five and not a hundred. Then I had a rich lawyer, but he was afraid of his wife, who was also a lawyer, and a Hindu who said he was a maharaja. And a—"

"Hortense, you got the gift of gab."

She turned her deadpan face on me. "Up in the sky you only met the birds, Air Force?"

"If you want to call the *Luftwaffe* birds, go ahead."

"I had a Nazi in the war who wanted to fox-trot like an American."

"A spy, of course, naturally."

"Yes. He asked a lot of questions, like you." She pushed her empty glass at me.

When I came back with our drinks she asked me if I'd looked in on Maxie. "No," I said. "But he's not in sight. He must still be sleeping." Her mention of Maxie hit me like ice water. "Tell me about you and Maxie, Hortense," I said hurriedly, and my voice sounded strange in my ears. Strange and awkward and yet sincere, like the voice of the Hugh Pierson who had always done the right thing.

She drank and then she smiled. "I'll never forget the day my butcher boy introduced us."

"Butcher boy?"

"Supervisor. It's a nickname we have. My supervisor thought Maxie was somebody, the way she was putting on the dog. The dog in blue ribbons. It was Mr. Dehn this and Mr. Dehn that and 'We make it a practice to select our teachers to suit the personality of our pupils, Mr. Dehn.' " Hortense laughed. "He had the personality of a sponge soaking wet. Mopping his face with his handkerchief, nervous. He's still that way. When he has to blow his nose he turns his head away to blow it soft and quiet. What gets me is that I fell for his line—Maxwell Dehn, Junior!"

"Any girl'd fall for a line in a night club."

"No, private eye. I fell for his line because he looked like the type who did-n't have a line."

"Is that it?"

"What then? Some of you have line written all over your face. But Maxie? There's a face a mother could love. Speaking of mothers, hasn't he got the prize? All she needed was a shawl when she blew into the studio. Right off the boat, that old crow!"

"She raised hell, didn't she?"

"She would've, but I managed to get her into one of the private studios. She was walking behind me, and you know what? I felt hard luck following me."

"What do you mean, Hortense?"

"Oh, believing Maxie's goddamned line, and who shows but a peasant off the boat. You're all phonys!"

We had another drink and another, and I forgot about Maxie sleeping it off in the bedroom. I wanted to forget and I did. Hortense and I got drunk togeth-er, and at the controls of that stolen evening sat ex-waist gunner Hugh Pier-son.

In the cab to her apartment she whimpered like a little child. "I'm drunk, I'm drunk. Why do I get so drunk? Who the hell're you, anyway?"

"Hugh," I said. "You feel sick? Want to get out a minute?"

"What for?"

"If you feel sick—"

"Never feel sick. I'm drunk, and what for? Nobody cares I'm drunk. If I had somebody— But nobody. Nobody!" Her eyes closed, her head falling onto my shoulder.

The cab driver asked me where we were going. "Hortense, you asleep?" I said.

"No."

"Where do you live?"

"Twenty-sixth off Fourth," she whispered so faintly I hardly heard her.

I repeated the address. I put my arm around her shoulders. The stars were over Riverside Drive and the black river reflected the lights of the big signs on the Jersey shore. Behind those gleaming signs, the highway led in starlit rib-bons to my home town. Home town? In the moving darkness of this cab with Hortense, I had no home. No past, and no future either, as if I were once more with some Italian girl in a room stinking of *vino*, tomorrow's mission between her breasts.

I shut my own eyes, and when I looked out of the window again I saw the high, blind, lightless walls of the downtown city.

"We're getting there," I said to encourage her.

She groaned. "I better walk a few blocks."

We got out at 29th Street and Fourth Avenue. Hortense shivered. The wind was cold. The false springtime was over. It was autumn.

"How do you feel, Hortense?" I said.

"Lousy."

I supported her, my arm around her waist. Her heels clicked on the empty dark sidewalks, clicking out some strange message that I had heard before on the sidewalks of London and Rome. The hour was late, her heels clickety-clicked, later even than you think.

The deserted office buildings towered above us. And on the deserted sidewalks our black shadows chased the shadows of all the other couples who had preceded us.

"We'll soon be there, Hortense," I said.

"This fresh air's poison," she tried to joke.

"Are you feeling better?"

"A little. Why do I drink so much?"

There was no answer to that. No answer to anything I felt.

We came to 26th and Fourth Avenue—three huge buildings on three corners, and on the fourth, a shabby hotel that looked like a furnished rooming house. Hortense lived in the middles of the street, in a row of remodeled houses opposite an armory. The remodelers had imported a narrow strip of lawn and a white colonial doorway.

The copper roof of the armory shone the palest of greens in the light of the street lamp, while the grass on the lawn glinted like metal. We stepped in to the hall and I watched her fumbling in her bag, her fingers all thumbs.

"Can't I help you?" I asked her.

"Damn it! It's gone! My keys—"

I took the bag from her, searched for her keys. She had a small alarm clock in her bag, I discovered. I found the keys, unlocked the door. Her face was ghastly. I suggested we go outside, but she shook her head and held onto my arm. I helped her up three flights of stairs to her floor, unlocked the door of her apartment. We went inside. She switched on a lamp and, slipping out of her coat, rushed for what could only have been the bathroom.

I lit a cigarette and stared at her coat, crumpled on the floor like a drunk on the sidewalk. I picked it up, tossed it to a chair. "Hortense," I called. "Can I help you?"

"No," her muffled voice answered me. I examined the room. I was in a combined bed-living room. The bed was against the wall, disguised as a couch and covered with gaudy red and green Mexican serapes. On the couch there sat an elegant cloth doll in a Marie Antoinette costume with painted leering eyes and a wicked smile that somehow reminded me of Mrs. Maharaja. There were other knickknacks on a low maple table. A beer mug whose handle was a naked girl, four or five miniature glass animals, and an unaccountable decoy duck, battered from much use, with red eyes. On the wall above the table there was an abstract oil painting. It was surprising, especially since the other pictures were a print of Whistler's mother and a conventional cabin in moonlight.

"I feel better," Hortense said, coming out of the bathroom.

"Do you really?"

"Only a splitting headache." She flopped down wearily on the couch.

"Why don't you take an aspirin?" I asked.

"That's no cure." She gathered herself up from the couch, slim in her black cocktail dress, her face white as only a sick drinker's face can be, and over her shoulder that white face turned, a sickish reckless smile on her lips. "Want a nightcap?"

"You better take some aspirin, Hortense."

"You take it," she said from the end of the living room, and pivoted out of sight into where I guessed the kitchen was. My advice to her echoed mockingly in my head: You better take some aspirin, Hortense. What a faker, I thought. Take some aspirin! Dr. Pierson talking.

She came into a the living room, two glasses of whiskey in her hands. They were water glasses. Each was half full of straight whiskey.

"That's some nightcap," I said.

"Yeah," she said, as if she weren't listening to me, as if concentrating on the sick feeling inside of her. She blinked her eyes, tilted her glass, drank. I thought, What the hell, and followed suit. The whiskey was a little nauseous as I swallowed it all in one dose. I coughed. I looked at Hortense and she looked at me and the room was suddenly very quiet. So quiet I could hear the silence beating against my ears.

"Thanks for bringing me home," she said.

"Forget it."

"What happened to Maxie?"

I shrugged and again the room was very quiet. I walked over to her, slid my free arm around her waist, and kissed her. When I stepped back from her, she was smiling, a smile like a sneer.

"Say it!" I said.

"You're all bastards, aren't you?"

What she said wasn't important. What was important was that we were alone, the city locked outside her door. "I'm Maxie's best friend. Go ahead! His best friend. But let's not kid each other, Hortense."

"They're not kidding when they say a dog's a man's best friend."

I flushed. I felt like retorting, Look who's talking! Pure, untouched, and undefiled! But it wasn't important. I knew that after a few more drinks, Hortense would accept me, or anybody else. Not for a second had I forgotten how casually she'd gone off with those artists a few weeks ago. It was that easy. I said, "I haven't been able to get you out of my mind."

"Mind!" She smiled with that smile of hers. "Is that what they call it now?" She looked at me and I was suddenly conscious that I was wearing my topcoat. Suddenly it was more than a topcoat. It was the test of my loyalty to Maxie. I felt that if I took it off I would be naked. I put my empty glass down on the maple table next to the decoy duck, got out of my topcoat, and threw it over to the chair where Hortense's coat was. "How about a drink, Hortense?"

In the kitchenette, the bottle of whiskey was waiting for me on a white enamel table. On top of the refrigerator there was a black brier pipe with a silver Y shining on the bowl. I laughed, and from the living room Hortense asked me what the joke was.

We had a few more nightcaps and the evening began to blur, to spin like a colored wheel. I remember picking up her decoy duck and asking if it belonged to the man who'd left the pipe. I remember arguing with Hortense about Mamma Dehn, and Hortense doing an impersonation of Mamma Dehn that had me in stitches. And somewhere in the blur, a retake of the maharaja act, and then there was no more whiskey. She wanted to fling the empty bottle out of the kitchen window but I wrestled it from her. Why she insisted on playing the record *"Bésame Mucho"* I can't remember at all, but I remember sitting down on the couch as the tango music flowed like a dark light around the fixed light of the standing lamp and staring at the girl in the black dress. *"Bésame Mucho"*... a dark music, a dark light in which I could almost see the shapes of unseen men gliding after unseen women and Hortense all the women. I remember her tangoing in front of me, a dancing doll come out of the Fifth Avenue display window and bringing with her the broad green leaves of some Cuba or Florida.

How long I watched her I don't remember, but it couldn't have been very long, a minute or two, perhaps five minutes. I remember rising from the couch and going toward her. She seemed far away. I was going toward her as if through the dark music, the dark light of *"Bésame Mucho"*....

Later, I woke up. I'd been sleeping on the couch; Hortense was sleeping on the inside, next to the wall. I woke up and wondered if Maxie were still at Tommy Nivens' apartment. Maxie Dehn—I remember him now. Or rather, the Hugh Pierson with a conscience was remembering. I forced myself to get out of bed and into the bathroom. I switched on the light. For some reason, the white walls reminded me of the base hospital where I had sweated out my Purple Heart. Again I thought of Maxie. I stared through the bathroom door at Hortense sleeping on the serapes. The cloth doll had been tumbled to the floor but one of its leering eyes met mine as if to say: Now you've had her and was it worth double-crossing Maxie for?

Downstairs, a fog-in-the-morning deadness lay on the city. I had to walk to 23rd Street before I could find a night owl cab. We must have made Tommy Nivens' apartment house in fifteen minutes, where a few drunken survivors were still carrying on. They said Maxie'd gone home. I went downstairs and took the Broadway subway. Hortense's keys were in my topcoat, but I wasn't returning to her place until morning, I thought. I was going back to my own room. I tried to think. Did Maxie know about me and Hortense leaving the party together? And what'd he thought coming home with me not there? I knew I had to have some kind of alibi. The truth had to be covered up. Maybe he was crazy wanting to marry Hortense. Maybe I'd only done the same as the man who'd left the decoy duck, and the Yale boy, and all the others, but I wasn't some anonymous woman hound loose in the city. I was Maxie's best friend, at least that was the theory. I felt exhausted and yet I had to think. I thought that I'd better stay as close to the truth as I could. I'd admit escorting Hortense home. "Of course, Maxie," I rehearsed it to myself. "She was tight and somebody had to take care of her. I took her home and then I went on to Rita's." It was a good alibi, I thought. Good because it was logical. Who but Maxie's friend would take Hortense home? And then what was more natural for the friend to go on down to his own girl friend? On Saturday night, what was more natural than a fellow wanting to sleep with his girl? It was very good reasoning and it was nauseating.

At 50th Street I got off the subway and walked west. The night air was cold and I felt the coming dawn in the hollow sockets of my eyes. In the empty ending night I thought of Hortense sleeping on the other side of the city. The wind was chilly on my skin and I thought of her warm body, and in the night it was nameless, the white body of love itself.

On Eighth Avenue the neons of the green-for-Ireland bars were no longer shining, and the last drunks'd long disappeared into the side streets. I thought of Maxie and Hortense and the important thing was that he wouldn't find out about me unless she told him. And there was no reason for her to give me away. The white stars twinkled between the black lines of the tenements on 47th Street and everything was exactly as before. I was still Maxie's best friend and Hortense was still the girl he hoped to marry. I looked up at those white stars, thinking of all the secrets they had kept over the ages. They would keep mine, too. I thought of all the people who'd come and gone on this street of railroad flats. Old-time Irish and Germans, Italians, Jews, Greeks, and now the Puerto Ricans' staying a year, ten years, a lifetime, and every last one of them with some secret or other, and in the long run, going, going for good. So I'd slept with Hortense tonight. Who knew, who cared? Only Maxie cared, and if he didn't know, what was the harm? Life was a thing gone before you knew it. Life was a cold blowy street like West 47th with nobody in sight, a meaningless key in the door of the house owned by Mamma Dehn, the house that would be owned by others after her as it'd been owned by others before her.

The banister was old and smooth as glass and on it was my hand. My own living hand following the hands of a thousand forgotten people in a world where nothing had ever been true but the living moment. I thought of Hortense and wished I were with her. "I love you," I whispered under my breath, and in that blind and sleeping house only my whisper, only the feel of my hand on the wood of the banister had any meaning.

The next morning, at ten, I was awake. I showered. I dressed quickly. Mamma wanted to make me breakfast but I said I had a breakfast date. Maxie was still sleeping, as he had been when I'd pulled in. Mamma followed me to the door, hinting broadly about young men who turned night into day, and how whiskey was bad for the liver. Her face was sad. Her pale eyes were bright with an intense curiosity I refused to satisfy. "Hugh," she said desperately as I opened the door. "Was Maxie with this dance woman?"

I evaded her question. "Mamma, I was at an N.Y.U. party," I said.

When I turned into East 26th Street again, children were playing in front of the white colonial doorway. A gray-faced man walked a brown-faced dog and they both looked at me as I went into the vestibule. I unlocked the door with Hortense's key, went up three flights. At her door I hesitated. I thought I ought to knock and not sneak in like a burglar and frighten her. She might be awake. Then as if my sleeping with her last night had given me certain rights, I unlocked the door and entered. She was asleep on the couch, a green and red serape over her body. The morning light tinged her eyelids a faint violet color and last night's raja baja waja Hortense was a sleeping girl.

I stood there, wondering if I weren't romanticizing her. Suppose she did look like a schoolgirl, I said to myself. Her real face, her true face, was staring up at me from the floor where the cloth doll had spent the night. I stared at the doll's painted eyes and smeary whore's smile. "Hortense," I said. "Hortense." She grumbled in her sleep. "Hortense!" I called.

Again we looked at each other in a meaningful silence. She said nothing. "Good morning," I said.

"Why'd you get me up?"

"I thought I might have to shop for breakfast."

She groaned. "Wakes me up for breakfast. For breakfast!"

"Do I have to buy anything?"

She tapped her temple with two fingers and yawned. "What you need you can't buy."

"Congratulations, Hortense. You're only up a few seconds and you've cracked your first wisecrack."

She smiled a little. "Go crack some eggs, and lots of coffee."

In the kitchen, the Y on the Yale man's pipe shone silver in the sunlight, the windows golden with noon. I found eggs and bacon in the refrigerator and half a loaf of bread. In the closet there was a tin of coffee. I sniffed at the rich dark smell of the ground coffee and I started to whistle.

When Hortense walked languidly into the kitchen, I tried to kiss her. She pushed me away. "Charge last night up to experience, honey, will you?"

There was a tough little grin on her face. She had never seemed more beautiful to me than she did then, with her hair damp from her shower, a red robe tight around her body. She grinned again. "And don't ask me for a rain check."

"That's one hell of a good morning," I said. She glanced at the breakfast I'd prepared, the scrambled eggs on a platter, garnished with strips of crisp bacon, the buttered toast, the coffeepot between our two settings. "Let's eat," she said.

"Did I do something, Hortense?" I asked as we sat down.

"Act your age, Pierson. Last night was last night. It's over, forget it!"

"Hortense—" I protested, but she cut in on me.

"Complaints! The nerve of you bastards! Complaining when I'm even giving you breakfast."

She made me wince and I hated myself for showing how I felt. "You're right, I just had the wrong idea," I said. "I thought last night was the beginning of a great friendship."

"Yes, one for the ages," she said, the tough little grin on her face. "Don't forget, Romeo, I'm a woman engaged to be married. What happened to Maxie? Was he still at Tommy Nivens'?"

"You knew I left last night?"

"Sure, I knew. What'd you do? Take my keys?"

"Yes."

"What happened to Maxie?"

"He was gone when I got there. I went home myself. He was asleep. He was asleep when I left this morning. It'll be O.K."

"What're you going to tell him?"

"I'll say I took you home because you were tight. I had another party last night—I'll tell him I went there after I took you home."

"Sounds all right."

"Hortense, I have to see you again!"

She shook her head no.

"Why not?"

She poured herself a cup of coffee. "Don't you understand? No, Romeo." Her eyes were cold and hard, a perfect match for that grin of hers. Only her body outlined under her red robe belonged to last night's Hortense.

We began to eat, both of us silent. The silence was a mistake, I knew. I had to talk, to say something. That silence was like a big hold between us, getting bigger and bigger by the second.

"Hortense," I said. It was all I could think of.

She sipped at her coffee, studying me coldly.

"Maxie doesn't know and he doesn't have to know," I said.

"We've gone over that, honey."

"Hortense—"

"Have some of those scrambled eggs, and promise me you won't blow your brains out because I love another," she hammed, grinning.

For the first time I felt like slapping that grinning face of hers. "You remind me of a girl I used to know in Rome."

"Honey, write me about it, will you?"

"She was a bitch! Like you!"

"Don't you think it's odd for you to talk about bitches?" she asked. Her soft full lips tightened and almost seemed thin. But there was no anger in her face.

Only contempt. "Maxie's big buddy from the war. Sees me once and right away plans how he can get in."

"I didn't plan!"

"No? Sees me going off with a couple of barflies and he thinks, the big war buddy, Why shouldn't I get mine, too?"

"It's not as simple as that! That's not all there is to it."

"Of course not. You want to get in again. Maybe after breakfast?" Her smile, for a second was like the smile of the cloth doll in the living room. And then she was tightlipped, contemptuous again.

"I want you, yes! I wanted to phone you from the night I first met you, but I didn't."

"Please!" she cried out as if in pain. "Please don't give me the love-love. Stay the wolf you are."

"What's made you so goddamned bitter?" was all I could say.

"'He didn't come to the studio to hear your biography,'" she rattled off as if reciting from some book—the Teachers' Guidebook, as I learned later. "'He'd rather you remained a mystery.'"

I was getting nowhere with her, but at least we were having a conversation. After we had finished breakfast, she said, "The subway's waiting for you, honey."

"Why don't you walk me to the subway? The fresh air'll do you good."

"Now, now, don't get so considerate. On you, it's not becoming."

"Hortense, the walk'll do you good."

"If I have to walk to get rid of you," she grinned, "I'll walk."

I sat smoking in the kitchen as she dressed, the Yale man's pipe on the refrigerator seeming like my constant companion by now. I wondered if Joe Yale'd breakfasted with Hortense, too, on some Sunday morning.

"Let's go," she called to me from the living room. I went in. She was wearing a dark green tailored suit. Her hair and eyes seemed darker, almost black.

"Hello, greenie." I smiled.

"That's gratitude. I let you stay with me and so I'm greenie?"

"You hurt my feelings. I meant your suit. You look so fresh in that suit. It's the green—like a green leaf."

"I may be a green leaf, but not for your salad."

"Ugh," I said. "Hortense, why the hell don't you relax and forget the comebacks?"

She glanced at me for a second and then stepped to the closet for a camel-hair sport coat.

"Can I help you with the coat?"

"Stay where you are."

"Suspicious! I had no intention of kissing you. Not a woman about to be married. Pure, untouched, and undefiled."

She laughed and we went downstairs to the street and over to Madison

Square, where the leaves were yellow and red in the wind. The wind blew a faint pinkness into Hortense's pale cheeks and she seemed like all the other Sunday girls strolling with the Sunday men. We stopped to watch a woman feeding the pigeons on the sidewalk bordering Madison Square. "I've seen her for years," Hortense remarked. "All these pigeon women're alike."

An empty grapefruit-juice can full of bread crusts stood on the sidewalk, the pigeons pecking at the stale crusts the pigeon woman'd already tossed to them. She was hatless, with stringy graying hair and a face the color of a soiled dish towel. Her coat was made of cloth, patched on one elbow, the fur collar mangy-looking. She wore brown shoes with low mannish heels, but when she spoke to her pigeons she sounded like a worried mother. "Ruby," she said to a pigeon in the gutter. "Ruby, will you please get on the sidewalk?"

Hortense grinned. I was grateful somebody else was the target for that grin of hers.

The sun glinted on the pearly feathers of the fat pigeons. On their necks, the feathers had a reddish-purplish glint to them, shining like metal hammered thin and fine. There were twenty or thirty pigeons in all, pecking at the bread crusts or strutting about, the males after the females. "Ruby, please get up on the sidewalk," the pigeon woman said. She retrieved the crusts the wind blew into the gutter, cooing to her pigeons. "Get up on the sidewalk, my darlings. Ruby, do you hear me?"

"I never heard of a pigeon getting run over by a car," Hortense remarked innocently.

"You never can tell," the pigeon woman answered, not looking at Hortense directly. "Get on the sidewalk, my darlings. Ruby, do you hear me? You'll get hurt, my darlings."

I whispered to Hortense so the pigeon woman wouldn't hear me, "She acts as if they understand her."

"Sure. She's a pigeon too. A little on the damaged side."

I whispered. "Sh! You'll hurt her feelings."

Hortense pointed at the courting males. "Look at them with their big chests. Like drum majors!" She eyed me suddenly. "Like some other birds I know."

I laughed. "At least they're not interested in eating when they're making love, not like the females."

The pigeon woman muttered angrily. She was offended.

"Excuse me," I apologized.

Hortense smiled at the pigeon woman. "Do you call them all Ruby?"

"What do you care what I call them?" the pigeon woman said moodily. "What's it to you what I call them?"

"I like pigeons," Hortense said. "When I was a kid I used to watch them over the roofs. Keeping the bread in the can's a good idea."

"I can't get pigeon food, and the wind blows all the bread away." She sighed and flapped her arms, her bony wrists sticking out of the cloth sleeves. "Ruby, get on the sidewalk. Get on the sidewalk, my darlings. Ruby."

"Have you any other names for them?" Hortense asked her, smiling.

"That bothers you?"

"No, of course not," Hortense said.

"What're you talking to me for, anyway? You don't want to talk to me."

"Why—"

"Why don't you quit molesting me?" the pigeon woman shouted. "Quit molesting me or I'll call a cop!"

"Go ahead and call a cop!" Hortense snapped at her.

"We don't mean any harm," I said in my best soothing voice.

In a fury, the pigeon woman flapped her arms at both of us as if we were a pair of huge birds she was trying to drive away. "Molesting me with your little remarks. Think I didn't hear them! Drum majors, dirty things like that." A pigeon flew to her shoulder. "Pigeons're cleaner than you two any time!" She fondled its pearly folded wings. "Ruby, darling, how are you?" she cooed gently.

"Let's go, Hortense," I said.

"Good-bye, pigeon lady," Hortense said maliciously to the gaunt stringy-haired woman.

The pigeon woman stared at Hortense and in her eyes there was a kind of pity. A pity gone daffy. "I used to be a lady. I used to get dressed up like you and they broke my heart. I was a lady." Her eyes overflowed with that half-mad pity. "Listen to me," she said to Hortense. "You can't trust no man."

"You're right."

"You can trust no woman!" the pigeon woman said fiercely. "You can't trust no one in the human race. There's no true love in the human race. Someday people'll learn the only true friends're the birds and the animals."

Hortense's eyes flashed at me. "Hear that, Pierson? Man's best friend is his dog, and that goes for Maxie."

"I used to keep four dogs and six cats when I had an apartment on Lexington, but they stopped me," the pigeon woman said, "and now I'm in a furnished room and they won't let me."

"Good-bye, lady," Hortense said to the pigeon woman. There was no sarcasm in her voice.

We walked away. "That old girl's not all there," I said.

"She's not so old," Hortense answered quietly.

"She looks older than the hills."

"She's about thirty-five."

"No!"

"Yes. Did you notice her features?"

"Not especially."

"She was pretty in her day."

"I doubt it."

"You're talking from ignorance. I've seen women in worse shape than that pigeon woman who used to be glamour girls. The hell with her. How about a drink?" she said suddenly.

There was a connection between this abrupt invitation and the change in her attitude toward the pigeon woman. I wondered if Hortense was worried about getting old. But that seemed ridiculous. Not Hortense, the raja baja waja girl, with more energy and a greater drinking capacity than most men. Over the first Martini I stopped thinking about Hortense's contradictions. She was smiling at me as people do before the first drink of the evening when every excitement, every wish, every hope still seems possible, poised on the rim of a lifted cocktail glass.

MAXIE

I started out by saying that maybe I was a jerk. Now what makes a jerk? Tough breaks, right? Bum luck, right? And when you get right down to it, another way of spelling jerk is j-i-n-x, right? A guy who's supposed to be a jerk might be only a guy who's been jinxed, and if ever a guy was jinxed, that guy was me. Listen.

A couple of days after I put the convincer on the Shaw sisters, Doyle rings me. "Maxie," he says, "I have to see you right away. How about the Astor, like the last time? The mezzanine lobby, O.K.?"

He had no right to ring me at the office. I'd warned him plenty of times that I'd do all the ringing. I couldn't figure it. Waiting for him up there in the mezzanine of the Astor, I got a little nervous. The Astor's no place for somebody who's nervous. All around me were well-dressed guys with nothing to do but smoke cigars and read the papers, dropping their cigar ashes in the ash trays they've got up there in the Astor that look like cannon shells set on end. These well-dressed guys were so calm that watching them was enough to make me sweat. You couldn't imagine those characters ever sweating. They had nothing to sweat about and never would, smoking their cigars and reading their papers. They were the morning papers. But up there in the Astor, what with the soft light and all, it's always like evening.

I walked to the rail on the mezzanine and looked down on the main floor. A couple high-class dames were buying some theatre tickets. The room clerk was talking to a man who could've been Doyle but wasn't. It was just a regular picnic down there, and I got more and more nervous.

When Doyle did come in from the street, I jumped back into my chair and made like I was one of these well-dressed characters myself. He came up to the mezzanine and when he smiled I knew something was wrong. His smile wasn't the big glad-hand smile I was used to from Doyle. It was a tricky little smile that went on and off his face.

"Hello, Maxie," he says. "Beautiful fall weather we're having." He spoke like he was the one personally responsible. He sat down next to me, taking off his Homburg. His hair shone like it was hand-polished. He had straight dark hair like in the hair ads. He was good-looking, this Doyle, with his long-chinned Irish mug and his bright blue eyes. Down our office, Eckstein called eyes like that "Irish operator eyes." It's true. All these big Irish politicians and contractors or even coppers collecting a little honest graft have eyes like that.

"Hello, Mr. Doyle," I says.

"Who's this Mr. Doyle? My name's Joe, Maxie."

"Mr. Doyle, why'd you call me at the office?"

"Oh, that," he says, the trick smile going on and off. "Now, Maxie, don't Mr. Doyle me. My name's Joe. Just plain Joe." He was about as plain as a hundred thousand in cold cash. He wasn't even old, around forty-five.

"You never should've called me at the office," I squawked good and loud.

He laughed and lit up a cigar, one of those long Havanas. "Will you have a cigar, Maxie?"

"No. You shouldn't've called me at the office."

"Maxie, you know I wouldn't have called your office if I didn't have to talk to you right away."

"About what?" I says, and I swallowed the lump in my throat.

He looked at his wrist watch. "Fifty-five minutes ago I had a conference with my associates." He puffed on his cigar and his trick smile made me feel I was turning green inside.

"Well," I says. "What about your associates?"

"I won't waste your time, Maxie. My associates think that the bonus we agreed upon is a little too high."

I'd expected bad news. But expecting it is different from getting it. Doyle was watching me like a hawk, so I held my face together. There was only one thing left for me to do and I did it. I bluffed. "O.K., Mr. Doyle, if that's how you feel. The deal's off." I was bluffing with ulcers, like old Jacob used to say when he told us about some of his deals. "The deal's off, Mr. Doyle!"

"Now, Maxie," Doyle says.

"Now nothing. The deal's off!"

"Don't mistake me, Maxie. I don't think it's too high. It's my associates think it's too high."

I stood up. "You tell your associates the deal's off, Mr. Doyle."

"Sit down!" he says, but I wouldn't sit down. So he got up too. "Maxie, let's talk it over."

"There's nothing to talk over. Good-bye, Mr. Doyle."

"Hold on! What about compromising it, Maxie? Don't be a stubborn Dutchman."

"What do you feel is a compromise?"

"It's not what I feel. It's what they feel, Maxie."

"O.K., what do they feel?"

"Something around twenty thousand for you."

"Nothing doing," I says. He tried to keep me, talking fast and smooth, but I walked out on him. I knew that if I gave in and said yes to twenty, that crook'd be chiseling me the next day. What I'd end up with would be a box of his Havanas. I knew that Irishman inside out. He followed me downstairs to the main floor and I only shook him on Broadway. I felt sick. The crowds were parading up and down, laughing and joking. But to me it was like the morgue. Things'd been too good to last. That forty-thousand bonus was a pipe dream I could forget. And I could forget all about Hortense, too. I felt worse than sick when I thought how lately we'd been out a couple times, and no mob scene either like the party at that fag Tommy Nivens', where I'd passed out cold. Just the two of us. She'd let me stay over her place each time like I was her real boy friend. God, when I thought how I made the grade at last only to have Doyle start chiseling, I could've broken down and cried like a kid. When I thought of how beautiful and loving she was, with the radio going like we were already married, just Hortense and me— Aw, what's the good of talking?

I moped along, not caring if I lived or if I died. That's how I felt.

Then three or four young guys, playing hockey from school, bumped into me. "Watch where you're going!" I said to the punks. They laughed and gave me the Bronx cheer. But it made me stop moping. Maxie, I says to myself, you better do a little thinking. So I think about Doyle and his associates, which is just double talk. Because Doyle's associates're nobody but Doyle himself. What his game was exactly I couldn't be too sure. For he could be trying to chisel me on general principles. Or maybe something really was up. Maybe there was another property that'd be just as good for television as the Shaw property and he was playing one against the other. If that was so, I might be out on my ear altogether. Out, but out.

I walked back to 42nd Street, to the office. But as soon as I stepped out of the elevator I knew I couldn't go in. I was too sick to work. A woman in black, an Italian woman, came out of Dr. Presto's office. I thought I could use a doctor myself. I thought how all day long Doc Presto had himself a cushy deal, with every sick ginzo in the West Side at five bucks a head. He didn't have to worry about money, Doc Presto. Or Saul Lipson, in the office next to Doc Presto's. Atlas Stamp Company, that was Saul Lipson. I thought, Leave it to those kinds, the ginzos and the Jewboys, to be in the money.

I was so full of hate, I wasn't human. For Doc Presto was my own doctor and Saul Lipson was a friend. I thought I better forget Doyle or I'd be tearing myself and everybody else to pieces. So to kill time, I went into Leo Edwards' office. The Edwards Times Square Messenger Service, Leo calls himself. He was a guy usually good for a laugh. Leo was inside at his desk, reading a racing sheet. Standing behind him and reading it was Aury Taglia, the window cleaner who had his office on the floor below. They looked up at me quick, two coked-up horse players, and looked down at their racing sheet even quicker. "Maxie, you know a good horse?" Leo, he says to me with a grin. "And don't give me Big Crap in the second."

He was coked up, this Leo Edwards, but once in his life he'd been smart. Why, I'll tell you. Everybody's seen the Western Union boys running around town, but it was Leo who'd come up with the idea of a special Times Square messenger service. He tried a couple more gags on me but I couldn't even joke a laugh to be polite. For I was thinking how everybody in the whole world'd started up something or other except me, and when I did, who do I draw but Doyle, the chiseler supreme?

"Maxie must've been hit by a truck," Leo says to Aury the window cleaner.

"Never mind him," Aury says, picking up the racing sheet. "In the second I like Stone Marten."

"In the second, there's-only one li'l hoss, and that's Black Ribbon!"

That started one of those horse arguments. I couldn't stand it. "You're behind on your rent," I says. I hadn't come in to ask Leo about his rent, but here I was asking him anyway. And the more beef and noise I made, the more I wanted to make. "What do you think we run in this building? A charity bazaar?"

Leo Edwards didn't say a word. He waited for me to finish. "Maxie, what's eating you?" he says.

"Nothing's eating me."

"So the Giants lost the World Series—"

"What about your rent?"

"Maxie, I've got a story for you about the two guys who bet on how many girls there were on square between Times Square and Herald Square."

I says, "Never mind that! Get up your rent!"

"Holy jeez, I'm only a week and a half behind, Maxie!"

"You're supposed to pay on the first, Edwards."

"Edwards, huh! O.K., Mr. Forty-second Street. You own this building, I know."

"Don't get personal unless you want a dispossess," I yelled at him, slamming the door on my way out.

In about half a second I was sorry for shooting my mouth off. Yet, on my way down in the elevator, when Phil the colored elevator boy said he'd never seen me going downstairs so much in one morning, I shot my mouth off all over again. "None of your business if I go down or up or sideways!" I says.

I was sorry for jumping on Phil. But the sorry was later. I walked down 42nd Street to Ninth Avenue, just walking. In my head, I went over everything Doyle'd said, but I learned nothing new. All I could be sure of was that he'd led me on, the mick fox, and just as I was reaching for the bait he sliced it in two. If I could've been sure of at least thirty thousand, I'd've compromised it. But how could I be sure Doyle wouldn't give me another slice—right across the throat? He had me by the throat, all because of Hortense.

I guess what I should've done was phoned the office I was sick and gone into a bar. When you're bluffing with ulcers, the only cure's whiskey. But instead, like the jerk I was, I went into a luncheonette for a cup of coffee. The place was empty. The late-breakfast truckers and shipping boys from the garment lofts were all gone. There was only a skinny guy without a necktie at the counter, reading a racing sheet. Why I had to sit down next to him, I don't know. Maybe because he reminded me of how snotty I'd been to Leo. Maybe because I wanted company or something. Who the hell knows? Anyway, this skinny guy had a hold on that racing sheet like he was afraid somebody was going to swipe the damn thing. His eyes in his head were squinting fierce as he read the horses. Another jerk trying to figure out how to win two for one.

"What you want?" the counterman says, coming over to me. He'd been talking with the Greek prop down at the cash register.

"A cup of coffee," I says.

"Black or cream and sugar?"

"Just a cup of coffee."

"You want black or you want cream and sugar?" He sounded real peeved.

I looked at this guy. Another jerk, with a mug all chipped and worn like the white china cups on the shelf behind him. A prize jerk, because even though he was peeved at me, he was smiling. Because he had to smile. I was the customer. And the customer's always right. "Take it easy, bud," I says to him.

"I'm taking it easy! Black or cream and sugar? You want it black, say you want it black."

"Black Ribbon!" I said for the hell of it, don't ask me why. Only Bellevue could've told me why.

"That's it!" the skinny horse player says, all excited. "That's the sweet ole hoss in the second for me!" He smiled at me and the counterman and the Greek prop. A dippy smile. That skinny horse player yacking about Black Ribbon was plain nuts!

The counterman curses under his breath and slaps a spoon down in front of me. "Wise guy," he says, like it's my fault the other guy's a dip.

"Who do you think you're talking to?" I knocked it straight back at him.

"Aw, cool off!" he says.

"Cool off yourself!"

"Looka, wise guy, I can't ask you all day long. Black or cream and sugar!"

"Cool off! You'll last longer."

"Who's asking you? You want it black or how do you want it?"

"You ask me in a nice way if you want an answer."

"O.K., wise guy!" he yelled. "I'll ask you in a nice way. Want it black or what the hell do you want?"

"That's some nice way."

"Just make up your mind!" he screamed like a lunatic. "Just make up your mind. Don't rush yourself! We don't close up here never! Open twenny-four hours a day, so don't rush yourself! We're gonna get some cots in here, and a cuppa coffee'll get you a cot besides cream and sugar and a toothpick on the way out!"

I didn't waste any more time on that lunatic. "You call this service?" I hollered down at the Greek prop. But the Greek, he looks at me like I was the one talking Greek. He's standing there next to his cash register. His eyes're wide open, he's even breathing. But he doesn't say a damn thing.

"Not even a doughnut with his cuppa coffee, so give'm service!" the counterman is screaming. "Give'm a cot to lay on!"

"Don't you hear him?" I says to the Greek prop. But the Greek, he only looks at me. I got up from the counter and rushed down to the cash register. "Don't you hear him?" That Greek doesn't say boo. "You'll never get anywhere this way, you dumb Greek!" I says.

That did it. "Me dumb Greek," he says. "You smart man." He wasn't mad even now. He'd said his say so quiet it was like he hadn't said anything.

But it stayed with me. All that day I kept thinking, yep, I was smart. Ask Doyle.

All that day I went around like a dead man. I knew I couldn't do a thing. I had to sweat it out until Doyle phoned me. But who knew when that'd be? I collected some rents. I had three shots of whiskey at lunch and checked in at the office around four-thirty. At five I was bound for home. I'd thought some of telling Hugh about this new development with Doyle. But then I decided not to. I didn't want any I-told-you-so from him. I wished I could've gone to Hortense and told her. But she was no girl to go singing the blues to. Especially the money blues. I just had to keep that Doyle sonofabitch to myself.

When fluky things happen, they happen in a series. Now if I'd've found that wallet any other time I would've chalked it up to luck. But finding wallets when I'm waiting for Doyle to phone me—to me—to me, anyway—it had a meaning. Like it was some kind of a sign.

That morning I left the house by myself. Hugh had a cold so he was staying home from class. I went down Eighth Avenue like a thousand times before and between 45th and 44th I noticed something out of the ordinary. A gleam, a shine, a shine of leather from inside a cardboard box. If the flaps of that cardboard box hadn't opened, I wouldn't've noticed anything. I edged over and what I see I can't believe. It's a wallet in that cardboard box. A wallet!

The last place you could expect to find a wallet is on Eighth Avenue. Eighth Avenue's where they carry their wallet buttoned down in their inside pocket. Me, I'd never in my life ever found a wallet. A couple pennies, a couple nickels, maybe once a dime or a quarter. Not believing I was seeing straight, I headed for that cardboard box like a light. Just then who do I spot but another guy going for that box. I get there ahead of him by inches and put my meathooks on.

"That yours?" he says in a tone of voice that says I'm a liar if I say yes.

"I'm lucky I found it again! Gosh, I'm relieved!" That's how I answered that would-be chiseler. "I never expected to find it again!"

He looked at me suspicious and then he says, "It's not fair."

"What's not fair?" I says.

"The guys finding things're always the guys heeled," he says, bitter as hell.

"It's mine."

"Yeah, it's yours," he says. "So's Central Park."

He shuffled up Eighth Avenue. A guy in an old coat he must've salvaged from a rag pile, his wrists out of the sleeves, his hands raw and red from the wind like he was wearing gloves, red gloves. It was the kind of a day when a guy wonders if he shouldn't switch into the winter overcoat. I had on my top-coat, one of those solid brown styles you can wear in business or on a date, fly-button front. My suit was almost new. Freshly pressed. My shoes had the shine, not the seat of my pants. To that scrounger, I must've looked like a million.

Anyway, as he shuffled up Eighth, I shook my head hard just in case any-body else'd been watching the argument. Like I was saying, this is the box I lost and ain't I one lucky guy finding it again!

I didn't see anybody who might've been interested. But you have to protect yourself, just in case. Everybody was on the move, bound for the garments south of 42nd. All of them time-clock punchers: seamstresses, cutters, pinkers. Wearing their eyes turned in like on the subway. Only that scrounger with nothing else to do'd smelled a rat. I wrapped my arm around that box with the wallet inside. I was feeling so good I could've sung. I thought that finding that wallet was a sign I'd outbluff that foxy Doyle. Then me and Hortense'd get married, then— Aw, what's the use of talking? I had myself a pipe dream that morning on Eighth Avenue.

When I reached the corner of 42nd and Eighth, the traffic light was red. I looked inside the flaps of the box. I saw no wallet. The traffic light blinked green. Everybody rushes forward except me. Some jerk yells I'm blocking traf-fic and am I color-blind? But I couldn't move. I was paralyzed. Then I shake that box and the wallet slides into sight out of nowhere. Like a seven out of a crapshooter's heaven. A brown wallet with a fine gold stripe along the edge.

I ran to catch the light and crossed to the other side of Eighth. Before me was 42nd Street, the World's Greatest Movie Center, like the sign painted on the side of the Selwyn Building says. Now 42nd'd never given me no thrill. Just a street where I had a job. Maybe it was the World's Greatest Movie Center to the jerks who come in mobs to see the movies and shoot rifles and eat hot dogs. To me it was just a jerk's paradise. But now it was like I'd never seen it before. Like it was striped with gold like that lucky wallet I'd found. Opening up like the biggest door in the world. And the guy all the movies were starring was nobody but me, little Maxie Dehn. I tell you there's no money like finder's money. Finder's money is the money you dream about, a real sign your luck is changing for the better.

I hugged that box. The crowds on the sidewalks all looked swell to me. Everything looked swell. The sky was cold gray, one of those November skies. But to me it was a sky in Florida. I was dancing only I didn't know it. I went by the Hotel Dixie entrance, which is next door to our building. A hundred lit-tle busy guys were already rushing in and out of the lobby. That's the Jacob Groteclose Building for you. Packed from the street to the roof with typewriter repairs, novelties, glassware importers, employment agencies, and anything else you can think of. I looked at all those busy little guys, some of them smok-ing big cigars like they were big time, and some of them were. And I thought that none of them, in fact, nobody on 42nd Street, was as lucky as me with my lucky wallet and my forty-thousand-dollar deals and Hortense topping off all my good luck like a piece of pie à la mode after a seven-course steak dinner. So Doyle was playing a fast one. And so what? You couldn't expect forty thousand to fall into your lap just like that.

I put my hand into that cardboard box, shoved the wallet into my coat pocket. What a thrill! Then I walked to the curb and was about to chuck that cardboard box away when a copper stopped me. "Hey, what's the big idea!" the copper says. Where he came from, search me. When you want a copper, you can't see one in a mile. "What you throwin' that cardboard into the gutter for?" this copper says, giving me the big copper eye.

For a second, I was jittery. Because the wallet wasn't mine. For a second I thought, Maybe I should turn it over to be on the safe side. "I'm sorry, officer," I says.

"You're sorry! What about keepin' the city clean?" he broadcasts as if he went around with a broom and shovel himself.

"I won't do it again, officer."

He ate up all that "officer" soft soap, for he says not so mad, "There's a trash can up the street."

Over to the trash can I go. I was burning up. What burned me was that I'd thought of turning the wallet in. I could've kicked myself from 42nd down to South Ferry and back for being such a jerk. I dumped the cardboard in the can and lit me a cigarette. I stood there smoking. And I can't help it, but I begin to smile at the whole damn world. I patted my coat pocket with the wallet and I feel swell again. There were some fat pigeons in the gutter, eating away at hunks of hot dog rolls that'd missed the trash can. I looked at those pigeons and thought what a soft deal they had. A million guys buying hot dogs and chucking the bread parts away! But who chucked wallets away? I asked myself and I had to smile.

I hurried back to the Jacob Groteclose Building and the Hotel Dixie doorman says to me, "Good morning, Mr. Dehn. You're coming from Broadway this morning?" He was dressed like a South American general, in his blue uniform and red-striped pants and gold braid. Strictly a jerk. And this morning Mr. Dehn from Broadway was too busy to be bothered. I must've smelled like money, for Phil the elevator boy, he asked the people to step back when he saw me coming. "Make room for one more, please," Phil says to them.

I squeezed into the elevator. Yes, sir, make room! For this was Mr. Dehn coming. Excuse me, Mr. Maxwell Dehn, Junior. That's how good I felt. I could feel that lucky wallet of mine in my pocket. And I think of all the stories in the papers about ragpickers and hackies finding wallets with fortunes in them. A regular miracle, me finding that wallet, for if it hadn't been inside that broken-up box, somebody else would've seen it long before me. What was it doing inside a cardboard box, anyway? I wonder. Was there a reason? Kind of fluky, wasn't it? I think. Fluky wallet, fluky dough. Suppose that wallet's loaded with folding money, with hot money, with the big easy money? I think a mile a minute.

The elevator stopped at my floor. The people getting off scooted down the corridor to the offices, but I stayed behind. Was I excited! I was boiling! I pull some business letters from my pocket and make like I'm looking them over. When there's nobody in the corridor, I shoved those letters the hell back and scuttled for the fire escape in the rear. I went out on the fire escape.

In the whole city of New York I couldn't've found a more secret place. All around were fire escapes and more fire escapes. Walls and ventilators. With the big clock on the Paramount Building up in the sky. I was in the center of New York, between 43rd and 42nd, but from the fire escape, it could've been some empty alley. Yet, a funny thing, before taking the wallet out of my coat, I played it safe anyway, facing the brick wall.

Aw, the hell with all the suspense.

There was nothing in that goddamn wallet. Nothing in the main fold. Nothing in the side folds or side pockets. No money. No licenses. No papers. I went through it a second time. There was nothing. A big nothing. Talk of luck. To go find a wallet and then have nothing in it. A goddamn wallet, lying around in a goddamn cardboard box. And for what? Just to make a jerk out of me. Then I guessed the real reason. That wallet must've been one of a bunch of wallets being delivered somewhere. The errand boy must've chucked the box away thinking it was empty. Or maybe he'd left one wallet behind. Deliberately on purpose, for the laugh. Hiding himself in a doorway and watching me arguing with the scrounger for the big booby prize. Hiding in a doorway and laughing to beat the band. All for the laugh. The whole goddamn town was full of people who'd do anything for a laugh. Talk of jerks! I was the prize jerk with my phony little act, making believe I'd lost that cardboard box, and glad, so glad to find it again. And brown-nosing the cop, calling him officer. Talk of jerks! I was the world's champion jerk.

I heaved that wallet down into the yard. Let the super, some other jerk get gypped finding it.

Luck? Yeah, luck.

Doyle, he didn't ring the next day. The food I ate could've been sawdust for all the good it did me. Then it was Thursday and my dancing lesson. When I stepped out of the elevator into the reception room, Hortense was already waiting for me. I had the funniest sensation, like it was all something I was seeing that nobody could understand. When my old man'd died, that was how I'd felt at the funeral. The minister and everybody sad or crying, Mamma and my own family, and what was it all about? A long wooden box, a closed wooden box, the coffin with my old man in it. Hortense was waiting for me, smiling and talking, and all the pupils and teachers were smiling and talking, but what it was all about I couldn't've told you.

We walked into the tango ballroom. She put my Course Book down on a chair and nothing was real. The Course Book wasn't real, she wasn't real, and I wasn't real. For how could a jerk like me be marrying a girl like her? I couldn't believe I'd ever kissed her or she'd kissed me. Because the only thing real was Doyle and what Doyle said up the mezzanine of the Astor.

We tangoed and she asked me why I was so quiet. And I said, "Am I quiet?" Then, after some more lame-brain talk like this, she asked me the question I'd been expecting. "How's the deal coming, honey?" she says, and she smiled. That smile ruined me. I could've cried like a kid. For that smile wasn't for me but for the deal, and if it was for the deal, it was for Doyle. A guy she'd never even seen. But not for me.

"O.K.," I says to her. "Just a coupla li'l headaches you can always expect." I hadn't meant to say that. I'd intended bluffing with Hortense. But I felt so funny and all, I simply had to give her some hint of what I was feeling. Even if it killed me.

"What kind of headaches?" she says.

"Oh, nothing serious, Hortense."

"Are you sure, Maxie?"

"Always some headaches when you float a big deal," I says quick, because her eyes were real worried. "The lawyers have to straighten out the damn legal complications. But nothing serious, Hortense. Honest!"

"You had me scared for a minute," she says.

I could've cried like a baby. For what'd scared her wasn't how I was feeling, wasn't me at all, but the deal. That goddamn deal. "Forget it," I says, bluffing with ulcers. Ulcers? Those ulcers were big as watermelons. "Forget it. That forty thousand's as good as in the bank."

"As long as it's in your bank, honey," she laughed. "Now let's concentrate on the tango, sweetheart."

We were doing Step Number Six, The Conversation Pizzarro, which, what with Doyle and all on my mind, I was messing up. "Keep your feet straight," I heard her saying. Only it wasn't her and it wasn't me. It was something happening that made no sense. "Make believe there are spurs on the backs of your shoes," she says, "and those spurs'll trip you up if your feet aren't straight."

We tangoed around a bug guy standing in the middle of the floor while his teacher gives him a lecture that the tango is three long steps and two short steps, all timing, and he has to pounce on the two short steps. "Take your hands out of your pockets, Mr. Maurice, and pounce!" this teacher says to the big guy.

It was a laugh, but I couldn't laugh. Because in that ballroom nobody and nothing was real. Like overseas before a mission when we'd get up in the middle of the night, dress like hell, and try to eat. The food and the coffee with no taste to it. And then run to the briefing shed and assemble near our ship. The Flying Rat Hole on Wings, we called her. She'd be shining like silver, her bomb bays loaded, her ten guns stripped for action. She was real enough and yet she wasn't real because we weren't real.

At the half-hour bell Hortense said we ought to rest a few minutes. So we sat down in a couple ballroom chairs and talk a lot of bubbles, all about nothing, and then she says, "Maxie, your poker face is pretty good but the trouble with you, you haven't got poker legs. You're dancing like you danced in the beginning. You didn't keep those spurs on for a second. Even coming to these chairs, you walked like a duck, like in the beginning."

"Can't a feller have an off day, Hortense?" I says to her.

"How much off can you get? Something's not so good. What is it, Maxie?"

"Hortense, if you had to listen to lawyers all day long with their lawyer hot air, you'd be a little groggy, too." I looked her square in the eye the way Doyle did, like my eyes were bright blue like his, and I gave her the big glad-hand Doyle smile.

But I guess I wasn't Doyle, for she says, "Maxie, what's worrying you, honey?"

"Nothing serious, baby. And that's the truth."

"You sure?"

"Sure as fate. How about meeting me tonight when you get off?"

But she couldn't make it that night. Which was lucky for me. I wouldn't have been able to bluff her a whole night through. Not Hortense.

When my lesson was over, I didn't go down in the elevators. The elevators were packed with pupils. I didn't have the patience to wait. I just had to get out fast. All I could think of was what a terrible mistake it'd been coming to the studio tonight. Passing on my worry to Hortense like some dumb jerk. I just had to get out fast. Like some criminal leaving the scene of his crime in the movies. Nutty, huh? You bet! I could've given myself up to the Chock-Full-of-Nuts eating places. For who the hell walks down eleven flights in an elevator building?

It was like the tomb on those stairs. Quiet. With nobody but me. And Doyle. Yeah, Doyle, inside my head, beating my brains out. Everything he'd said and I'd said at the Astor, it was inside my dumb splitting head. And things he'd said other times. All kinds of things. Like once when I'd argued it was the privilege of the Shaw sisters not to sell if they didn't want to, he'd yacked, "What privilege? Two old spinsters from the Civil War. There ought to be a law to make them sell, holding up progress. Don't look at me so funny, either. Sure, I'm out for a dollar, and who isn't? But when you and me, not mention the Shaw sisters, are deep under, there'll be a television city uptown there, and that's progress." That whole yacking speech of his, and others like it, came to me now.

I was just a jerk. And if I needed more proof I got it that very same night. I'm not superstitious, but when things happen in a series, there's a reason.

Anyway, I was on my way home, minding my own business, when in this

side street between the Avenue of the Americas and Broadway I hear this
spieler barking out of a store that your hair is important and to come in for a
demonstration. It was strictly hick stuff. Made to order for the hicks you see
wandering all over Broadway. She had a crowd of them hypnotized, mostly
men, but plenty of women too. Her store was jammed and more coming in
from the street. Now, me? Sure, I'm sensitive about my hair. I admit it. But feeling the way I did that night, I wouldn't have cared if I was as bald as Bing Crosby. The only reason I stopped was to kill a little time, to forget how dumb I
was, getting Hortense worried about the Doyle deal. What I'm driving at is
that stopping like I did was natural but what happened after I stopped was on
the fluky side. Almost like finding that damn wallet. Like it was a sign.

This spieler was on a high wooden platform in the rear of the store. She had
an amplifier on her, the long black wire hanging from her neck. A big dame
she was. No chicken, but ripe and curvy, in a black suit striped with a white
pencil line that made her seem more curvy than she was. And she had plenty
of hair. Thick and fluffed up and bright as brass. But nothing compared to the
hair in the two life-size photos on each side of the platform. In one, there was
a beautiful dame in a white swimsuit, with hair reaching to below her hips. In
the other, there was a couple saying sweet things to each other and also with
hair out of this world.

"Come on in!" this big dame spieled. "The weather man predicts snow for
tonight, any minute now. Come on in and warm up. Don't block the doorway!"
She had a voice that would've stopped a truck. Without the voice, she would've
stopped a truck. She was that ripe.

I still wasn't going in but all those hicks rubbernecking behind me were on
the move. I tried to get from under. But just my luck, that spieler spots me.
"Where you going, mister?" she says. "You came in here of your own free will.
Least I expect is the courtesy to hear what I have to say, or didn't you ever hear
of courtesy, Mr. Vishinsky?"

All those hicks let out a big laugh, They were all moving forward and I
moved too. Because I didn't want any more debates like with the counterman.
I thought, what the hell, I'd kill a little time anyway.

"This is a public platform open to criticism at all times," that big tomato was
spieling away. "I'm not a hairdresser or a beautician." She waved her hand at a
little table on the platform. On the table there was a goldfish bowl full of
water, but with no goldfish. "Please observe this simple demonstration," she
says. Picking up a slip of paper, she dipped it into the bowl. "Watch the water
run off!" she says, holding up the slip of paper for us to see. "That's how erl"—
she was a New Yorker, all right, this big tomato, and oil was erl—"runs off your
head. We'll talk about erl a li'l later. Your hair's an asset, although I can see that
with a lot of you out there it's a shrinking asset."

The crowd laughed. She was as good as a show to that hick convention. You
know how they are. They laugh easy.

"You meet a new girl," the spieler she spiels, "and you don't say I met a girl in a blue coat, do you? You say you met a blonde or a brunette or a redhead. So what do you men do? If hair's important on a girl, it's important on a man! You bet your hair's important. Don't you spend millions on your hair every year? Ask your bald barber! So the bald barber says you got to put the erl back into your hair if you want to keep it—so you douse your hair with erl!"

She reached for a bottle of olive oil on the table and took a drink. Just like that. The crowd split its side but I'd heard about enough. I started to ease out but before I'd gone a second step she had me. "Erl belongs in the stummick and not on the head and that goes for the head of Mr. Vishinsky!" I stopped dead and turned around. She was smiling at me like a sister. Maybe I shouldn't have given up, but I just didn't have the energy to buck that big dame.

"Don't the Mayo Clinic use it for the intestines?" she spieled. "It's good for the intestines! For the insides! But don't put it on the outside!" She began to massage her scalp. "Now you girls think this is funny! You girls're so much wiser than the men. The hairdresser says you need a hot-erl treatment so you get doused with erl. They put a steaming helmet on top so hot it could cook your dinner. Don't laugh, you men! Your bald barber fingers his hot towel, but it's too hot to handle so he throws it on your head to get rid of it! You bake and you stew and you sweat! Don't laugh at the truth! All of you have wasted your money on erl, but don't get me wrong. I'm not knocking olive erl! Olive erl is good for you. Good inside of you! The Mayo Clinic uses it! But did you ever see hair grow on an olive? What do you want, anyway? Hair or vegetables?"

The crowd let out another big horse laugh, but she didn't act satisfied. She looked them over without a smile on her face. When they quieted down, she says, "You can't afford to laugh! You put erl on. You put brilliantine on. All kinds of colored junk. Did you ever read the labels? Nearly all that junk contains alcohol!" She grinned like a bar fly and when she got her laugh, she turned around to a carton on a chair behind her. She reached in and held up a small jar. "We sell a product that grows hair. Don't laugh! I'm not crazy, unless I'm crazy as a fox. I got brains and I use psychology. Maybe you think I'm crazy, but you'll remember me tonight when you look at your hair. But it's all in the comb, your hair! Not on your wise little head! In the comb! I don't sell erl what's good for the glandular system, I don't sell a product with alcohol for a base, I sell a product that grows hair on the head! It costs one dollar and your money back if you're not satisfied!"

I didn't have to do it, but she was looking right at me. And I'd had enough free publicity from that spieler. I pulled out my wallet. What was a dollar, and maybe her junk had something, I thought. One of her shills took my dollar and gave me a jar.

I'd bought my right to beat it, which I did, with all those hicks grinning at me because they still remembered the Mr. Vishinsky wisecracks.

I walked out to the street. It was snowing like the weather man predicted. And not even winter yet. But I didn't get a kick out of it, and I'm one guy who loves it when it snows. For one thing, I knew I'd been had. I knew that hair grower I'd bought was just no damn good. Worse than that, I started in thinking about Hortense worrying, and Doyle.

I almost tossed that jar of hair grower into the gutter. Then I shoved it into my coat pocket and hurried toward home. On Broadway the crowds were coming out of the movies. They were looking up into the sky all full of snowflakes and getting a kick out of it. The wind was blowing a mile a minute and the snow was dancing. When you have a snow on Broadway with all the lights shining, you've got something to look at. But tonight nothing looked good to me. Because nothing good was real. Only the aggravations. Like Hortense worrying, and Doyle sneaking around, they were real. And when I put my hand into my coat pocket, that jar of hair grower was real. I'd let that big tomato in the black suit rook me into paying out a dollar. And for what? It wasn't the dollar either that burned me up. It was just the idea that everybody was always playing me for a jerk. That big tomato. And Doyle. And Hortense, too. Without the money, I didn't rate for beans with her. I felt terrible. And all I could think of was to get rid of that damn hair grower like it was that'd put the jinx on me.

I crossed to Duffy Square, meaning to toss the jar over the railing, when what happens? A guy with nothing else to do, even with the snow coming down thick, stops to watch me. That's New York for you. It could've been the blizzard of '88 and some guy'd still be snooping around to see what he could see.

"Maybe you want it?" I says, real sarcastic.

"Want what?" this nosy guy says, walking closer to me.

"This jar."

"Jar of what?"

"It grows hair is what!"

"It grows what?"

"Hair! Yellow hair, red hair, or brown hair. Any kind you want."

"You're kidding me."

"No, it's all yours for being nosy."

I thought he might've got sore, but these noisy guys haven't any feelings. He only says, "What's the matter with it?"

"Nothing's the matter with it, Nosy. But if you're losing your hair—"

That burned him. "What's it to you, I'm losing my hair!" he yacked, getting excited. Can you beat that! This nosy character with a skin like an elephant, he was getting to be the insulted one. "My hair's none of your business."

"Aw, go lose yourself with your hair."

"What's it coming to when it's everybody's business a man's losing his hair!" He was making a speech now, in the snow and all, like it was the Fourth of July.

"Lose yourself, Nosy!" I says.

"Never mind that!" he says. "Why don't you use that jar yourself? You give away ice in the winter, don't you?"

I was sick of arguing with him. It was a jerk's argument, anyway. You can't win with these nosy characters. Why, they want to know. Why! "Look!" I says to him. "This is a racket. Just an advertising stunt. We give these jars away to passers-by. Samples!"

"When it's snowing?" he asked.

"Snow or rain, what's the difference in advertising!"

"Oh, I see," he says. "Why didn't you say so in the first place." He held out his hand and I gave him the jar. He went north, Nosy did, and I crossed to the west side of Broadway.

I should've gone straight home. You know how it is when things go off? They all go off. Just listen to this.

On the corner of Broadway and 47th Street, a blind accordion player was playing "White Christmas." No harm in that, right? Just wait a minute, though. When I got there some woman'd dropped a coin into his tin cup, and the blind guy was smiling. Blind and all, with the snow flying in his face, he could still get up a smile. A guy who had nothing. It kind of hit me. Here was a guy whose breaks'd been a hundred times worse than mine. He couldn't see the snow or have fun like the crowds from the movies. But he could hear them yacking about the snow, the white snow he couldn't see, and he was with that crowd all the way. Playing "White Christmas." Maybe he was thinking of Christmas when he had eyes, when he was like everybody else. Now he had nothing. But he could get up a smile. I thought of the buck I'd wasted on that jar of hair grower and how I could've used that buck a helluva sight better, and the next thing I know, I'm hauling out my wallet and pushing a dollar into the tin cup riveted onto the accordion.

It was a mistake. The wind blew that buck out of the cup. I tried to catch it, but it went into the gutter. I ran after it and smacked into two fellows. "Where you going?" they hollered, and I was so excited, I explained about the buck blowing away and how I'd wanted to give it to the blind accordion player. They said they'd get it for me, those two fellows. Don't ask me why I believed them. The old Christmas spirit. Yeah, and I'm just a jerk. But with all that snow, so clean and white, and the blind accordion player standing there on the corner, puzzled by what was going on but still playing "White Christmas"—anyway, I believed them. I went back to the blind accordion player and explained about the dollar blowing away and the two fellows.

I had one nosy before. But now there must've been a million of them, asking questions and making remarks. I pointed out the two young guys in the middle of Broadway. Everybody looks. The snow is coming down. The taxis are beeping. It's a sight. One of those guys, he bends over for my dollar and he straightens up. And keeps on running, the other crook after him. "Hey!" I yell.

"Stop! Stop, you thieves!" I started after them but a car misses me by an inch. The traffic is too heavy. I gave up and went back. And what a crowd now! Out of all the cracks in the sidewalk, and yacking. God, they were yacking.

"What a shame!" says a guy with an umbrella. "Didja see that? A shame!"

"I saw'm give the money myself."

"How much was it?"

"Five bucks!" This was one of the kibitzers that comes in every crowd.

I said it was only a buck. But nobody is listening to me, for when a crowd gets that big, the kibitzers take over. Not to mention the guys who have to prove how much they know, the big authorities. The guy with the umbrella tried to push through to talk to me. But his umbrella was a nuisance and started an argument. "Five bucks!" the kibitzer says. And another says, "For five bucks I would've chased after that money myself." And another guy with a voice like a foghorn says, "He must be rich or screwy or something." And the crowds look at me, a whole stack of eyes under their hats, like I was the biggest jerk in the city of New York.

"The wind blew it out of your cup," I says to the blind accordion player. "It wasn't five bucks. It was only a buck."

"Thanks," that blind guys says, and he smiled, and his voice was— How shall I say it? His voice was smiling, too. A sad smile, a regular blind man's smile. A smile like he'd made up his mind he was making the best of being blind and all. It gave me a queer sensation. Like it was that dumb yacking crowd that was blind, and the blind accordion player, he wasn't so blind, at that. I felt I had to help a guy like that. So I slipped a dollar into his hand. Don't ask me why. Don't ask me nothing. I don't understand all of it myself.

He thanked me and asked if there was anything I'd like for him to play. I could hardly hear him, for that crowd couldn't get over the dollar I'd given him. Yacking! God, what a yacking!

"He must be rich," some guy is saying over and over.

And the kibitzer says, "What's money to some people! What we all need's a tin cup."

That crowd's talking to beat the band. But the blind accordion player, he's looking at me like he could see me almost. "Anything you like," he says. And the kibitzer laughs, "Play 'Brother, Can You Spare a Dime'" and that whole Broadway bunch let out a howl like they had nothing better to do than hang around in the snow laughing at me. What the blind accordion player plays is "White Christmas" and the kibitzer hollers, "For Santa Claus!" and they laugh louder.

I'd had enough. I scrammed the hell out of there, sad and mad all together. Thinking how lately all the wise guys were laughing at me. They could be somebody like Doyle. Or that big tomato with the hair grower. Or that guy on Duffy Square, Mr. Nosy. And this bunch of nosys. All the goddamn wise guys were getting a laugh out of me. And what were they all but crooks at heart, from Doyle down to the two guys who'd lammed off with my buck?

The sign on my block was covered with snow so you couldn't see it was 47th Street. The one-way traffic arrow, it was pointing down a street without a number. It wasn't my block, I thought. Only a place where I hung my hat. Where I ate and slept. What was the good of that? I thought of Mamma waiting up for me, ready to nag me for being out in the snow. As if that was important. And if Hugh was home, he'd be studying his N.Y.U. books. Lately, he seemed to be kind of ducking me. Like he didn't want to be bothered about my troubles.

It was just the kind of a night when a fellow should be with his girl. But Hortense couldn't make it tonight. For all I knew, she was out on one of those famous Hortense dates. With that redheaded heel of a Dexter Rolfe. Drinking herself stinking drunk in some bar. What I ought to do, I told myself, is get stinking and pick up a dame and the hell with everything.

There were places I could go to, dames. So what if they were bags? When it's snowing and all, a fellow needs a woman. Even if she is a bag.

I walked by my house. With that snow, it could've been any old house. Even the green lamps of the police station across the way looked different in the snow. And yet who do I think of now but my old man? Ninth Avenue, it looked haunted. Haunted's not the right word. But when it snows, especially the first snow of the year, and I get to thinking of how my old man used to pull me in my sled on Ninth, when the El was still there.... Oh, well. Anyway, Ninth Avenue doesn't look right without the El. The old El—the big iron pillars holding up the tracks, the uptown locals, the downtown locals, with the express on the middle track going by like thunder. Ninth Avenue's too wide, too empty now, not like when my old man'd been alive. Those were the days. The snows would last all winter and we'd build snow forts in the gutters and my old man'd pull me along with the snow coming down on Ninth, and I'd kind of make believe the snow was falling from the El trains like they were snow trains or something.

My old man should've seen me now. Ninth Avenue was still a big street to me. The street of the bags. This Katie O'Toole lived off 39th Street and Ninth while Madame Shouria was on Ninth itself. I thought how I hadn't gone near either of them in weeks. And here I was slipping back into the old habits. But like the old-timers say down the West Side: When you can't get good whiskey, bad whiskey's next best.

I went to Madame Shouria's because she was the nearer one. The sign she had over the doorway where she lived was covered with snow. But I knew every word on it backward and forward: "Madame Shouria" was the first line. Then, "Fortunes." Then, "3rd Floor." Madame Shouria was what we in the real-estate line call a permanent fortuneteller. She wasn't one of those fly-by-night gypsys who rent an empty store for a couple of weeks or months and then blow out. She was a good tenant. She'd moved into one of the properties I managed, a year before the war. She was still there when I was mustered out of uniform.

I looked up at that sign of hers, covered with snow, and I had a funny feeling in the pit of my stomach. Like there was some meaning to it. Like it meant I shouldn't go up and start in all over again. That snow on her sign was like a blot through somebody's name. A big blot. For what's the use of kidding myself? Madame Shouria was the old sickness Hortense had cured me of.

Yeah, sickness. That's what it was, the bag sickness. They could be Irish like Katie O'Toole or part Egyptian and part Syrian like Madame Shouria said she was. But what they were wasn't important. What was important was how old they were. This Madame Shouria was in her forties and she had two kids. She was fat and big and her skin was greasy from eating those Greek lamb dishes. What you'd call a real Turkish harem beauty, only in reverse. And Katie O'Toole could've been her twin sister. Another big tomato in her forties. She was a widow and a lush who sewed trim on hats in the busy millinery season. She was another tenant of mine. I'd met her like this. One day when I was collecting her rent, I saw she was a little drunk. We got to talking and she asked me to bring her a bottle of rye, which I did. That was my speed. Katie O'Toole and Madame Shouria. When I was with a young good-looking girl, like Frieda Amberg, for instance, who I wanted to marry before going overseas, I was numb. I couldn't even kiss them without getting numb. Frieda was smart to turn me down. Our marriage, it would've been a fizzle. Like when I dated this Eyetie over in Italy, beautiful and only seventeen and stacked, but it was no go when I tried. A fizzle. But let them be ripe like Katie O'Toole or Madame Shouria and I was O.K. What do you call that but a sickness? And while I'm on the subject, I might as well give you all the rest. Before the war I'd tried to find out what it was. I'd go into those bookstores around Times Square where they sell sex books on how to consummate your marriage and stuff like that. But what I read there only mixed me up worse. Those bookstores had a lot of books about faggots and Lesbians and perversity, but I wasn't queer. I could do all right with women, providing they were older than me. Until Hortense straightened me out.

Listen, I know what's wrong with me better than any doctor. In fact, I know exactly when it started with me. It was like this. I must've been about fifteen when I first tried it. It was with a girl who'd been around plenty. She was about thirteen when I went up on the roof with her. God, was I scared! I kept thinking of my folks down a few flights and how they might come up and catch me at it. I kept wishing I'd gone to some other roof. Then this girl starts getting ready like I wasn't even there. Like she was undressing before going to sleep. I couldn't do a thing. She kidded me fierce. What she said I don't remember. But how her voice sounded I'll never forget to my dying day. Even when I was in high school and the guys got to bull-sessioning about girls, I'd hear the sound of that voice. I stayed away from girls until I graduated from high school, when a bunch of us went to a cathouse. I went in to the whore and she took off her robe, and what do I hear? That damn girl on the roof. The whore laughed at me and asked me if I'd had a big night the night before. Some joke! But I didn't hear her like I heard the girl on the roof, if you know what I mean. God, that was when I knew I was jinxed. I just stayed away from girls after that, working my head off in the Jacob Groteclose office. Everybody had women, but not me. I was jinxed, sick. Then I met some married tomato whose rents I collected. She was twice as old as me, a bag. But I was O.K. I was O.K. with the bags. When they were on the ripe side, I was a great little lover. Until Hortense opened the door for me and showed me what I'd been missing all my life.

Where was I? Oh, yeah. There I was looking up at that sign of Madame Shouria's. I'm not superstitious. But there're meanings to things. That sign was covered with snow like I shouldn't go up. Like I'd be taking too much of a chance. I thought, Suppose there's, no return ticket for somebody like me! What a payoff! To outbluff Doyle in the long run, pocket the forty thousand, marry Hortense, and then on the wedding night to fizzle it like the other times when I'd fizzled it.

"Hell!" I said, and ducked into the vestibule. With my passkey I opened the vestibule door. A radio was playing somewhere, and the house smelled musty like all these old tenements. I thought of Hortense and how maybe she was with some guy, drinking herself stupid and then going to sleep with the bastard. And I wished she was dead and I was dead into the bargain. I didn't give a damn any more what happened. When you're jinxed like me, it's no use worrying.

I went up to the fourth floor. In the rear, over Madame Shouria's door, she had another sign. This one had a big white hand painted on it like the hand of a traffic cop. I looked at that white hand and it was like a hand made of snow, kind of. And I thought there was a meaning. But I didn't give a damn any more.

I knocked on the door. No answer, so I tried the doorknob. The door was closed. I used my passkey and went inside. It was quiet but somebody was still awake, for on the table inside the door the light she had there was lit. It was one of those brass Buddhas with a yellow electric bulb screwed into the top of the head. This Buddha was one for the jerks. For all the guys who when they go to a fortuneteller expect mystery like in the old Charlie Chan movies. There was some incense burning in a copper dish next to the Buddha. That was Madame Shouria for you. Buddhas and incense, and claiming she was part Egyptian and part Syrian, when all she was was just another hundred-and-ten-per-cent phony.

"Madame Shouria!" I called down the corridor.

She came out of the kitchen. When she saw me she smiled. She was real glad to see me. For like I said, I hadn't been around except to collect her rent in a long time. "Mr. Dehn, Maxie!" she says, and she even walked a little faster than she usually did. I watched her coming to me. She had on an old blue and gray bathrobe and old slippers. Her black hair was piled high on her head and she was all smiles. But what I noticed most was how round and fat her neck was, and how thick her ankles were. She stopped not a foot from me, waiting for me to say something, smiling. Her smile looked fatty to me, like all the rest of her. I yanked her to me quick or else I don't know what I would've done or said. Under her bathrobe, she felt soft and fat, like she had on a corset made of jelly, and I had a feeling that in about another second I'd be turning into something soft and fatty myself. And old.

I must've let out a groan or something, for she says, "Maxie, you sick?"

And I says, "No, no. Who's sick?"

Down the West Side they say that when a drunk falls off the water wagon, the splash can be heard in bars a mile away. That was how it was with me and Madame Shouria. I started in, not only with her, but with all the old tricks I've been ashamed to even mention until now. French picture cards, for example. I began buying them again like I used to before I met Hortense. And the dirt you buy to read when you look at the pictures. I even bought some of the poems the hicks buy, which I'd never done before. I was walking along Eighth, and in one of those souvenir stores near Madison Square Garden where they sell Statues of Liberty and cowboy leather goods, I saw this poem in the window. It went like this:

> I'm tired of whiskey, I'm tired of gin,
> I'm tired of virtue, tired of sin,
> Tired of the rumba, tired of truckin',
> And after last night, boy, am I tired.

Nothing to it. But I bought this poem anyway, like I was turning into a hick myself. I kept the French pictures and the rest of the dirt on the top shelf in my closet, inside a carton of old books. Inside an old Tarzan book that had the name of a kid I used to know in high school written on the front page. That old Tarzan was the alibi I'd thought up when I was still in high school. You see, although Mamma never bothered with the top shelves in my closet, I had the alibi ready. I could say the French pictures and the rest'd belonged to that kid and I didn't know they'd been inside his Tarzan book all these years.

Disgusting, huh? I disgusted myself. More than that, I hated myself. If I were to tell you the things that popped into my head about girls, and what you could do to them—Well, never mind. I wasn't kidding before when I said I had a sickness.

A couple weeks went by and not a sound out of Doyle. I was so chewed up inside, I wasn't human. Legal complications, I kept saying to Hortense, but who the hell was I kidding? Not Hortense. She was always too busy when I asked her for a date. Said she was taking private dancing lessons after she finished at the studio and that left her tired. These private lessons were supposed to be with a rumba specialist. According to Hortense, she was thinking of trying to get a job as a rumba dancer in some night club. Maybe she wasn't stringing me. All I know was that she didn't have any more time for me.

Doyle, Doyle, Doyle. That foxy mick was eating me up alive. But when you start a bluff you've got to go through with it. Hugh, who I'd finally got around to telling about Doyle, Hugh's idea was that I ought to forget Doyle, and Hortense, too. That's what you call advice. Advice and a half! Lately, I couldn't seem to get close to Hugh. When he wasn't busy with this girl Rita from N.Y.U., he'd bury himself in his schoolbooks.

God, I'd feel so lonely I'd go walking by myself nights. One night I walked from 47th Street along Ninth, wondering if I shouldn't give in and ring Doyle in the morning. At 34th Street I stopped. I stood there on the corner of 34th, and what do I think of? Doyle? Nope. I thought of how when I was a kid, 34th and the Pennsy tracks were the boundary of Hell's Kitchen. None of us kids'd dare go below 34th when the Chelsea gangs were waiting to mobilize us.

I went back but I couldn't get my mind on Doyle. All I could think of were the days when I'd been a kid. That's not so hard to do on Ninth. Because even with the El gone, the buildings're just about the same. Three- and four-story bricks, some of them built in the Civil War. It's only in the side streets that the garment lofts have come in. I passed J. Blomeir's Drugstore, and in the windows there were the same red and brown and green drugstore bottles like when we'd lived on 38th Street. You jerk, what about Doyle? I said to myself. Cherry candy drops from Blomeir's—that's what my jerk's mind thinks of. Cherry candy drops, and the camphor bags Mamma tied around our necks in the year of the big flu epidemic, and the cod-liver oil with the picture of a fisherman on the bottle carrying a fish as big as himself. When I passed our old block, 38th, I kind of half closed my eyes so I wouldn't see the lofts too clearly. What with the night and all, it was almost like the same solid German block it'd been once. I thought I'd go home and have a cup of coffee with Mamma like I used to. We'd talk a little maybe about my old man and the way things used to be. I passed the real-estate office of Crosby and Blemly and the real-estate office of Foss and Dohm. Oldtimers like Jacob Groteclose, but they'd stayed behind on Ninth Avenue. I thought of when my old man'd worked for old Jacob in the Ninth Avenue office. My old man, he'd been wonderful to me, and now I was letting him down, letting them all down in the office, by trying to pull a fast one with Doyle. I think to myself that if my old man were alive, I wouldn't be such a crumb. If he were alive, I'd have somebody to talk to.

I hadn't felt my old man around so close and so near, kind of, like I did now. I remembered a thousand things about him. His dark blue suits, his gold watch that my brother Pete had now. His big brown pipes and his mustache and the way he'd wipe the beer suds from his mustache with a flip of his finger. Saturdays, I'd go shopping in Paddy's Market with my old man and Mamma. The horse-and-wagon peddlers lining the curb under the El, the smell of oranges and apples in the cold air. "Smell the fruit!" my old man used to say to me. "It is like the old country, Maxie." And he'd buy me a bag of hot chestnuts from the hot-chestnut man on the corner. Boy, they tasted wonderful.

Aw, what's the use of remembering things like that? My old man was gone and the old days are gone. Gone with Paddy's Market underneath the El. All gone. The El sold for iron scrap to Japan. The peddlers' horses sold to the glue factory. Ninth Avenue's a one-way street and you can only go south on it. All that was left, I think to myself, is Mamma and me. For my brother Pete's married, and my sister Johanna. And Mamma's waiting up for me, I thought. Poor Mamma.

I crossed 42nd Street, passing the barbershop where I got my haircuts and the Washland where Mamma fetched our laundry and Salomone's shoe repair where we fixed our shoes, and Carroll's bar and Sheehy's bar on 47th Street, where I sometimes had a beer. Irish bars, like the old days when Hell's Kitchen'd been nearly all Irish. I went up my own block. Inside Larry's candy store there were a bunch of Puerto Rican kids hanging around. From a doorway some Puerto Rican was playing spick music on a guitar. I thought how the Puerto Ricans were pushing the Italians and Greeks out, like the Italians'd pushed out the Irish, and only a jerk like me could still be making believe things were like they used to be. This going home to drink coffee with Mamma? What was that but a jerk's idea? I wouldn't be able to sleep, worrying about Doyle. Worrying about Hortense. I'd toss around and get to thinking of her and me. I'd get into a lather, and think of the French picture postals. Aw, I thought, why be dumb? I heeled around, passing Larry's candy store again. There were Puerto Rican girls with the boys inside. They could be made, I thought. They were jail bait, but they could be made.

You guessed it. I was on my way to Madame Shouria's and to hell with Hortense. So what should jump into my head out of nowhere but a story Mamma used to tell us when we were kids. The story of the peasant shoe and the princess shoe. How the peasant's shoe was just what you could expect, worn out and covered with mud and dirt. But just the same, the peasant's shoe was always dreaming of pairing up with the shoe of the princess in the castle. That was a shoe! All shiny red leather and with a little diamond stitched above the toe. In Mamma's story, the peasant's shoe also turned into shiny red leather with a little diamond on it, and they lived happily ever after. Just like Disney.

I couldn't think why I should remember that story all of a sudden. Then I knew. It was a sign I should forget all about Hortense. All the fluky things happening to me were signs I should forget Hortense. I was jinxed. I'd been born jinxed and I'd die jinxed. My head began to go round and round like crazy. Forget her? I'd sooner be dead.

I just had to talk to somebody. So the next night I made Hugh leave the house with me. Over a cup of coffee, I first told him about the wallet I'd found. The jar of hair grower, everything. You know how it is when you begin. There's no stopping. Walking home, I even worked up the nerve to tell him what I'd kept secret my whole life: About how it was with me and women. My sickness. I couldn't've got that off my chest in a cafeteria, but in the night, in the dark, it wasn't so hard.

Hortense

I had the misery blues.

When I woke up that morning, in my own room for a change, I knew I was going to say yes to Dexter. How long can a girl hold out with nothing happening?

O.K., Hortense, I said to myself, you've never been a pro but there's always a first time. That day, friend Maxie was due for a lesson at seven o'clock. I made up my mind I was unloading Maxie for good. He could ask for another teacher or raise hell, but I was through teaching him. And I was through with friend Hugh. On Sunday, when that free lover was next due, I'd give him his walking papers, too.

Yes to Dexter, no to Maxie and no to Hugh. Just like that. Bang-bang-bang like out of a pistol. Some girls make up their minds, but they have minds. Me, I must've dreamed up my mind. When I'd gone to sleep the night before, nothing'd been definite.

I wasn't any happier now. I didn't feel any better. But at least I was wising up to myself. I guess I should've known all along that the only real money I could depend on was what I earned myself. Milly, working four nights a week for Dexter, was making three hundred a week. Claudia, working only one night to pay her liquor bills, was picking up a neat seventy-five. Two nights a week'd net me one-fifty. I thought that I should've said yes to Dexter weeks ago. "You're sleeping around town," he'd pestered me almost every day at the studio. "Why not get paid for it?"

Why not was right. What was the percentage floating around like some of those victory kids nobody'd bothered to tip off the war was over. I knew the score. But here I was traveling the same old circuit from barroom to bedroom. Reserving Sundays, besides at least one night during the week for Hugh Pierson, who didn't own a dime, all because he said, "I love you," as if he meant it. In the hockshop, what can a girl get for those three little words? Hugh and Maxie, they were a pair of I-love-yous. I-love-you and I. O. U.—they were the same damn thing. A hundred and fifty in cold cash wasn't forty thousand, but at least you could deposit it in the bank. I'd been stupid for believing for one second that Maxie and forty thousand could even be mentioned in the same breath.

I had myself a coffee breakfast. Last night I'd been drinking with Claudia. Just the two of us, or should I say the three of us? O.K., the three of us, Claudia and me and Mr. Bottle. I went downstairs. It was about half past twelve and the sun was a sick yellow color like the chilled grapefruit I hadn't touched up in my place. I walked by the Elton Hotel on the corner. The misery blues, this morning, had a different beat to them, because I knew I was saying yes to

Dexter. I looked at the Elton and thought that when I was twenty-eight I'd be living there, and when I was thirty I'd be living in a furnished room between Lexington and Third. I might be worth seventy-five now, but what would I be worth in two years? In four? Bong-a-bong-a-bong, give the honey seventy-five, give her twenty-five, give the old bitch five, five's enough, too much, bong-a-bong-a-bong.

I thought how I'd lived for two whole years on East 26th Street, with the Armenians over on Lexington, and the taxi drivers piloting the out-of-towners to the girls in the furnished rooms. Maxie and his forty grand'd given me ideas about moving to Tudor City or Central Park West. Sure, I'd move. From East 26th to East 27th. I was twenty-six, the same number as the street where I lived, and in July I'd be twenty-seven and then twenty-eight. And then what? Some girls can lap up the whiskey, the late hours, and the men, but I wasn't the type. I was no lady Frankenstein like Milly, but one of those little cutie pies, worse luck. Just a little cutie pie who'd believed a little too long in the law of averages. Guaranteed. But the only thing guaranteed was the rat race. The only sure thing was your hair turning gray.

This was a morning. I was going to say yes to Dexter but without cheers. I never was one to kid myself, and I felt so blue. So damn blue. The misery blues, I had them bad. I felt as if something'd gone out of me for keeps. Maybe believing in the law of averages was dumb. But it'd kept me hoping. Maybe it was only a shot in the arm, a private little morale-booster. But what did I have now? Dexter? There was no guarantee he wouldn't try to cut the seventy-five to fifty or even less. I knew myself well enough to know that once I was call girling, I'd just drift along. Dexter Rolfe was an operator, and you can't trust a man who's going up just as you can't trust the slob going down. I thought I'd keep my job at George Lawrence like Claudia had for insurance. Milly'd quit teaching, but not me. Quit, and Dexter'd think he owned me body and soul with the accent on the body—you can have the soul. Oh, that bastard Maxie, I thought, with his forty G's, now you see them, now you don't.

It was a perfect morning for the Blooms. Winter was in the air. In Madison Square there wasn't a leaf on the trees. I looked at all the typists and stenos hurrying to lunch, with their dumb laughing and their dumb boy friends, full of hope like a junkie full of heroin. I wished I could've been a dumb steno myself, in a Woolworth chinchilla, engaged to some white collar. Marrying someday and living out in Brooklyn or Queens in two and a half rooms.

On Fifth Avenue, I took the bus as I always did to work. The misery blues, they were driving me mad. To stop thinking, I looked at the advertising sign on the back of the seat in front of me. Don't report this to the bus company, but I was so miserable, the next thing I was scratching on that sign with my nail file, and the next thing I knew, I'd scratched a couple little words on that sign. The little words you see all over the city, on posters, on the sides of trucks, everywhere. They're famous.

I pushed my nail file down into my bag and tried looking out of the bus window. And all the men I saw, I thought to myself, suppose they're Dexter's customers. From where I live on 26th Street up to 34th Street, it's business. Lofts and office buildings, fabric houses, rug marts, and corner cigars, cheaper than cheap. The sidewalks were crowded now with all the bastards who'd got old chasing a dollar, picking their yellow teeth after their eighty-five-cent luncheons. Manufacturers, salesmen, clerks. It was bad enough having them as pupils at the George Lawrence School of the Dahntz, but God, I thought, taking those cripples into bed.

It was a relief when the bus passed 34th Street, where the department stores begin and where the women shoppers take over. But then I started asking myself, what did all those women have that I didn't have? I looked at them, down on the sidewalks, in minks and in Persians, with nothing to do but spend money, carrying their brassieres and their rears high off the sidewalks as they stepped into the stores where the salespeople would treat them like queens. Seventy-five a night was real money, but it was piker money to what one of these rich married bags collected from a night with hubby.

It was a perfect morning for the Glooms. When the bus went by the library on 42nd and Fifth, the white stone stairs and white stone lions reminded me of when I used to come here and read all the books. Just a kid who loved to read. It gave me a needle, for I hadn't thought of the 42nd Street library and me in years. I hadn't dreamed, back then, that I'd end up as a call girl. I was such a skinny little kid, and for years I didn't have any more sex than an old maid. None of the girls in our family had any sex when we were kids. My mother used to say it was because we were born coal-patch kids.... The bus rolled north on Fifth Avenue, but I wasn't looking out of the window any more. I was thinking of my mother, who had tried so hard to make a home for us. She'd planted violets and Sweet Williams in the flowerpots as she used to do when we were living in Pennsylvania. And my father, that dumb Polack, would laugh like when he was still a miner and not a janitor in New York. "Flower tings no grow by coal tipple!" he used to say back in Pennsylvania, and in New York, "Flower tings no grow by skyscraper!" A dumb Polack if there ever was one.

I hadn't thought of my family in years. There's no point to it. There's no point to anything, I say. The only smart thing's to let your life go by. Let it go and let it go, for you never get what you want.

Shirley Rollins, up in the reception room, had her usual little dig for me. But I said nothing to the bitch. I was too miserable. I went into the teachers' lounge, which was on the move like the subway express at rush hour, the men putting on their dancing shoes and cardigans, the girls mugging at the mirrors, the wise guys wisecracking, the weepers weeping. "Dex," I said as I passed him, "will you hang up my coat for me, honey?" He smiled and followed me to the lockers in the rear, where I got rid of my coat. He watched me. He was smiling as if to say: I'm not going to keep asking you forever.

"Dex," I said. "Dex—" I'd made up my mind to say yes, but I couldn't stand the sight of that face of his with that smile like a price tag tied onto me. "Dex," I said. "Go away, honey. In fact, go to hell!"

"What's the idea?" he said, his smile coming off.

"I'm in the market these days. Stocks're up and utilities show a marked improvement."

He got sore. "Cut the crap, Hortense! What'd you call me over for?"

"I can't say a thing until I see my lawyer."

He wasn't sore any more. He was smiling again. "Your lawyer? Who knows? You might get a Wall Street lawyer today for a pupil. He'll fall for you, honey, and whisper in your pearly ear, 'Dream girl, how'd you like a convertible to match your eyes?'"

That was one morning when the comebacks didn't come when I wanted them. Dexter walked off, and then the warning bell went *bonggg.* "General meeting," Claudia said as we left the lounge. It was Thursday and I'd forgotten.

We hurried into the main ballroom, we girls lining up on the left, the men on the right. Up front like a fourstar general, G.L. as usual was waiting for us with his secretary, Miss Ambers, whom we called Miss America. She was really a knockout, a pale blonde. A couple of steps behind Miss Ambers, Tibson the porter was posted in a good position, as usual. This Ambers kid had a rear end made of solid glass, the kind you have when you've just turned twenty. Tibson did his peeping-Tom act every Thursday. He'd stand behind Ambers and his fat face sometimes would get flushed. Of course, he never imagined anybody noticed him. Maybe because his uniform was green to match the drapes, he thought he was in disguise. Like a green worm. I looked Tibson over and I asked myself the $64 question.

Seventy-five dollars didn't seem so big.

This Thursday meeting began on a health note. "The air is bad in here!" G.L. said. "We don't want colds in this weather! Miss Ambers!" She smiled and waved Tibson over to the windows. Tibson opened one, looking back for further instructions. G. L. lifted two fingers, and Ambers, to make it official, nodded at Tibson. Up went a second window. G.L. treated himself to a deep breath and said, "Miss Ambers, will you have Tibson notify Dr. Mayer we're ready?"

It was definite by now we were in for another G.L. production. A dancing school with green drapes, and Course Books with golden nymphs on them, and mirrors and glamour brings out the ham in everybody concerned. You can't put on a daily act for the cripples seven hours a day without having a little of good old Broadway get into your system. Even Tibson marching across the ballroom floor—it was his big moment—was like a stage super carrying a spear. As for G.L., he was staring up at the ceiling like King Lear. "The weather's been treacherous lately. Very treacherous. Snow and sunshine!"

A man in white stepped out of the side door. Even if he hadn't been in white, he couldn't have been anybody but Dr. Mayer. There was nothing about him that was the George Lawrence School of the Dahntz. He walked with his feet spread out like a duck's. His head was down on his chest, his shoulders stooped, like he'd never read in the Guidebook: "To be upright is a visual delight—*Never* slouch."

"Does it matter which arm they roll up, Dr. Mayer?" G.L. asked him.

"I prefer the left arm, Mr. Lawrence."

"Roll up your left arms!" G.L. said. "As you have gathered, Dr. Mayer will give you all a cold shot."

A nurse, escorted by Tibson, pushed a white table on wheels through the side door. The men began taking off their cardigan jackets. The whisperers began to whisper and the gigglers to giggle. Johnny Byrne, near me, whispered we were getting embalmed: Claudia said why not, when the cripples were half dead anyway? What the occasion needed was somebody to yell out those two little words I'd scratched on the sign in the bus.

"Get on line!" G.L., our M.C., ordered. "Please get on line, and quiet, please!"

The nurse dabbed some alcohol on the first arm. The doctor jabbed his needle.

"Quiet, please!" G.L. said. "This meeting will continue, if you don't mind. I have some reports on my desk from Allentown, Pennsylvania, and San Francisco, but perhaps we aren't interested here. This is Fifth Avenue and we're different on Fifth Avenue. We don't contract colds on Fifth Avenue!" He sounded sulky, Papa did. He reminded me of another production of his when he'd turned the general meeting into a dress shop, with Ceil Chapman dresses for every girl ahead of her quota and a cheap Seventh Avenue special for every girl behind.

"Ouch!" a girl yelled after being jabbed.

"Next!" said Dr. Mayer. "Next! Next, please!"

"Out there in Allentown and San Francisco," G.L. was saying, "they look to us to pioneer new developments, but we don't care, do we, on Fifth Avenue? Not us, we're on Fifth Avenue."

It was too much for me. Twisting my head sideways so G.L. couldn't see my face, I let out a stage whisper—"Ouch!" That was all I said, ouch, but the timing was just right. The whole place rocked. When things quieted the nurse asked, "What's so funny?" Everybody laughed again and G.L. said sarcastically, "Who is our humorist?"

"Next!" said Dr. Mayer. That started the laughing again.

Papa shook his head sadly and said, "There's no use in being serious today, is there? Will the supervisors meet me in my office immediately." He walked out of the ballroom, followed by Miss Ambers, who was followed by Tibson and the supervisors.

"Odd sense of humor these people have," the doctor said, turning to his nurse. "I guess we chose the wrong profession."

The nurse said, "What profession is the right profession, Doctor?" Or maybe

I only imagined it, for Claudia, on the line behind me, was shooting a lot of questions in my ear. Claudia and the others behind her had seen me. Already the news was humming on the old grapevine. "Hortense," they called to me, grinning or shaking their heads.

"For God's sake," Claudia was saying to the teachers behind her. "Forget it, will you! The butcher boys might be back." She hushed them but I knew it wouldn't stay that way.

"Will you please be still?" Dr. Mayer said to us. "Next, please." The nurse dabbed while he jabbed. Dab, jab, dab, jab. As I moved up on the line, I wondered at what I'd done. Goofy? Worse than goofy. Some teacher was sure to rat on me. I could see myself downstairs with G.L. And what could I say? That I'd become so frightened at the idea of the hypo I'd become hysterical? I thought I'd better not wait for someone to rat on me. I better go see Papa and rat on myself. Appeal to Papa's good nature. Apologize and promise to behave myself in the future. Every family has at least one bad girl, and with Christmas around the corner, what was a bad girl for if not to be forgiven? Since I wasn't booked at four, I could go down then and let Papa forgive me.

Bonggg.... It was the five-of bell. Full of preventive cold bugs, we ran with our new little friends—isn't science wonderful?—into the teachers' lounge for the Course Books of our two o'clocks. *Onggg....* "Hortense!" a dozen grinning apes called to me, and I knew that the grapevine was wrapped around my little neck. "I sneezed," I said as Dexter reached me, and we all ran for the reception room.

"Hortense!" He grinned like all the rest.

I said, "I'm in!" The bell was fading and it sounded like my own heart. "I'm in, Dex!"

"In what? In Dutch?" he said, and then he got what I meant. "Swell! See you at dinner."

"Hortense!" they called to me as we flew down the corridor.

"I can get another job at Arthur Murray's or Fred Astaire's," I said. "Now smile, all you handsome bastards and lovely bitches! That's what our devoted pupils expect. White teeth! White teeth like in Allentown, P.A."

Dexter laughed and said something, but I didn't hear him. I didn't hear any of them, for my heart was beating fast and loud, with a private little bong and ong. "How are your fallen arches this wonderful day, dear cripple?" I hammed like mad, thinking I'd said yes to Dexter. "How is junior's fever? Down to a hundred and ten? Why, that's practically normal for a child, Mr. Schmohawk. You'll be able to rumba with a carefree mind!" But it wasn't me talking. I had a goofy notion it was the bells.

My two o'clock was a Mr. Colby, interested in what he called "a smooth fox trot." As we went into the fox-trot ballroom, he said he was worried about his wife coming up one of these days for a look-see. Seemed his wife thought he was paying only two dollars an hour for instruction, and one peek at our swank and she'd know he was lying. I thought of the instruction I could give

Mr. Colby for seventy-five bucks, and just then the two-o'clock bell bonged. I laughed, for it wouldn't be me instructing him, but the bells.

Mr. Colby became irritated. "I don't think it's funny, Hortense."

"Mr. Colby, everything's funny. Including you and me."

He stared at me like he couldn't believe his ears. Neither could I. It was a bit of dialogue not in the Teachers' Guidebook. We fox-trotted, doing the Rainbow Beat with Turn, and it was bong at the half hour and bong at the hour, and good-bye to Mr. Colby. "You were very good today, Mr. Colby," I said. "And don't worry, I won't ask you to think of another course." I smiled at what I could sell him.

"You are in a good mood today," Mr. Colby said with a smile.

"Don't worry," I said. "I won't ask you to think of another course. All you professionals are hard to sell. The doctors have no regular income, the dentists have no money. The lawyers want to see a contract. And none of this, Mr. Colby, is out of the Teachers' Guidebook."

"Teachers' Guidebook?" he said puzzled, for he hadn't heard of our bible.

"Someday they'll publish a Teachers' Gripe Book, if you want to know, Mr. Colby."

He laughed. "You're one girl with a sense of humor, Hortense."

"Sure thing," I said. Get a reputation for having a sense of humor and you can get away with murder.

My three o'clock was a Mr. Immer, and although this was his fifteenth hour in a twenty-five-hour course, he was still shy. One of those thin quiet types who only wear brown suits, white shirts, and maroon neckties. I tried to imagine Mr. Immer paying out seventy-five bucks, but even my imagination couldn't make it. He was a tango fiend, Mr. Immer, so we tangoed. In the middle of the ballroom, I saw Dexter fanning about his three o'clock. This three o'clock had her hand raised over her foolish head, pointing one finger at the ceiling. Dexter was giving her the Statue of Liberty. Pure corn. But when they're forty-five, like this cripple was, they don't complain. In fact, they beg for second helpings. I thought that Dexter ought to hire himself some call boys, too, and I laughed. I was just wowing myself that day.

Mr. Immer stared at me.

"Nothing like romance," I said.

"Romance, Miss Walton?" He was frowning, this white collar in a brown suit.

"The tango, Mr. Immer."

"I suppose so, Miss Walton. But excuse me, I don't get the—"

"It's not important, Mr. Immer." I let up on the comedy, for suddenly I felt tired as hell. It was only a few minutes after three but it seemed as if I'd been dancing for years, dancing nonstop to some nonstop tune. I thought of G.L., whom I'd be seeing soon, and I thought that working for Dexter I'd be doing a Statue of Liberty myself. One finger pointing to heaven as every bastard with seventy-five bucks to his name fanned about me. "Hell!" I muttered, not giving a damn what I said or did.

"Excuse me, Miss Walton—"

I said nothing.

"Excuse me, Miss Walton. You're pale, excuse me. Quite pale."

"The tango only has five steps, Mr. Immer," I said, giving him the routine patter. That's where the Teachers' Guidebook is a lifesaver. "If you can count to five, the tango's easy, Mr. Immer. Did you know that, Mr. Immer?"

Bonggg and *onggg* and *nggg*, again the bells.

I'd intended seeing G.L. at four. But no sooner did I file away Mr. Immer's Course Book when my butcher boy, Lila Rand, grabbed me. "Hortense," she said. "We've just signed this cripple up for fifty hours. He's practically illiterate but he wants to rumba. You work him right and he'll renew in a couple weeks."

"I'm beat, Lila," I said. "Get somebody else."

"This is an order, stinker!"

I wondered if the grapevine'd reached her, but I decided it hadn't or she would've been dragging me down to the tenth floor instead of into one of the private studios, where the cripple and Bunny Saunders, the interviewer, were having themselves a chat. "Mr. Anargaros." Lila said, "I want you to meet Miss Hortense Walton. Miss Walton is ideally suited to your personality, Mr. Anargaros. We make it a practice, you know, to select our teachers to suit the personalities of our pupils."

He was a dark hairy type, this victim, in a bright blue suit, a white shirt, and a hand-painted necktie with an Indian in a purple canoe. Lila's speech worried him, but he smiled and said, "I say hello."

I gave him the big charm smile. So did Bunny and Lila. This dark type blinked. It was a spectacle when you think of it. Three pretty girls all smiling at a joker in a hand-painted necktie. The show must go on, I thought. Goddamn the show.

Bunny walked over to the desk, picking up Mr. Anargaros' new Course Book, reading the results of her interview in a voice that could've been set to music. "Rhythm, excellent. Balance needs development. Self-confidence will develop. Natural ability, above average."

"I thank you," this Mr. Anargaros said, wiping his face with a colored handkerchief big enough to be a tent for the Sheik of Araby. Somehow he reminded me of Maxie.

"I can see you doing the rumba, Mr. Anargaros." Lila glowed like a six-coil electric stove. "I can just see you doing a perfectly wonderful rumba."

This Mr. Anargaros only began to recover a little when Lila and Bunny left the studio. I walked to the canned-music dial and pushed in the fox-trot button. "Let's see how you dance," I said, and offered him my smiling torso. In about a minute he stepped on my foot.

"See!" he said, excited. "See! I no do American dance! In old country we dance like this." He showed me how, by spinning his forefinger around in a circle.

"All we'll do now is walk to the music, and don't worry about stepping on my feet," I said, soothing as a mother. "Put your hands on my shoulders, Mr. Anargaros. And I'll put mine on your shoulders. All we'll do is walk to the music. That's very nice. Now your name is hard to remember. What's your first name?" I smiled at him like the heroine in the last few seconds of the feature as she hustles down Paradise Alley, into the big clinch. The show must go on, I thought. But if there'd been anything to this thought-wave theory, Lila Rand would've dropped dead that second.

"Xenocrates," he said as we walked to the music.

"Xenocrates," I said. "Imagine! What a fine name! Have you a nickname, Xenocrates?"

He laughed. "Not for lady."

"Please tell me your nickname. Is it Blacky?"

"No, Shorty."

"O.K., Shorty, listen to the music."

We walked and I talked. The victim from the old country didn't say much at first. But in the Teachers' Guidebook we have a solid page on the subject of silence.

"Remember there is nothing so embarrassing as silence. Ask him why he really wants to dance. Ask him about his wife or girl friend. Ask him about his job. Remember every pupil has a life of his own outside the studio."

Well, Shorty was a window cleaner, and I begged him to enlighten me about it and not to leave a thing out. We were still walking to the music, my hands on his shoulders. "Window cleaners not for lady," he said, apologizing.

"What's a nicer job than keeping things clean, Shorty? I want to hear about your job. I really do."

"Company send man in," Shorty said. "No come, drunk. I work for myself. No afraid big company. I make good money."

"I'll bet you do," I said, thinking who could tell, this window cleaner might be a likely bet after all—for Dexter as well as for G.L.

I pressed a button inside my head as I'd pressed a button for the canned music, and a canned smile came out on my lips. And Shorty talked and talked and talked.

At five, when I was rid of Shorty, I went downstairs to G.L.'s office. His secretary, Miss Ambers, said he couldn't see anyone today. His appointment book was full up. I hesitated for a second only. It wouldn't hurt Ambers to be the one to have the information for G.L., to be ahead of the supervisors. Besides, she had the reputation of being a nice kid. "You might help me explain matters," I said. "I'm Hortense Walton."

"What matters, Miss Walton?"

"Have you a sense of humor?" I asked her.

"A little," she smiled.

"I was the one who yelled, 'Ouch.'"

"You!"

"Me." I was watching her like her mother never had. First she stared at me and then a smile showed. I breathed easier. "Miss Ambers, I'd appreciate it if you'd say I was sorry. I came down to apologize. This is the first free minute I've had, and no one sent me, either."

"I'll do what I can," she said.

I felt so good at supper about that Ambers kid helping me I almost ordered a drink. But I never drink when it's business. And Dexter Rolfe, my new boss, was nothing but.

I wasted no time on Maxie. Five minutes after we walked into the rumba ballroom I said he should find himself another teacher.

It was brutal.

His face went white, his eyes wet. His mouth moved like a fish without a word coming out. He began to sweat. Not the honest sweat from doing the Cuban Fantasy, but a sweat half blood. I could've let myself feel sorry for him, but I didn't. At dinner between five and six, Dexter and I'd had a serious talk. I was a pro from now on.

"Maxie," I said, "things couldn't go on."

"You and me—" he said. He was unable to say any more, his mouth moving like a fish again.

"There is no you and me, Maxie. The deal's laid an egg and you know it, Maxie."

"No!" He managed to choke it out of him. "No, no! For God's sake!" he said, so loud that the nearest rumba dancers stared at us. When rumba dancers out of this world can hear anything, it's time to run for the exits.

"We'll talk in one of the studios," I said quickly. I picked up his Course Book and he followed me out of the ballroom, down the corridor to one of the private little studios. He didn't say a word and neither did I. But as soon as I closed the door, he grabbed me, kissed me. "Maxie!" I stopped him. "Somebody might be peeking through the peephole! Maxie, want me to lose my job?" With this kind of chatter and a little armwork, I managed to break out of his grip.

He stood there like a corpse, his face white. I brought the chair over. "Sit down, Maxie. Sit down, Maxie." He didn't seem to hear me, like he'd gone into shock. But I wasn't letting myself be sorry for him.

"Maxie," I said, "you'll be better off with another teacher."

He began biting his knuckles.

"Take your hands out of your mouth, Maxie!" He did so and it was so quiet in that studio, his breathing sounded like a mile race. "Maxie, there are lots of nice teachers."

"No, Hortense. Please—"

"Forget it, Maxie."

"Give me one more chance, Hortense. I'll ring Doyle first thing in the morning."

"Maxie, you and me're through. We're through!"

He was like a fish again, his mouth working and nothing coming out. A sweating fish. I didn't have the heart to say another thing. We just looked at each other. His eyes filled with tears, but I paid no attention. I wasn't weakening a second time. I knew he wouldn't ever be in the real money and neither would I. It was seventy-five a night for me right now, but next year, what would it be? It was the rat race for both of us.

"Hortense!" he said, like my name was some kind of a strange sound. An unnatural sound, awful, like a fish that'd somehow learned to talk one word, and had to get it out of its system before it died. "Hortense, Hortense—"

I went over to him and patted his head like you would a child. He had some sticky stuff on his head that made my fingers sticky. And a peculiar thing happened. As soon as I felt that stickiness on my fingers, I wasn't so sorry for him any more. "We can't stay in here forever, Maxie. My supervisor'll be after us."

"What've I got to live for, without you?"

I had to stare. It was like I'd never expected Maxie to talk normal again.

He was talking low. "Without you, what's the good, Hortense? Hortense, give me a break. Keep on being my teacher. That isn't too much to ask. For God's sake, Hortense!"

I gave in, and yet all the time I knew that if I were to touch his hair again, getting that stuff on my fingers, I wouldn't've given in. Isn't it queer what we know about ourselves sometimes? So why didn't I touch his hair?

Because I'd weakened on friend Maxie, I was that much tougher on Hugh. When he dropped in Sunday around noon, I gave it to him like a machine gun.

HUGH

I couldn't believe I had heard straight. "You might have waited until I'd taken off my coat, Hortense," I said.

She smiled at me from the couch where she was sitting, the couch where we had slept together, covered now by its daytime serapes. She was wearing dark gray lounging pajamas. There was no make-up on her face. The cloth doll on the couch with its black eyes and exaggerated smile seemed more of a call girl than Hortense. I couldn't believe *that* either, and yet it all had a sickening logic.

"Hugh," she said as I'd come in through the door, "Maxie tell you I'm through with him?"

"Yes," I had said. "It's a good idea."

"I'm through with you, too, honey," she had said, smiling. "Starting next week I'm working for Dexter. What the papers weep circulation tears over. I'm going to be a call girl, honey. Business is business, you know. No more free love, honey."

In my coat, I sat down opposite Hortense. "Yes, you might've waited until I'd taken off my coat," I said for the second time.

"Want a drink, honey?"

"What's the drink for?"

"For being smart. Maxie threw a fit."

In those gray pajamas, everything about her that was young and schoolgirl-ish was somehow played up. Never had her eyes seemed so large, so pure, as if she had announced her coming wedding. And in a sense she had. She was leaving one kind of life for another, and the brightness, the youngness of the bride-to-be shone from her in a radiance that I knew was entirely imaginary, a trick of my own imagination. I was aware that I was again romanticizing Hortense. It struck me that I had always seen her with Maxie's eyes as well as my own. Maxie's eyes! The thought was a revelation. And the time had come to throw Maxie's eyes away forever if I wanted to hold on to her.

"Can I have that drink, Hortense?" I said.

She got up from the couch. I had an urge to grab her as she passed, to kiss some kind of passion, some emotion into those cool dark eyes of hers. I controlled myself. I knew that it would be useless appealing to her emotions, to her heart. I could only reach her by appealing somehow to the Hortense going into business. But how? I asked myself. The thought, the hope, went through me that if we could get drunk I might change her mind.

But when she returned from the kitchen, she had only one highball. For me. "Thanks," I said. "So you'll taper down on your drinking, too? A good idea, Hortense."

She smiled. "Why wait for the New Year to make a resolution?"

I lifted my glass. "Here's luck, sweetheart." I felt like adding, 'and don't take any wooden nickels.' But I controlled myself. Sarcasm was a luxury I couldn't afford now. I sipped my highball and forced myself to remember that this being a call girl was a practical affair and somehow I had to be practical too. I drank my highball slowly. We smoked and talked. I asked her about Dexter and her new career and what the tariff would be, because, said I, perhaps I might become a customer. We laughed, and after some more talk the practical answer I had been groping for burst into my head like a rocket.

It was practical, all right, and low down, so low down I couldn't see myself taking advantage of it. There must be some other way, I thought. I said, "Hortense, we had fun, didn't we?" I heard my wistful downbeat voice as if listening to a stranger. Here I was appealing to her emotions after all. It was a mistake, and yet I said, "I can understand why you want to make money. But why can't we go on as before, Hortense? All work and no play isn't much fun, sweetheart." She was watching me, a tough little grin on her lips. She was polite enough, she didn't interrupt me, but that grin beat on my nerves like a warning drum. I was on the wrong track and abruptly I said, "I'm talking like a damned fool, Hortense. I wish you luck, sweetheart."

"Luck?" She shrugged. "Hugh, I'll tell you the truth. I'm not cheering. But what's a girl going to do? You know that story about the chorus girl who told everybody that when she'd be twenty-eight she'd either be fixed with some rich sucker, or else she'd have to kill herself because she'd be too old for her profession? Know it?"

"No."

"Well, she didn't land her sucker, so on her twenty-eighth birthday she jumped out of the window. The coroner looked her over on the sidewalk. There was a note in her hand and the coroner read the note. It explained that it was her birthday, she was twenty-eight and too old to go on being a chorus girl. So the coroner turned in a report. Death from natural causes."

"And that's how you feel at the ripe age of twenty-six?"

"That's how I feel, honey."

I thought to myself, Hugh, either you want her or you don't. If you want her, you'll have to be practical, just like her, practical and low down. The thought hurt. How low down could a man get? I wondered. Or go? And I knew as I'd never known until this moment that there were no limits. There were only the stairs going down, each stair lettered: "Be Practical" or "Be Realistic" or "That's the Way It Is." And somewhere an invisible line that if once passed barred all return. I knew as never before that there were actions that once undertaken were irrevocable. I could bring Hortense back into this room with me, the Hortense I'd had fun with, but if I did, I would never leave it. Not as long as I lived.

"Hortense," I said with a desperation she could never have guessed at, "why don't you let me see you once in a while?"

"Hugh, must we go all over that again?"

"No, don't." I drank from my highball, drank air. It was empty. But I felt as if I'd swallowed a glassful of straight whiskey, for I'd made up my mind to be practical.

Her face was pale and lovely and cynical, the face of a girl who trusted no man. I thought of Alice in Charlestown, whom I'd wanted to marry, and of Beatrice in Rome, and the feeling I'd had for both of them, the sweet little Southern girl and the English bitch. Looking at Hortense, I remembered them, girls of the past, and all I had left, like some GI with his souvenirs, was my own beating heart. "Hortense," I said, "the very first time we met you said you hated all men. I remember another remark of yours, on our last date. You said all a man wants to do is break open a girl like a clam, like there was a bonus in it."

"What're you getting at?"

"This. You don't trust me, but you do trust Dexter. Do you trust him more than me?" And with each word I felt myself leaving behind the Hugh Pierson who had been mad and foolish with love and who had never been practical as I was now in this room with the girl in the dark gray pajamas. "Hortense, you might need somebody you can trust a little bit, anyway."

She was staring at me, silent. She had made the connection. "This call girl racket," I said. "It's like anything else. Even if you trust nobody, you still have to trust somebody." As I spoke, little pictures flashed through my mind—the whores of Europe with their little thieving pimps, the painted smiling whores who sometimes also had other protectors, their lovers or husbands. "Dexter might try to take advantage of you. He wouldn't if there was a man around." I gritted my teeth, silent as she was silent. Then I managed to say the rest of it. "I don't want any of your damn money, Hortense. I love you. That's all I want."

Before that Sunday was over, we understood each other. The next day I packed up my suitcases and left West 47th Street for good. To Mamma Dehn, I said I was sharing an apartment with some other N.Y.U. students. To Maxie, who helped me with my suitcases over to Eighth Avenue, where I whistled a cab, I explained I was going to live with Rita. He believed me, but even if he hadn't, I wouldn't have cared much. Conscience, in the beginning, is all hard sharp edges. But then it becomes as round and soft as a rubber ball, and like a rubber ball it can be bounced all day long without any perceptible wear or tear.

I moved in with Hortense and our affair shifted to a different level. Up to now, we had played around. From the night when I'd escorted Hortense home from Tommy Nivens' party, we had literally played as lovers, two drinking companions whose love-making was only another highball. Drinkers on a binge don't fuss overmuch about the contents of their glass. Although I was curious about Hortense and had asked her the usual questions about herself, she had told me very little, calling me a private eye. It was as if she'd liquidated her past and been born fully grown to dance at George Lawrence. Even when she was very tight, she had revealed next to nothing, muttering about someone who cared—the sentimental drunken confidences of any hard-boiled operator.

But now that we were partners of a sort, and living together, I learned more about her in a few days than I had in all the previous weeks. When she returned home from one of her call girl dates, I would be there in the darkness. And in this private darkness we really got to know each other. In this darkness, Hortense had a past.

I didn't have to coax her to talk. She was eager now.

She had been born Hortense Pavlec in a small coal town outside of McKeesport, Pennsylvania. In 1932, in the depression period, her family had come to New York. Hortense was twelve then, the oldest in a family of six children. Her father had managed to get a job as a janitor taking care of three tenements in the East Fifties between Third and Second Avenues. As she told me this, I'd thought of Maxie Dehn, who in those years had lived almost directly west on 47th Street. Those two had been separated by all the anonymous millions of the city, separated by time, but not separated by the casual fate that brings a man and a woman together.

From 1932 to 1934, the ex-coal miner's daughter Hortense Pavlec had been a child, reading books and dreaming a child's dreams. "I must've believed in a fairy godmother," she said to me one night. "I was sure that when I grew up I'd marry a wonderful man. I was sure I'd be happy, a great dancer." When she was fourteen, she was working as a bus girl in a cafeteria. Bus girl, then hat-check girl and dancer in third-rate night clubs. "I was ambitious," she said. "I could dance and I had looks. I learned fast. Too fast, maybe. It was lay for the guy who could help you up. But I don't know—my luck was bad. I never got up into the top clubs."

When she was eighteen, she was dancing in a Greenwich Village club, her name Hortense Walton. Her visits to her family began to space out, and when her mother died, her visits stopped. "My father, that dumb Polack, didn't give a damn about me. By this time, three of my brothers and sisters'd flown the coop. The ones who stayed were like my father. Dumb Polacks! All they wanted from me was money. My mother used to cry when I came home. She always wanted to do things for me. I should let her wash my clothes, sew, anything."

When she was dancing at the Del Rio night club, she met an actor, Ronny Culver by name. According to Hortense, Ronny was better-looking than most Hollywood stars. He was tall and dark haired, "with chiseled features, the chiseler!" They were married and she became not only his wife, but his meal ticket. "Ronny used my money to take out other girls, and when I complained, he slapped me around." Yet it had been Ronny who'd walked out on the marriage—all the way to Hollywood, where his agent had landed him a bit part in a horse epic. She had written him letter after letter, how she loved and would always love him. "Real sucker stuff!" Hortense confessed bitterly in the darkness that was ours and nobody else's.

The mementos of her forgotten lovers were all over the apartment, the pipe with the silver Y on the bowl, the decoy duck, the abstract painting on the wall. Quickie lovers gone forever who had left her nothing, unlike Ronny. "One thing I got from Ronny was the bug to be an actress. I caught it from him. I had a crazy idea I'd get to be an actress and prove something to him. Crazy!"

Only about Ronny's agent, the man she called The Bastard, was Hortense reluctant to speak. "You should've been a private eye, Hugh!" she said to me. I didn't urge her. I knew she would get around to The Bastard sooner or later.

I was working at Gimbels these days, as a temporary salesman. Christmas was close and I'd been hired when I applied. I took the job mainly because I didn't want any of Hortense's money. She had plenty of money now, teaching at George Lawrence and working for Dexter twice a week. It gave me some satisfaction when I bought the groceries now and then or paid for our tickets when we went to a midnight movie after she was through teaching. And it was at the movies that she began to talk a little about The Bastard. She would criticize the acting on the screen. "I can act as good as most of those sex pots," she'd say, and point out actresses whose careers, according to Hortense, had been helped by The Bastard.

And then one night as she lay in my arms in the breathing darkness she said, "Hugh, you're a smart boy. Tell me, how many times do you have to take a reaming in this goddamn life before you get wise? How many times do you have to play the sucker? Take Ronny. He at least was normal, even if he used his hands, the son-of-a-bitching slapper. But The Bastard. I hate to tell you what he made me do and what I did. Goddamn it, Hugh, still want me to tell you?"

"Yes," I whispered.

She said, "Like you know, I got the acting bug from Ronny. He loved to act, but he had no part when we got married, no audience. So I was elected audience. Audience and sucker. When he became a Hollywood cowboy, like a sucker, I thought maybe I could get some kind of job acting, too. I could dance. I wasn't beautiful, but as beautiful anyway as most of those sex pots. And I was still on the young side. Twenty-three. So I went to see Ronny's agent in his office. There he was, sitting at a desk big enough for the President. A fat little guy like he was a king, wearing one of those ten-dollar neckties all zigzags and dots like that painting I've got. There he was, ten stories up, with Broadway down below, like it was at his feet. And on the walls, dozens of autographed photos of actors and actresses. 'When they write those books on show business,' he said to me, 'they left out one word only, the key word. Patience!' I wasn't falling for that, not after all the men I'd played sucker for. The key word! But I listened to him like any other sucker while he waved his hand at the autographs on the walls. 'See this stable of boys and girls, their names in lights, Louella Parsons interviews them, Hollywood contracts them. Your own husband, Ronny! They didn't make good without patience. In this business you've got to have patience!'

"While he was talking all this crap, he was sizing me up with his frog eyes. Ronny'd told me he loved the girls. But he was very careful, Ronny said. He never touched a married woman with an active husband. So I explained that Ronny and me were separated for good. The Bastard knew that, but he wanted to hear it from me. 'You want to act like Ronny?' he said, and I said I did, and then he did something I'll never forget. One of those stunts show business is full of. One of those stunts that the mental midgets who run show business like so much because it proves they've got Temperament and Artistry and Genius. He unknotted that zigzag and dots necktie of his and whipped it to the desk while he shouted, 'Flair! That's what a girl needs besides patience.' He didn't fool me for a second. God, Hugh, I thought I was so damn wise. This flair, like this patience—more crap. Another word for bed. I thought, O.K., I'd pay off in flair, providing he'd help me. He helped me, all right. He loved the girls like he loved his Turkish baths. Oh, well, before you wise up it takes time."

Her voice was bitter and yet it sounded strangely cheerful, as if at last, finally, she had received an acquittal from some court.

And that night as she slept in my arms I went over all she had said, and I kissed her sleeping face. She was so wise now, Hortense, or so she thought. Earning one hundred and fifty a week as a call girl and banking almost every cent of it. Wise with all the experience she had paid so dearly for. The final verdict—wisdom—granted by the court in session so long. A court without any official name, but all-powerful in its authority: the Nameless versus Hortense Walton, born Hortense Pavlec. I thought of the coal miner's kid coming to live in the fabulous city and remembered my own excitement in the fall when I'd moved into West 47th Street. I thought of the coal miner's kid walking from the tenements between Second and Third into the crowds on Lexington, to Park, Madison, and Fifth, into a world of elegant restaurants and department stores. To the kid going to the library on Fifth Avenue, it must have been a magical experience, like turning from a drab chapter in a book to a chapter all blazing light. She had dreamed of marrying a Hero when she grew up, of being a Dancer, and married Ronny Culver and become a dancer, and the books were all closed. Poor Hortense, I thought. When she looked back at the little sucker Hortense Pavlec, she believed herself wise as the ages, wiser by the years, wiser by the men who had come with the years, never realizing, not even now, that she was still a Broadway moth fluttering her life away. A little Broadway moth, wise. Yes, wise. Wise without wisdom....

The next day I phoned Maxie at his office and arranged to see him in the evening. He invited me to dinner, but I declined. At nine o'clock we met and went into a bar, and as we drank our first beer, I wondered how I could convince him once and for all, to forget Hortense. For that was why I had phoned. That much, anyway, I owed to Maxie Dehn. He smiled at me and said I looked thin, wisecracking in a feeble kind of way about what my girl Rita was doing to me. I felt like the biggest fraud on earth and it was hard to remember that even a fraud, even a hypocrite, could be capable of a good deed. Page the boy scouts! I had phoned Maxie to do him a good turn. I swear it. Once and for all I felt he had to realize Hortense wasn't for him.

"I miss you, Hugh," Maxie said. "I've got no one to talk to these days."

"What do you hear from Doyle, Maxie?"

"Nothing."

"You're still bluffing?"

"Yep," he said stubbornly. "I've made up my mind. I'll give him to Christmas week. If he doesn't phone by then, I'll phone him. You know—I'll wish him a Merry Christmas and see what the crook says."

"Maxie, you ought to forget that crook."

"Easy to say."

"You ought to."

"I need Doyle, I need the money."

"You mean for Hortense?" I said. This was the opening I had been waiting for. "Maxie, the best damned thing you can do is forget Hortense."

"Hugh, don't be dumb! Forget Hortense, you say. How? I've just got to have her, Hugh! I see her once a week, dancing lessons. She won't listen to me on Doyle. But if I get that piece of change— Aw, what's the use talking? She's like no other woman ever was for me. I've told you, Hugh!"

I couldn't look at his pleading humble face. Poor Maxie, I pitied him as I'd pitied Hortense the night before. I was just rotten with pity. In that Eighth Avenue bar, smelling of beer, I felt I understood Maxie as I'd never understood him when living in his house. His whole life seemed to streak through my mind. Maxie Dehn, the son of Mamma Dehn. Another biography written by another loving mother's ever loving hand. I thought of the stewed fruit Mamma served on Mondays, Wednesdays, and Fridays, the orange juice on alternate days. Of how she put out Maxie's pajamas for him, the blues one week, the yellows the next, the browns the third. A calendar of the weeks, a calendar of the days. I thought for the first time that the furniture in Maxie's bedroom, bird's-eye maple, was rather delicate for a man. Undoubtedly select-ed by Mamma. Yes, Mamma had done everything a mother could do for her son except sleep with Maxie in that bird's-eye-maple bed. Poor Maxie. He had been cheated so, only able to feel himself a man in the fat motherly arms of the fortuneteller on Ninth Avenue whose name I couldn't recall. But the name wasn't important, as the names weren't important of the fatlegs with mus-taches he'd gone with in Italy. They were sisters, all, the shadows of the woman who squeezed orange juice for Maxie Dehn so faithfully every Tues-day, Thursday, and Saturday. Yes, Hortense was like no other woman for Maxie Dehn. She had taken him by the hand and led him out of Mamma Dehn's house, out of the old-fashioned Groteclose office, and shown him the vast and glittering city, whispering the magic of another personality and another life in his ear. Maxwell Dehn, Jr., the big shot. A big shot in the city where every man had his price, even Jacob Groteclose's honest rent collector, little Maxie Dehn, and every woman could be bought, even the dream women.

What was there to say? Nothing. But I said it anyway. "I know how you feel about Hortense, Maxie. She's something special to you. After women like that fortuneteller."

"Women! Bags!" he said violently. "Hortense, she saved me. That's what she did!"

I thought that even if I blurted out the fact that Hortense was a call girl and living with me, it wouldn't have made any lasting difference to Maxie. He was committed to her as much as a man could be committed to any woman. For her, he'd invented the Maxwell Dehn, Jr., razzle-dazzle, and when that collapsed he'd gone into the Doyle deal. For her, the facts of his life had been knocked out like so many binding nails.

"She saved you," I agreed. "But things don't stay the same, Maxie. She thought you'd be in the money."

"She'll settle down if the Doyle deal can be salvaged."

"But Maxie, that's only a hope."

"What else is there but hope? I can't forget her. She's the best thing ever happened to me. That first time—I haven't told you that, Hugh. But maybe you'll understand better if I tell you."

I didn't want to hear him. I was suddenly sick of staring into the secret rooms of other people's lives.

I finished my beer and ordered another for myself and Maxie. "This job at Gimbels—"

But he wasn't listening to me. His eyes were shining, withdrawn. He wasn't aware of the drinkers at the bar, the tired and worn and greedy faces. "That first time, Hugh," he said almost as if to himself, heartening himself with the memory. "We went to the Cotillion Room at the Pierre. I had an idea she was going to let me take her home, see. All through dinner and the floor show, I was in a sweat. I couldn't even look at her without feeling panicked. It was the old sickness, Hugh. She was too young, too pretty. She had on a red cocktail dress, and two little red rubies in her ears. No other jewelry, only those two little red rubies in her ears. She was beautiful and ritzy, like she ate in the Cotillion Room every night. But me! What a joke, Hugh! What I ate and what the floor show was all about, you've got me. Know what I did to get a li'l courage, Hugh? I kept saying to myself, You're not Maxie the jerk, you're this Maxwell guy, and a pretty babe's just what you deserve. You're this Maxwell guy who takes his girl to the Pierre. But the more I tried to tell myself I was Maxwell, the more I remembered the times I'd fizzled, the time on the roof, and all the other times. That's over with, I kept telling myself. You're not the same guy, you're this Maxwell, no jerk like you've been all your life. Well, when we left, we went to her place. She made some drinks and we had a couple. But it didn't do me no good. I was shaking inside. I was panicked I'd be the same old Maxie. We sat down on the couch. She sat close to me. But me, I held onto my whiskey glass like the jerk I was. Afraid to put it down because she was waiting for me to put it down and kiss her. But me, I held onto that damn glass like a lifesaver. She must've guessed something or had a hunch or something. Or maybe she thought I was shy and needed encouragement, because she started to play some records. Blues and rumbas. Aw, what's the use of talking, Hugh? I couldn't give it to you how it was if I yacked all night. You couldn't understand unless you were a jerk like me in the first place. The music is playing and she's smiling, and me? I'm praying to God to take the damn jinx off me, and let me be like this Maxwell who I'm supposed to be. Then she took the glass from me, and we kissed, and I felt the old sickness in me like I was going dead inside. Hugh, she must've had an instinct or something, for she said what we should do is dance. Hugh, how can I give it to you how it was? What with the dancing and everything, I was able to— The first time in my whole life."

I had heard enough, too much. I didn't pity Maxie now. When he'd spoken of the blues and rumbas Hortense had played for him, I had thought of the *"Besame Mucho"* record she'd played for me after Tommy Nivens' party. It was singing inside my head now, the *"Besame Mucho"* of that passionate and mournful Spanish tenor. He had danced mockingly into this bar, invisible as ever, to hook one arm through Maxie's and the other through mine. He had watched Hortense give Maxie the gift of young love and with the same invisible eyes observed me with Hortense. And Hortense? Where was she tonight? Her lips parted for whose kiss? Not Maxie's, not mine, but for the kiss of the somebody who cared—who cared enough to pay seventy-five dollars.

"I've got to go, Maxie," I said.

"Let's have another beer. I hardly ever see you."

"Can't. I'll phone you, Maxie."

We separated and I walked down Eighth Avenue to 42nd Street. I thought of Hortense and to myself I cursed.

The peons of 42nd Street shone in a hundred empty colors. Jerk's paradise, jerk's alley were some of Maxie's names for it. But in Italy, Sergeant Maxie Dehn'd been sentimental enough about this street.

On the corner of 42nd and Eighth Avenue, the revolving clock of the Franklin Savings Bank turned and turned, the time on one side, Ben Franklin's golden profile like the profile on some huge golden coin on the other. Seventy-five bucks was seventy-five bucks, I thought, and time was money. I wondered if maybe I shouldn't go home for Christmas instead of spending it with Hortense, or rather spending Hortense's nonworking nights with Hortense. Spending, a significant word in more ways than one.

I looked up 42nd Street, a street for sale, promising everything and giving away nothing. A blazing neon candle to light the path for the emptyhearted into a neon paradise of false red and green and purple light, and if you didn't like what was on at the Thrill Theatre or the Liberty, there was always the New Amsterdam or the Laff Movie. Ten movies, 42nd Street, promising everything, and giving away nothing. I thought of how I had parted from Maxie tonight, almost hating him because my vanity'd been touched. Suppose Hortense had played her records for both of us? Was that a reason to hate? Vanity was all I had left. No pride, no decency, only the vanity of a call girl's little boy friend.

Love, I thought bitterly. Love? My brand of love was the 42nd Street brand, a perpetual lovers' midnight of double features. I looked at the men on the crowded sidewalks, all the little dreamers of the big city, dreaming of love as I had dreamed of love in the fall, and settling for a sixty-nine-cent seat in the darkness as I had settled for Hortense. Love? It would come someday, but in the meanwhile there were the neons and the darkness, where for sixty-nine cents you could make love to a beauty in Technicolor. At least the Technicolor women let you go when the movie ended. They let you go and their celluloid hands left no stain.

After that talk with Maxie, I felt that the change in me was a permanent one. There were still two of me, but the—shall I say better?—Hugh Pierson seemed to have thinned down considerably, becoming less visible and occupying less space in that secret center of being which my folks in Hightstown would have called soul.

I began to see the city with Hortense's eyes and with Maxie's or rather Maxwell's eyes: Hortense the would-be actress become a call girl, and Maxie, who had walked away from his roll-top desk in the Groteclose offices to become a would-be operator. Their city became my city. One afternoon, for example, after a big night with Hortense when I'd been too tired to report to Gimbels, I had wandered around town, walking on Broadway. The very pretty girls I saw were no longer the bright and romantic faces washed along on the crowds whom I had so naively admired in the fall. Their lives were known to me now. They were singers or actresses or dancers like Hortense, driven by the ambition that'd driven Hortense, and perhaps doomed also to the narrow frame of any man's bed. Maybe they had been born in small towns like Hortense, but on Broadway they had no past. Their snatches of conversation that I overheard could have been the very same words Hortense herself had used two or three years ago. "This thing in *Variety*..." "When I was up at my agency last..." They were young and beautiful and perhaps they even had talent. Perhaps they had everything but luck, the same luck that'd slipped through Hortense's fingers. Almost I could hear them exchanging the knife-edged repartee of Broadway in the offices of the people sitting at the controls. I could imagine them becoming meat for the vultures.

City of the big stem and not so big heart, with the December wind blowing down Broadway and the Santa Clauses ringing their bells on the corners. Hortense's city and Maxie-Maxwell's city. For the men in the side streets, gossiping on the curbs in the chilly sunlight, I knew them, too. I knew why their eyes were so sharp. They were afraid the main chance might slip by even as they spoke. The main chance, the big chance, the big deal. They were Maxwell's cousins, heartless and dollar-crazy, the big-deal boys, showing off their new overcoats if they were in the money, and in the money or out of the money, always ready to stick a knife into friend's or foe's back. The Doyle deal, what was it but a knife in the back of Jacob Groteclose? And a knife in the back of Maxie's dead father? And in the back of the equally dead Maxie? And hadn't I pushed a knife of my own into Maxie's back? City of phonies where Maxie'd become Maxwell the Rich Man, and Mamma posed as a Good Mother, and Hugh Pierson as a Best Friend. Only Hortense was honest. "I'm a call girl two nights a week," she had said to me once. "I'm not cheering, but what can you do? You can't breathe unless you have money. It's different with you, Hugh. You're going to school, your folks have money. You don't know what it is not to have money. No Gimbels Basement for me when I'm thirty."

I had seen another city in the fall and it was gone. Brilliant and varied, city of love and of dream, it had shrunk in size, no larger than the face of the tiny alarm clock Hortense carried in her bag. A city ticking like a clock when the rainbows in which it had been wrapped were stripped and thrown away. City of time where time was money and money was timeless. Where the hours and the minutes were scissors of time constantly snipping away at the hurrying crowds on the sidewalks. At old ladies and smooth young numbers in furs, at faded bankrupts and powerhouses in two-hundred-dollar suits, at giggling teen-agers and serious college students, the scissors were busy with all of them. Where did they come from? Where were they going? What did they all want? It didn't matter. No questions were necessary once you had become aware of the scissors. The questions had all been answered even before they had been asked. All the silly romantic tourist-like questions about the hurrying people who piled up on all the Broadway corners. They had come from everywhere to the heart of Manhattan, where Broadway and Seventh Avenue crossed at 42nd Street, like the blades of a pair of scissors made of stone. Come in their multitudes, and in their multitudes they would go, and if time pursued them all, there were some among them who pursued the others. For in this Manhattan of many-nations, there were only two nationalities: the hunters and the hunted.

I knew now that I was one of the hunters.

III: THE VERDICTS

Hortense

If you ask me, Hugh should've been taking classes, not in management and law like he was doing at N.Y.U., but in the Meaning of It All, in caps. Or else he should've gone to one of those schools where for a hundred dollars they give you a diploma saying you are hereby qualified to be a private eye if anybody's sucker enough to hire you. Living with a natural-born private eye like Hugh is an experience very, very wearing on the tongue. About myself, I didn't mind telling him, but he had to know about what went on when I worked for Dexter. "Hugh," I used to say, "leave a girl some privacy." But when he kept on asking questions, I said, "Hugh, I'll tell you about this one date. It's typical and it could be called an evening in the life of a call girl, pun intended. But after this, honey, let me alone."

If you want the low-down on anybody, say I, find out what they're doing to make a buck.

It was my fourth date. After Dexter collected the money, Milly, me, and the boys piled into a cab. Right away my happy boy, the big one, Jack, lifted me onto his lap. He wasn't wasting any time. I'd given him about three minutes to start in feeling his way, but I'd guessed wrong. It was closer to three seconds. "I'll warm you up, sister," he said with one of those rugged laughs you get from the he-man type.

"I didn't say I was cold," I said.

"No? It's snowing!" he said, and made with the laugh again. "It's not much of a snow. You don't know what snow is in this town, what's your name again?"

"Fifi," I told him for the sake of a little variety. I'd been Gladys on my last date.

"French, huh, or are you kidding me?" he said, giving me a couple more feels.

Milly laughed. But when Jack asked her if I was really French, Milly said I was French on my father's side. Call-girling is like anything else. You have to stick together. Milly and her date were on the pull-up seats in front.

Her date, Jim, a perfect gentleman, was holding nothing but Milly's hands. We really should've swapped men and everybody would've been satisfied.

That night there was a light rainy snow coming down, and the bright lights on Broadway were shining like a Christmas tree. We were traveling up Broadway because our dates were out-of-towners and wanted to get in a little sightseeing besides all the rest.

"I know a place with the best drinks in town, Fifi, if that's your name," my date said, bragging like most of these out-of-towners do, as if he had his dope from the Mayor himself.

"Let's skip the drinks, honey," I said. It was a standard remark with me whenever the date suggested drinking. The sooner I finished up the evening, the better I felt. Besides, Hugh always waited up for me. I'd told him not to but a lot of good that did. He would wait up because he was bothered when I was working. He wasn't getting any money from me, but his conscience wouldn't let him sleep. When I'd come in from my first date, he not only was awake, reading a magazine, he was also fully dressed. I'd asked him what was the matter and he said, "Nothing." He had even smiled, making like he was the big sophisticated type, back from the wars, who'd seen everything there was to see. Only his eyes'd give him away. "Hugh," I'd said to him, "you can't see the guy. I didn't bring the bastard home."

"What're you raving about?" he'd said.

"You know damn well what I'm raving about."

"You've got me all wrong," he'd said.

That night I was wearing a very tight form-fitting dress, and Hugh, he'd looked at me with those giveaway eyes of his. And what he was thinking I could've put down on a piece of paper. He was thinking how I must've looked to the guy I'd been with.

"How about a drink?" I'd said. He said no, but I fixed two drinks anyway, two stiff ones, and he eased up a little and began to talk.

"It's my damned pride," he'd said. "Here I am your little household pet and I want it that way, but still I don't like it."

"Forget it," I'd said to him. "So what if I've come home from another guy? Isn't it over?"

"Maxie should see us now," he'd said with a funny laugh.

I didn't want to discuss Maxie but I asked him anyway, "Why should Maxie see us?"

"We're a perfect triangle," he'd answered. "With Maxie the innocent bystander who doesn't know about you and me, or that you've become a call girl. And me the biggest crumb of all. Maxie's Maxie and you're you."

"Are you calling me a crumb?"

"We're all crumbs, but the biggest's me," he'd answered. "I'm the biggest because I've got the nerve to gripe about my poor little injured pride."

Yes, Hugh Pierson had a conscience, not too much, but enough. That was why I'd gone for his proposition that Sunday instead of kissing him off.

Where was I? Oh, yes. In a cab with this he-man, Jack. He wouldn't listen to my idea about skipping the drinks. "We're not going to skip a single thing," he said, giving me an extra feel so I wouldn't miss his little joke.

We pulled up to this place with the best drinks in town and we went inside. It was another side-street tavern between Broadway and Sixth. I've been in a dozen like it. There were four or five soldiers at the bar with a couple of Broadway bobby-soxers. And the two kinds of beer drinkers, the schmoes who wear their hats pushed back on their heads and the schmoes with their hats pulled low over their eyes. The cigarette smoke was heavy, the jukebox was juking, and the joint was just rocking with gay conversation such as, "Hey, where's my Tom Collins?" It was pretty clear that our two happy boys, after splurging for Milly and me, were going to cut all their other expenses down to the bone and then cut the bone in half.

"They have the best rye highballs in town," my honey, Big Jack, said when we sat down.

"Jack," I said. "Suppose you like to drink Scotch?"

"Scotch," he laughed. "What's that, Fifi?"

"Some people must drink Scotch even where you come from, honey."

"Where do I come from, you cute French doll, you?" He slammed the table playfully with a hand that belonged on the wheel of a truck. Except that he was wearing a diamond ring, a big one set in a flashy setting.

"You come from the great Middle West."

"You said it, you cute kid, you. Now what's a cute kid like you doing drinking Scotch?"

"I wouldn't ask for Scotch here, honey."

"Why wouldn't you ask for Scotch here?"

"This is strictly a rye and gin ginmill, honey."

"Now look here, Fifi, if that's your damn name!" he said. "They've got better drinks here than the Waldorf. That's why we're here! For the drinks! Not for the atmosphere or the entertainment."

"The entertainment's not bad, Jack," I said. "You should've been a movie star."

Milly got worried. "Jack, don't mind her."

But her date, Gentleman Jim, laughed. "Jack, this girl's got you tied up in knots."

Big Jack grinned what they call sheepishly in the magazines and he said, "You're a great little joker, aren't you, Fifi? Let me tell you about how I found out about this place."

"You read the address on the wall in the railroad station where you went for—"

"Will you stop!" Milly almost shouted at me.

"I don't mind her," Big Jack said. "I like a girl with a sense of humor." He slammed the table again. His diamond shone like a million and I wondered what he did out in the great Middle West to sport a rock like that one. From his big square face and two little eyes with thick brown hair cropped close, you couldn't guess much.

He was about forty, dressed in a dark blue suit and white shirt, with only the necktie loud enough to scare a little baby. But it was an expensive necktie, too.

"Honey," I said, "it's none of my business, but what do you do in Chicago?"

He laughed. "You're not so far off. Ever been to Detroit, cutie?"

"A great town, Detroit," I said.

"You bet it's a great town," he said, while his friend Gentleman Jim came in on the chorus with a "You bet!" of his own. He was about forty, too, Gentleman Jim, a quiet type, and maybe he was smart. He looked smart, but since he said practically nothing all that night, I never did find out for sure.

"What do you boys do in Detroit?" I asked them.

"We're in the union," Big Jack said. "We're negotiators as good as they come."

"Even better," I said.

But he didn't hear me. He was too busy blowing his own horn and the noise was terrific. "We're in New York to negotiate for the union with this lawyer. He's a lawyer and we're not, but we'll have him over the barrel, won't we, Jim? He's the one brought us here, only last night. Why, cutie, this lawyer, he can sit down anywhere in this town of New York, and I mean anywhere. He's in the chips. But this is where he brought us."

"For the best drinks in town?" I said to Big Jack, the negotiator.

"That's right! And let me tell you something else—"

Sometimes I think that the worst part of this call girl racket, like in dance teaching, is the listening part. "Where's our drinks?" I broke in on that blabbermouth.

The waitress was busy and it was another five minutes before she reached us. Big Jack ordered four rye highballs. I said I wanted Scotch. But he grinned and said that when the guy eats onions, the girl should eat them, too. So rye it was. When the drinks came he asked us to tell him the truth if they weren't the best drinks in town. "All I want to know is the truth," he said. "The plain unvarnished truth."

I shut my eyes and lifted the glass to my lips. "Varnish is right," I said. "Varnish and neutral spirits!"

"Stop horsing around," Big Jack yelled.

I took another sip. I swished it around in my mouth and after a while I swallowed it. "It's good rye," I said. "But I wouldn't call it an important rye."

Milly and Gentleman Jim laughed, but not my honey. He was mad, like he owned a half interest in the bar. He certainly ordered like he didn't have to pick up the tab. At the third or fourth drink I said maybe we ought to be going. But I was wasting my breath. Back in Detroit, Big Jack must've read a guidebook on how to have a big time. And the first chapter said the first thing to do was to get drunk, which we did. Milly got so she couldn't see straight. Whenever she stubbed out a cigarette, she'd miss the ash tray two times out of three, stubbing the butt out on the table. As for Big Jack, he began to investigate my knees. I was feeling drunk as a fly swimming around in a glass of whiskey myself. And when the next round came, I thought to myself, Kiddo, better nurse it.

In this call girl racket, at least one of the girls has to stay halfway sober.

"Honey," I said to Big Jack, "you own the bar, I know. But let's skip a round."

"Do you want this bar, cutie? Just say the word and I'll give you this bar." He laughed and laughed. "She can call it Frenchy's Tavern."

"Not bad," Milly said.

"Where do you get all the money?" I said. "Not from negotiating?"

"That's a drop in the bucket. It's the horses, you li'l cutie from Paree."

"Horses? I thought they made autos in Detroit."

He laughed like I'd killed him and then he said, "Horses're what the boys bet on. Horses and numbers. They bet right there in the plant on the line, and who do you think the hoods have there to take it, cutie?"

"So that's how you got that big diamond ring," I said to him.

"Never mind how. Where's that waitress?"

I tried to count myself out, saying I still had a drink, but he made me drink it down. He was roaring by now, and when he asked me again if I wanted the bar, I said no, and for a gag I said I'd settle for the ring. And what does my happy boy do but take the ring off his finger and slip it on my ring finger. It was too big. So he tried the middle finger and it was still too big. So he said he'd keep it for me and I was to remind him later and he'd give it to me. That ring got me excited and I said to Gentleman Jim and Milly they were my witnesses that Jack'd given me the ring. Sure, we're witnesses, Gentleman Jim and Milly said, laughing like it was one hell of a joke. Maybe it was just a joke to them. But it was no joke to me. I'm a sucker for jewelry. Besides, in this call girl racket, anything you can get by hook or crook is strictly legitimate.

I could hardly keep my eyes off that diamond ring, all shining and white, with little blue lights shooting out of it. Those little blue lights were shining right into my heart. I asked Big Jack to let me wear it and he put it on my middle finger.

"Where's that waitress?" he hollered. When she walked over, she asked him not to holler like that. But Big Jack was riding the big-shot special. "Who the hell're you?" he said.

"Please, mister," she said.

Gentleman Jim said, "Jack, she's right."

The waitress fetched us four more highballs and Milly was so drunk she stubbed her cigarette butt out on the table. Jack laughed and said why didn't she use the ash tray for a change. She said she did, and he said she didn't. I heard them arguing but what did I care with that big diamond ring shining on my finger? Milly yelled that what she didn't like were guys who went around tearing a girl down. She was so mad she spilled her highball down the front of her dress and when Gentleman Jim mopped it up, she got mad at him for rubbing so hard. I pushed my highball over to Milly. "Here, honey," I said.

"You're a honey," she said, and drank it down in two gulps, but it didn't console her. That Milly was so full of whiskey she could've been poured back into the bottle. She reached across the table and took my hand, the hand with the diamond on it, and begged me with her eyes swimming in her head like she was half angel and half spaniel to never, but never get married, no matter what else I did. "What does it get you?" Milly sobbed. "I got married to that Dexter bastard and here I am being insulted for a lousy stinking ash tray." At this, Jim, the silent one, revived enough to ask Milly if she was really married, and with a sob she said she was. She shook her blonde head like Dexter was in it and she was trying to shake him out. She hit the table with both hands sobbing she was married, oh, yes, she was married, all right, and would die married, just look at her. Gentleman Jim put his arm around her shaking shoulders and promised he'd take good care of her. Big Jack liked that. He smiled like a father at those two drunken sots and he said there was nothing like a good union man to take care of a girl.

Now, I'd been keeping myself out of this madhouse as much as I could. But that last remark of Big Jack's was too much for me. My father'd been a union man, in the mine union, and a dumb Polack if there ever was one. And here was this Big Jack, the big negotiator, negotiating himself diamond rings and seventy-five bucks for call girls. "Milly," I said, "it's O.K. for Jim to take care of you. But you have to watch your pocketbook when a friend of the working man's taking care!"

"You're too damn cute!" Big Jack yelled at me. "If you had any sense in your head you'd know you're nothing but a working girl yourself even if you're a call girl. If you call girls had a closed shop you'd make more than you do now!"

"You're just the lad to organize us," I said. "Organize us and mobilize us!"

He laughed. "That calls for another drink!"

"Pul-leaze!" I said.

But the drinks were coming out of the union treasury. Big Jack and Jim and Milly must have been at least three or four up on me. But by this time all of us were over the hill and going down on the scooter, and I didn't care any more, with that big diamond shining on my middle finger. All their faces were spinning around like the fruits spinning on a quarter slot machine, and when Big Jack kissed me, his little eyes were gone like they'd dropped out of his face.

"I expect some sweet loving, cutie," he said. "I gave you a ring, remember."

"I'll give you the sweetest you ever had," I said.

"You got boy friends, plenty boy friends, but how many give you diamond rings, cutie?"

"They all give me diamond rings," I said like a goof.

"Who, f'instance?"

I imitated him. "F'instance, this man I know on Park Avenue. F'instance this maharaja."

"This what?"

"This maharaja. A maharaja's a big wheel who lives in India and owns all the diamond mines."

"You're a great joker," he said. "Diamond mines! All a call girl gets is the sweat offa you know what."

"All a call girl gets is the same your wife gets."

He lifted his big hand as if he were going to slap me but I just looked at him. He didn't scare me, Big Jack didn't. After Ronny, a beating was no news to me.

"Jack, honey," Milly said. "She don't mean a thing."

"Tell her to keep my wife out!" Big Jack hollered.

Another round of drinks and the argument was forgotten. Except by me. I was thinking that this he-man Jack probably manhandled women like Ronny. I thought that if he tried it with me, I'd crack his head open. And thinking of Ronny, I thought of The Bastard. Every once in a while, out of the clear, out of nowhere, I think of The Bastard. Ronny and The Bastard, the two guys who'd played me for a sucker. To forget, I lifted my hand, and the diamond on my middle finger shone with its blue lights like some kind of blue fire. It had me hypnotized almost. And then what do I feel but Big Jack's hands on my knees under the table. Ring or no ring, no one was going to do that to me in public. "Push off before I get you arrested!" I said to him. "You've got too damn many hands for one guy!"

He stared at me, silent, like he hated me. And for the first time that evening I had a personal feeling about him. I hated him, too. His hands'd jumped off my knees but he'd only brought one into sight, the other one still under the table somewhere. I had a goofy idea that the one under the table wasn't a hand but a lobster claw. Big Jack still hadn't said a word and I began to worry a little. When the blabbermouth type shuts up, a girl never knows what's ahead. And sometime this night I was going to be all alone in a room with him. "What I mean," I said fast, pretending I was so drunk I didn't know what I was saying. "What I mean! Every single bit of it. When a guy has hands, he ought to be arrested. Hands, lobster claws, goddamn lobster claws—"

"You goddamn French whore!" he said in a low mean voice. "Give me back my ring, you!"

There was nothing to do but give it to him. He snatched it out of my hand, and he was so drunk and mad, he shoved it into his coat pocket. "I won't even let you see it!" he yelled spitefully. "You goddamn whore!"

I felt sick because my act hadn't worked so hot. It was my turn not to say anything.

"Let's have a drink." Gentleman Jim smiled like he'd come up with a bright idea.

"Let's have a drink, honey?" I said to Big Jack. I hated to talk to him, but after all the big bastard'd paid for the night. And I hadn't forgotten that ring. He didn't know it, the big negotiator, but I intended negotiating that ring. "Let's have a drink, darling," I said to him. "Darling, honey—"

"The hell with that!"

"Let's have a drink and make up," I coaxed, and after a while he did me a favor and we all had another, and another. While we are drinking, I prayed he wouldn't remember to put the ring back on his finger. He didn't. Who says there's nothing in prayer?

I'll skip the details of Big Jack's love-making. He was out to get his money's worth and he got it, or thought he got it. What I gave him, of course, was nothing but the animated-corpse treatment known to every girl with any experience, and to practically every married woman. I gave him the Old Zombie, patent applied for back in the Garden of Eden by a little girl by name of Eve.

He must've had his suspicions, for when he conked out finally he groaned as he slept.

This was one date when I hadn't bothered setting my alarm clock. Because I still had a date—with Big Jack's diamond ring.

As soon as he was asleep, I got out of bed and headed for the bathroom. I left the bathroom door open so I could see into the bedroom. I dressed and then in my stocking feet I sneaked into the bedroom to where his clothes were hanging on a chair. I picked up his coat and tiptoed back into the bathroom. When I felt the ring in his pocket I thought I'd drop, I was that excited. I took it out and pushed it deep down into my bag. And on the bathroom mirror I wrote with my lipstick, "Honey, thanks for the Christmas present you gave me."

I signed the initial of the phony name I'd been using that night, F, and started to laugh like I was crazy. I had to slap my hand over my mouth.

There wasn't a sound in the bedroom, but I could imagine what'd happen to me if I woke him up. What could I've said if he'd caught me with his coat in the bathroom? That I was cleaning the whiskey off? What whiskey? It was Milly who spilled the whiskey. I could imagine him making with the laugh, and coming at me mean and beating the hell out of me with his big fists.

My heart was pounding so hard I thought I'd drop dead. I thought of Milly, whom I'd tipped off in the lady's john back in the bar that I was heisting the ring. She'd been awful jittery. I'd told her to scram out of the hotel as soon as she could, and she'd said what would happen if the men go after Dexter? And I'd said, "Chances are they won't. They won't want publicity." I'd said not to mention the ring to Dexter unless we had to, that I'd sell it and give her a cut. Wasn't that what we were in this racket for? The money?

I didn't even dare look into the bedroom. But I knew I wasn't giving up that diamond ring. Even if he awoke now, I'd hide it. I actually searched the bathroom for a place to hide that ring if I had to. But where can you hide anything in a hotel bathroom? I thought the best place'd be inside the hollow cardboard in the middle of the roll of toilet paper. That's how panicked I was. If you have any imagination, crime doesn't pay—much.

I got up the nerve to see what was doing in the bedroom. Big Jack from Detroit was sleeping on his side, one arm over his head. Maybe I'd only given him the Old Zombie, but it'd worked like a charm. He was all zombed out tonight, Big Jack was. I got all my things together. Carrying my shoes in one hand, I tiptoed into the bedroom and over to the door. It was a last mile to the door, but I made it and let myself out into the corridor.

There was nobody awake in that whole hotel but me. The doors were closed. I put on my shoes and went over to the elevators.

I pressed the button and waited. My nerves were screaming. I thought, what if my boy friend missed me and got up, running to the door, opening it. What opened was the elevator door. The elevator boy sized me up. He smiled a nasty grin and said, "I'll have to ask you who you were visiting." I'd heard of this racket, elevator boys and hotel dicks all together, making it rough on people who sneaked out in the middle of the night. I didn't want any trouble. I opened my bag and without a single word I handed the little bastard five bucks. He didn't say anything more, either. He didn't have to say anything. I didn't have to say anything. Money talks. You can say that again.

Down in the street the sky was just getting light. The early-morning suckers who have to be at work somewhere at six o'clock were shuffling along. It was a cold and gray and miserable morning but I felt like spring was around the corner.

You guessed it, or maybe you didn't. That diamond was a good imitation worth about twenty bucks. The first hockshop I didn't believe. But when the second uncle said the same thing, I knew I'd been had. Negotiated.

Well, I started off by saying I'd give you a typical evening in the life of a call girl. My date with Big Jack was typical enough when it came to the drinking and the loud talk and the hotel room. The diamond ring, of course, was one in a thousand. Yet that ring and how I felt about it and what I did to get it should give you the low-down on this Hortense Walton, alias Fifi the Diamond Kid.

MAXIE

This is going to be hard to believe. Me, a guy who'd laughed up his sleeve at all this palm-reading and crystal ball stuff. Me, I got around to asking the advice of Madame Shouria. I had to talk to somebody, that's why, with Hugh dropped out of sight.

What a buddy he didn't turn out to be! O.K., I could understand his not giving me the address or phone where he was living with his N.Y.U. girl. O.K., he didn't want to embarrass the tomato because she's supposed to be a nice girl. But the least he could've done was see me once in a while or phone me. Even if he'd parroted what he'd said the last time about forgetting Hortense and Doyle, that would've been something. A guy has to have advice from a friend when he don't know whether he's coming or going. The advice can be no good, it can even stink on ice. But the important thing is knowing there's somebody listening to you. So Madame Shouria was elected.

It was about nine that night when I got up to her place. Upstairs, I looked at the big white fortunetelling hand she has there over her door. I felt like the prize jerk. Like that white fortunetelling hand'd been made especially for me, waving at me and saying, Step right in, jerko. The door was open. I went inside. The incense was burning in the copper dish. The Buddha with the yellow electric bulb screwed in his head was sitting there on the little table, with a big fat smile for all the suckers on his Buddha face. Down the corridor in the kitchen, I heard voices arguing: "She's got more shishkebab than me!" This was Madame Shouria's kids. And a man's voice. "You stop grab sister's shishkebab or I break the head." This was Chris, who's supposed to be her cousin, and whose job is to bring up shishkebab from the Greek restaurants in the neighborhood. The rest of his job is taking care of Madame Shouria. I listened to them arguing over the shishkebab. They ate supper late at Madame Shouria's. What you could expect from gypsies. Permanents or transients, they're all alike, gypsies.

I walked down the corridor and knocked on the kitchen door. The arguing stopped. And Chris, he says, "Fortune, clairvoyance, spirits." That's how Madame Shouria's got them all trained from Chris down to the two kids. Somebody comes in and they spiel, "Fortune, clairvoyance, spirits." I heard Chris's footsteps moving quick like he was afraid the customer'd beat it before he got there.

He opened the kitchen door and he smiled when he saw it was me. "Mr. Dehn," he says. "She with customer, Mr. Dehn." This Chris is a little dark Greek who could've been anywhere from thirty to fifty. He was in his socks, white socks, his shirt opened at the collar. Madame Shouria's kids were looking at me, too. The boy in a sweat shirt with "Dodgers" on it, his sister in a night-gown like the middle of summer. The boy was about eight, the girl about ten. They should've been in bed asleep, not eating shishkebab. But time means nothing to kids like that. Or maybe gypsy kids don't need the sleep like other kids.

"I'll wait," I says, feeling queerer by the second, with all of them smiling at me. Anybody would've felt queer in that kitchen. The shishkebab on the table, and the two army cots where the kids slept. That kitchen was a regular junk-yard. There was a small trunk with canned goods on it. There were two clocks and clothing on the shelves besides bread and fruit, a radio, and a big statue of Venus, the one without the arms.

"You wait, Mr. Dehn?" Chris says, smiling funny. Like he was letting me know that although he was only a Ninth Avenue Greek and I was Mr. Dehn from the landlord's office, we were maybe even pals, kind of, because of Madame Shouria. "Why not sit down, Mr. Dehn?" he says. "Some shishkebab, maybe? Some coffee, Mr. Dehn?"

"I'll wait in the waiting room," I says to him. I shut the door and went down the corridor, thinking that this Chris certainly had his nerve smiling at me that way. Then I remembered I hadn't come here tonight to get fixed. I'd come here tonight to ask Madame Shouria's advice. It was strictly business tonight.

The waiting room wasn't much bigger than a big closet. It was lit up with the twin of the Buddha in the foyer, only the bulb in this Buddha's head was green. The next room was the fortunetelling room. The door between the waiting room and the fortunetelling room'd been taken off and the space hung with heavy dark drapes. I should've heard voices from in there, her voice and the customer's. But it was like the morgue. It made me suspicious. I thought, If she's hustling, I'll dispossess her. I was working myself up into a lather before I remembered that the fortunetelling room didn't have a bed or even a couch because Madame Shouria slept in the waiting room on two mattresses piled one on top of the other and covered with Turkish rugs. Then I thought, Suppose she's on the floor? I couldn't stand the suspense, so I tiptoed over to the drapes.

I put my hand on the drapes. My hand was greenish in the light. Spooky. I pulled on the edge of the drapes a little until I could peek through. Inside the fortunetelling room, it was purplish from the purple electric lights Madame Shouria has in there. I saw her kneeling on a pile of pillows in front of a low table, the customer on the other side. It was strictly business and I felt better. The customer's hand was on the table, palm up. They didn't notice me so I kept on watching them. Madame Shouria was reading the customer's hand, and in that light it was purple. This Madame Shouria was a smart dame. She didn't have to wear red and green veils or great big earrings in her ears. All she need-ed were some different colored electric bulbs. Yellow when the sucker came in off the street, then green, then purple for the big act. Here in the purple room, she had the windows covered up and draped, with all kinds of Turkish rugs thrown around, and more incense burning on the table. It smelled like fortunes, clairvoyance, and spirits besides looking like it. I'd never spied on Madame Shouria before. It was none of my business. But I couldn't stop myself now.

I watched her squinting at the sucker's hand, and it was so quiet I could hear my heart beating. Then in her singsong gypsy voice she says, "Gods of fate, Madame Shouria iss on the knees to the gods and spirits."

But the sucker wasn't so dumb, for he says kind of sharp like he's impatient or in a rush, "What I wanna know is about this certain party, this lady."

"Please!" she says. "No talk now, mister, when with gods of fate—"

"Mind you," he says, "I'm not criticizin', but what I wanna know is like what I said. Does my hand show she only wants to marry me because of this truckin' business of mine?" He sounded like he was only half a sucker. The worst kind.

"Mister," she says to him, "in your business, the truck, you know the best. In my business, the fortune, I know the best. For fortune I must—"

"I don't want my fortune, I'm trying to tell you! That's just the pernt! What I wanna know's about this lady."

"What iss lady but fortune?" she came back at him. "Can be good, can be bad." She tightened her grip on his hand and spread his fingers flat, looking down into his palm. Just as I was wondering how she could read hands in that light, she unsnapped one of those fountain-pen flashlights that had been clipped to her dress. She aimed the light on the sucker's palm. "Gods of fate," Madame Shouria began again.

He didn't like it one bit. He squirmed around like he didn't want to buy any of this gods-of-fate jibber-jabber. All he wanted was some advice, like I wanted some advice. I had to feel sorry for that guy. He was stuck like when I'd been stuck in that hair-grower dive. When he tried to butt in on Madame Shouria, she rolled over him like a Mack truck. When it came to talking she could give him two for one. Besides, she had the lights and the incense on her side. "The gods of fate," she says. "They have given you big trouble with this lady. She iss your trouble, this lady, mister. Venus, star in the sky, she speak to Sagittarius the Archer in the constellations of heaven. This lady she will go on journey with you, mister. Here iss written. Equeleus the leedle horse iss the journey."

I watched her massaging the meat on this sucker's thumb. "Here iss written," she says to him. "You are favoreet Venus and can be big lover. Lover the blonde lady, the dark lady, the red lady." She aimed her flash into the middle of his palm. "Iss clouded here. Taurus the Bull walk here. I see Capricornus the Goat. They make war with Columba the Dove." She closed her eyes like she was praying. "Gods of fate of man, what you say? Will Taurus the Bull step the hefty foot on Columba the Dove? Will Capricornus make the jealousy? Gods of fate of man, Madame Shouria iss on her knees."

There was a ton of this kind of stuff. Then she was silent and so was the sucker. She'd put him into a tailspin. He didn't know where he was. She was the first to speak. "You are favoreet Venus. You will marry the lady, yes. You will marry her, mister, but she must bring money into truck business. Yes. The true love iss to spit on the money. The true love, it iss for the future. Yes. This lady has money. Two thousand dollar she must bring, mister. Two thousand iss enough."

She got up from the pillows on the floor, "Five dollars, mister, please."

I walked away and sat down on a chair, next to the two mattresses. From inside the fortunetelling room I could hear them bargaining. The guy was arguing how he'd been sent here by Pete the locksmith on Ninth Avenue and 39th Street. He said neighborhood people should get a discount. They settled on four bucks. The sucker went by me, on his way out. His face was green in the light of the waiting room so it was hard to tell what he really looked like. When the door closed, Madame Shouria herself came into the waiting room.

"Mr. Dehn," she says to me, smiling. "Iss a pleasure to see you."

"So that guy's from the neighborhood?" I got up from the chair and she stepped over to me.

"Yes, my sweetheart," she says, and she patted me on the face with her hand.

"Don't do that!" I warned her, getting mad.

"No, Mr. Dehn?" she says, smiling.

"I'm not one of your kids. Remember that!"

"Do not make noise. Iss late. Come, we sit down, Mr. Dehn, yes?"

But I hadn't come tonight for any of that. I'd come to ask for advice. But somehow I couldn't get the first word out. I kept thinking how I was a sucker like the sucker with the trucking business. I tried to make myself talk. This Madame Shouria was a permanent gypsy, I told myself. She might be able to help me. She must be good, giving the neighborhood people their money's worth, or they wouldn't be sending up people like the guy who'd just left. "I heard a li'l of what you said to that guy, Madame Shouria," I says to her.

"What you hear, my sweetheart?" She sat down on the two mattresses and patted the place next to her and smiled up at me.

"How the girl has to bring two thousand into his business."

"He iss a man of forty-seven. She iss woman twenty-nine. Twenty-nine, can she love the forty-seven? Maybe. Iss no, iss yes. Maybe she loves him and loves his business together, yes? Come, sit down, my sweetheart."

"Is it a good business?"

"McGuire truck business. Sit down, sit down."

I sat down next to her. She picked up my hand and held it between both of her own. Her hands were green in the light. Her face was green and her smile was green. In the beginning it used to give me the creeps, all that green, like I was with some monster or something. But you get used to things. She started in now, petting my hand, and her big soft leg was on mine, and I thought, what the hell, I could ask her advice later on.

That Madame Shouria could've been a real-estate broker. That's how good her advice was. I didn't give her any real names, of course. Not Doyle's or Hortense's or anybody's. I said it was a friend of mine in the real-estate line who was up against it, with a girl who loved money, and he didn't know what to do. When I finished she had the answer. All she did was put two and two together, which was why her advice was so good. I'd seen the two and two myself. But putting them together, I'd never dreamed. This was Madame Shouria's advice: that if a big shot wanted to pay my friend in the real-estate line a big bonus for his help in buying the property, the property must be worth it. So why didn't my friend buy the property himself and sell it at a profit? That was what Madame Shouria said to me. I wouldn't've thought of it by myself. Not me. Not in a million years. I was like my old man in that respect. He'd been with old Jacob all his life but he'd only bought the house we lived in. And wouldn't've done that if Mamma hadn't nagged him into it.

Madame Shouria's advice was just perfect. I didn't have the money to buy the Shaw sisters' parcel. But money could always be promoted. O.K., so I'd never promoted before. What did I have to lose? I could make the try, anyway. It'd be better than moping, waiting for Christmas week to ring Doyle, and Hortense at the studio like a stranger. Worse than a stranger, because from a stranger you expect nothing.

The next morning I woke up without Mamma calling me. It was only a few minutes after seven. But I didn't feel sleepy or tired, although when I'd left Madame Shouria's it was two in the morning. I felt peppy, ready for anything. There was Leo Edwards down the office and Saul Lipson and Doc Presto, who should be interested in a sure-fire real-estate deal. For years they'd been saying if I had anything good, they'd be interested. But me, I'd been more conservative than the Bank of England: Just like my old man. Parroting the same line he had used: "I'm in real estate. But I never speculate. I never buy stocks. I put my money in the bank." The Shaw sisters' parcel was no speculation. Even if Doyle was thinking of some other property, the Shaw property was located right. Television'd be needing more than any one man's holdings. Like the garment industry.

I lay there in bed, figuring that as a start I'd talk to the boys down the office. Then I'd see my Uncle Gus. My Uncle Gus was my mother's oldest brother and he owned a secondhand record shop on the Avenue of the Americas. He was loaded with money, my Uncle Gus, and so was my other uncle on my mother's side, my Uncle Julius, who owned an ice-cream parlor in Queens. But Uncle Gus was the best bet in the family because he already owned real estate. My Uncle Gus'd bought four or five tenements in the West Side on my old man's say-so, when prices'd been low. He'd lost a couple houses in the depression, but he was still ahead.

No, I didn't have to have Mamma waking me up that morning. I got out of bed and the first thing I did was walk over to the dresser and kiss Hortense's photograph. She was going to have her eyes opened, I thought. Maybe I'd been sort of licked. But who was coming up swinging at the count of nine? Nobody but Maxie Dehn. I thought how I'd promote the money to buy the Shaw sisters' property, resell it, and marry Hortense. I'd outfox Joseph Henry Doyle. Not to mention the satisfaction of cutting out all the under-the-table stuff. I'd be buying out in the open, a deal on the level, and old Jacob couldn't have any objections. I wouldn't have to worry about risking my job if it leaked like before. Tell me, could anything be more perfect?

I felt so wonderful, I kissed Hortense's photograph again. Then I went in for my shower. For a shower and a pipe dream. They both came out of the jets. I could see us married already, Hortense and me, living in a little house out on Long Island where there was grass and trees and sun. We'd have a kid, Hortense and me. I could see it clear. Me taking my shower before breakfast, the coffee perking in the kitchen. Then me and Hortense and the kid all having breakfast together. The kitchen, all gleamy white, with all the gadgets, electric washing machine and dishwashing machine, the kid in his high chair, round and fat and blond like I used to be. That's how it'd be. And the kid'd grow up and go to school, and maybe there'd be another kid in the high chair, and me kissing Hortense before I went to work in a brand-new Buick convertible. For I'd be in the money by then, with a lot of real estate, besides being a partner in Jacob Groteclose....

Whoa, I said to myself. Get off the horse, jerko!

It was too perfect to be true, I tried to tell myself. The only dame I was marrying was Madame Shouria. The only kids I'd have would be those shishkebab twins of hers. I thought of how she'd looked, like a barrel of lard, only the lard was green. I had the old sick feeling of being locked up inside of my own body and never being able to get out. Jinxed. Jinxed in everything.

But that morning I couldn't put a damper on my spirits no matter how I tried. How could I lose? I wasn't depending on Doyle any more, but on myself. And this Shaw deal, with me promoting it, was a natural. Money? I would promote the money.

I dolled up in my best clothes, my number-one suit, the gray worsted, which gave me the shoulders you see on the prize fighters who hang around Madison Square Garden. I took my best hat out of its box, a snappy gray beauty with that dashaway-style brim. I put it on and looked at myself in the mirror. No kidding, I was Maxwell Dehn, Jr.

Mamma couldn't believe her eyes when I walked into the kitchen. "Maxie! What is it? Sunday?" she says.

"Good morning, Mamma."

"Where is the good-morning kiss, Maxie?" she says.

After a date with somebody like Madame Shouria, I hated to kiss her. But she insisted, so I gave her the regular good-morning kiss.

"Maxie, you have on the best suit," Mamma says. "What is it, Sunday?"

"It's always going to be Sunday from now on, Mamma." I smiled and sat down at the kitchen table.

She was puzzled, wondering why I dressed up like a fashion plate, and if it had anything to do with my date of the night before. I knew Mamma like a book. Suspicious! Boy, is she suspicious when it comes to me! She'd been in her room when I'd returned last night. But I knew she was awake. Mamma always waits up for me to get home. She shouldn't do it, but she does, and it always makes me feel bad to know she's waiting up. Especially when I'm out with a bag like Madame Shouria.

She went to the refrigerator and brought the stewed fruit. And as we ate breakfast, I explained why the suit, and about the gilt-edged property of the Shaws, and how I had the inside track. I didn't tell her about Doyle or the bonus or the conniving. But everything else.

This being a promoter is something. I hadn't thought of asking Mamma to come in on the Shaw deal. But while I'm explaining things, I get to thinking of the money Mamma has in the bank and the house, which she owned free and clear and no mortgage. "Mamma," I says to her, "here I'm going to see my business friends. And Uncle Gus and maybe Uncle Julius. But what about you?"

"Me!" she says, like I'd tossed the hot coffee in her face.

"Mamma, you own this house, don't you?"

"Yes?" she says, like she's saying no.

"It's free and clear, Mamma. You could easily raise a twenty-thousand-dollar mortgage on it."

"This house I will not mortgage, Maxie! Never!" she says, her face getting all red.

"It'd only be for a short time, Mamma."

"Short time, long time, this house I will not mortgage!"

But when you're a promoter you follow two things, as they say. Your tongue and the other party's dollar. The more I spoke, the more I felt, Why shouldn't Mamma make some easy money? "Mamma, it's an opportunity that comes once in a lifetime! The television people're buying locations now, like I've explained to you. They're not buying forever. We wouldn't have to hold onto the Shaw property more'n six months or a year."

"Television, what is this television? Talk, talk!"

"It's not only talk, Mamma. Our friends at the bank tipped me off. Television's coming in north of Times Square. Into the Fifty and Sixty blocks. Remember when nobody believed the cloak-and-suiters'd locate in the West Side? Only old Jacob, he saw it. The tenants call us collectors Mr. Forty-second Street. But it's old Jacob who's the real Mr. Forty-second Street."

"I do not want to be rich, Maxie. I only want for my son to be happy and not in the middle of the night from no-good dancing girls to be coming home."

I cut it short before Mamma could warm up. Downstairs in the street, I thought I could work on Mamma through my brother Pete and sister Johanna. Pete and Johanna didn't have too much money themselves but they had pull with Mamma. Yes, sir, when you're a promoter the angles keep angling, like they say.

A promoter, that's what I was. It made all the difference. Eighth Avenue with its cheap store fronts and cabs honking wasn't the Eighth Avenue of yesterday. What I saw were the pretty holly wreaths, and all the red and green for Christmas. And 42nd Street, it was like that morning when I'd found that damn wallet.

First thing I did after cleaning up my desk at the office was go into Leo Edwards' office and tell him to chuck his racing sheet out of the window. He looked at me. "Maxie, where'd you steal those clothes?" he says.

I picked up his phone and phoned Saul Lipson down the hall to come on over.

"Hey, Maxie," Leo says. "What's the big idea?"

"I'm too busy to see you bums separately," I answered him. When Saul Lipson showed up, I asked him to shut the door. I had them looking at me with big goo-goo eyes. I could've laughed at how easy it was, and they were two cagey guys. All you had to do was pull a Doyle. Dress like the big money, act like the big money, and people fell all over themselves. "Listen, boys," I says. "I have the real estate deal you've been after. You boys've known me a long time so I don't have to sell you a bill of goods about whether I know real estate or not. Just listen and don't ask me no questions until I'm through. O.K.? I've got a hot tip. I know where the television people're buying property. It's more than a tip. Columbia Broadcasting wants a certain property bad and I've got the inside track." I'd invented the company, but when you promote you might as well promote it good. Follow your tongue is right!

"Columbia Broadcasting!" Saul Lipson says, lifting his eyebrows.

"This television's not ready yet," Leo Edwards says, being cautious.

Him I slapped down right away. "Neither was radio ready. Listen, I'm not twisting anybody's arm. This television'll be ready in about a year and a half. The wise boys're getting set. I'm not twisting anybody's arm. I've got the inside track to this property. It's owned by a private estate who won't sell to nobody but who I advise them to. Boys, this is in strict confidence. I don't want it leaking to my office, get me."

Leo yanked off his glasses to wipe them. They'd got all clouded. He wasn't excited. Not much. While he's wiping his glasses Saul Lipson pulls out his pack and offers the cigarettes. "We're your friends," Saul says. "You know that, Maxie."

"Sure, sure. To cut it short, boys, what's good for Columbia Broadcasting's good enough for me!"

They wanted to know more details. I hadn't even thought exactly what I could offer the Shaws. But now I had to name figures. Doyle's top offer'd been four-twenty. I might get the Shaw sisters to take four, maybe a little less. I had to name figures because promoters never hesitate a second. It can be the wrong figures, but you don't hesitate. "I can buy this property for about three-fifty."

"Three-fifty what?" Leo says nervously.

"Three hundred and fifty thousand. Maybe a little more. Resell to CBS for a hundred thousand over what I pay. A hundred fifty, if I wait a year. My relatives're coming in on the deal. But I need more cash. That's why I'm talking to you boys."

I must've been with them an hour. They asked all kinds of questions and I built it up big. Invest ten grand, I says, and make ten grand clear profit. I had them reeling. "Give us a li'l time to think it over," Leo Edwards says, still being cautious. "A week."

"I can give you a couple days," I says. "No longer." I flashed the big Doyle smile and breezed out. I had to laugh, thinking of how it would be Leo Edwards, that coked-up horse player, to be the cautious one. I walked down the corridor and pressed the elevator button with the little finger of my right hand, like I'd once seen some big shot smoking a dollar cigar doing. I put a cigarette into my face. For a face under a dashaway-style hat doesn't look right without at least a cigarette in it. "I've got a big deal on the fire," I says to Phil the elevator boy when the door opened. There was no one in the elevator except me and him. Everybody was going up, not down at this hour in the morning. "This party has to fly in and settle it one way or another!" It was a scream, me showing off like that to an elevator boy. This being a promoter was something!

But Phil was listening to me like I owned the building and not old Jacob. "That's the way it is, Mr. Dehn," he says, like he was a promoter himself on the side. Maybe during his lunch hour.

When I was down on 42nd Street—I just had to laugh at myself. Boy, was I coked up! And why not? I thought. That Shaw deal was a natural.

I went into a phone booth at the Hotel Dixie and made an appointment to see the Shaw sisters at three o'clock. Then I phoned my Uncle Julius in Queens and made a lunch date with him. Everything was clicking. I felt so cocky I phoned Hortense at her place on 26th Street. She couldn't believe I had the nerve ringing her and neither did I. "Don't hang up," I says. "You know I wouldn't ring you unless it's important."

"Important! Damn you, Maxie—"

"Listen first, Hortense. Give me a chance and listen." I heard my voice going over the wire so big and strong I could hardly believe it was me, only it was me, and I felt almost that she could see me. Like there was already television, and more than television. So when you talk to someone on the phone, they can see you. Me in my best suit. "Hortense, you never thought I could do it."

"Do what? Wake up people when they're sleeping?"

"Hortense, I'm sorry if I woke you."

"You woke me, all right."

"I'm sorry, Hortense. But I had to tell you the deal's moving. How about a date tonight when you're through teaching?"

"A date!" she says, mad.

"Hortense, baby, the deal's moving and I thought we could celebrate."

"Only thing's moving is your mouth!" she shouted at me.

"Don't hang up, Hortense," I says. "Honest, the deal's moving and I'll have the money."

"What money? Two-ninety-eight?"

"No, real money, or I wouldn't've called. Honest to God, Hortense."

"God, God, God!" she shouted, mad as hell. "Lay off on God! You sound like somebody inside a strait jacket," she shouted. "Maxie, you listen to me now. I'm glad you phoned. Find yourself another teacher! I'm through! I'm through teaching you. Thursday you find yourself another teacher, because I'm not teaching you any more, Maxie!"

Any other time, I would've folded at that kind of talk. But now I says to Hortense, "I'm too busy to take lessons right now, Hortense."

"Maxie, we're through. You find another teacher!"

"Hortense," I says, and again I heard my voice going over the wire big and strong. "You don't understand me, Hortense. I'm too busy to take lessons. But I'll be around when this deal's cinched and you'll change your mind."

"O.K. When you get that million, honey, look me up!" She hung up on me. But I wasn't sore or anything. I was thinking that it was just like a movie between Hortense and me. Things all snafued between the boy and the girl, one damn thing after another, but you know they'll get straightened out in the end. I reached for a cigarette, then I shoved the pack back.

I went over to the cigar counter in the Hotel Dixie. "Give me an Uppmann Havana," I says to the clerk. He handed me the box and I selected one. I lit up. Under that dashaway hat of mine, a fifty-cent Uppmann Havana went better than a cigarette any day.

I thought of Hortense and her wisecracks over the phone and how mad she'd been. I thought that when I had the Shaw deal cinched, I'd go see her and push those wisecracks down her throat. I loved her and all, but for putting me through the wringer she deserved a little punishment.

My next stop was my Uncle Gus's record shop. I walked toward the Avenue of the Americas feeling like a millionaire. The stores were full of Christmas and I wondered what I'd give Hortense for Christmas. There were furs in the windows, jewelry, silverware, women's clothes. I passed a liquor store where they had a big bottle of brandy inside a green silk box like a candy box. A little sign explained it was "Louis XIII Brandy, Age Unknown $37.50." I thought that was the kind of stuff Hortense and me'd drink when I saw her next. Nothing but the best.

My Uncle Gus's store was between 44th and 45th Streets on the Avenue of the Americas, which my Uncle Gus still called by the old name, Sixth Avenue. "Who is this?" he says to me when I went inside. "The Prince of Wales, maybe?" I was dressed as good as he was dressed bad. He was wearing old pants and a black sweater buttoned down the middle. The knot of his necktie was an inch or two under his collar, which was frayed. That's my Uncle Gus for you, his regular outfit. "Well," he says, grinning, "how is Maxie? How is my sister, your mother?"

I asked him about his family and we chewed the fat about one thing and another, as the phonograph played and the amplifier took the music out into the street. We were standing at the cash register talking. With my Uncle Gus you have to lead up to business by degrees. Now and then somebody stepped into the store and bought some of his secondhand records. Bebop or classical or religious, my Uncle Gus had them all. At seven for a dollar. That was what he charged. He'd figured out that seven for a dollar was just right. Four or five for a dollar was no bargain, my Uncle Gus told me once. Six for a dollar was better, but seven was better yet, because seven was a better number for business. That's my Uncle Gus for you. He dresses like a tramp but he's smart.

"How's tricks?" I asked him after a half hour or so.

"Business, you mean, Maxie?"

"How is it? Should be good with Christmas coming."

"Stinks business. This location's terrible, Maxie."

"You say that every time I see you, Uncle Gus."

"I mean it, Maxie. This Avenue of the Americas, huh! Avenue of American Bankrupts, maybe."

That's my Uncle Gus. He always has to prove he's in the gutter with the rest of the bums before he can relax. Some more customers came in, and when they were gone I says, "Uncle Gus, how would you like to make twenty thousand on an investment of twenty thousand?"

My Uncle Gus forgot all about how poor he was. He kept me there until close to eleven, when I had to leave so I could get out to Queens for lunch with my Uncle Julius.

That first day went off like a song.

My Uncle Julius was interested, like my Uncle Gus and the boys down the office. When I kept my appointment at three o'clock with the Shaw sisters, they threw up Doyle's four-twenty offer. But, I said, he offered it, but where's the cash? At three hundred thousand they'd be doing good, I said. And three-fifty was finding money. They said if I advised it, they'd sell. I felt so good I would've treated Hugh to dinner at Luchow's if he'd been around. But since he wasn't, I went to dinner with the boys, Leo Edwards and Saul Lipson. By the second cocktail I had them eating out of my hand.

The next morning I was so happy, what do I do but go over to Hortense's building on Fifth Avenue. It wasn't even nine o'clock and I knew the teachers didn't come until one. But I just wanted to be near her, sort of, I was feeling that good. The sun was bright and you could hear the Santa Clauses ringing bells on the corners, and when I looked at the George Lawrence display windows, at the one where the girl doll reminded me of Hortense, it was like a dream. On the other side of Fifth Avenue there was Cartier's, and I thought of what I'd thought the day before. Of what I'd buy Hortense for Christmas. A ring from Cartier's, I thought, laughing at myself. But why not? If I promoted the Shaw deal I'd be promoting something else, and in a couple years, say five years, why shouldn't I be shopping at Cartier's. I crossed over and looked into the Cartier windows, at the jewels, the sapphires, the diamonds. I was in a dream. For I was seeing myself a few years from now, the clerks whispering, "Here comes Mr. Dehn, Mr. Maxwell Dehn, the big real estate operator." And me going inside and pointing the tip of my cigar at a diamond ring or a sapphire bracelet and saying, "Wrap it up."

Fifth Avenue's the street to dream on if you have the money. For right next to Cartier's there was a window all travel, with maps and tours and a model of the Queen Mary and a card saying: "32 Days, $963 up." And another card: "47 Days, $1,302 up." I thought if the Shaws sold at about three-fifty and we could resell at a hundred profit above that, my share as promoter ought to be able to finance a little trip. For what I intended doing was organizing a corporation to buy the Shaw property and to give myself 10 percent of the stock without investing a dollar of my own. Yes, sir, this being a promoter is something.

I hung around in front of that travel window, thinking how I'd reserve Queen Mary's own suite on the Queen Mary someday. How me and Hortense'd go on a little cruise, with me saying, "Hortense, honey, shall we rumba, Mrs. Dehn? We can go to the royal ballroom, Mrs. Dehn, honey, and show the limeys a rumba or two. Maybe you ought to wear those Cartier things, Mrs. Dehn, honey."

Whoa! I thought. Get off the horse, Maxie.

I had to shake myself. No kidding, I had to shake myself to snap out of it. But I didn't get off Fifth Avenue right away, as I should've done. I wanted to keep on dreaming for another couple minutes. How often in one life does a guy get to feel he owns the whole goddamn city from the biggest skyscrapers down to the last matchstick on the sidewalks?

HUGH

Although Hortense had laughed when she'd told me of Maxie's phone call, her laugh had been a little uncertain. "Wouldn't it be a joke if he does make out?" she had said.

A joke? I wasn't so sure. I was less sure after I phoned Maxie myself. He was so excited, so bubbling over, I arranged to meet him the very next night in the same bar where we had talked not so long ago. "Have a cigar," he had said when we met. "Hugh, you ought to smoke cigars instead of cigarettes. They're the best. This is an Uppmann."

So with one of Maxie's Uppmanns in my mouth, I had listened to the details of his scheme to buy the Shaw property myself. I was too worried to listen carefully. But I remember Maxie saying he hoped to pay only three hundred and fifty thousand, fifty thousand in cash, the balance in mortgage. He was still dickering over the terms with the Shaw sisters. The fifty thousand in cash would come from his family, from his uncles and perhaps Mamma, and from business people in the Groteclose building, a stamp man called Lipson or Liebson, I've forgotten which, and several others. Maxie wasn't investing a cent of his own money. As a promoter of the deal, he'd have 10 percent of the stock. "I've about eight thousand of my own in the bank," he had said. "But I'll have to have that to live on until we resell." I was stunned at his certainty that Hortense would marry him. "When I have the contract money, I'll go see Hortense and show her fifty thousand on deposit in my bank. That ought to convince her the deal's moving. I've got Doyle where I want him!" He had laughed with sheer joy. "I've got him, but that bastard's costing me money. You see, Hugh, here I've talked four-twenty to the Shaw sisters when I thought Doyle was buying. I had to convince them that talk money's not money on the line. But naturally they want the most they can get. That property cost their father about a hundred twenty thousand. Three-fifty's a good price and it'll cost Doyle four-fifty! If I sell to him at four-fifty, my ten percent'll be worth ten thousand. It's not as big as the bonus he promised, but what're promises worth? Ten thousand isn't bad."

No, it wasn't bad. And in the meanwhile, Maxie had hinted at other real-estate deals. I had asked him if it wasn't sharp practice to convince the Shaw sisters to sell for a figure so much less than Doyle's offer. "They're still making a big profit," he had retorted, and I was ashamed for trying to prod his conscience. Who was I to preach? Hortense's little lap dog, whining because he was about to be tossed out into the cold.

But if Maxie had to have Hortense, so did I.

The next day, in the afternoon, when I knew Maxie would be at work, I went to see Mamma Dehn. As we sat in the kitchen over a cup of coffee I explained the reasons for my visit. I told her everything I knew. "Maxie wants to marry Hortense," I said. "And she'll only marry him if he's a rich man." Before I left I asked Mamma to promise me to never mention my visit to Maxie.

It was a dirty thing to have done. Maxie had been my best friend. I tried to rationalize it by saying to myself it was a world of hunters and hunted. Hadn't Maxie himself abandoned the solid old-fashioned virtues symbolized by his long years with the Groteclose firm? By becoming a Maxwell Dehn, Jr., so to speak, hadn't he also turned hunter? The answer was yes. Part of the answer was yes. Only a part, for in the long run a man, every man, must be judged on his own private actions and not the world's. My going to Mamma was a dirty thing that could never be entirely rationalized. I had done what I could to break up not only Maxie's hopes, but Hortense's also. True, she was a call girl and had about given up hope of getting a rich man. Still, Maxie, as Hortense herself had said, might have "made out." Christmas was still coming and I had given Hortense, although she would never know it, another false diamond ring.

That Christmas week with the holiday bells ringing and the stories of the three wise kings and the Babe in the manger, I thought of another Biblical character, Judas, and I had no regrets. That was the astonishing self-revelation, that a man could turn Judas and have no regrets.

Maxie

You expect headaches in a big deal. That's why, in the beginning, I wasn't worried about my family. You take the boys down the office, for example. Here they'd begged me for years to give them a good buy. I give them a good buy. So what happens? They have to get cagey at the last minute. Leo Edwards, that coked-up horse player, ended up by coming in with a cheap five thousand. Saul Lipson with ten. So I had to go to Doc Presto for another ten. I'd hoped for more from the boys, but I couldn't ask everybody in the building. Only the ones I could trust. That's what I mean by headaches. Then, you take the Shaw sisters. Because Doyle'd offered them four-twenty, it was all I could do to knock that price out of their heads. Three-fifty wasn't enough for them. They did me a favor with three-seventy. Satisfied with fifty thousand in cash? Oh, no, a hundred thousand in cash was what they wanted, and I couldn't budge them. That goddamn Doyle was jinxing me even now. A hundred thousand in cash! That's what I mean by headaches. All the little things you don't expect to happen but do.

With only twenty-five from the boys, that meant I had to raise seventy-five from my family. Big money. But in the beginning things went smooth. My Uncle Gus promised twenty-five thousand. My Uncle Julius said that he and a friend of his would put in another twenty-five thousand. When I had them promised, I went to see my brother Pete and sister Johanna, who worked on Mamma for me. Pete could only raise five, Johanna couldn't raise a dime, but they talked Mamma into coming in, with only ten at first. Then when Pete and Johanna and me put the pressure on Mamma, she upped it to fifteen. Her fifteen, and Pete's five, and the fifty thousand from my two uncles, made seventy thousand. I was still short five thousand of what I needed. I had to put in myself, which I hadn't intended. But what can you do?

I deposited the boys' twenty-five thousand and my five thousand in the corporation's name. And here Christmas was three days off and I still didn't have a dime from the family.

There's no rush, they kept saying.

When I phoned my Uncle Julius, he says, Soon. When's soon? I says. When Uncle Gus's in, he says. Uncle Gus is in, I says.

No rush and no checks. I began to get real worried. One night I went to see my brother Pete. He tipped me off that the family were all waiting for Uncle Gus to start the ball rolling. Because Uncle Gus was the one who'd had the real-estate experience. Now this sounded reasonable to me, and it also sounded a little fishy. I told Pete that the one with the real-estate experience wasn't Uncle Gus, but me. Why don't you talk to Uncle Gus? Pete says. There's a little trouble, Pete says. What trouble? I asked him with my heart in my mouth. But he wouldn't say.

I left Pete's house and walked to the subway station, where I bought a box of aspirins in the drugstore. My head was going a mile a minute. It's an hour ride from Brooklyn, where Pete lived, to the city, and the whole way I'm beating my brains out. The only reason I can think of for my family's cold feet is that putting cash down on the line always hurts. Even my Uncle Gus, who owned real estate, was still only a storekeeper used to squeezing nickels.

When I reached Uncle Gus's store, I couldn't go in for a minute. My head was that bad. I thought how a couple days ago, when I'd asked my Uncle Gus for his check, he'd given me a load of hot air how he'd quit working on his first million, which he'd never made, so he could start on his second million. That's my Uncle Gus for you. Always crying how broke he is. Twenty-five thousand was money, but he had more than that salted away. The tenements he owned, what with the housing shortage, were practically a gold mine.

I stalled around. The music was loud out of the amplifier and it made me think of Hortense. I didn't want to think of her, so I looked into Uncle Gus's window. He had a new sign for the Christmas trade. "Connoisseurs of Records," it said. That's my Uncle Gus, a sucker for signs. The window was full of them. "Blue and hot jazz," it said on one sign. "Bargains in Chicago and Sepia," it said on another sign. There were at least a dozen smaller signs that said, "7 for $1."

Aw, hell, I thought, and I went inside. From behind the cash register, inside the door, Uncle Gus smiled at me. "Maxie," he says. "How is my sister?"

"Mamma's fine, Uncle Gus. I was in the neighborhood so I dropped in."

He smiled at me and I smiled at him. He was wearing a big gray sweater tonight, which made him seem bigger than he was. He's a big heavy man, my Uncle Gus, and with his thick gray hair, and in that sweater, he could've been a retired wrestler or a truck driver who's now on relief. It's his store, too, that gives him that busted look. The brown paint on the walls peeling through in spots so you could see the oyster white of the picture-framing business that'd been there before. And although Uncle Gus, like I say, is a sucker for signs, he never throws the old ones away. There were dirty old "7 for $1" signs tacked on the walls and stuck up on the four long counters where the records were.

We spoke about the family for five minutes maybe, although it seemed like five years to me. Then he says, "Not a customer in the place. Some Christmas rush!"

"That's why you should be giving me your check, Uncle Gus, so we can get going and make some real money."

He changed the Guy Lombardo and put a Louis Armstrong on the phonograph. "This is what they call the Christmas rush, Maxie," he says, like the original gloomy Gus himself.

"It's a bad night."

"That's what it is. Bad!"

Aw, hell with it, I thought. I might as well find out where I stood. "Uncle Gus," I says, "I just came from Brooklyn. Pete says there's a little trouble. I should talk to you."

"To me?"

"That's what he said. They're all waiting for you, the whole family, to start the ball rolling. Uncle Julius, all of them."

Uncle Gus scratched his head. "In the family, who always has to be the bad one?"

"What do you mean, Uncle Gus?"

"Who always has to be the bad one?" he asked, getting mad, not at me, but at the family. I felt terrible. I had the feeling you get when something's about to break. Like flak before it breaks. "Pete!" my Uncle Gus snorts. "That brother of yours, Maxie! What is he? A man or a mouse? I always have to be the bad one! O.K., I will be the bad one. But remember, Maxie, it is for your own good!"

I couldn't talk. I was paralyzed.

"This dancer is the trouble, Maxie! Mamma, Uncle Julius, me—we are all worried about this dance girl."

For what seemed like an hour, I couldn't answer him. He was scratching his head and looking at me, waiting. Then he says, "Maxie, believe me, it is for your own good. Ach, I have to be the bad one. Maxie, the family, we would like to make money, and for you to make money. But this dance girl. She will spend your money like a drunken sailor."

I couldn't stand it any more. "What has she got to do with it?" I yelled.

"I will be the bad one," my Uncle Gus says, gloomy but stubborn. "Maxie, this dancer, what does she want but your money? For your money she will marry you. Yes!"

When he'd first dragged Hortense in, I'd been so surprised and excited, I couldn't think straight. But now it grew on me in letters nine feet high. Mamma! It was Mamma! Mamma spoiling everything like the time when she'd gone up to the studio. It was Mamma thinking that if I bought the Shaw sisters' property, I'd be after Hortense again to marry me. It was Mamma! But why couldn't she have said no right away? And the family could've said no. Instead of stringing me along and then pulling the rug like Doyle'd done. "What a family!" I yelled. "What a family! What a lousy family!"

Uncle Gus, he'd never heard me talk that way in my whole life. "Lousy!" he yelled back at me.

"Lousy bunch of renegers!"

"Maxie!" he yelled. "Be respectful, Maxie."

"How about being respectful to me? Saying yes and then reneging."

"Ach, I have to be the bad one." My Uncle Gus began to sing the blues all over again. "Maxie, this dancer—What is a dancer? The big day in their life is when the husband drops dead so they can collect the insurance."

I couldn't answer him. The heart was out of me. I was in a sweat. I was burning alive. My eyes were full of tears. But Uncle Gus didn't know that because I was busy wiping my face all the time.

"Maxie," he says, like he's sorry for me.

"Don't bother me."

The next thing I know he's out from the cash register grabbing me by both arms and speaking in German like I was a little boy again. Saying how my life and my future were more important than money and what a shame it'd be to waste my life on a dancer.

"Let me alone," I mumbled at him.

"Maxie—"

"Let me alone! I've got thirty thousand in the bank from people with sense. Thirty thousand! I can raise the rest without you or the family."

Just remembering that money, saying it like that—thirty thousand—made me feel less low.

"*Gott,* Maxie!" he groaned and started speaking in English again. "Maxie, like my own son I ask you to forget this dancer. You can raise the money, yes! But who will spend it like a drunken sailor? Maxie! With a million girls in the city, why, for a wife, must there only be this dancer?"

"Never mind that, Uncle Gus!" I yelled. "Never mind who I should or shouldn't marry. All I want to know is this: You want to come in or don't you want to come in?"

"I want to come in, Maxie. Julius, he wants to come in."

"Then come in."

"How can we?" he says, real sad. He picked up my hat where I'd laid it down near the cash register. He began to brush off a spot of dust that wasn't there with his sweater sleeve. "How can we, Maxie? How can we?"

"Don't listen to Mamma, that's how you can. Don't you want to make money?"

"The family comes before the money, Maxie. This dance girl, she is not for you."

"What do any of you know about that?" I yelled at him. "She'll settle down once we're married. I know that, Uncle Gus. She won't spend my money crazy. She'll settle down and we'll have a family."

Uncle Gus said nothing. He kept on brushing my hat with his sweater sleeve. I took my hat away from him. He still said nothing.

"Can't you speak any more?" I asked him.

"So we can make big money in this real estate maybe," he says.

"There is no maybe! It's a sure thing!"

"Maybe yes, maybe no. Lose we will not. But what I wish to say, Maxie, is even if we make big money, it is the future I worry for you. With this dancer—"

"What do you think she'll spend the money on, champagne?"

"Who knows, Maxie?"

"Uncle Gus, you're talking like *a dumkopf!*"

"*Dumkopf,* huh? Now I am a *dumkopf!*"

"I'm sorry, Uncle Gus," I tried to tell him.

"All my life I work for a living!" he began winding himself up. "Seven for a dollar we got to sell! Sell like hot cakes."

"I said I was sorry."

"French champagne and Russian caviar!" he yelled at me. "For this you make insults, Maxie!"

Two customers stepped into the store and he controlled himself. When the customers left, he started shaking his head real sad again. "Maxie, I ask you like your own father. What are you, Maxie? A playboy to marry dancers?"

"Uncle Gus, she's a dance teacher. Not a dancer. Let's get that straight, Uncle Gus. Hortense's a dance teacher like your own daughter Charlotte in public school. A teacher just like Charlotte."

"I am ashamed of you, Maxie," he says.

"Why're you ashamed of me, Uncle Gus?"

"Your nerve! The nerve to say this common dancer is like Charlotte, your own cousin. I want an apology, Maxie."

I guess I must've gone psycho for a second. For what I did was to pick up the nearest record and smash it on the floor, yelling, "There's your apology, Uncle Gus!"

He looked at all the broken black pieces of the record on the floor. Then he looked at me and there were tears in his eyes. He was that sorry for me, my Uncle Gus. But I couldn't take his being sorry for me any more. "Seven cost a dollar!" I yelled at him, a real psycho for the Army medics. "That means I broke fourteen cents' worth. Say fifteen cents!" And like a psycho, I hauled out a dime and a nickel and slapped the coins down near the cash register. Uncle Gus just looked at me, tears in his eyes and shaking his head. In another second I would've been crying too. So what I did was get the hell out as fast as I could.

Aw, what's the good of talking? What's the good of rehashing what you want to forget? What I said to Mamma and what she said to me was more of the same that'd passed between my Uncle Gus and me. Only more so. She was my Mamma. I'd leave it all out if there wasn't something I learned from her that has to be told.

From Uncle Gus, I walked back to the house. First, Mamma tried to make believe everything was like always, saying she'd saved me supper. I could smell the roast and baked potatoes in the kitchen. But who the hell could eat? I let her know what'd happened between me and Uncle Gus and she began to cry and explain. But I wouldn't listen to her. She was crying like a baby and trying to hold my hand. I pushed her away. Yes, that's what I did. But I had to push her away, for she just kept on reaching for my hands. Hysterical. But I didn't care even when she got to screaming. I didn't care, for I was screaming inside, too. Then she stopped carrying on and looked at me and I looked at her. And it was like she was on one side of the Hudson River with me on the other. Like she was all alone in the world. The kitchen light was shining on her face. Her lips were white, her hair like a wig or something, and I'd never seen her so old. Older than in the first few weeks after my old man died. Older than the hills. She was like a little old gray shadow, not saying a word, only looking at me and breathing hard, almost panting like she'd drop dead in a minute. Aw, what's the good of talking? I wouldn't't've mentioned any of this except that all of a sudden she lets out a shriek like she was crazy or I was dead or something and she says in German that I couldn't only blame her. That even my friend, my best friend, Hugh Pierson, didn't think I should marry Hortense. Or else why'd he come to her, my best friend, saying I was going to marry Hortense and maybe throw away my partnership. Crying like a baby, she said all that and how she'd promised Hugh never to tell me about his coming but she couldn't help it, for her heart was breaking.

I felt awful. I rushed into my own room and locked the door. And Mamma had the sense to leave me alone.

Hugh, Hugh Pierson.... What's the good of talking?

How long I lay there on my bed I couldn't say. It was the fire engines rolling out of the firehouse up near the corner that made me snap out of the fog. All my life I'd heard those fire engines clanging away. When I was a little kid I used to think the fires were all in my own block, in my own house. I wished now for the house to burn down for real. With me and Mamma in it. Let it all burn, I thought, and teach them all a lesson. Only what lesson? If I'd learned anything, it was that people never learn a lesson. Never learn to mind their own business, to live and let live. I thought how Mamma and Uncle Gus would've sworn on the Bible that the reneging was only for my own good. And Hugh would've sworn that he'd gone to Mamma for my own good. But what was my own good if not Hortense? Uncle Gus and Mamma didn't know that, I thought. I couldn't blame them so much. They were the older generation. But Hugh, he was smart. Hugh, he knew I loved Hortense and needed her like a guy needs his right arm. Hugh I'd shown what was in my heart, and yet he'd run to Mamma like any alley stool pigeon.

I was jinxed. I thought that no matter what I did, I was jinxed. I could try and raise the reneged money, but even if I raised it, something else'd pop up to queer me. For I'd been born a jerk and a jerk I'd die. Who but a jerk'd be lying in bed, in his coat, with his hat for a pillow? I asked myself, sitting up. It was my best hat, too.

My head felt so dizzy, I went over the window and opened it for some air. The cold air hit me. The shaft was black and I got twice as dizzy. I didn't know what was making me so dizzy. All I knew was that I better get away from that window. Or who knows? Maybe I would've not jumped exactly, but let myself fall out, sort of, like it was only half on purpose, half accident.

I walked to the dresser. There was my jerk's face staring at me out of the mirror. I couldn't believe that me, Maxie Dehn, I'd been on the verge. My face was all white. My nose was red and my eyes were wet. Those wet eyes of mine surprised me. For I didn't know I'd been crying. I looked at that crybaby mug in the mirror and I wondered who would've been the biggest jerk, Maxie Dehn who killed himself, or Maxie Dehn who didn't. A toss-up.

Hortense's photograph was on the dresser, the new one she'd given me after Tommy Nivens' party when things'd been so rosy. Across the bottom she'd written: "To Maxie, My Best Pupil and Sweetheart, Hortense." I read it over and thought that if I'd had the nerve to jump out of the window I could've written under that line of hers a couple of my own. Such as: "Hortense, I cannot live without you. I'll always love you, Maxie."

That would've been love. Real love. Real jerky love. For I'd be dead and she'd go right on sleeping with all kinds of bastards.

"Hell with you too!" I said, and I ripped her photograph in half and threw the pieces on the floor. Then I picked them up and pushed them into my overcoat. Give Mamma the satisfaction of finding them? Not me.

I straightened out my hat and left my room. Mamma, she heard me. She hurried into the corridor from the kitchen, "Maxie, eat some supper," she said so quiet I hardly heard her. She spoke quiet but somehow she sounded like before, like she was screaming. Like she knew it was all over and was just going through the motions.

I didn't say a word to her. I went downstairs. When I reached the corner of Eighth Avenue it was like a circus. The big red hook and ladder from the firehouse in my block was turning around. There were four or five other fire engines on Eighth Avenue, and half a dozen precinct cars along the curb. Coppers and fire inspectors were parading around in the gutter like they had nothing else to do, while on the corner a crowd of people watched the free show, yacking and pointing. A firebug'd turned in the alarm and a couple of coppers'd nabbed him. You could see it for yourself. The coppers and the firebug were off by themselves, on the sidewalk on the opposite corner. This firebug was a skinny guy, real nervous, without a hat, in a windbreaker. He was behaving like he'd expected to be beaten up but the coppers were just asking him questions. He'd expected action, so what he got were a few questions. He was a prize jerk, of course, to ring the alarm right around the corner from the firehouse, but I was sorry for him. I knew how he felt. Here he'd set off the alarm because he had nothing else to do. No girl to date, no friends to sit around with, nobody. Just like me. I thought of Hortense and how the Doyle deal'd been for her, and when Doyle'd sat on his hands I'd cooked up my own deal. And that deal, too, wasn't worth a plugged nickel. Three times—it was three times counting the first time when I'd said I was Maxwell Dehn, Jr.—I'd been breaking my neck to satisfy that dame. And Hugh, he'd listened to me and all my grief like a stool pigeon listens.

Yeah, if I could've helped that firebug, I would've done it in a minute. But Roy Rogers on his big horse is only for the movies.

I walked up Eighth to 50th Street and cut east. I didn't know where I was going or what I was going to do. My head was that numb. In fact, I didn't have a head. I was just a numbness on two legs. When I passed the Greyhound Terminal, I thought of pulling out of the city. The Greyhound busses were lined up in front of a dark brick wall like they'd been left for scrap. Like they couldn't travel anywhere. Besides, without Hortense, who wanted to go anywhere? Dance music sounded down on the street and I looked up at the lights of the Majestic dance hall, and the sign they have there: "75 Glamour Girls." It made me laugh, the kind of laugh that tears your insides. Glamour girls, I thought. The town was full of glamour girls, all right. I'd had one myself.

On the corner of 50th and Broadway, I stopped for the light. It was cold but the crowds were almost as thick as ever, the big signs flashing, and up in the sky the dame on the Bond sign was looking things over. Glamour girl number one, I thought, with a third wire and no heart. I hung around on the corner a minute, watching the secretaries stepping out with their bosses, the out-of-town dames with their pickups, all the third-wire dames. I'd fallen for one myself. I still loved her, worse luck. I thought that if only she'd backed me up, maybe I would've been able to do something with Doyle. Compromised the forty-thousand bonus. Something. For all a guy has to have is a little backing from his girl. Only a little, not much, only a little heart, not much. Just a little heart. Then I thought to myself that blaming Hortense was a jerk's game. For she was what she was, a glamour girl, and money was like the blood in her veins. She was the red leather shoe of the princess with a diamond stitched on the toe. Like I was the peasant's shoe, a jerk. And whose fault was it but my own for giving myself a pipe dream, a little old Broadway pipe dream of a glamour girl and a pile of money?

Get a move on, bum, I told myself. I moved. On the Avenue of the Americas, high up, the little golden windows in Radio City were shining, and I thought that way up there on the twentieth and thirtieth floors, the big shots were working late on the big deals. They needed a little extra dough before Christmas, I thought, an extra little million or two, and who was to stop me from going up there and jumping myself into the biggest deal of all?

Two men, their collars raised against the wind, looked at me, and one of them laughed. "Bud, you better go home to this Hortense."

I felt like I'd been socked in the jaw. Guys who spoke to themselves, mumbling the names of their girls, were a dime a dozen on Sixth Avenue, even if it was called Avenue of the Americas. But I'd never thought I'd ever be one of the mumblers.

I hurried into the nearest bar. When the barkeep asked me what I wanted, I read the answer from one of the signs over the mirror. "Mount Wilson special 20c. Big shot 25c." I ordered the big shot. Just what I deserved, I thought, a big shot for a big shot. I had a second and a third.

There should be a law against mirrors in bars. I might've drunk myself unconscious if not for that mirror reminding me I was the jerk supreme, who'd been double-crossed by all his relatives, not to mention his best friend.

I blew out of that bar into the middle of the night. I gulped in the cold air to sober myself up. One thing I knew. Nobody on earth was going to make me a phony three times in a row to Hortense.

I didn't need Madame Shouria's or anybody's advice. All the shining windows full of Christmas was all the advice I had to know.

HORTENSE

I've got to say this about Maxie. He was like the ten-year itch. There was no getting rid of him.

When he phoned me again, it wasn't altogether unexpected, although since that other wake-up call of his, he had been the invisible man in person, Mr. Inviz himself. He hadn't tried to see me once, and he hadn't shown up at the studio, for I'd checked with Lila Rand. When he phoned again, I was alone in the place like the last time, Hugh at Gimbels, and I was goddamn sleepy and mad, too. But I didn't hang up on him, because sleepy or not, he was talking big money with his first breath. And who hangs up on money?

"I don't believe you," I said to him, which was a lie.

"Will you believe a bankbook? I'll bring it in cash if you want."

"You will?" I said, still not believing him. But what did I have to lose?

"I'll meet you now, Hortense."

"Not now, I'm due at the studio soon," I said. "You say the deal's in the bag?"

"It's in the bag and I've got ten thousand deposit, Hortense, like I've told you. Honest to God, Hortense! Hortense, I'm crazy about you. I want to marry you. I love you, Hortense!"

There was more of this love-love, but I finally got a word in. "You've got ten thousand deposit?" I asked him.

"In my pocket, right this second, Hortense."

"Ten thousand?" I said.

"Ten thousand," he said. "And more coming. We can do what we want. Want to go to Florida, sweetheart?"

"Maxie," I said, "meet me at five. Downstairs on Fifth Avenue, Maxie."

Even when I hung up, I could still hear the kisses he'd blown into the phone. Or maybe it was the noises in my head. I wondered if Maxie could be telling the truth for once.

That day was one of the longest in my life.

What worried me the most was that Maxie might be walking around with ten thousand in cash and get himself knocked on the head. He was just dumb enough to walk around with all that money on him. Then I thought not even Maxie could be that dumb. Ten grand! And that was only a part of it. As I remembered it, there was forty thousand in the deal for Maxie—and me. Yes, me, I thought, as I took the bus to the studio.

They had done me such a big favor at the studio, only putting me on probation for saying ouch at general meeting. And now I could say ouch at the studio, and ouch to Dexter, the hell with them all. It was simple arithmetic, as Dexter himself would've been the first to admit. Ten grand was money. Forty grand was even more money. G.L. could go shove his wages, I thought as the bus traveled up Fifth Avenue. Even Dexter's seventy-five a night wasn't money. If I worked every night of the year, instead of only twice a week, I still couldn't earn forty grand. It was simple arithmetic. A hundred nights would've cleared me seventy-five hundred. Four hundred nights—stick to round figures, kiddies—was only thirty grand. And who but Milly could've worked four hundred in a row?

What a day!

The day wasn't Thursday. But after fifty minutes of Lila Rand screaming renewals and quotas, there was a surprise ten-minute general meeting anyway in the main ballroom. G.L. does that once in a while to keep us up on our toes. He was waiting, Papa was, with his secretary, Miss Ambers, and Tibson the porter, posted as usual a few steps behind her. "The phone book!" G.L. said, and we all looked at Tibson walking to a chair with a phone book on it. That was how this morning's surprise production began. Tibson brought the phone book over to Miss Ambers. She told him to hold it. He turned himself into a living magazine rack while she thumbed through the pages. But that day everything seemed just perfect to me. G.L. and Tibson and Miss Ambers, they were like some kind of a skit. Even Lila's screaming act was a laugh. Ten thousand dollars are the original rose-colored glasses, or should I say green-colored glasses?

G.L. began with a speech how he had received reports that morning from the branches in Kansas City, Spokane, and Boston. There wasn't a teacher or a supervisor out there, G.L. said, who wouldn't be happy to be in New York, in the Fifth Avenue studio. As for me, I thought of what Maxie'd said about going to Florida. I wanted to laugh. I wanted to cry. I couldn't believe the day had come at last when I could kiss them all good-bye.

"You all know what this book is," G.L. said, pointing at the phone book. "It's the Classified. It's the where-to-buy book. A quarter-of-a-page ad costs two hundred and fifty dollars a month. We have a quarter of a page in the Classified. But how many here know that ten other dancing schools in New York can afford that too?" He walked over to Tibson and read out their names. "Do you know why they can afford the Classified? It's only because we're not getting the renewals we should! It's because we haven't got the proper spirit here on Fifth Avenue! Yet our people out in the branches speak of us with pride. They envy us. How little do they know of the true state of affairs in Kansas City or Spokane or Boston!"

"Mr. Lawrence," Miss Ambers said to G.L., "you asked me to remind you a minute before the bell."

G.L. speeded up, the words rushing from his mouth like he was on his deathbed making a last statement to the press. His words began to combine but all I heard was noise because what I was hearing was Maxie saying: Ten thousand... and more... Florida....

Then *bonggg.* It was the five-of-two bell. Nobody moved because G.L. was still speeching. He looked angrily at his wrist watch and then he threw in the sponge. Maybe he was the big mastermind of Fifth Avenue, not to mention Kansas City, Spokane, and Boston, but when it came to the bells, he was no better than any of us.

"That's all for today!" G.L. said, and walked out of the ballroom.

The supervisors and teachers flew after him. Only me, I was in no hurry. Not today, I wasn't. Not when I was kissing off the rat race for good. I took my own sweet time, although I had a two o'clock myself. I watched Tibson the porter sneaking a last farewell look at the Ambers rear end as she followed G.L. It would have to last Tibson until the next general meeting, Tibson in his green uniform, green like the drapes and the walls. I began to laugh. I laughed and wished to God it was five o'clock.

I wasn't breathing when I picked up my two o'clock. But the cripple didn't notice a thing wrong. All I had to do was recite from the Teachers' Guidebook. I recited. And when I asked my happy boy if he had ever been to Florida, he thought I was making ballroom conversation. I wasn't booked at three, so I returned to the teachers' lounge. My butcher boy, Lila Rand, spotted me and said if I had nothing to do I should write my cripples who'd been playing hookey. She reminded me I had two cripples like that, and for good measure she tossed in a few insults. Lila's never forgiven me for reporting myself to G.L. The way Lila thought, I had no right to rat on myself when there were butcher boys paid good money to do that. But this day I smiled at her insults. I even felt sorry for her. She was caught in the rat race and I wasn't. When she left me, Tommy Nivens came over and said, "There's so much writing to do, isn't there, honey? Why do we have to write all these pupils? They ought to know what they're doing if they decide to quit. I find it so boring, don't you? Dexter never has to write letters, does he? None of his pupils ever miss a lesson, do they?"

"To hell with Dexter!" I said, laughing. "And to hell with the George Lawrence School of the Dahntz!"

"Honey," Tommy smiled. "If you feel like that, you better write some letters. For the therapy, you know. Or would you rather do some weaving, honey?"

"I'm weaving myself out of this rat race, Tommy," I said, and I walked to the rear of the lounge. Near the lockers, the desks were lined up for the pen-pushers. G.L. had thought of everything. Everything. That was what hurt.

I sat down and pulled a sheet of stationery out of the drawer. The stationery was green, too, the George Lawrence nymph in gold, on a shield with a golden L. Writing to backsliders was a painless operation. The paper and ink were supplied, and so were the words. All you had to do was open your Teachers' Guidebook to the section "Sample Letters," where everything was spelled out. I nearly always used the one that began: "You simply have no notion of how much you are missed at the studio. My supervisor"—blank space—"and the receptionist"—blank space—"have asked me several times where you are. Do I have to tell you you are due for the grandest welcome...." But this was one day I wasn't writing to backsliders. While talking with Tommy, I'd had the notion that maybe I ought to write to Hugh. Writing would be better than a scene with a lot of arguments.

But what could I write him? I wondered. I closed my eyes for a second and wished it was five o'clock. Five o'clock and Maxie and ten grand and Florida. Would Hugh understand? He knew how I felt. Or did he really, private eye that he was? My thoughts drifted, and I thought of the bell at five and the last bell at ten. How there really was no last bell, for even as the ten-o'clock bell was bonging, the next day's first bell was being readied. Readied by whom? Yes, by whom? And if Hugh could understand that, he would understand everything. The bells always bonging us in and out of G.L.'s happiness factory. "Don't You Know That Wallflowers Go to the Wall and Flowers to the Sun?"—that was the latest gem out of the tenth floor. Coast to coast, in Kansas City, Spokane, Boston, on the hour, every hour, the happiness factory was humming like mad. And was that anything to write about? How I was sick and tired of my cripples who wanted to be happy? Sick and tired of putting the polish on? Glamour, Popularity, Love? Name your own brand. We had them all. And was that anything to write about? And Dexter's happiness factory? Was that anything to write about?

I thought that if I wrote Hugh about the bells he'd think I was cracking up. If I wrote him about the law of averages working out for me at last, he'd think I was money mad, and who isn't? If I wrote him that I wanted to loaf in the sun down in Florida, with not a care in the world, and how there were worse than Maxie, he'd only feel bad. He was the official boy friend, after all.

So what I wrote was that I loved him and only wished he had the money instead of Maxie and that he should be a good boy and work hard at N.Y.U. so he could get a job someday and make himself some money. And I signed that letter: "I love you, Hortense."

I folded the letter and put it in an envelope. I didn't intend mailing it just yet. The mailing could wait until I saw the color of Maxie's ten thousand. That beautiful green color. It was green everywhere that year.

HUGH

What else is there to say? A little more, perhaps. But before I begin I want to stress the fact that Mamma was my sole source of information, for I never saw Maxie or Hortense again. What Mamma told me she had from Maxie after his return to New York.

Maxie and Hortense flew to Miami the day before Christmas: They had ten thousand dollars, eight thousand of Maxie's savings and another two thousand he had borrowed. Evidently Maxie had some peculiar need to go with ten thousand rather than with eight. Anyway, according to Mamma, the money was spent in five or six weeks. "They lived like kings, and that prostitood, she was what you could expect, crazy for the gambling." In February Maxie had returned to New York alone. As for Hortense, according to Mamma, Hortense was in Toledo or Cincinnati, where she'd gone with a manufacturer or banker whom she had met in the gambling casinos. Mamma wasn't sure of the city or the rich man's occupation. "That prostitood!" she raved to me. "Maxie had one luck that she wouldn't marry him." It seemed that Hortense'd refused to marry Maxie until he had all the money from the deal. At least, that was what Mamma said. What was true, what was false, I will never know.

After I received Hortense's farewell letter, I'd rushed to see Mamma. But she was hysterical. She was still hysterical when I visited her after Maxie'd struggled back to town. "Hugh," Mamma had wept, "this is what I have from my own son—the money he throws away on this no-good dancer, this common woman, the money I do not grudge. He has his job again at Jacob Groteclose, thank God! That old man, Mr. Groteclose, he is a saint when you consider Maxie went away without a single word to nobody. But in the office they remembered his father. Maxie himself, his record is good until this no-good dancer, she turns his head."

Then, painfully, between fits of weeping, Mamma told me what she knew of the Miami trip. Maxie, it seemed, had been outspoken. On his return to town, he had gone to see Mamma, and among other things announced he was moving into his own place. "The money I do not care," Mamma had mourned. "It is the change in him that breaks my heart. Who cares for the money if only a lesson he should learn?" But Maxie apparently hadn't learned his "lesson." He had referred to his five or six weeks with Hortense as a "honeymoon," and, even more unforgivable from Mamma's viewpoint, he had no bitterness against Hortense. She had deserted him when his money began to drain away and he'd been terribly unhappy but he had no bitterness. "Hugh!" Mamma had shrilled at me, the tears raining down her cheeks. "You will not belief this! Maxie, he said to me, about this prostitood, 'How can we blame her?' That is what he said to me. 'Can we blame a cat for going to another house where there is cream?' A cat is God's truth!" Mamma had cried in fury. "A common street cat of a whore, you will excuse the expression."

Before I left I made Mamma promise not to mention my seeing her to Maxie. For although Maxie was out of the house, he still visited Mamma now and then, as she tearfully confessed to me. "He was always such a good boy, my Maxie, until this common woman." Yes, Mamma's rating as mother was a continuing proposition. But I had no rating.

Four or five times I visited Mamma. Then I stopped. I had hoped for some news about Hortense via Maxie. But there was no news. Hortense had vanished to "another house" where there was "cream," while in the house on West 47th Street, the mother cat lived on alone, her nest empty.

About a year and a half after Maxie's Florida trip, Mamma Dehn sent me a note, care of my folks in Hightstown. For I'd long since lost contact with her. Maxie had married a good German girl, Mamma wrote proudly, a niece of one of the men at the office, Mr. Platt. I replied and asked Mamma to give Maxie my congratulations. I'd considered writing Maxie myself and even thought of sending him a wedding present. But I couldn't, not when the possibility existed that Hortense might have revealed our relationship. Perhaps when they were becoming estranged, before she deserted him. I would never know.

Six years have gone by, and although I've been in New York most of this time, I still haven't bumped into Maxie Dehn. For one thing, I rarely get over to the West Side or even to the Broadway area except when I go to the theatre. As for 42nd Street, between Eighth and Times Square, where the Groteclose Building is, it could almost be a street in another city. My firm, Aeroflex, Inc., has its offices on Madison Avenue. So it goes. I've done all right at Aeroflex, where I am one of the brighter of the bright young executives. Married, too, with a fine wife and two kids out in commuterville, in Rye, New York. So it goes. Sometimes I won't think of either Maxie or Hortense for months on end. But in late September, that first autumn of mine in New York rustles in memory like an autumn leaf itself. And during the hectic weeks before Christmas, Hortense's last words to me, written on a sheet of George Lawrence stationery, again print themselves in my heart.

This Christmas was no exception. There'd been the usual Christmas party at the office, and toward four-thirty I felt the need for some fresh air. I'd gone downstairs to Madison Avenue, to the Christmas city. In the hazy winter twilight the skyscrapers had the look of fabulous toys, while the Santa Clauses, with night coming on, looked like the real thing. As real as the false diamond ring Hortense had laughingly presented to me in 1946 and that I'd kept all these years in a corner of my desk. I thought of Hortense again, and again I speculated where she was this Christmas and what she was doing, and whether the law of averages'd held good for her in the Middle West. Had she married her rich man, the manufacturer in Toledo or Cincinnati. Mistress, call girl, whore? And Maxie? Had old Jacob Groteclose died and was Maxie now a partner in the Groteclose firm? A Maxwell Dehn, Jr., in reality? Who knew? But this I did know: Maxie Dehn would never again be as happy as he must've been on that Florida "honeymoon" with Hortense.

As I say, I needed fresh air. In fact, I was drunk, drunk and mellow. So on the impulse I walked west toward Eighth Avenue, the first time in six years. Again I came to the old corner of West 47th Street and Eighth Avenue. I went down the block, passing the firehouse, and across the street Molfeta the Greek's cafeteria. Again I looked at the long rows of tenements. They were the same and yet not the same, for there is no return to the streets of our past, to the dreams of our young manhood. I glanced at the public school, the police station, the Jewish Actors' Temple with its Ten Commandments in stained glass, and I lingered a second in front of the brownstone house where I had lived that first time in New York. I thought that maybe this very second Mamma Dehn was busy in her spotless kitchen. Or with Christmas so close, maybe she was visiting her oldest son or daughter or Maxie. He could forgive his mother what he could never forgive his friend. Then I thought that perhaps Maxie, being Maxie, had no hard feelings against me. Even if Hortense had told him of our affair. I would have had hard feelings, I knew, if I had been in Maxie's shoes. But not Maxie, not after so many years.

I walked to Ninth Avenue. Winter glowed in the darkening air and the stacked pines made forests on the city sidewalks. The windows gleamed, happy and splendid with Christmas, and in the gay light, Christ held out His hands, His forgiving hands.

I saw Maxie in the little boys tagging after their Christmas-shopping mothers— Maxie tied to Mamma Dehn's apron strings. He hadn't known back then that he would go to war and return to meet Hortense or that I would come to live with him. And with Hortense.... Don't have any hard feelings, Maxie, I thought to myself, and I looked up at the winter sky above Ninth Avenue, searching for God alone knew what. Maybe for that lost autumn when we'd still been friends. For it is in the tinted twilight sky, where we look for the autumns that will never come again, for our vanished ideals and hopes, in the tinted warehouse of the sky. Maxie and Hortense and me.... Of the three of us, Maxie had been the most admirable. Not Hortense, as I'd thought once. True, she had faced the facts of life and called them by their right names without hypocrisy or self-pity. But only Maxie had been brave enough to go tilting against the facts that'd shaped Hortense and shaped himself. Only Maxie had been brave enough to hope.

On and on I walked until I reached the westernmost boundary of the West Side, and here with the river smell in my nostrils I turned and looked through haze and darkness at the glittering towers of Manhattan, the airiest of all fables in the night. Gone was the city of steel, this city where the skyscrapers were always abuilding, where the guns of the riveters were an iron singing, the one true song of the city, perhaps its only song, like steel-throated woodpeckers in a steel-branched jungle leafed with the shining glass of all its countless windows. City of the hunted and the hunters. I thought of Hortense, who was thirty-two now. Of Hortense, who when drunk had sighed for someone who cared, in love always with that ever elusive someone. Never knowing, for who was there to tell her, that her phantom lover had been with her all day long, crooning out of the George Lawrence amplifiers. Someone who cared—the lover who was every girl's lover and no girl's lover, with those rumba eyes and tango personality and that mamba-samba virility. Every girl's lover and no girl's lover, hiding in the smoke-wreathed jukebox behind the last table, in radio and electric player, showing himself on a TV screen. Someone who cared, someone with money to care for a slightly used, misused, and self-abusing little moth called Hortense. I thought of Maxie, who had hoped a great hope. But I had to wreck his plan to buy the Shaw property. Maybe if Hortense'd seen his plan become fact, she might have stayed with him, married him....

The city of steel was gone, this empire city, this massive consumer of boroughs and nations, habits and customs, dreams and hopes, consumed in turn, and reduced to a wirelike tracery, brilliant with light. Where was the old Hell's Kitchen of Maxie's youth or today's 42nd Street or the East Fifties where Hortense Pavlec, the miner's daughter, had dreamed her child's dreams? Towns for a day, a year, a lifetime within the town on the Hudson. Gone now in the night as the Town itself was gone, with nothing remaining but a promise in the sky, the towers of Manhattan become a gate opening now before my enchanted eyes....

It was time to go home. I had a wife and family waiting for me. I walked back into the city and the gate in the sky was blocked out of sight by houses, black roofs, and the sound of footsteps, mine and those of others on the sidewalks. The gate in the sky—it would open again someday, I felt. In another autumn, another Christmas, in another time when we would dare follow our dreams and hopes into the universe revealed no matter how momentarily in every man's and woman's heart, to ascend, always to ascend, instead of walking our lives away, with our dreams and hopes dragging behind us like unwanted shadows, mourners following us down the dark sidewalks of cities left to us by our weaker selves.

THE END

LIFE AND DEATH OF A TOUGH GUY

BY BENJAMIN APPEL

To Sophie Again

ONE • *IN THE GANG*

Downstairs was the street. Downstairs was the Bogeyman with his bag, Jack the Ripper with his knife.

The boys on the street yelled at him when he walked by with his mother:

"Scarey Cat, chase a rat;
Kick a jewboy inna slat."

He was only four and his mother's explanations confused him. The boys were bad. God didn't like bad boys.

God was the Man who lived in the sky.

There was another Man who lived in the red house with the cross on top.

His mother said he couldn't go into the red house.

When he was five his father began sending him on errands. The boys would try to stop him; he was a good runner. Once they trapped him and said, "Hey, Joey. Wanna shoe shine?" They polished his high button shoes with watermelon rind, and laughing, shined up his face, too, for good measure.

Downstairs was the street. At night from the front windows of his family's flat, he watched the silent lamplighter lighting huge white cats' eyes in the darkness. Everywhere there were eyes. Down in the cellar, the coal in the bin glittered with many eyes; he hated to go down there. "The eyes of the devil," his mother would say as she filled the coal scuttle. He knew who the devil was— the devil was the Man who lived in cellars and burned up all the dead people.

Of all these things Joey thought when he lay in bed with his younger brother Danny, listening to the street's mysterious and frightening sounds. A woman crying, a man shouting, the whistle of a tugboat from the river, brought up images of the bad boys, of Bogeyman and Jack the Ripper, of strange men called God and Devil.

Street of the dark voices. It could come through all the locked doors and there was no hiding. It would find him.

He didn't know that one day this street of a hundred fears would narrow down to two rows of red brick tenements and that instead of answering to the name of Scarey Cat, he would nod indifferently at the respectful greetings of mobsters and gunmen. "That Joey Case's tough," they would say of him. "He's one of the toughest guys in the whole West Side."

"Tough and smart, guy. Don't forget the smart. He'd be pushin' up the daisies long ago if he wasn't smart."

That summer, his name was still Joey Kasow, and the man he would become was still far away on the other side of the night.

"*Yussele*—Joey," his mother said in Yiddish, looking up from her sewing machine. "You cannot stay in the house a whole summer long, hiding in corners." Her voice was soft and tender for her first-born. On the kitchen floor his younger brother Danny played with some clothespins, his baby sister Sarah sucked on her bottle in the crib.

He stood there with hanging head, his dark blond hair still wet from a dousing in the kitchen sink. He wore no shirt, no stockings, only blue knee pants, his feet in scuffed shoes with soles so thin that when he walked on the summer sidewalks he felt the heat coming through.

"Have you lost your face, my dear one? Let me see your face," she coaxed him. His gray eyes were the same color as his mother's. She kissed him, then stared at the drawn window shades. Spider webs of light glowed in the cracks.

"You will be six in another month, *Yussele*," she said. "You will go to school. You must learn to play with other children. Go downstairs and play," she begged him. The boy's eyes were as wet as his hair. She, too, felt like crying.

Downstairs, were the streets of the Irish. The saloons on the corners, the bums sleeping in the hallways, the gangsters robbing the stores on Ninth Avenue. When Mrs. Radisch, the butcher lady on Thirty-Eighth Street had first told her that the neighborhood was called *der Teufel's Kuche*—Hell's Kitchen—Mrs. Kasow had smiled, thinking that everybody wanted to fool a greenhorn. She knew better now. The streets were no place for an innocent Jewish child.

Her husband laughed at her. "You are making a woman out of him with your salty tears and your stupid pity!" So spoke her husband. He was becoming a half-Irisher himself, she would think; yes, he could be brave, he was big like a peasant, with hands like the blocks of wood he cut through with his carpenter's saw, and a tongue in his head sharper than any steel.

She got up from the sewing machine and embraced her son, whispering, kissing his cheeks. But when she managed to lead him to the door she felt as if she had betrayed her oldest-born. She closed the door between them and thought with tears in her eyes: so, we drive our own flesh and blood into the cruel world.

The boy outside sobbed. He knocked and when she didn't open the door, he banged it with his fists; he started to shout. She let him in. But that same week, cowed by her husband's arguments, the door remained shut.

The door was painted dark blue. It had a white china doorknob that gleamed like a cold and monstrous eye.... Joey began to scream. From one of the flats on the floor, a woman hurried over to him. She said, "What're you cryin' fer?" And when he didn't reply she murmured to herself, "Good Lord, always cryin' them Jews."

He flattened against the wall. The woman said, "I'm not gonna hit you, sonny. Why doncha go downstairs and play?"

Mutely, he stared at her.

"Don't wanna do that, huh? Lemme see—you like pigeons? Can't talk, huh? Now you go up onna roof and see the pigeons. Me boy's up there with his pigeons. Gwan! See the pigeons, don't hang around cryin' or I'll belt you one for sure."

When she was gone, he remembered that he wasn't supposed to go on the roof. The roof was bad. Mama is bad, Mama is bad, he singsonged to himself, climbing to the top floor. There, an iron ladder angled up steeply to a square of blue summer sky. To his worried eyes, the ladder was a stair with big holes.

Fall-through holes! Mama is bad, he chanted to himself and ascended the iron ladder. Stepping out on the roof, he was blinded by the sun. It spread, a yellow sky in size, then shrank, becoming round like the fire in the stove when his mother lifted a lid, a yellow circle. Big! He was overwhelmed by the bigness of the sun and the blue bigness of the heaven, the tarred tenement roofs stretching far and wide, another city in the sky, the pigeons flying. Then as a voice hollered, the universe contracted: three faces were watching him.

Two boys of fifteen or sixteen sat in the shade of a lean-to of white pine planks propped up against the chimney, while a small boy ran over to Joey, hollering.

"What yuh doin' on my roof, Scarey Cat?" Joey knew him. His name was Georgie.

Georgie scowled. He was Joey's age but bigger. He had stripped out of his clothes except for a pair of homemade underpants cut out of his father's old Sunday shirt, a gaudy green silk shirt striped in red. As he brandished a fist under Joey's nose, he looked like a miniature flyweight. His black hair was cropped close, a bulletheaded boy whose right fist was fanning a steady breeze into Joey's face.

"His mudder said," Joey was stammering.

"Whose mudder?"

Joey pointed at the two big boys under the lean-to.

"I know'm," the pigeon-flyer said. "He's on my floor. Hey, jewboy, should we let yuh stay? Or kick yuh off."

"Let'm stay," his friend said. "He's jus' a lil squirt—"

"Since when d'you love the Jews? I thought your name was Dineen?"

"Go fly a kite, Flaherty!"

They let him stay there, out in the bright sun. A limitless no-man's land stretched between Joey and the three of them sitting cozy under the lean-to. After a while he dared lift his head to the flock of pigeons flying as if a single gray wing supported them all. Their easy motion was hypnotic. His arms lifted from his sides, his fingers fluttered. Up, up, up, he flew from Flaherty and Dineen and Georgie. Georgie couldn't catch him, nobody could ever catch him.

Up, up.

Safe.

He was startled when Flaherty yelled, "Hawk!" Flaherty ran towards the coops on the roof. He picked up a twenty-foot bamboo pole and circled it in the sky. The white decoy rag tied to the tip-end waved, a warning flag. Dineen cursed, Georgie hopped up and down, shaking his fists. And far up in the blue reach, too high in dazzle and sky to be a pigeon, a black speck was becoming larger. Still, the flock coasted in the blue, not a worry in their heads. "Come down!" Flaherty implored them, "Come down you dumb bastids!" Three or four pigeons flew lower to investigate the white rag. Flaherty slowly sank the pole to the roof wall. A dozen pigeons alighted, nodding their gray heads, as the black speck now clearly a bird, sped down the blue racetrack of the sky.

Joey gaped, his mouth a flytrap. Flaherty lifted the bamboo again, the white rag fluttered. Rag? It was a leader, a mighty white pigeon to be followed when it dropped to the roof wall and skipped over to the coops. The pigeons crowded onto the wired top of a coop, stupid birds of a sudden, the flash of brain lost, lost with the mighty white pigeon. Flaherty's pole shooed them into the coop.

He was too quick, too nervous with the pole. Two pigeons escaped him. They flew up from the roof. Higher, higher. The hawk wheeled slowly, thirty stories up. Flaherty wiggled his pole but the two pigeons, as if missing the numbers and safety of the flock, giddy at the two of them alone, flew up and up and up. The hawk dropped, a feathered stone. "Dumb bastids!" Flaherty wailed, for the two pigeons didn't see the hawk. City birds, coop-dwellers, they were too petted and spoiled to know a hawk when they met one.

The hawk was no longer falling through the sky, but climbing, flying with his prey toward the Jersey Palisades. The two joined birds became one bird, a black speck again, a colorless dot so tiny it might have been an air bubble in the sky.

Flaherty lured the surviving pigeon into the coop. His unhappy eyes fixed on Joey's tilted head. "Hoodoo," he grumbled. "Ain't been a hawk around all summer."

"Ain't his fault," Dineen tried to say.

Flaherty called to Georgie: "Kick the jewboy off the roof! Bust'm one, Georgie! Damn hoodoo!"

Georgie ran over to Joey, he hit him in the face, socked him in the jaw. Joey's arms stayed against his sides. A third fist hit him high on the forehead and Georgie faded out of his vision. Georgie vanished, hidden in the pain smoking out of those swinging hard little fists.

Dineen pulled Georgie off. Flaherty shouted insults at his friend. One helluva Irishman that one was, Flaherty informed the world. Joey heard voices, sound, not meaning.

"Fight back!" Dineen was shouting at Joey, backslapping at Georgie to keep the blackhaired batter away. "God damn it, doncha hear me?" He grabbed Joey's shoulders and shook him while Georgie circled the two of them like a terrier knocked off from his victim.

"Give the lil jewboy a big kiss," Flaherty jeered at Dineen.

"Kiss my ass!"

"Wait'll I tell the gang!"

Dineen cursed him and he cursed the limp boy in his hands. "Fight back, damn you!" But he might have been talking to a bundle of old rags.

"Kiss'm," Flaherty advised mockingly.

"Kiss'm!" Georgie echoed.

Dineen slapped Joey across the face. "Fight or I'll knock your head off!" While the mocking chorus sang at him, "Kiss'm, kiss'm!"

"I'll throw you off the roof, damn you!" Dineen hollered, and suddenly he picked up the boy and carried him to the roof wall. Christ, Dineen thought, he'd show those mutts who was kissing jewboys. Over the edge, he lifted the hysterical boy.

Joey saw the bottom world hurling up through space at him like an elevator car gone mad and then with a dizzy speed sliding down on cables that might have been attached to the intestines in the sinking pit of his stomach. Dazzling white sheets flapping in the breeze, red brick walls, back yards. Down, down, down. No hands seemed to be holding him above this awful bottom world. "Mama!" he screamed.

Dineen swung him back onto the roof, still holding onto the boy's arm. "Stop your damn cryin'! Lissen you! I'm gonna t'row you off the roof you don't fight. You hear me! I'm gonna t'row you off you don't fight!" And out of the corners of his eyes he glanced at Flaherty. There wasn't a peep out of Flaherty and with a furious sense of satisfaction, Dineen thought, Flaherty could tell the gang any old story he wanted to now.

"Mama, mama," Joey bawled helplessly.

Dineen grabbed Joey's leg and began lifting him. Joey kicked, punching with his free hand. Dineen dropped him back on the roof, and with a mighty shove pushed him towards Georgie. "Fight you lil yeller bastid or I'll t'row you off for real!"

Georgie like a pebble off a slingshot whirled at Joey. Joey kicked wildly, meeting the fists with his scratching fingers.

Kicking and scratching at all the terrors in his life.

Five stories up, the street had found him.

All he ever told his mother was that he had been in a fight; he was afraid to tell her he had been up on the roof. "Georgie hit me, Mama. He hit me...." As for George Connelly, he had won another fight. "I coulda licked him wid one finger," Georgie had bragged to Fats Smith and Paddy Burley and Cheater Riordan and all the other little shanty micks down on the street. They didn't believe Scarey Cat could put up any kind of fight until they had given him a bloody nose themselves.

But what was a bloody nose or a black eye? If the street could knot like a fist, it could also open a hand of friendship. Georgie and Fats, and the others, began to play with him when they all trooped home after school. In the autumn afternoons they played ringeleveo and Red Rover, cowboys and Indians. Joey learned to shoot marbles. He kept his champ shooter, banded with swirls of gold and dark green, in a piece of soft cloth. He collected the pictures of prize fighters that came with packs of cigarettes. John L. Sullivan, Jim Jeffries, Gentleman Jim Corbett—the heroes of all the pint-sized kids in Hell's Kitchen— became his heroes, too.

"My Joey plays in the street all the time," Mrs. Kasow complained to Mrs. Radisch the butcher store lady and to Mr. Buff the grocer whose store was also on Thirty-Eighth Street where the Jews for a mile around shopped for their kosher meat and smoked pink salmon and pumpernickel bread. And the Jewish storekeepers clucked their sympathy.

Oi, the street, they condoled with her. The street of the *goyem*, the street of the Irisher pogromchiks. Perhaps, some day, the storekeepers hoped piously, there would be enough Jews in *der Teufel's Kuche* for a Hebrew school where Jewish children could go and learn their *aleph, beth*—their a, b, c's.

"My Joey will not speak Yiddish in the house," Mrs. Kasow unburdened her heart to the storekeepers. "If I talk to him in our tongue he does not answer." And she would sigh, staring at her friends in bewilderment.

Yes, something had happened to Joey all right. Flaherty the pigeon-flyer could've given her the lowdown or Dineen or Georgie Connelly. But between herself and the Irish there were too many screens. Even if she had been Irish herself, there would still have been the separate screen of a man's world. Between all the mothers and their sons, the street lifted like a giant wall. He was growing up, Joey Kasow, and the street had become his new mother. A mother of red brick, her heart the iron sewer covers in the gutter where he played marbles, her voice the thunder of the Els on Ninth Avenue, her name, no name at all but a number, cold, inhuman, mathematical: Thirty-Seventh Street.

On the stone step leading into the vestibule of the tenement where he lived, Joey sat wedged between Georgie and Cheater, watching the girls playing patsy on the hot and yellow sidewalk of another summer. He was almost nine now. That summer morning on the roof, with the pigeons flying and the hawk and the fight with Georgie, was almost forgotten. Sometimes, at night he dreamed that great big birds with human heads were eating him up. Sometimes, the past flapped its huge and silent and eternal wing.

But now the girls were playing patsy while in the gutter the dusty sparrows scattered when a wagon lumbered by, stirring no memory of birds undulating in a blue sky to the wand of Flaherty's bamboo pole. "See Mary's drawers when she jumps," Georgie whispered, grinning at Cheater and Joey Patsy players and sparrows, the sun a sheet of yellow tin fastened across the gutter under the rainless sky, and three small boys sitting in the street like fishermen on the edge of a magic river.

Oh, there was so much to see down on the street. Drunks, happy as kings or sobbing like babies as they walked a crooked line from the corner saloons on Ninth Avenue:

> "You're a stinkin' drunk
> You're a cheesy junk
> You're an ugly monk
> Whiskey is the bunk."

Some unknown Hell's Kitchen poet had invented that epic and a dozen others like it that the kids were always singing. They would tag after a drunk, baiting him with their rhymes. They would throw sticks at the painted women and yell, "Hoors! Doity hoors!" And listen of a night to the big guys chewing the fat: "The Badgers killed a copper over on Tenth Avenoo...."

Nobody had to tell Georgie or Joey that the Badgers were the toughest gang in the whole West Side. "Oney one in our gang who's gonna be a Badger when he's big is me," Georgie'd boast.

"Me, too," Joey'd say.

"Nah! You ain't game enough, Joey."

Late one hot August morning when the sky was full of little white clouds clean as soap suds, they saw the witch who lived in their block coming up the sidewalk. They had been sitting in the shade, sweaty after a stickball game, seven or eight of them, Georgie, Cheater, Angelo, Fats and Joey. "Who wants-a see me put the horns on that ole witch?" Georgie said.

Joey listened to him uneasily. When he had asked his mother about the witch, she had shaken her head sadly. "Old Mrs. Pierce is not a witch. People have hearts of stone. Cannot they see what I see?"

"What do you see, Mama?"

"Her children have left her. She lives alone. Will you be a good son to me when I am old and gray like that poor old woman, Yussele?"

"Don't call me Yussele!" he had shouted and rushed downstairs where Georgie and the others would've laughed for an hour if they could've heard his old woman with her *Yussele....*

His mother's voice was a thousand miles away now as Georgie pressed his two middle fingers down on his thumb, the forefinger and pinky finger pointing out stiffly—the horns. Angelo whispered, "Them witches talk to the devil inna night. They make people die, them witches."

Was Mrs. Pierce a witch? And if she wore black, didn't the old Italian women wear black, too? But she wasn't an Italian, she had no family. She was different from everybody else on this street of Connellys and Flahertys, with a few odd-lot Italian, Jewish, German, Polish and God-knew-what-else scattered among the Irish. And that was enough for somebody to begin whispering about witches. So, Mrs. Kasow might have spoken to her son.

His mother's voice, the voice of reason, snapped like the thinnest of threads. "Ole witch!" Georgie cried and darted out at the woman in black, pointing the horns at her. Angelo followed Georgie and the two of them ran around her in a big circle like kids around a bonfire in the winter. "Ole witch!" they hollered while she lifted her dead white hands, begging them to leave her alone.

"Ole witch makes you die!" Angelo screamed. "Gwan an' die yerself, yuh ole witch!" Two or three other stickball players were sucked into the mad dance. And only Joey and Fats gaped as the old woman called for help. Angelo's shoemaker father rushed out of his store. He chased the kids away and led his son off by the ear.

Safe in their backyard, Georgie turned on Fats and Joey. "You guys shouldn' be inna gang!" he yelled. "You was scared stiff! Scared-a that ole witch! Yeller jewboy!"

Jewboy.

It filled the air like a black cloud, it rammed down his throat, a black lump. It was all the blackness in the world.

"Georgie," Joey pleaded, "I'll holler on her nex' time I see her—"

"Yeller belly!" Georgie taunted him. "You and Fats—"

"I'll holler on her inna night!" Joey promised recklessly. "Inna night. Up her house!"

They all looked at him unbelievingly, for it was in the night, as everybody knew, that she changed into a witch, in the night, when old ladies' faces became witches' faces.

"I'll show you who's the game guy!" Joey challenged them. His gray eyes were moist, but there was a chip on his shoulder that hadn't been there a second ago: a chip to last a lifetime. "Who'll go with me tonight?"

Only Georgie met Joey in the hot breathing darkness, the men sitting on wooden boxes smoking, the women sucking on ices, waiting patiently for the breeze that might come from the river four avenues to the west. There the Hudson flowed to the sea and the piers, like the teeth of a comb, held the flowing starlit waters. Toward midnight, the women would comb their hair, too, and look at their aging faces in the mirrors, the street quiet, all footfalls fading, all voices sinking back in the red caves of throats quiet in sleep, with lust a drying spot on a sheet, and hope the smallest and whitest star in the tenement sky.

But now an Irish kid and a Jewish kid, who waited for no breeze, hurried silently down the sidewalk as if the night were a huge and menacing ear that served the witch. They passed the cellar bakery where ghosts white as flour sometimes sat on the barrels. They passed the house in the middle of the block from which a woman with a slashed neck had run on an autumn day, and the lamppost that marked the spot where gang murder had been done, and the hallway where a girl of ten had been dragged on a winter night. They came to the witch's house and the Irish kid whispered softly, "Whatta we haffa do it for, Joey?"

"I'm game if you are—"

Georgie said nothing, he shook himself like a wet dog. He made the sign of the cross as he followed Joey into the vestibule. Under a bowl of frosted glass, the blue gaslight burned, the brass-edged stairs gleamed. They had never been inside the witch's house before, but they knew she lived on the top floor: on the streets of the poor there are no secrets.

They went up the stairs to her floor. From one of the front flats, a phonograph record was playing the song of the stone villages and shepherds. The two kids listened to the wailing music of the Greeks. From behind the door of the other front flat, they heard a man's voice. Joey walked to the two doors in the rear, Georgie behind him. "Joey," Georgie whispered.

"I'll show yuh!" Joey muttered shakily.

From behind one of the rear doors, many voices rose and fell. There was only one door left. Joey pointed at it and Georgie looked at him with despair. "Joey—"

"I'll show yuh!"

Georgie crossed himself and suddenly he knocked on the last door. He was showing Joey now! Joey felt as if someone were rapping on his heart. He choked, he was afraid. Furiously, Georgie continued knocking with his left fist while his right hand described convulsive crosses in the semi-darkness of the hallway. Joey's hand shot up with a jerky jellying life of its own, and in frantic imitation he too crossed himself. And crossed the pit between *goy* and Jew so that for a stunning second he seemed to be looking across at the other side, at his mother and father. Jewboys, he accused them and accused himself, his mouth twisting, his eyes blind in their sockets. Madly he kicked at the door. "Jewboy!" he cried incoherently. "Witch, you witch you!"

But the dark and mystic door on which a cross had flamed to destroy the six-pointed Jewish star remained shut. No witch flew out on a broomstick, no witch in witch's black, blacker than coal, the black of hell, no witch with great white teeth smeared with blood.

A woman in a bathrobe rushed out from the flat next door. The Greek flat emptied into the corridor. The woman slapped at the retreating boys, one of the Greeks shouted in the most reproachful of voices as if aroused out of sweet sleep himself, "Wake up peepuls!"

"Greaseballs!" Georgie hollered when he was halfway down the stairs. And in the street, he crowed triumphantly. "We showed 'em! Didn't we, Joey?" He laughed and laughed. "Who's the gamest guys onna block?" Georgie asked the whole wide world. He put his arm around Joey's shoulders and in the clear pure light of friendship, they walked down the long dark street.

When Joey couldn't sleep at nights for thinking of the cross he'd made up in the witch's house, he was consoled a little by the memory of Georgie saying, "Who's the gamest guys onna whole block!" And when the Jews in the neighborhood finally launched a little Hebrew school for their sons over on Thirty-Fifth Street, he wouldn't go. His father beat him a dozen times, giving up finally with a bitter curse, *"Goldene Amerika* where the sons of Jews desert the customs of their fathers!"

Other customs, other fathers.

They were eleven and twelve years old now, Georgie Connelly and Joey Kasow, Cheater Riordan, Fats Smith, Angelo Esposito, and eight or nine others who had grown up on Thirty-Seventh Street. They had a real gang now called the 1-4-Alls. Georgie was the leader and he'd picked Joey as autocratically as Kaiser Wilhelm over there in Germany as Next. The Leader and Next Leader had led the 1-4-Alls on raids against the Dutchies on Thirty-Eighth, against the wops on the other side of Ninth. Shouting "Christ killers!" they'd chased the jewboys coming out of their school on Thirty-Fifth, with only Joey silent, only Joey thinking he was no jewboy like those Hebrew school jewboys. Silent was Next Leader, silent. He felt better when they went after the Dutchies again or swiped fruit from Paddy's Market on Ninth. There, every Saturday night, the horse and wagon peddlers lined the curbs. Saturday afternoons, the 1-4-Alls would sit in the Eighth Avenue nickelodeons, watching Pearl White escape the clutching hand as the pianist hit the keys and an usher sprayed cheap perfume to kill the stink of the sleeping bums. They all loved Pearl White and Angelo said when he was a man he'd marry her. "Marry this!" they hooted, goosing him, itchy with the lusts of their adolescence. And in the cellars and on the roof tops, they lined up one behind the other, waiting their turn at the little sluts of the tenements. It was easier finding girls when they had their own clubhouse.

Their clubhouse was a backyard shed. It was also their true home, their inner city, the secret ghetto of their youth.

KEEP OUT, some long ago proprietor had painted in white on the 1-4-All shed door. And in fading yellow paint another former occupant had notified everybody: J. RIORDAN PRIVIT. Underneath the misspelled PRIVIT, there was a legend in dark red: 1-4-ALL CLUB. That winter evening, behind their locked door, Georgie, Joey, Angelo and Fats sat smoking in the tiny yellow glow of a candle. On a shadowy shelf there was a cigar box full of cigarette butts retrieved from every avenue on the West Side; Sweet Caporals from in front of the pool parlors on Eighth, fancy Helmars and Hassans picked up outside the Broadway cafes. Next to the box was a carved wooden ship, its hull stained black out of a bottle of stolen shoe polish with a single mast whose white sail had been scissored out of some housewife's missing pillowcase. On that white sail, Fats, the best letterer in school, had printed 1-4-All in square black-ink letters. Without a keel or a rudder that ship could only have sailed on an adolescent's faraway and dreamy seas.

Now in the smoky shed, Georgie was saying, "We'll raid that greaseball tomorrer!"

They all nodded. Yeh, raid him and teach him a lesson for being such a tight-wad! The Greeky frankfurter man! The stingy greaseball! All they'd asked him the other day was to trust them for a coupla lousy pennies and he wouldn't do it. So they sat smoking and planning in the candle-lit wintery darkness with their dream ship on the shelf above their heads.

And outside in the backyard, the old newspapers whirled round and round between the sheds and the fences like crazy prisoners, wearing the crazy black and white of that year's newsprint:

KAISER DELIVERS ULTIMATUM
BECKER ELECTROCUTED

Outside was the huge and waiting world that the German Kaiser wanted for *Deutschland Uber Alles* while Becker, the New York police lieutenant, had only wanted to line his pockets with a little graft.

But all Joey Kasow wanted was to belong to the 1-4-Alls. West Side, East Side, all around the town, all that any of the kids in the kid gangs wanted was to belong.

The next day, toward evening, they found the Greek frankfurter man on his usual corner. He stared frightened at the crowd of boys with snowballs in their mittened hands. A lank dark man, the Greek, a brown scarf wrapped around his skinny neck, his long nose drooping over a thick black mustache. His frankfurter pushcart was as rundown as he was:

FRANKFURTERS 2c
SAUERKRAUT, MUSTARD

A charcoal fire under the iron plate kept the franks red hot. The Greek stared; he sensed disaster; he shouted for help. The first snowballs thudded into his body, his face.

"Raid the greaseball!" Georgie bellowed and sprinting close to the cart, he knocked the mustard pot to the sidewalk. A dozen 1-4-Alls charged, whoop-ing and yelling like the redskins in the nickelodeons. They snatched at the frankfurters, the Greek hitting at their hands. But there were too many hands.

Nobody stopped them on that winter corner. One or two storekeepers watched from inside their doors, afraid to interfere, afraid the kids would return on another evening and smash their plateglass. Laced with frost, those store windows, an icy night coming on, and outside in the steely blue winter a grown man crying like a baby. "Help, help!" the Greek frankfurter man called. "Help! Poleese!" Calling, sobbing, he rushed at the boy who had led the raid, the biggest boy of them all. He seized Georgie by the collar of his macki-naw. Georgie kicked him in the leg, but still the Greek held on, punching with his free hand. The 1-4-Alls's piled on the Greek, knocking him off his feet, but still he held onto Georgie. The two of them tumbled into the gutter. Still the Greek held on as if his fingers had frozen tight.

"Get the greaseball!" Joey commanded and whipping forward, he kicked at the Greek's head. The booting feet of a half dozen boys made the Greek let go. The gang dashed around the corner. Now the storekeepers came out of their stores and picked up the bleeding and unconscious man.

And if Joey Kasow lay awake in the bedroom he shared with his kid brother, Danny, who was to know. And if his eyes filled with tears over a no-good tightwad greaseball, who was there to see.

Down on the street nobody had seen Joey Kasow cry in a long long time.

Down on the street, the street of the raiders....

There where Becker the police lieutenant had been the silent partner of a gambler called Rosenthal. On orders from the reform police commissioner, Becker had to raid his partner's place. "I was doublecrossed. Becker was my partner," the gambler had written to the newspapers. Hired killers had shot him dead on Forty-Third Street off Broadway outside the Metropole Café. Their names were Gyp the Blood, Dago Frank, Leftie Louey and Whitey Louis. They were all electrocuted, with their employer.

"Imagine a policeman hiring killers!" people had said all over the country, more excited over a cheap gambler's murder than the assassination of the Archduke Ferdinand in Serbia. Where was Serbia anyway and who cared. Soon, on all the streets of the land, marching doughboys would be chanting "Hang the Kaiser!" Soon, there would be war and war would drag in on its bloody dragging skirts a freak with two heads looking in two opposite directions, talking out of two mouths, that men would call Prohibition. Soon the slum gangs—Five Pointers, Hudson Dusters, Badgers—scratching out a hardworking dishonest living, existing from pickpocket hand to plug-ugly mouth, would be riding de luxe, coast to coast, on the Bootleggers' Special.

"There's some good kids comin' up. From Fortieth, you got Billy O'Connor and Red Riley. There's Billy Muhlen on Thirty-Eight'. And Georgie Connelly and a jewboy, name of Joey Kasow, on Thirty-Seven'."

This was Spotter Boyle talking, and next to Clip Haley the Spotter was the biggest man in the Badgers. Clip was the roughneck leader, Kid Knucks himself. The Spotter wasn't much use in a brawl. His heart, as everybody in the gang knew, was on the blink. But the Spotter had a pale blue eye on him that could case a store in a minute flat. Was the money in the cash register? Or hidden in a sock? That was the kind of thing the Spotter was A-1 at. Sizing them up—whether they were Ninth Avenue storekeepers or the tough kids coming along in every block.

"A jewboy?" Clip Haley asked unbelievingly. They were talking it over in a saloon. Clip was drinking boilermakers, a shot of rye washed down with a beer; the Spotter was sticking to beer. "We never had one in the Badgers!"

"Some of them foreigners got the Irish beat," Spotter Boyle had to admit as if his old man and old lady hadn't come over in the steerage themselves. "If the guy's good, what the hell?"

"You're a queer one, Spotter."

He could've said that one again. The Spotter'd popped up out of nowhere nine, ten years ago. The Badgers were all Hell's Kitchen boys, Manhattan born and bred, but the Spotter was from Brooklyn somewhere. Nobody knew him from a hole in the ground, and there he was with a story of an old miser across the bridge who kept his money in the house. Johnny Burke, the Badger leader then, had smelled a rat. Who the hell was the long beanpole with the skinny face anyway? He wasn't much to look at but when they followed his pointing finger there was more than a thousand in cold cash. That gave the Spotter his nickname and made him a bona fide Badger sure enough. And the old miser? Some guys said he was a relative of the Spotter's. Others said the Spotter came from a big family out there in Brooklyn and was going to parochial school to be a priest when his heart went bad and he began running wild to get even. The Spotter only laughed and said it was all mullarkey. They couldn't get much out of him, and over the years they'd stopped asking questions. Johnny Burke, who'd given the Spotter his chance was in Sing Sing. Boxcar Johnson, the new leader had been killed in a fight over a woman. There weren't many Badgers left, only Clip and a couple others, who had been in the gang nine, ten years ago.

"Why don't you get a Greek for the Badgers?" Clip was asking now with a sarcasm heavy as a piece of leadpipe.

"Just a jewboy this time, Clip."

A couple nights later, he brought Joey Kasow and Georgie Connelly up to Clip's furnished room. The Badger leader let them in, he sat down again, putting his shiny brown buttoned shoes up on the table. Clip's sandy hair was perfumed, his rocky jaw powdered. A golden horseshoe tie-pin shone in his necktie. "Who's the jewboy?" Clip asked, playing a game of cat-and-mouse and turning toward Georgie who was black smoky Irish as even a blind man could see. "You?"

"Me?" Georgie was amazed down to the core of his pugnose soul.

Clip had to laugh. The Spotter flopped down on the double bed in the room; the Spotter was a great one for resting. "It's the Bum Ticker," he would explain, as if his heart were a living and separate thing following him around like a kid brother nobody wanted.

"Then it's you," Clip said to the second fifteen-year-old. He saw a kid who, although two inches shorter than Kid Irish, was five foot seven or eight and solidly built. The kid's hair was dark blond under his cap, his round face on the small side, all his features neat, the nose narrow and straight over a mouth like a girl's with only the jaws strong and square.

"He don't look like a jewboy," Clip announced. "Some mick must've corked up his ol' lady on a dark night. Didja say your name was Kasow or Kelly?" Clip roared at his joke, Georgie laughed while the Spotter watched them all like a hawk.

The kid's gray eyes hadn't wavered, his face hadn't changed, and for the first time Clip felt that the Spotter hadn't gone off the deep end about picking a jewboy for the Badgers.

Nothing that Clip could have said would've fazed Joey. Was Clip saying dirty things about his mother? Enough that a guy who was somebody big was knocking his name around.

They became Badgers. They were somebody now. Badgers! The Spotter started them in on the department stores. Work good enough for young punks. Rosie Mafetti, the Spotter's girl, taught them the little things a good shoplifter has to know. "Always keep your face innercent," she advised them, who had long lost her own innocence. "When you're goin' to the counter be sure the store bull ain't around. Stick close to some woman what's shoppin' like you're with her. And wear hats, youse guys. Real hats, not them caps from Nint' Avenoo." She demonstrated the sleight of hand so necessary in the profession. "A quick swipe, see! And only swipe stuff that fits in your hand. No pianos!" Rosie had them practice on the bottles of perfume on her dresser. And when the lesson was over, she smiled at their flushed faces. "Don't let the Spotter ever catch you lookin' at me like that, youse guys."

One day they would work R. H. Macy's on Thirty-Fourth Street and Broadway, the next, Gimbels on Thirty-Third. It was at Gimbels' necktie counter that they were almost caught. Joey noticed the bull slipping in on them through the crowd of men. "Cheese it!" he hissed in warning. They edged away quick from the shoppers busily ferreting out the bargains that surely had to be on the bottom. They moved fast, so fast that the bull quit approaching them like a pickpocket, sneaky and without elbows. Straight at them, the law rushed. They ran, big Georgie in the lead, socking at any woman who didn't get out of his way. The store blew up with noise like a crazy balloon, with a shrieking and a screaming. A tight mad grin showed on Georgie's face. He seemed to have forgotten that a bull was hot after them, as if he'd been dropped into a gym where all the targets were soft faces and softer bellies.

The newspapers printed a story about two shoplifters who had run amok.

"They're a coupla fightin' fools," the Spotter said to Clip.

"They should have work where they can be tough as they want."

Their next job was plumbers. It was a famous cold winter, that winter of 1917. The tenement plumbing, new in the year of another war, in 1898, began to give way. The water in the pipes froze, the pipes cracked, the plumbers were busy around the clock. They went after the plumbers at night, led by a Badger two or three years older than they were, a heavy muscled blonde kid of seventeen with a pair of mitts on him like two bricks. His name was Moore but the Badgers had nicknamed him Bughead because he'd go bugs one drunk out of three and start wrecking things.

That night they met Bughead on the corner of Thirty-Ninth Street and Ninth Avenue. The black pillars of the El lifted up into a sky of white polished stars shining like the glass Christmas stars put away now for another year. Their breath was steam, they kept their gloved hands inside their mackinaw pockets. They crossed under the El tracks, hurried down Thirty-Ninth. The sidewalks were empty with only a slow-footed two-footed whiskey barrel rolling homewards from the saloons, so drunk he seemed to be strolling in the springtime. "We could roll him, Bug," Joey whispered to Bughead.

"Not tonight," Bughead said.

They passed the wobbling drunk and Joey laughed, he didn't know why. But on these winter streets he felt as if he could do anything he wanted, knock over any man for his dirty money, pull any woman into a doorway. He thought of Rosie Mafetti and the long dark street suddenly seemed to glow with the memory of her. The flashing emerald eyes of a slinking cat were her eyes; the deepest shadows, her black hair. Behind all the yellow windows, she was waiting for him, naked in the winter night, and if not her, another like her, prettier....

Into the tenement spotted for them by Spotter Boyle, walked the three Badgers, silent, treading softly. The cellar door in the rear was open. Bughead called, "Hey plumber!" He descended the wooden cellar stairs. They groaned under his heavy step. "Hey, plumber, the landlor' wants yuh over 418 Fortieth Street right away. The pipes all busted there. 418 Fortieth," he kept repeating while Joey listening to the ominous creaking of those stairs wondered what kind of warning did a God damn plumber have to work.

Sometimes the plumber would lift a face shadowy and suspicious in the light of his candle. Sometimes the plumber would joke and ask if it was zero out in the street. But once the Bughead had his wrestler's grip on him, with Georgie pounding down, a hunk of leadpipe in his fist, it'd be over in jig time. With no one to hear a shout for help, or if anyone heard, no one with the nerve to unbolt and unlock his door to come hunting trouble. In the winter night, in the Hell's Kitchen night, the shouters for help were like the doomed in hell.

Creakity creakity creak, said the stairs. Be careful, said the stairs. Watch out, said the stairs. Tensely, Joey listened. "Help!" the plumber cried once in a choking voice. Down Georgie thundered. Joey leaped into the doorway. He saw the plumber trying to pull free from Bughead. He heard the plumber moaning like a stunned slaughterhouse bull. Bughead must've sloughed him one in the kisser, Joey guessed. The plumber's glazed eyes lifted to Georgie closing in with the leadpipe, and as the Bughead spun him around his eyelids, like the wings of a trapped bird, fluttered, eyes meeting the eyes of Joey on top of the stairs. For a second before Georgie smashed him one, those eyes seemed to speak. "Help!" they begged and were answered. "Damn you!" Joey's eyes said. Yet he felt a sudden pressure on his temples: pity touched him with its gentle fingers.

The leadpipe thudded against the plumber's head. He dropped, Georgie kicked him in penalty for calling for help. Then staring down at the man's fat mustached face, Georgie muttered, "Looks like a sauerkraut," and patriotically kicked the plumber a second one. Bughead was picking up the scattered tools. Georgie helped him dump them into the plumber's bag.

Up they came, while down below in the steady light the unconscious plumber pointed at them all with one outflung limp arm.

"Bug," Joey said in the street, "when do I get my chance with the leadpipe?"

"You're tough, ain't you? Here's your chance!" Bughead laughed, and unslinging the heavy tool bag from his shoulder, he slipped the leather strap over Joey's shoulder.

But if Bughead, like Clip Haley, carried a spite against him because he was a jewboy, most of the gang treated him fair and square. The Spotter was always preaching to the new Badgers. "You guys gotta get along good. And no scrappin'." Billy Muhlen, the dutchie from the dutchie block on Thirty-Eighth Street, used to grin at Joey and Georgie. "Remember when we usta fight like cats and dogs?" Billy Muhlen was a good guy, they were nearly all good guys, Joey thought. Still Georgie remained his best friend. Between jobs they would loaf along Broadway, darkened now to save electricity for the war, lingering in front of Liberty Hall, on Times Square, listening to the speakers. Buy bonds, the speakers all said. Joey and Georgie would yawn after a while and take in a burlesque. There in the male darkness that somehow smelled of both a whore-house bedroom and a kennel, they pointed out their favorites among the bespangled girls.

It was a feeling to be a Badger, to be one of the gang at a beer party when the smoke was so thick a guy could hardly see the next guy's mug. Yet those smoky faces were the only real faces to Joey Kasow. If he still slept at home, still shared a bed with his brother Danny, his family wasn't real to him. Faces that didn't count as if cut out of brown paper with the eyes and mouths paint-ed on like the masks he'd made as a kid. A bunch of dumb Jews, was how Joey Kasow appraised them. His old man working like a dog, his old lady always sewing and cooking and washing, his dumb brother and sister only trying to get good marks at school like the dumb Jewish bookworms they were.

Jew, jewboy, sheeny, kike? Maybe he was one, but he was also a Badger as he had been a 1-4-All. It was a feeling! Like the last day in school when every-body ran out into the street singing:

> "No more classes, no more books
> No more teachers' dirty looks."

And no more swiping stuff from Paddy's Market! No more swimming off the docks! No more crowding into a shed with a dumb old boat on the shelf, 1-4-All scribbled on it! Yet sometimes when he and Georgie walked down Thirty-

Seventh Street, down the old block, passing a bunch of little kids roasting sweet mickeys in a fire in the gutter and yelling in foghorn voices like the runts they were, he would glimpse the boy he had been and hear the voices of his abandoned boyhood.

By March, Joey and Georgie were broken in on their new work—robbing stores. One rainy night when most stores on Ninth Avenue had already closed, Joey and Georgie and Bughead, a team since the plumbers of the winter, hurried down the wet sidewalks, Joey carrying an empty suitcase. A trolley, lit up like a huge yellow box on wheels, rattled underneath the elevated tracks. Far away, an approaching El sounded like an iron beast loose in the middle of the dark wet sky.

"That's the joint," Bughead said as the three Badgers neared a little candy store, its window a lonely square of light. "Joey, you lay Butso—" To lay Butso meant to watch out for a cop, for danger.

"Let Georgie lay Butso—"

"Aw, pipe down!"

"You never gimme a chance—"

"Some other time—"

"Always some other time."

Georgie put in his nickel's worth too. "Bug, give'm a chance."

Ahead of them, the candy store window loomed, solitary and shining among the locked-up stores. Its window was full of tops and balls, rows of toy soldiers; but in the lonely night, it seemed there would never be any hands to spin those tops or throw those balls, no generals in knee pants and black stockings to play with the soldiers, no voices anywhere to shout, "I'm the 'Mericans, you can be the Huns."

"Hey Joey, you still game?" the Bughead asked out of a corner of his mouth.

Game.... It was the word of his lifetime. It rang now like a bell, a ringside bell where one round followed another in a match that had no end.

"Sure."

"I'll lay Butso," Bughead decided. "Gimme the bag." He took the suitcase and said, "Georgie, you'n Joey know what to do."

Joey.... His name had a new sound to him. Joey! That's who he was, neither jewboy nor mick. He felt himself to be anonymous, like the toy soldiers in the candy store window, a Badger with two other Badgers.

Already Georgie was at the door. The doorbell tinkled; they stepped inside. Electric bulbs hung on long wires from the corrugated metal ceiling, empty spots of light. Joey stared at the cigar counter. Five sleepless dolls on a shelf behind the counter stared back at him. His eyes leaped to the rear where a dark green velvety curtain separated store from home.

"Hey!" Georgie hollered down the store.

"We ain't got all night!" Joey cried brashly.

That'd show Georgie, show 'em all, he thought.

LIFE AND DEATH OF A TOUGH GUY   **177**

Georgie looked at him with surprise. Joey, intoxicated by what he'd done, almost forgot that they were waiting for the storekeeper to come out from behind the curtain. His racing mind jumped the mile of time; he could almost hear Georgie telling Bughead, "Know what? Joey, he yells, 'We ain't got all night!'" And Bughead telling it to Clip and Spotter and all the Badgers, and all of them saying he was a game guy. He breathed in the candy store smell of licorice and chocolate and tasted the strong good salt of his own courage, hearing the praise of the only guys in the world from whom he wanted praise.

The drunken second vanished when the curtain in the rear parted. The storekeeper hurried forward in slipper feet, on his tired face the wired-on smile he displayed to all his customers.

"I wanna box of chalklits for my mudder," Georgie said. "Somethin' 'round a dollar."

The big blackhaired boy was parroting the Spotter who had the right line for every wrong move. The Spotter knew that a storekeeper would look twice at a couple of tough kids blowing into his store at the tail-end of the day's business. You had to give a storekeeper a hunk of sugar if you were smart. And the Spotter was smart. He knew there was no song and dance as sweet as the one with a mother in it. The Spotter had seen roaring dock wallopers and teamsters get soft as putty when they got onto the subject of Their Mothers. True, these same men when they staggered home would knock the bloody hell out of the little mothers of their own families, which only proved that a square peg could fit a round hole and that a man had to give the boot to somebody in this bloody life.

The storekeeper nodded, he padded down the counter, returned with a box wrapped in violet paper and tied with a green ribbon. "This is good chocolate. Your mother'll like it." And added as sentimentally as the next man, "The best for a mother—"

Joey reached across the counter, his arms diving before him, his hands locking tight on the storekeeper's throat. Like a huge round snake that he had caught, it thrashed wildly between his tight pressing fingers. Then Georgie had his blackjack out—the storekeeper slumped and Joey let go his stranglehold. He peered, frightened suddenly, at the curtain in the rear. Nobody! Only Bughead coming in with the suitcase, coming and going so fast, he could've been a ghost. Georgie'd already gone behind the counter, emptying out the storekeeper's pockets. Nimbly, Joey took from Georgie's hands a worn brown wallet, a watch with a gold lion fob. He opened the suitcase, dropped them in. Georgie passed him cigar boxes, toys. Georgie passed over himself, for one second he'd been behind the counter and the next he was at Joey's side, grinning. Joey felt the numbing heaviness lift, he felt light and giddy and triumphant, and as he tagged after Georgie, he snatched at the box of candy wrapped in violet paper that everybody'd forgotten about.

Behind them the door bell tinkled in warning. Bughead was waiting. They legged it for the corner. "Joey, you done good," Bughead said.

"What about that guy's family? They deaf?"

"Deaf, me eye! Leave it to the Spotter. The guy ain't got no fam'ly. So, you were worried, huh, Joey?"

"Not on your life, Bug." He became aware of the box of candy in his hand. "Here. Got sometin' for you, Bug."

"What?"

"A box of candy for your mudder!"

"Sonuvabitch joker."

Georgie laughed. "A box of candy for your mudder! That's good, that's good."

Their heels hit the sidewalks, a night-owl truck rumbled down Ninth, and everything Joey heard, all the sounds of the great sleeping city that never really slept seemed to be saying one thing:

For your mother, for your mother, FOR YOUR MOTHER....

"Mama, I can't look for work if I don't feel well," he shouted the next morning. But he managed to eat a big bowl of stewed mixed fruits, some scrambled eggs and a couple of the big fat poppyseed rolls she had bought at the Jewish grocery on Thirty-Eighth Street.

His mother stood there in her scrubbed kitchen, watching her oldest born. *Gott,* she asked herself, why did this son alone have to be such an *ausworf. Ausworf*—it was Yiddish for outlaw. His brother Danny and his sister Sarah had left for school long ago, her husband for work. Only this one slept like a king and then he had paraded into the kitchen for her to serve him. Sick? Yes, he was sick as a *goy,* she thought bitterly.

"No school, no woik," she mourned, speaking in English because this son of hers, this *halber goy*—half Christian—wouldn't listen to her if she spoke Yiddish.

"Aw, don't bother me! Do I ask *you* for money?"

"Your father will drive you out of the house like a dog!" she cried angrily in her own language.

"Who cares," he said, thinking that he'd had about one breakfast too many in this house anyway.

He felt better down in the street. With Georgie. With the Badgers.

Later that week, after the story of The Box of Chocolates for Your Mother had gotten around, the Spotter invited the kid to have a beer with him. He led Joey through the Ladies' Entrance of Quinn's saloon to an empty table in the backroom. "There's some cockeye law about minors," the Spotter explained. He smiled, the gentlest of lawbreaking fagans, at Joey's eyes opening up like Sambo himself. Maybe, the Spotter mused, Quinn's backroom did look like heaven when the guy looking was sixteen. The Spotter was twenty-seven but what with the Bum Ticker and all, he sometimes felt like a hundred.

Joey had tried to keep a pokerface on him as if he wasn't really a minor but a grown man used to stepping out with Spotter Boyle every second night in the week. But he couldn't control his eyes.

Women in flowered hats sat at all the tables, their long skirts brushing the gleaming hardwood floor as they drank with the cigar-smoking Eighth Avenue sports. Ladies of the evening, their rouged cheeks glowing like sunsets, cigarettes in their fingers. Smoke hung from the antlers of a stuffed deer's head and through it Joey peered at the paintings on the wall where veiled and naked sirens, the sisters of the women at the tables, displayed their pink and rosy thighs and breasts. "Genuwine hand-painted hunerd percent erls," boasted Quinn, the proud owner.

A baldheaded Irish waiter in a spotless black coat came to the Spotter's table and said, "Boyle, you know we can't soive nobody underage."

The Spotter chuckled. It was a low and throaty chuckle, as if he didn't have the strength to laugh hard these days. "You mean him? Why next week President Wilson's draftin' the poor bastid into the army. You ain't gonna begrudge him a schooner of beer?"

When the waiter brought them two schooners, the Spotter's toast was, "For your ole mother." The Spotter'd become curious about this Joey Kasow. It was plain the kid was more than a fighting fool like his pal Georgie. Fighting fools came a dime a dozen. And they didn't interest the Spotter much. In his nine years with the Badgers, he'd seen tough guys galore, the tough guys who'd rather fight than eat. There were the ones too dumb to know better, their brains put in backwards. Others were tough because they were fighting a yellow streak. Joey's cross, the Spotter guessed, must be his being a jewboy. But after he'd asked the kid a few questions, the Spotter decided that the jewboy was only a part of it. "So all you want's a chance?"

"I can do anything anybody else can," Joey said in a shaky yet reckless voice, as if borrowing himself a tongue out of that hairy-chested and bawdy backroom smelling of whiskey and French perfume.

"How about usin' the old bean?" the Spotter asked, tapping a bony forefinger against his temple. "The guy who's tough ain't in the same class as the guy who's tough and smart. Don't let the Bug get you down, kid. Be smart. He's worried he'll be drafted so he has to pick on somebody. He's even gonna get married to beat the draft." The Spotter lazily lifted a thumb at the door leading to the saloon out front. "Quinn and his fat-ass politicians fixed up Clip with a fake wife and four kids, but that's for Clip."

Joey's face had flushed at the Spotter's easy confidences. The Spotter, a cigarette dangling from his thin mouth, almost felt like laughing. Here was another punk acting like he'd been handed the big red and white peppermint stick. For the pure hell of it, the Spotter said, testing Joey, "Bet I could trust you with a gun, kid?"

Joey nodded, his gray young eyes shining, and suddenly the Spotter's heart, that sick heart of his, tightened in his chest. Here was another punk ready for anything, the Spotter thought. All these God damn punks were strong as horses. Smart or dumb, they were ready. "Not so fast," the Spotter said, thinking that for himself going fast was over with forever. He tilted the derby on his head back on his forehead, his sunken eyes searching the young face across the table, and suddenly his exposed forehead seemed too broad as his peaked face seemed too meager under the full-blown yet rigid contours of that black iron kelly, its blackness shadowed now in the searching, pale and envious eyes.

The kid noticed nothing. All he could think of was that the Spotter didn't hold his being a jewboy against him. "I'll do anything you say, Spotter," he said gratefully.

"Why?"

"Because you're one fair guy."

That the Spotter was—in his way.

During the next few months he brought the kid along like a prizefight manager with a good meal ticket. When the kid showed up after the flu had knocked him for a loop, the Spotter treated him to a pick-me-up over at Quinn's. A glass of milk, a raw egg broken in, laced with two inches of cognac. He had one himself, Spotter Boyle, although the flu epidemic hadn't been able to squeeze a single bug into his skinny frame. He loaned the kid a few bucks in the lean stretches between jobs and always he was saying, "Use the old bean. You got no police record, so keep it clean, kiddo." When Joey complained how sick and tired he was living at home, the Spotter shook his head. "You blow out now and your ole man, he'll go to the cops. Steer clear of trouble, kiddo. You stick around 'til the ole man gets sick of you and tells you to go to hell. He will, too. Use the old bean, kiddo." He was grooming Joey Kasow as a stick-up artist, the Spotter was, but he was still leery about giving the kid a gun. Shoot a storekeeper and the coppers buzzed out like flies. The Spotter was always warning the Badgers with guns, guys like Bughead. "Don't pull the trigger unless the guy's got a gun too. Let them cops keep warmin' their feet. Remember there's nothin' like a killing to put a firecracker under their fat ass."

With the first warm days when the amusement parks opened again, the Spotter suggested that Joey practice shooting out in Coney Island or across the river in Palisades Park. "You get the feel of a gun that way," the Spotter said. Joey asked Georgie to keep him company. Two or three times a week they shot at lead ducks and clay pipes. "There goes a Hudson Duster," Joey'd grin at Georgie when he scored a hit. Hudson Dusters and coppers, all the enemies broken into pieces like the clay pipes they shattered with their bullets. And in the spring, too, as the Spotter predicted, Joey's father'd finally thrown him the hell out of the house. It happened during the week of Passover when Mr. Kasow asked his son to come with him to the synagogue. Joey refused; he'd refused every year, but this time his father didn't beat him or shout or curse. In a quiet voice he had parted with his oldest child while his wife and younger children wept: "Go your own way, Joseph. You are no son of mine."

That was the signal for Georgie to blow, too. "A bad end to yuh, yuh scut!" Georgie's father had bellowed at his son. The two kids moved into a furnished room on Forty-Sixth Street, off Eighth Avenue, a room not much bigger than two closets joined together: small and yet big as the world.

It was a world sick of war and when the armistice was announced, the first false armistice, the people of New York went wild with joy. Fifth Avenue was closed to traffic. A paper rain of torn newspapers fluttered down from the windows. Whistles and bells split the air shaking with the voices of a multitude. "Down with the Kaiser!" they shouted while the signs in the stores proclaimed *Closed For The Kaiser's Funeral* and a thousand flags danced the red, white and blue of victory.

"Down with the Kaiser!" the crowds shouted at the shrine of pylons and palms on Forty-Second Street that had been named a Court of the Heroic Dead. And all night long colored searchlights played on the weeping, laughing, praying, screaming, drunken faces.

"Down with the Kaiser!" those crowds cried deliriously and if someone, some bluenose, had cried, "Down with Drinking!" the crowds, even the drunks, would have agreed with equal moral fervor. All over the country prohibition sentiment had mounted with the war fever. Sober soldiers were good soldiers, the temperance ladies had stated with temperate tears in their eyes. The country needs the grain, the patriots had thundered, and weren't most of those brewers and distillers Huns anyway? "Down with the Kaiser.... Down with Whiskey...."

It was a war to save democracy, a war to usher in utopia, a shortcut to a better world.

Marching down all the avenues of the cities, the returning doughboys paraded, and state after state voted prohibition. In the saloons, the heroes of the Argonne and Chateau-Thierry swallowed their beers and whiskies in big gulping drinks and killed the Huns all over again. And over in Hell's Kitchen, Spotter Boyle lay awake at nights thinking that a big change was coming sure as fate, and it might be a good idea to get a wad of dough together. There was nothing like green money to help a guy in the clutch, was the Spotter's ten commandments.

The Spotter put a gun into Joey's hand and sent him out on his first armed robbery.

Joe Kasow, age sixteen and a half, had graduated finally out of blackjacks into the champion class where a finger on a trigger could cut anybody down to size.

After Joey's third gun job, the Spotter knew the kid had a cool head on his shoulders. "Another guy might've pulled the trigger when that crazy wop butcher took a poke at Georgie," the Spotter praised Joey, and to demonstrate his appreciation, he brought him up to a tenderloin sporting house. There, in a parlor hung with plushy curtains and shiny with gilt mirrors, the Spotter asked the madame for Nora. To Joey he said, "She's the one I always have. What's good for me's good for you!" The Spotter winked slyly, his lips stretching in a man-to-man smile. But behind his pale blue eyes, like some calculating prize fight manager, he was wondering if he couldn't use Joey good but good. He'd been thinking lately of sticking up a gambling game or two. True, the Hudson Dusters were protecting a lot of poker parlors down the West Side, and if anything went wrong, he was risking a gang war, but if the risk was big, so was the money....

A blonde woman in a flame-colored evening gown walked into the parlor. "Spotter Boyle himself," she said with a smile.

Joey stared at her. He'd had two-dollar whores, he'd had free stuff—but this was a woman! She was tall, her breasts were full and creamy, a million dollar dame. He'd seen women like her in Quinn's backroom, on the arms of the Broadway swells in the burlesque shows, in the penny movie machines, in his dreams.

"You haven't been around in a dog's age," the tall woman was saying to the Spotter.

"I'm a man with three wives," he joked. "Nora, how 'bout bein' good to Joey here?"

Her golden head moved on her powdered neck, she smiled at the kid who was holding his cap too tightly in one white-knuckled fist. "I'm old enough to be his mother, Spotter."

"You oughta know, Nora," the Spotter said maliciously. "Poysonally I thought you were under thirty."

"Bye-bye, Spotter," she smiled. "C'mon," she said to Joey. He followed her out of the parlor. Her golden hair, the back of her neck, her naked white shoulders, her wide hips sheathed in flame-red silk, burned in his eyes. She stepped into a bedroom where only the big bed, without a blanket or a spread, covered by a fresh white sheet, had a plain workmanlike look to it, like the bed in a hospital. The dresser glittered with mirrors, the chairs were studded with brass tacks, the lamps fringed with strings of colored glass beads. She shut the door. "Under thirty! The nerve of that Spotter bastid." She glanced at Joey. "How old're you?"

"What the hell do you care," he said flushing.

She glanced at the kid indifferently, not seeing him any more as a separate person. To her, he was neither young or old, goodlooking or ugly. Just another marcher in the male parade in and out of this room. "Put your clothes on that chair," she said, and without another word, silently, efficiently, like a hospital nurse, she slipped out of her evening dress and onto the bed.

He hadn't budged, some inner ear still deafened by that question of hers. *How old are you?... I'm old enough to be his mother....* He dropped his cap on a chair, he wanted to say something. What? He felt dizzy. Out of the corner of his eye he glared at her full heavy body, strangely faceless like the whitish headless body of a pig in a butcher window. His mother's face flitted over to that naked body, vanished, but he remembered. Images of his mother's breasts accidentally seen, images of his mother's body haunted him.

"I ain't got all night," she said without emotion. It was as if she'd never spoken. Or as if the waiting body, this apparatus of flesh had jingled out words only because somewhere a coin had been dropped in. "I ain't got all night." She had recited the whore's words as if under the big breasts where her heart had been scooped out there was now a little hidden phonograph.

"Aw ri," he muttered and began to undress. She was silent, he was silent. The silence roared, *I'm old enough to be his mother. Mother, mother, mother,* his own heart echoed insanely. He stood up, and the bed and the woman on the bed lifted like a wave, and on the wave she was naked, with only the face dressed up, two round circles of rouge on the cheeks, lipstick on the lips. *Old enough to be his mother....* "You hoor!" he shouted.

She thought she knew what was wrong. Another kid rushing a mile a minute into being a man. She thought he needed babying. The painted lips parted in the imitation of a loving smile. "Don't you wanna kiss me?" she said, her words cloying and sweet like the titles of the silent movies.

The gray eyes of the kid didn't seem to be focused on her. She realized he wasn't looking at her breasts or thighs. He wasn't looking at her at all but at some shadow that had crept into the room, the shadow of his hate.

She had seen that look before, on the faces of the wild ones, the woman-beaters, the perverts. Then she thought angrily what a fool she was to let a kid worry her. Still she felt she had to snap him out of it. She cupped her breasts with her hands in a gesture that was almost automatic like the movements of a wax fortune teller in an amusement park. Waxy whore's hands under waxy whore's breasts while her eyes, human, still worried, waited for his eyes to find her.

They found her. She sighed, she lifted her arms to him, offering herself to another customer. She stopped being a woman who was a little afraid and again became a bed-machine.

Joey felt himself falling down a hot and panting darkness although the light glowed through the colored stringed beads of the room lamps, falling through the darkness of forgotten roofs where the stars, like bright beads, lay tangled in dark and wanton hair, falling, falling, through the mother darkness, through the woman darkness, falling....

When the Spotter thought it over, he nixed the idea of sticking up poker games protected by the Hudson Dusters. Why should he? There was the East Side, free and clear. True he'd have to use the old bean and locate the joints. But that was what a bean was for. The Spotter snooped around and got all set. Then Clip Haley, Ted Griffin, Sarge Killigan, Lefty O'Connor and Billy Muhlen, the dutchie, stuck up a poker game on Rivington Street. Three thousand bucks plus watches and rings was what that little job was worth. "We don't want 'em to remember our mugs," the Spotter said. So for the next job, he picked a new bunch led by Bughead. This job, too, went off like a song. "We better lay low a while," said the Spotter.

It was summer before he was ready again. "This is a job for three guys," he said to Joey. "The idear's to get there 'round seven before the game gets goin'. Should be only the house guys, two of 'em. You'll say Davey Finkel sent you. That's how I got in. This Davey Finkel, he runs a saloon on Allen Street." The Spotter was a great believer in knowing exactly where you were. He had Joey con the neighborhood and the sidestreet where up on the third floor of a tenement lady luck could be chased with a pair of galloping dice. Joey reported back to the Spotter who said, "Now let's see who ain't been in on any of this East Side stuff. You'll need a coupla guys—"

"How about Georgie?"

"You and Georgie're glued together ain't you?"

"We can do it ourself. We don't need no other guy."

"You sure, Joey?" The Spotter grinned. "Or you only want one guy so you get a bigger split?"

On a warm August day, the two Badgers hit the East Side. Sheenieland, Georgie was thinking, while the gray eyes of Joey Kasow glinted with the same sense of difference that showed in the Irish kid's blue eyes.

East Side, West Side, two sides of the poor man's coin. Pushcart peddlers lined the curbs shouting their wares in Yiddish. A beggar tap-tapped down the crowded sidewalk, his cane striking the stone heart of a world with eyes. A mob of small punks tailed two soldiers. "Hymie," a small voice shrilled. "Why doncha lemme see der medal again, oney dis time, Hymie." Sewing machines hummed in sweatshops above the stores on the street, still taking a stitch out of the long day.

The two Badgers turned into a narrow vestibule, walked up three flights to the crap casino spotted for them by Spotter Boyle. Joey pressed the doorbell. His finger felt stiff, frozen. He stared down at it as if it were some strange sixth finger that had come with the gun in his hip pocket. He heard footsteps behind the door. Felt his body stiffening, tensing. He glanced at Georgie standing there like a brick wall except for the spreading nostrils on his pug nose, as if Georgie were sniffing out the smell of those unseen footsteps.

The door opened a gambler's wary inch. In the greenish-yellow space between the edge of the door and the dark wall—Eyes!

"Davey Finkel sent us," Joey said.

"Finkel?" Inch by inch the door widened, the eyes became part of a face, a fat dark face with a neatly trimmed General Pershing mustache.

"Finkel says you run a straight game. You're Ganzer, ain't you?"

"I'm Ganzer—" dubiously. "You fellers're kinda young—"

The Spotter had thought of the answer to this one too. Joey recited, "We got the dough, what more you want. We got the dough."

To that magic word, the door swung wide and they walked into what had been a kitchen. On the unused rusted coal stove stood a whiskey bottle and glasses. At the kitchen table, Ganzer's partner, the second house man, was playing solitaire. He raised his brown eyes to the newcomers and then they fell back, heavy as lead pieces, to the rows of cards.

"Wanna wait 'til the crowd comes?" the man with the mustache asked. He was jacketless, in an immaculate pearl gray vest, his snowy shirt sleeves banded by purple sleeve-garters. Gold cuff links shone in his snowy cuffs; a tie-pin in his necktie, a tiny golden hand whose thumb and forefinger held a diamond. A true gambler, this one, gleaming like a false diamond himself.

"Sure, the night's young," Joey said to him.

The man with the mustache laughed. He appealed to the solitaire player: "Sam, you hear? Nothink like a young sport." He was studying them, smiling. "So you know Finkel? What you doink in dis neighborhood? You're Irish," he said to Georgie. "You, you're a Polack," he said to Joey.

"Not me," Joey replied and wondered what he was waiting for. The coast was clear just as the Spotter'd said it'd be. But the Spotter hadn't foreseen a room spinning like a wheel. Stove, solitaire player, man with mustache. Joey's eyes shifted from Ganzer's smiling and suspicious face to his tie-pin, and suddenly as if that golden hand had given him the signal, he swung his arm behind him, heard himself saying. "Stick 'em up, you guys! Stick 'em up!" There was a revolver in his fist and the spinning room had come to a stop. With a shocking stop. Still the room was, and yet vibrant, with the iron muscle of that gun of his that had already knocked Sam, the solitaire player's hands away from his cards and over his head, and tossed Ganzer's plump hands high toward the mouse gray ceiling.

"Keep 'em up, sheenie!" Georgie warned as he tapped at the solitaire player's pockets, pulling out a wallet and a gold watch. Georgie hurried over to Ganzer, tapped him, unbuttoned Ganzer's back pocket. He hauled out a wallet thick with the fading money for this night's crap game while Joey floated the eye of his revolver from target to target, smiling a little, as if they were only a couple of white ducks in a shooting gallery after all.

"The tie-pin!" he ordered Georgie.

Georgie reached for the golden hand, but it was held in place by a safety-bead.

"Take his tie off!" Joey said.

Ganzer's face had been a deadpan, but now he ground his teeth as if they had stripped him naked. Georgie stuffed the necktie with the golden hand into his pocket.

The door bell rang. It rang, it rang. The solitaire player sat straight in his chair, but Ganzer's upper body leaned forward as if he were about to answer the door.

"Stay where you are!" Joey warned them. "Georgie, let the bastid in. I'll take 'm!"

Georgie went to the door, he opened it, the newcomer stared at the gun pointing at him. Joey said, "Stick 'em up!" And turned to see the kitchen table leaping at him, the cards fluttering to the floor, red cards, black cards, the table coming at him.

The solitaire player, playing the table like a hidden ace, charged the kid with the gun. The newcomer grappled with Georgie. Twice Joey pulled the trigger, but the table didn't drop, coming at him two-legged, headless, like an apparition out of the dark streets of his childhood. He fired a third time and when the horror smashed into him Ganzer plunged forward, grabbing at his gun arm, kicking. A fourth bullet whined into the ceiling and Joey fell to the floor, his groin throbbing from Ganzer's boot who stooped and yanked the gun out of the kid's unnerved hand.

From the floor, biting on his lips to keep from crying, he saw Georgie slowly lift his arms and hands over his head, and cursed himself who'd lost his gun to a pack of sheenies.

Ganzer, the man with the gun now, kicked the kid on the floor in the belly. Joey felt his insides break like glass. With a boneless weak hand, he rubbed at his chin. His chin was wet, his fingers smelled of death. He realized he'd puked. Who? He? It couldn't be true.

"Momser—bastard!" Ganzer cursed in Yiddish. He nodded at the man Georgie had let in. "Max, a favor I ask of you. Go outside the door and when the people arrive, tell the people there will be no play tonight. Do me this favor, my friend."

Georgie had averted his head. He couldn't look at Joey whose shirt was covered with greenish vomit. Christ, what luck, Georgie was thinking dumbly. He blinked when the gun was aimed at him; he submitted to a search. The solitaire player found a blackjack in his pocket. He squatted down next to Joey, patting at him with the seeking quick flats of his hands, straightened, sniffing at his fingers. There was vomit on them. He walked over to Georgie and toweled his fingers clean on Georgie's jacket.

Ganzer's eyes hadn't shifted from the kid on the floor. The one on the floor was the *momser* with the gun. "The friend of Dave Finkel!" he cried in a passion and kicked once, viciously.

Joey passed out.

"Sam, throw water on the *momser*," Ganzer said, and he aimed the wheeling gun at Georgie. Sam filled a glass at the sink, walked to the kid on the floor and flung the water out as hard as he could. The glassful flew. A bullet of water, it hit, drenching the kid's face and stinking shirt.

Joey felt a tearing begin inside his belly. Like a hand, like the golden and revengeful hand of the tie-pin. He pressed his fingers against the tearing, the pain.

"That's from Finkel!" the man with the gun grimly informed him. "*Verdar-mmte Irisher momser!*" Damned Irish bastard, Ganzer had cursed.

Finkel.... Joey, remembered the name, he remembered everything. The gray haze was going, the sharp black and white of memory remained. He peered at the three faces in the room, the two gamblers set against him, murderous. His eyes met Georgie's guarded eyes, and between one breath and the next, they opened to pity. He's sorry for me, Joey thought, he's sorry for me. For an instant he loved Georgie as once he'd loved his mother when only she could shelter him from the street.

Street of Jack the Ripper, of the bad boys, street of fear.... Street of the 1-4-Alls, street of the Badgers, street of love.

He heard the man with the gun questioning him about Finkel and knew that soon he'd have to answer. Answer what? Christ, what was the right answer?

"You coulda killed me!" Ganzer said, as if he'd been the rusher with the table. His dark eyes slanted unbelievingly at the gun in his hand. His meaty shoulders sagged as if only now had he realized how close he'd been to hurt, to death. He stirred himself, glanced at Georgie who was still reaching for the ceiling. "*Schwartzer Irisher choleria*—black Irish cholera—turn 'round to the wall!"

Don't tell 'em a thing, Georgie's eyes had said in a final message. Now those eyes were gone, Georgie was gone. The broad faceless back, the hands lifted in prayer, wasn't Georgie.

Joey felt alone.

"Who told you 'bout dis game, 'bout me?" Ganzer questioned him.

Joey said nothing. The solitaire player lit a cigarette, he puffed calmly and then remembering the blackjack, he fetched it out of his pocket, hefted it in his palm. His fingers tightened on the blackjack. He went over to Georgie, swung. Georgie collapsed.

The man with the gun flushed, but before he could speak the solitaire player explained in Yiddish. "I had the wish to give him a little knock, Ganzer. Is that so *schlecht*—bad?"

"*Grubber jung*—thickheaded lout!" Ganzer cursed him.

"For such dirt a clean burial in the river." The solitaire player wagged his blackjack at Joey and said in English. "How you like it? We shove your head in a milk can and throw you in the river. How you like dat?"

From between the solitaire player's gold-capped teeth, the river hurled into Joey's consciousness. He'd heard, and who hadn't, of the milk can dodge where the head of the guy to be dumped was pushed into the can like a cork into a bottle. He lay there on the floor, weak and in pain, covered with the vomit of defeat, seeing the river of the West Side docks, seeing the rivers of his dreams and nightmare drownings. It was a second of profound revelation, the world splitting into its two naked halves: those who stood strong on their feet, armed with gun and blackjack, and those who lay beaten and afraid on the floor.

"*Momser,*" the man with the gun was saying to him. "How you come here?"

Ganzer could have served on a plainclothes squad for he had to perfection the hammer-and-nail technique used by most detectives in questioning suspects. Keep hammering the same question and sooner or later the nail gives.

"How you come to Finkel?"

"Just went in for a drink."

"Finkel, he told you 'bout me?"

"Yeh."

"Irish *momser.*"

All night long he'd been hearing that chorus of *Irish bastard* sung out as if it were a single spitting word like *jewboy.* But in the fury of this night, no words, no insults meant anything. The guy with the gun was the top American of them all.

Ganzer said to him, "I'll tell you somet'ing. You keep lying, we'll kill you and dot's all."

On the floor, fear became cunning. "I'm Jewish like you. Gimme a chance."

The man with the gun roared out his disbelief, the man with the blackjack smiled and joked about circumsized *goys.*

"*Ich bin a Yid and my nommen is Joey Kasow,*" he said in a rusty Yiddish that was half English.

"In America, the Irishers go to *cheder,*" the man with the blackjack said in Yiddish to Ganzer. *Cheder*—Jewish school. He nodded at Georgie's back and asked Joey with a bitter humor, "Vot's his name? Cohn?"

They laughed, the two dark men who had met plenty of Irishmen and Poles in the East Side with a smattering of Yiddish. Then Ganzer said, "How you came here? Who send you?"

"We heard from Finkel—"

"Enough with Finkel! Who send you?"

He knew now they wouldn't stop until they had the name out of him, and the name they wanted was Spotter Boyle's. They were certain it was inside his head and they wanted it on his lips. "Finkel," he repeated stubbornly.

"Irish liar!"

"I'm not lyin'! He sent me, for God sake, he sent me—"

"No, no. Not Finkel! Sam, a lil knock, give him."

He cringed as the man with the blackjack neared him. He had tried being smart, tried to use the "old bean" but it hadn't worked. "No!" he cried at the man with the blackjack who was leaning over him now, silent as death. For all the talking that had to be done was coming out of the mouth of the man with the gun.

"The las' time, Irish *momser!* Who sent you?"

Spotter Boyle.

That was the name they wanted and it almost burst out on his lips, and in anguish and hatred at how close he'd been to turning squealer, he screamed. "Sheenies!" screaming like a madman, for in this kitchen where four bullets had pumped out of his gun, in this blackjack kitchen of vomited pain, there was only room for a squealer or a madman.

The blackjack whanged down at him, his arms sprang up, and the blackjack caught him on his forearm. His breath exploded in his lungs like a brown paper bag blown up by a kid and broken with a quick clap. The man with the blackjack jabbed his weapon like an exploring left, feinting like a boxer. Hit!

It was the little knock ordered by the man with the gun who said, "The las' time, Irish *momser!*"

Full tilt into a wall he'd run—that was how the knock had felt. Joey recovered slowly, he looked up helplessly at the two faces, the two weapons. The blackjack, the gun.

"Who send you?" the gun was asking.

Joey shook his head, tears in his eyes. The gun said, "Sam, a lil knock."

"Wait!" he screamed, names forming in his brain, other names.

"Who send you?"

"The Hudson Dusters," Joey said, naming the gang below the Pennsy tracks.

He had silenced that pitiless *who send you*. He said, "We're from the Hudson Dusters. The Hudson Dusters, the Hudson Dusters...."

The gun listened. "Sam, a lil knock," the gun said.

The blackjack lifted and the impulse to confess he was lying quivered on his lips, and then with all his might he cried. "What more yuh want, yuh damn sheenies! The Dusters, Johnny Murtagh sent us!" He'd named the leader of the Hudson Dusters. "Johnny Murtagh sent us—"

This wall hit harder than all the others.

His mind emptied of all fears and doubts, of madness and cunning, loyalty and betrayal, and he drifted away on a river wider than the river of the Hudson Dusters and the Badgers, limitless between the fragile banks of human brain and human temple.

TWO • *PROHIBITION—NO PROHIBITIONS*

"Least you didn't rat," the Spotter had admitted when the pair of beaten-up kids dragged back out of the East Side. Just the same he bawled Joey out for giving his real name. "Suppose them sheenies get after Johnny Murtagh and he starts huntin' the guys in his gang what give him away? He's got no Joey Kasow in the Dusters, but we have. All we need's the Dusters fightin' the Badgers! You guys stay outa sight a while. Don't come near me!"

It was Georgie who had said, "Joey, les hobo a while. I always wanted to see the country."

"Might as well," Joey had answered bitterly. This treatment of the Spotter's hit below the belt; he hadn't expected a gold medal exactly, but they hadn't ratted and they'd saved their skins into the bargain. "Nobody loves a loser!" he announced to Georgie as if he'd discovered this fact in person.

On a sparkling August morning, the two kids headed for the Weehawken ferry at the foot of Forty-Second Street. With only the West Side sparrows chirping them a farewell song, they walked off the street—the street of the Badgers—into the USA.

The continent swallowed them as it swallowed all its fugitives. Draft dodgers still on the dodge, soldiers homeless after the war, hoboes and bindlestiffs, all the highball wonders and freight car marvels.

The continent shuttled them up and down on its iron miles and good riddance too, while it went about its business, which that year included a little joker called the Volstead Act. Congress passed the Act and Prohibition moved out of the fat dictionary to become a new household word: the word with a dozen meanings. To the politicians, prohibition meant votes; to the pious old WCTU ladies, it was a vision of God with a glass of root beer in His hand; to the old-time brewers and whiskey distillers, it spelled bankruptcy or readjustment depending on how realistic they were. To the gangsters in the big cities, it would be the luckiest of lucky rabbit feet. Prohibition! With it they would kick open the door behind which the big dough was waiting.

"I smell money," the Spotter said when the saloons closed down in January 1920, and he'd grinned like a pale and half-starved cat left by mistake in a fish store.

The Badgers had been limping along on a little holdup money, a little whore money, a little gambling money. This prohibition was a gold rush! In the first wild days with every second man in town peddling alky and every second cop finding out how good it was to have his palm greased regularly, Spotter Boyle and Clip Haley opened their first speakeasy. Within three months, they were operating close to a dozen speaks, making their own gin and cutting the honest stuff. Five hundred bucks bought a still that could make fifty to a hundred gallons a day. Since the government permitted the manufacture and sale of industrial alcohol, what was to stop an up-and-coming bootlegger from hiring himself a chemist to extract the undrinkable elements such as wood alky? Since near beer was legal, and the only way to make near beer was to make real beer and then remove the alcohol, what was to stop an up-and-coming beer baron from seeing to it that the alky wasn't removed?

Wild days, with everybody in town breaking an ankle to get on the pie-wagon. A shot of bootleg whiskey fetched as high as a buck, and even at two bits the speakeasy prop wasn't losing. All the loss was in the customer's pocketbook, not to mention his stomach.

"Seven's my lucky number," Clip Haley had tooted when he and the Spotter opened their seventh speak. Clip'd bought a box of cigars and, drunk as a coot, he skipped up and down Eighth Avenue, passing the stogies out free to every cop he bumped into. Afterwards, when the Spotter'd asked him, "How come?" Clip explained fuzzily about cheap grafters. The Spotter left him alone, and Clip, with money to burn and two or three dames holding the match for him, was a hundred percent satisfied.

The Spotter watched Clip's antics with a cold eye. The trouble with Clip, the Spotter thought as he lay sleeplessly in his room at the Hotel Berkeley where he'd just moved, was that Clip was still a rough-housing Badger at heart, okay with the fists, but not so good on the headwork.

In his dark hotel room, the Spotter would grin mockingly at his doctor's advice to relax. Yeh, relax. Okay, so he wasn't touching a drop of booze and the Ziegeld Follies could march naked into his bedroom without getting more than a whistle from him. So he was in bed by midnight, okay, okay, okay. But tell that to the Bum Ticker, the Spotter thought. Someone had to do the headwork. How many quarts of whiskey were needed for the speak on Thirty-Ninth? For the speak on Forty-First? On Forty-Second, Forty-Fifth, Forty-Eighth? How much whiskey, gin, beer? How was their supply? With ten speaks operating, that meant a payroll of close to thirty guys. That meant figuring payroll money besides booze money and protection money.

By the fourth month of prohibition, the Spotter knew he had to get himself a partner if he didn't want to put down a deposit on a coffin. So when Tom Quinn, the ex-saloon-keeper, approached him, the Spotter who wasn't superstitious thought, "Somebody must care about my lousy ticker."

He couldn't have found a better man. Quinn had come over from Ireland in the steerage, swung a pick and shovel, worked himself up to a bartender with a handlebar mustache, saved his money to become the owner of a gild-edge saloon on Eighth Avenue. With prohibition, Tom Quinn had temporarily retired to see as he put it, "How the wind was blowin.'"

"You an' me, Spotter," the ex-saloon-keeper declared, "Can make ourself a good penny. Every Tom, Dick and Harry're makin' an easy penny but the lion's share'll go into the pockets of the boys with the connections. All we want's our share of the Kitchen."

It was one big Hell's Kitchen, five avenues wide, with Twelfth Avenue fronting on the Hudson River, then Eleventh, Tenth, Ninth and Eighth Avenues, the sidestreets numbered as regularly as the avenues. Over on Seventh Avenue, the wreckers were carting away the tenements, twenty-story garment lofts rising on the rubble; a building boom to match the drinking boom, with Broadway the drinking headquarters for a whole nation. "Broadway, we won't even try to break into," Tom Quinn said to the Spotter. "All we wants our share of the Kitchen and that won't be no leadpipe cinch neither." For there was Ownie Madden bootlegging, and Ownie had for a lawyer a slim good-looking smart Irishman by name of Jimmy Walker: that same Jimmy would be elected Mayor of New York. Arrested fifty-seven times, Ownie'd broken parole fifty-seven times and the wise boys down the West Side said with a wink that there must be two kinds of parole. "One kind the coppers hound you all the time. The other kind's the Ownie Madden kind with the coppers kissing your ass and thanking you for the honor." Besides Ownie, there was Larry Fay and Waxey Gorden and Big Bill Dwyer, the exlongshoreman: that same Big Bill would get to be the biggest bootlegger in the whole country for a while, with offices on Lexington Avenue, with a corruptions department in charge of paying off old friends and influencing new ones, a traffic department with experts in trucks and speedboats, a police department where bullets kept the chisellers in line.

Wild days! The old-time gangs moved wholesale into bootlegging. Mugs who thought Chile came in bottles became authorities on St. Pierre and Miquelon off Newfoundland from where the whiskey boats sailed to anchor off the Long Island and Jersey coasts. The bootleggers landed their whiskey, transferred it to trucks and if they weren't hijacked—that was a new word too—they had themselves a truckload of dough. If they were hijacked, they could recoup with somebody else's whiskey. NEW BOOTLEGGER KILLING, the papers reported, while a thirsty nation growled: "Whose business is it anyway if a man wants a drink on Saturday night?"

The Spotter and his new partner Tom Quinn doubled their speaks in Hell's Kitchen. Quinn knew the politicians, he knew the cops and he took over the job of keeping everybody happy. A fiver took care of the cop in the street, a tenner satisfied the sergeant, a captain had to have a weekly C-note and a fed had to be inhuman to resist a cool grand. Every few months the plainclothes lads were switched around, but the new men flew to the easy money with the instinct of homing pigeons. "I've got to make a pinch," Quinn's friends among the feds would confide in the most confidential of whispers, "so get yourself ready." And Quinn'd speak to the Spotter who would order his boys to drag a bum off the street.

"Any bum. Shave the bastid, stick him in a clean suit and bring 'm up this flat on Forty-Fourth."

The bum would become the owner, the raid'd come off, the feds'd get their man, and the owner'd become a bum again with plenty of time in the clink to mull over the mistakes of a lifetime.

"It pays to be smart," all the smart boys agreed as they communed with their souls which, like their cash, they kept snug and safe in their wallets.

"The speakeasy's here to stay like your whorehouse," the cinderbed prophets preached in the hobo jungles as Joey listened. "If you stiffs was smart, which you ain't or you wouldn't be stiffs, you'd be highballin' to L.A. or Chicago and get yourself on the gravy train."

"The Spotter must be in it," Joey had said to Georgie. "Bet he sent us six telegrams to come back only the shacks tore 'em up."

Georgie didn't go for this kind of talk, staring uneasily like a faithful dog at the sullen-faced kid with the gray eyes.

Joey'd had plenty of time for thinking on the road. He knew now what the Spotter'd meant about being tough and smart. He'd been smart to holler out the name of Johnny Murtagh, but dumb when he'd given the sheenies his real name, and even dumber telling the Spotter what'd happened. A real smart guy would've kept his big trap shut. Yeah! Being tough was no good without being smart. And there was no depending on luck, Joey brooded. Luck could be sliced two ways, good or bad. His luck'd been bad when that damn sheeny'd popped in out of nowhere to spoil the stickup. That was when a guy had to be smart when the luck was n.g. He'd been smart, but not smart enough, and this hoboing was the dumbest of the dumb.

"We oughta go home," Joey began urging Georgie.

"We ain't seen everything yet," Georgie'd protested.

Joey'd smiled. Georgie's brains must be drying up, he'd thought. Christ, what was there to see? More railroad yards, more railroad bulls?

They turned east in May, panhandled in Dallas, fought off five jockos in a St. Louis flop who wanted their white skin, stole a suitcase in Chicago whose contents fetched a dollar and a half at a hockshop, paid over that same dollar and a half to a South Side bootlegger for a pint without a label described as "real Canadian whiskey." That was hoboing for you, Joey thought in the clackety freights, everything happening and nothing happening, and he'd been doing it close to a year. Christ, about time he became smart. Like the Spotter!

YOUNG DEMOCRATS CLUB, the sign said. It was a big sign stretching clear across four windows on the second floor of a tenement in Fortieth Street between Ninth and Tenth Avenues. From inside an upholstery shop on the ground floor, the upholsterer squinted at the two kids out on the sidewalk looking up at the sign. A hulking kid and a kid with shaggy dark blond hair, wearing hockshop specials for coats. The upholsterer hadn't ever seen this pair before, but he cursed them anyway and cursed the club above his store, and prohibition that'd brought the club, and the whole country that was going to the dogs.

Georgie pointed up at the YOUNG DEMOCRATS sign. "What the hell's that?"

"Nothin'. They're the same old Badgers. Only with a different name," Joey assured him. "Don't you worry Georgie. The Spotter'll roll out the red carpet."

The street was darkening, the first lights blinking yellow, and Georgie felt about as big as the coins in his pocket where a lonely quarter was rubbing against a thinner dime. Georgie felt like thirty-five cents, no more, no less. "Red carpet," Georgie muttered. "Don't be such a wise guy—"

"Green carpet then," Joey retorted and asked himself what he was waiting for. A half hour ago, at Brenner's pool parlor, an old Badger hangout, they'd met some of the guys who'd given them the lowdown. How the gang was rolling in four-leaf clovers these days, how Clip Haley'd been found with a bullet through the back of his head, how Tom Quinn'd stepped into Clip's shoes. "Frig 'em!" Joey said and he walked toward the vestibule.

They went up to the second floor. The voices of the Young Democrats seemed to break out from behind the closed door to come on the run to meet them. They stepped into a room full of faces half of whom they didn't know from a hole in the ground, with even the old Badger faces on the strange side.

"Hey, Bug, wanna see somethin'?" Billy Muhlen hollered at the sight of them.

Georgie and Joey smiled as only hoboes can smile at the faces in a crowd they hope won't yell for the cops. Billy Muhlen shook hands with them. But Bughead Moore, a grin as cold as a railroad bull's on his lips, ordered the Badgers to back up. What for? they wanted to know, and he told them, grinning. "I'm the street cleanin' inspector." He was wearing a light blue suit that did everything but scream. He inspected the kids' broken shoes and ragged coats, announcing to his audience, "Yuh can see they pulled up in the flea express!"

Georgie laughed with the others, but Joey couldn't even force a smile to his lips. "The Spotter in?" he asked.

"Look who wants the Spotter!" Bughead clowned. "They think all they haffta do is show their maps." He sniffed at Georgie. "Here yuh got a flea what's a mick flea, and this one here's one of them kosher fleas...."

Kosher.... Almost he'd forgotten. On the road, that secret mark branded on his heart had faded in the hammering of wheel on rail. Christ, Joey thought, he'd been away all right and the friggen Bug was king of the hill. "We wanna see Spotter and not his errand boy," he said, not caring now if he was dumb or smart, answering with his heart, with his blood, in a fury that drained the color out of his cheeks.

The color he had lost washed, so it seemed, onto Bughead's reddening face. "Okay, jewboy," Bughead jeered. "Come back at ten yuh wanna see the Spotter, but don't bring no rabbi."

This time Joey controlled himself.

At the Forty-Second Street Automat, they spent Georgie's thirty-five cents on two pots of Boston baked beans, and bread and butter and coffee. They stayed on awhile. When the manager eyed them, they left in a hurry, losing themselves in the Times Square crowd. Georgie, still hungry, said they should've dumped a bottle of catsup into a bowl of hot water—hot water for tea was free at the Automat—and had themselves some tomato soup. Joey answered he wouldn't wash his feet in that kind of tomato soup and besides the Spotter wouldn't let them down.

They were back at the club before ten. A card game was on, the smoke of cigarettes winding in broken bluish chains between the players and the hangers-on. Bughead, without a word, led them out of the front room into a corridor over to a closed door. He knocked, and the last they saw of him was his grin floating behind as if disembodied.

Spotter Boyle smiled when they entered. He was sitting at a roll-top desk in a small room, once a bedroom, the walls painted green, with a gauze-draped Turkish beauty adorning the calendar of a bygone year. It was the same old Spotter, Joey thought with a relief so great he felt dizzy when the Spotter in a friendly voice asked what the trouble was with Bughead.

"I let'm get under my skin," Joey admitted. "I was dead wrong, Spotter," he whipped himself. "Just a sap. He said I was a kosher flea so I got sore and called him an errand boy."

The Spotter lit a cigarette and then offered the pack to the two kids. "Hoboin' didn't hurt you guys," he said. "You look strong enough to hitch to a wagon." They laughed. "I guess you want work," he said wearily. "You worked with Bughead before. You'll work with him again, okay?"

"Bughead's O.K. We can work with him," Joey said.

The Spotter laughed appreciatively. "You're a natcheral born assemblyman, Joey, 'cept when you blow your top." He fished a tenner out of his wallet. "Get yourself a room and a meal. This name-callin' gotta stop, Joey. I don't give a damn if a guy's a chink so long as he works for me. I gotta Jew runnin' a speak for me around the corner. My lawyer's a Jewish guy."

"I was a sap, Spotter."

"You oughta know," the Spotter said quick as a knife thrust, and then he added reflectively, "You're no sap, kiddo. Don't try and fool the ol' Spotter. And remember this. Bughead's got a grudge against you maybe, but grudges don't mean a damn until one of the guys takes a baseball bat to the other guy."

"Yeh."

"Okay now, Joey?"

"Maybe I shouldn't ask, but what happened with Johnny Murtagh and the Dusters?"

"Forget it, kiddo. This guy Volstead, he took care of everything."

When the voice behind the speakeasy door said, "Who's there?" Bughead answered, "We usta go to Gilroy's." Behind him stood his delegation of strongarms, Ted Griffin, Georgie Connelly and Joey Kasow.

Gilroy's had been a corner saloon on Forty-Fifth and Ninth, with two elk heads over the bar. The elk heads were in a second-hand furniture store now and Gilroy's patrons had scattered among a half dozen neighborhood speaks like this speak, up three flights of tenement stairs. "We hit the joints that don't use our protection and rough 'em up," Bughead Moore had explained to the ex-hoboes.

"Anybody from Gilroy's okay," the voice greeted, throwing out the welcome mat.

The door opened and all four Young Democrats piled through before the door-watcher could catch a second breath.

He edged away from the door, a middle-aged man with hanging jowls like flaps of pinkish leather. But his eyes, round and still in his head, didn't even show a glint of surprise as if long ago he'd become used to the idea of being cornered by fast-moving muscles.

"O'Hara, you bastid!" Bughead said with a wide grin and hustled him from the kitchen into the flat's front room. There, slowly turning his blonde cannonball of a head on his shoulders, the neckless Bug sized things up.

In the front room, absolutely neutral, five or six customers sat at almost as many tables. Those tables were a bargain-lot bought second-hand and the customers looked as if they'd come along in a second lot; two dock wallopers at a battered walnut table near the drawn window shades; a couple of neighborhood boys, caps on their heads at a wire-legged table whose best days had been spent in an ice cream parlor; an old fellow with a medium ripe plum for a nose drinking all by his lonesome.

"Beat it, you guys!" Bughead ordered O'Hara's customers. "There's gonna be a padlock on this joint in an hour."

"O'Hara—" the old fellow began when the Bug shouted him deaf and dumb. "Doncha unnerstan' no English!"

Plum Nose drained the last drop of whiskey in his glass; all the customers tilted their glasses. O'Hara's speak emptied like a pot of water heaved through a fire-escape window.

"What've I done to you?" O'Hara asked as if he felt he should say something, no matter what.

The Bug sneered. "Runs a speak in our territory and what's he done?"

"I can't afford no pertection. Take a look for yourself."

They all looked around at O'Hara's hole-in-the-wall proposition, with O'Hara the sole prop and chief bartender. O'Hara had been a foreman in a shut-down brewery. On the skids, now, O'Hara.

"You pay the cops doncha?" the Bug stated.

"Everybody pays the cops."

"Maybe you pay Ownie Madden?" The Bug winked at his silent strongarms and Joey thought, this was the Bug's speed. Putting the pins and needles into a guy licked before he started.

"Not a dime I swear to Christ. Only pertection I pay's the cops."

"You're in our territory, O'Hara," the Bug said and he was on O'Hara like a ten-ton truck. He was grinning, for there was nothing the Bug loved better than breaking noses and bottles. O'Hara would supply both tonight.

O'Hara retreated to the wall. "For Christ sake," he pleaded.

The Bug socked him one in the gut; his second punch caught O'Hara flush in the face. O'Hara fell. The Bug kicked him in the knee, aiming the boot with a surgeon's eye. O'Hara would have a gimpy leg tomorrow.

Ted, Georgie and Joey'd already headed for the kitchen; in the tenement speaks the kitchens were the liquor storerooms. Ted swung a closet door open. On the top shelf eight or nine bottles of whiskey stood in two rows like good soldiers. Georgie reached up. A bottle in each hand, he dashed over to the sink, smashed them against the faucets. "Wow!" Georgie chanted, Wow!" Joey, investigating the icebox, pulled out a jug of home brewed beer. "Lemme bust it!" Georgie called, grinning. Joey passed him the jug, Georgie smashed it, and the dark furry smell of beer mixed with the smell of the spilled whiskey. "Georgie!" Ted said. "Here y'are." He tossed over a bottle from the closet. "Fly ball, Georgie!"

When they returned to the front room the Bug was resting in a chair, his knife-edged trousers lifted high over his socks. A few inches from the points of his pointy yellow shoes, O'Hara's hands lay like rags on the floor. O'Hara was bleeding, a trickle of blood in a thin red ribbon seemed pasted to his lips. Even Georgie stopped grinning while Joey wondered what that damn Bug'd been up to alone in the room with O'Hara.

The Bug got up, he kicked aimlessly at the man on the floor, without any real interest like a kid about to throw away the dead mouse he'd been torturing. "We gotta coupla more of these bastids t'night," the Bug said lazily.

Georgie was staring, fascinated, at the man on the floor. Ted Griffin, the ex-pug said, "Wunna these days you'll kill wunna these guys, Bug."

"Maybe yuh wanna kiss his fanny?"

"Sure, like this!" Joey walked to the unconscious man. He kicked savagely at the flabby buttocks. Damn, he'd give the Bug something to blab about to the Spotter. Show them all, the whole damn clubhouse, the whole damn world. He fought down the sick feeling in the pit of his stomach; he turned around.

They were all looking at him: Joey's face could have been chipped out of the slategray sidewalks three flights down from O'Hara's wrecked speak.

Joey Kasow had made up his mind to be smart from this time out. Like a batter who has swung and missed, he was warier now as he stood waiting for the next pitch.

With fate in the pitcher's box. And no guessing how many chances a man would get in a lifetime. For many, one strike was out, while others, luckier, might be offered a round dozen.

Joey Kasow was taking no chances. "You gotta be smart even in the lil things," Joey explained to his sidekick Georgie when they moved out of their furnished room in a FOR MEN ONLY hotel on Forty-Second and Tenth, into a big furnished place in a Chelsea brownstone on Twenty-Fourth off Eighth right smack in the middle of Hudson Duster territory. "We don't wanna be near our dumb family, Georgie. Suppose we bump into 'em and they start askin' questions and maybe squawkin' to the coppers."

"Let 'em squawk," Georgie'd replied. "We eighteen or ain't we eighteen?"

"We ain't legal 'til we're twenty-one," Joey had answered sagely, if mistakenly, as if he spent all his spare time in a lawyer's office.

"Yeh, I guess you're right," Georgie'd said, impressed.

Their first furnished room had been a rathole, so small that Joey used to say, "No deep breathin' or we'll go through the damn walls, Georgie!" But that was in the spring after they'd just gotten in again with the gang and only rated a fiver for a night's work. By fall they were drawing a steady fifty bucks a week whether they worked or not. To the ex-hoboes, it was a regular fortune. Their room rent on Twenty-Fourth was six bucks a week, meals another couple bucks a day. Up at the Young Democrats there was often a keg of free beer, and Bughead didn't mind when they salvaged a bottle of whiskey out of some roughed-up speak. "Only don't be a hog," the Bug would warn his strongarms, a quart in each of his overcoat pockets, with a third quart under an armpit. Fifty bucks was big, especially in the beginning.

After a while, what with new clothes and dames who had to be paid in advance, that fifty was running like a racehorse out of their pockets. A smart guy got himself fixed up with private stuff, Joey began to think, as he listened to the guys bragging up at the club.

"This ginzo girl lives on Thirty-Nint! Her ole man thought she was gonna be strict. What a joke!"

"Thas nothin! I gotta girl never been with no guy except me."

Seemed that all of them, with the exception of Joey Kasow, had a private little dame somewhere. A girl who was no top-of-the-roof special, a girl one hundred percent clean until yours truly had stepped into sight, in a suit and tie and socks the color of a rainbow. In those loud duds, like birds slick in their plumage, they pecked away with greedy beaks.

Oh, the good girls, the good girls. There were no in-betweens down the West Side. A girl was either a whore or she was up on a pedestal a million miles high, wearing a snowcloud for a coat and burglar-proof locks at her buttonholes. And maybe that was why it was such a stunt to pull a good girl down into the gutter. As if there was a gold medal in it from The Society of Madames and Pimps, Inc.

All of Joey's girls had been everybody else's girls. Girls of the line-ups, dopey Doras, bitchos on wheels. Love? That was a word in a song at the vaudeville. A guy had to have a girl just as he had to eat or sleep, about summed up Joey's philosophy. But now that he was eating regular, he was thinking it made no sense making the whores rich.

Love? A song, a laugh....

On a November day, Joey left their room, a cigarette slanting out of his mouth, two suits on his arm, one Georgie's and one his own. He swaggered down the street, into the tailor shop near Ninth where they were bringing their clothes. The tailor raised his face from a pair of trousers he was mending. Joey hadn't ever seen him before. "Where's the tailor?" Joey asked.

"I buy the biz'ness from Mister Goldfarb," the man said. "Sadie," he called. The curtain in the rear of the store parted, a girl hurried toward them and the tailor bent to his stitching. It was as if he had dropped through a hole in the floor. Did he have reddish hair too; was the fuzz on his bald head reddish? He was gone where the work-worn and middle-aged go. The girl was young and pretty and redhaired. Joey stared at her. Against the dark blue serges, the chestnut browns, the iron grays of the pressed suits hanging on a long iron rod, her long hair, coiled around her head, glinted, a glinting red crown.

He'd seen a hundred prettier girls on the streets of Chelsea. But there was something flukey about this one that puzzled him. Then her downcast eyes, her lips too tightly closed reminded him of the way the nuns looked when you tried to catch their eye. Nuns? Joey had to smile at the idea of a nun by the name of Sadie. Sadie, the cherry, he thought, a virgin. A trap door in his mind opened and the street talk and the street superstitions flooded into his consciousness. The Jewish girls, the Jewish girls, they were built tighter, they were softer, they layed like dinges, they layed cold as icebergs.

"Press them suits good, will you, Sadie," he smiled.

He saw the color of her eyes now as they flashed at him, reddish-brown and round and indignant.

"Don't you want me to call you Sadie?" he asked innocently.

The tailor was peering up at this customer. Another boy who wasn't a boy. Another loafer dressed in the middle of the afternoon like for a wild party. "Give the receipt Sadie," he muttered.

"Yes, papa." She reached for a pad on the counter while Joey watched that moving hand of hers, slim and quick and covered with the palest of freckles. "The name, mister?"

"Don't call me mister, Sadie. Make that receipt out to Joey. Just Joey."

And that was how he began with Sadie Madofsky. That was how all the guys began with the good girls in the neighborhood. Georgie would discover her for himself. "Boy, Joey, that's some redhead down the Jew tailor!" All Joey had said then was, "She's okay, but that ole man of hers wouldn't let you get within a mile." That was more truth than poetry. Madofsky the tailor had an eagle eye on him like a honest detective's, soured at the price of being honest in a crooked world. Madofsky the tailor had never gotten used to hearing what he called "gangsters and bummers" joking with his sixteen-year-old daughter.

Besides, Joey wouldn't have admitted his interest in Sadie Madofsky for a hundred in cold cash. Not to Georgie, not to any of the guys. And have them razzing him! Christ, that's all he needed—the old razz about jewboys falling for jewgirls.

Falling? So far all he'd done was give Sadie a big smile if she happened to be in the store when he picked up his pressed suits. Anyway, he was too busy to break his neck over any hard-to-get dame. There were plenty of pick-ups, the speaks were lousy with them. The trouble with those whiskey lushes was that buying them a good time came to more money than a flying trip to a whore house. He started going with a waitress. But she was the original Miss Need-It: always needing stockings, perfume, even a suitcase. Also, you couldn't exactly call her private stuff.

He noticed that Sadie was never around mornings. "She goes to school?" he asked her father one morning with the politest of smiles that fooled nobody but the headless rows of hanging suits. Madofsky the tailor grunted. Joey persisted, "High school, huh?" And wormed out the information that Sadie attended Washington Irving over on East Sixteenth Street. Now he made it his business to bring in his suits in the late afternoons, and once when her father wasn't within hearing, he whispered, "Suppose I meet you at Washington Irving some day?" The girl blushed, shaking her head angrily, but that week he was waiting for her, laughing to see her cheeks redden. It was the cherry in her, he thought with pleasure and anticipation.

The eyes of her schoolmates darted at the two of them, the blushing girl in a faded dark gray coat, her dress sweeping below the coat line and reaching almost to her ankles, the boy cocky as a street sparrow in a stylish belted overcoat, his hands in gray suede gloves, a gray felt hat cocked over his left ear.

"Gimme those books, Sadie," he smiled.

She clutched them more tightly as if she felt her father's presence in the giggling crowd of school girls. But that embittered and observant eye was on the other side of town, confined to his store where it revolved as if in a second and larger socket. "Mister, please go away," she whispered and walked from him.

He was at her elbow. "How'm I gonna get to know you, Sadie? How about a movin' pitcher tonight? Gee whiz, Sadie, what's the harm?"

He wouldn't let her go home by herself. Together they crossed the roaring avenues and gray spaces of the winter city: Fourth Avenue, Union Square with its crowds arguing about the Russian Bolshevik Lenin who had killed the Czar, Fifth Avenue with its tall buildings of the 1890's. Everywhere, a thousand strangers hurried with them, indifferent to them. They walked west under the Sixth Avenue elevated tracks—a boy too old for his years and a girl without any experience with boys.

At Seventh Avenue she begged him again, "Please, let me alone. Somebody might see us and tell my father. Please, mister."

At that, he nodded and waved good-bye. He stood on the corner, watching her walk down Twenty-Fourth Street. She was like a figure sinking into a four-sided shaft of red brick, gray gutter and gray sky, a girl in a hand-me-down coat, her hair brave and coppery red like the wing of a bird.

"Dames!" he would say contemptuously to Georgie after a night in a side-street joint where a guy could have himself three different kinds of redheads if he wanted.

Sadie Madofsky wouldn't go to a moving picture with him, but he kept on meeting her after school anyway. "Call a cop," he would advise her with a smile. Once he bought a bag of pretzels and when she accepted one after five minutes of urging, he had smiled, thinking that sooner or later he'd have her eating out of his hand.

Outside the big stores on Fourteenth Street the Santa Claus bells tinkled, the clear winter sky hanging like a great blue bell over the Christmas city: a Christmas city and a Jewish girl.

The Jewish girls, the Jewish girls, the street refrain beat inside his head. She could have been Irish with her red hair and short nose, but when she looked at him with sad and fearful eyes, Joey wasn't so sure. It was a look that seemed to come from deep inside of her. Deep down she was Jewish, he had thought; and it's what you are deep down that makes you what you are.

Joey Kasow'd never had a lulu of a thought like that one before. It had shaken him up and he'd wondered about himself with his gray eyes and blondie hair and beak straight as any damn mick's. Straighter, for there were plenty micks with hooked beaks, and big beaks, and micks with black hair like Georgie. What you are deep down.... The thought had whirled through him, hot and red as his own beating blood and then it had vanished, lost in the maze of years in which he had tried to lose the Jew inside. Leaving the faintest and most cynical of smiles on his lips. "Next time I see her," he had decided, "I'll tell her I'm a jewboy too."

"How come you and Joey're buddies?" Bughead Moore was always asking Georgie when they were alone. Once he'd followed Georgie down from the club, catching up with him on the sidewalk. It wasn't late and it wasn't early, around ten o'clock, and they'd walked together toward Ninth Avenue. Far away an approaching El beat a pan of iron against the winter sky. "How come?" the Bug wanted to know.

"I told you a million times. I know Joey since we was kids on Thirty-Seven!"

"Be your age, Georgie. You don't trust them sheenies, do yuh?"

"Nope!" Georgie answered instantly.

"Then what the hell you buddies with Joey?"

They had loitered on the windy corner a minute, smoking cigarettes. A cat glided under the dark El pillars and all was quiet and still in the dark hollow hush of the week before Christmas. Soon the Prince of Peace would be walking the Hell's Kitchen streets again.

"You oughta forget that sheeny, Georgie. You and me, we could be buddies."

"I thought we wuz buddies—"

"Hell you thought! I mean real buddies."

"I thought we wuz real buddies—"

The Bug spat disgustedly and Georgie said to wait a minute. He went over to a penny chewing-gum machine in front of a candy store, inserted a penny in the slot, returned with two balls of colored gum. "I like this kinda chung-gum better'n the slicey kind," Georgie declared, offering the Bug his choice.

The Bug accepted one of the colored balls and shot it out into the gutter like a marble. "You're dumb, Georgie, but you ain't that dumb! I hate a guy what plays dumb, Georgie."

But when Joey heard the latest on Bug, he'd only laughed and repeated the Spotter's words of advice. "Grudges don' mean a damn 'til one of the guys takes a baseball bat to the other guy."

"He ain't called Bughead for nothin', Joey. One of these days, he'll get drunk and go bugs on you."

"Yeh?" And Joey added mysteriously, "Don't forget, Georgie, there's more'n one way to skin a cat."

He swung that same skinned cat when he was with Sadie. "Sure, I'm Jewish. I'm not foolin' you." Joey was glad she didn't believe him. Her surprised face reminded him of the two East Side gamblers who also hadn't believed him.

"You don't look Jewish," Sadie said.

"What about yourself? All that red hair and freckles! Wanna hear me talk Jewish? *Ich bin Yiddish wie du.*" I am Jewish like you, he had said and continued glibly, "I'm no *goy*, Sadie, just 'cause I live among 'em. Now with Christmas it oughta be *Chanukah*, too. *Rosh Hashona, Pesach!*" he named the great Jewish holidays; the Feast of Light and New Year and Passover. The holiday candles of his father's house shone in his mind, magnified a thousandfold by the golden office windows of the city. His father and mother and brother and sister leaped in his mind like candlelight, so that in a voice that was both remembering and mocking, Jew and Jew-hater, he said, "My mother's *gefillte* fish, yeh. Your mother make *gefillte* fish, Sadie?"

"My mother's dead."

That day, as he lingered on the corner as she went on by herself, the faint smile on his lips was like that of an old man. He stared after her, thinking he was using the old bean sure enough. His smile widened, predatory now, the smile of guys on a corner undressing every dame passing by. His eyes shifted from Sadie's red hair, to her hips and legs, to her hair again and with an animal joy he asked himself if she had red hair all over. Yah!

The Jewish girls, the redhaired Jewish girls....

She still protested when he met her. He smiled away her arguments. Even if her father was strict, did he have to know everything? Here she was going to school, working in the store, keeping house. Didn't she have a right to a little fun, what harm was there in a moving picture? She could say she was seeing a friend, one of the girls at Washington Irving.

Oh, the Jewish girls, the Jewish girls.... They could be dumb like any other kind, he was thinking. Here she was, sixteen and in high school, but she didn't have the brains of a fly. When he said his family lived out in Chicago, she believed him. When she asked him what his job was in New York and he said he worked in a warehouse, she believed him. When he said he'd written his mother about Sadie and his mother'd written back he should go out with a nice Jewish girl like her, she believed him.

The lonely have no other alternative in life but to believe.

The strong believe only in their strength. Joey was certain he'd get her—and not only Sadie—but anything else he wanted. As if courage and cunning were a pair of unbeatable dukes. Had he tasted his vomit on the floor of an East Side gambling joint? Chewed the green bile of fear? Sweated at the flashlight of a railroad shack, tightened his belt after kissing another meal good-bye, stared hungrily at women who didn't see him for dirt—the dirt and dust of the road that had covered him from head to foot? He was eighteen, with twice eighteen lives....

And the Spotter, with no such illusions, lay in his dark bed at the Hotel Berkeley, scheming up new schemes, always figuring, a bookkeeper whose numbers were men.

Early that December, the Spotter'd about decided to use some of his boys—Bughead, Joey, Georgie, a couple others—in a hijacking job. Ordinarily the Spotter was leery of hijackings. Even if you got away clean, it meant killing the truckdriver and maybe the guard with him. It meant cops asking questions, for a killing brought them buzzing like flies to a stiff. It meant riling up the gang who'd lost the load of booze. But when you get a real hot tip, what can a guy do? Fifty thousand bucks in wet money, ninety proof Canadian, was coming down in trucks from outside of Albany, fifty thousand in each and every truck. Booze for the Christmas trade. The Spotter had his tip from a federal who'd gumshoed the backroads upstate and uncovered the new route being used by Big Bill Dwyer's gang. This particular fed was earning eighteen hundred a year, he was married, with two kids. The Spotter paid him a thousand cash down, with another fifteen hundred promised if the hijacking came off okay.

From around the curve, the headlights of the truck opened two tunnels of white light in the darkness. Joey blinked, he was sitting at the wheel of a flivver inside a rutted side road. "Count to four or five when you see their lights," the Bug had said. "Gotta make it look real. Like you just come along and got yourself stuck like you was a hick farmer yourself." One, Joey counted. Two, three, Joey counted, the numbers springing into his mind, cut out of white light. Four, he counted. FIVE, and one two three four five, he drove out onto the main road, shutting off his gas, the truck roaring down at him, enormous, his heart swelling too fast in his chest like a balloon some immense mouth had suddenly inflated. Not fifteen feet away the truck braked to a stop, Joey hurled himself from the flivver's seat to the floor, while the bursting noise of shotguns boomed and the metal split of pistols washed across his breaking nerves.

Georgie ran across the road to the flivver. "Joey, you aw right? Joey Joey?"

"Yeh," he said shakily, rising from the floor, hearing the huge blast of silence after gunfire.

"I got the driver!" Georgie boasted excitedly as if he'd been hunting deer. Joey watched the Bug yelling orders in the light of the truck's headlights—the son-afabitch, Joey thought. In that white inhuman glare, they were dragging the bodies of the truckdriver and the guard into the brush. Joey thought of how he'd been a sitting duck in that flivver, a damn decoy. If the luck'd gone against him, if....

Forty minutes later, the hijacked truck crawled into an unused barn belonging to a farmer recommended by the federal with the hot tip. The Spotter's boys piled out of their sedan, walked into the farmhouse. It was warm inside, the potbellied stove a cherry red, the kerosene lamps shedding a mild golden light. To Joey, it was all a crazy pipedream. This farm dropping out of the middle of nowhere. The farmer and his wife bringing in platters of fried eggs and potatoes and pots of coffee, and then the woman following her husband upstairs as if she were used to having her home overrun every second night in the week by racketeers from the city.

"Spotter's got things organized good," Joey said and lit himself another cigarette. He was feeling a little better now although he was still hearing echoes of the night's gunfire.

"You bet!" Ted Griffin agreed and for a second the Spotter, a hundred odd miles away, walked into all their thoughts: Spotter the organizer, the leader of the racket. They sat down at the table, ate. The Bug, his jaws champing on a huge mouthful of egg and potato, winked at Ted Griffin. Ted followed the Bug outside, they returned with six bottles of Canadian whiskey.

"One for each-a you," the Bug said magnanimously. "We got plenty time to kill in this dump...." They started drinking the good Canadian stuff. Georgie produced a deck of cards and all six of the Spotter's boys began playing poker.

They had tossed their overcoats onto a battered red sofa, but they still wore their hats on their heads. Cigarettes drooping out of their mouths, they looked as if they had no home anywhere, this farmhouse some kind of queer railroad station where the whiskey was served in bottles. Time ticked off in a shuffle of cards.

The Bug, fortified with close to a pint of straight whiskey, said to Joey who'd just lost a pot, "I like to see you lose," the Bug announced, an honest drunk who deserved and got an honest laugh.

"Can't always win," Joey said.

"Shut up, jewboy!" the Bug yelled suddenly, showing his hate for all of them to see like a blackjack in his hand. The Bug's eyes were gone between his squinched-up narrowed lids, his broad face throwing off a heat as intense as that of the potbelly stove.

"Aw, Bug, lay off," Georgie said.

The Bug cursed him. "Yuh good-for-nothin' mick!"

Killigan smiled at the Bug; a careful smile guaranteed to arouse no anger. "I was goin' to drive tonight. The last minute you said Joey should. He done good. Let's have a drink, Bug, and forget it."

The Bug said nothing. They all liked Killigan whom they called Sarge because he'd been in the war. Killigan was older than any of them, and now as the Bug remained silent, Georgie and Lefty and Ted began to get their hopes up.

"Hell!" said the Bug. "The jewboy's gotta lotta buddies t'night!" He pushed back his chair, rising, and suddenly he seemed to have gained not only his own height but some huge stature. His head lowered on his chest, a rock. The jacket of his double-breasted blue suit wrapped around a body that could have been a solid cake of ice.

"Bug—" Killigan tried to say.

"Go to hell!" The Bug swung around, confronting Joey who was still seated at the table, his cards exposed before him, their faces up. Three jacks—they hadn't done much for Joey tonight. "Get out!" the Bug said.

"Lissen, Bug—"

"Yuh heard me! Get out!"

"The Spotter won't like it—"

"Never mind the Spotter, jewboy! Get out!"

Killigan spoke, Georgie said something, but what they said blew away like smoke, less than smoke as the Bug pulled his gun from its armpit holster. "Get out!" he shouted at Joey, and grinned with a clownish and cunning hatred. "Wasn't he once a hobo?" he asked everybody and nobody. "Walk back to Noo Yawk! Hit the road, jewboy!"

Sarge Killigan said, "Bug—" Georgie said, "Bug—" And that was all they said. The swinging point of the gun knocked all the rest of what they wanted to say down their throats. Ted Griffin, the ex-pug, stayed where he was and Lefty with the black patent-leather hair looked as if he were off in Hoboken somewhere. The Bug's gun, the Bug's roving eye, the Bug's reputation had them all licked.

"Put a leg on!" the Bug ordered Joey.

Joey walked to the sofa for his overcoat, wishing to God he had a gun cached in his pocket. A gun anywhere! Oh, he'd been kidding himself about the Bug. He, the smart guy, and Georgie the dumb guy! Georgie was right! The Bug hadn't been given his name for nothing. When the little screw broke in the Bug's head, the bugs had to come out, and the Spotter didn't count, nothing counted. Except a gun. Joey dug his overcoat out from among the pile on the sofa, swearing to himself he'd get himself a gun first thing.

"Don't pick no pockets!" the Bug clowned, drunk with his own humor, a mad funny man. He said, "That jewboy'd pick his old man's pants, pick his old lady's drawers!"

Joey dropped his overcoat. He pivoted slowly on his heel, he looked at the Bug, seeing Ganzer the gambler, seeing no man's face, seeing a man with a gun. And the possibilities flicked before him like so many hidden cards all the same kind: the ace of spades. Knuckle down, he thought. What else could he do? Nobody'd blame him. The Spotter'd be with him. But knuckle down once, meant knuckle down twice. Meant the Bug'd be on his neck for keeps, meant the Bug'd always be yapping jewboy. Yellow jewboy, yellow.... "Without that gun you couldn't make me get out," he heard himself saying.

The Bug rushed to Sarge Killigan and passed him the gun, passed away the iron ruler he'd held over all their heads. Right away Sarge Killigan shouted, "Now let's cut out all this stuff, Bug!" And Georgie shouted, "Bug, you're twice Joey's size!" And Ted Griffin jumped to his feet, "Georgie's right!" And even the silent Lefty said, "Yeh!"

The Bug spun around, sneering at his critics. "He asked for it, didn't he?"

"Yeh, I asked for it!" Joey heard himself saying and didn't believe he was speaking. For how could a guy sell himself out? He knew he didn't have the ghost of a chance against the Bug, but he couldn't back out now, he couldn't be yellow now.

"Joey!" Georgie protested.

"I asked for it," Joey said. "Damn right!"

They were all on their feet. Nobody stepped between the Bug and Joey. Only Georgie grabbed at Joey's elbow to stop him from fighting. Joey shook him off.

This night, the stakes were bigger than all the money on the table. And he had to play. There was no quitting in this fight of a lifetime: Joey Kasow, A Regular Guy vs Joey Kasow, The Yellow Jewboy. The whole damn mob was going to know once and for all he wasn't scared of nobody, not even of the Bug.

"You're gonna get a kiss of this," the Bug grinned and lifted his fist. If a screw had broken in his head, it'd mended in jig time for the Bug now stripped out of his jacket and vest. Clothes were clothes and no sense wrecking them.

Joey pulled off his own jacket and vest, flung them into the Bug's grinning face. The Bug swatted at the flying cloth, he kicked at the jacket when it fell to the floor. "Jewboy!" the Bug cried. "I'll kill yuh!"

"It ain't fair," Georgie groaned, but nobody heard him. Sarge Killigan, Ted and Lefty were staring intently at the Bug and Joey like fight fans at the bell. The Bug charged, Joey sidestepped, hitting out with his right at the blonde head hurtling by. The Bug wheeled, his cheekbone red from the kid's knuckles and before he could get going again, Joey plunked his right to the Bug's chin. The Bug only grinned as if to say: I'll take all the Sunday punches you can deliver. Lips white, but grinning, the Bug rolled forward slowly like a street grader into Joey's flying fists.

He's too strong, Joey thought in a spasm of self-pity, knowing that sooner or later the Bug'd clip him one.

Clipped he was. He tasted the blood in his mouth and, dizzy, he backed away from the fists swinging a mile a minute. His shoulders touched the wall, and still dizzy from the Bug's haymaker, he forced himself forward, to attack, like a fighter bouncing off the ringside ropes. He caught the Bug on the ear, on the nose. And caught a fist on his own forehead. He sucked in mouthfuls of air he couldn't hold, fighting without breath, feeling his punches floating away from him, light and inconsequential, soap bubbles made out of his knotted fingers. He dodged, he was past the Bug. Safe in the middle of the room, he turned. The Bug was advancing on him like a butcher with two meat cleavers in his fists and himself the meat. For a split tenth of a second, Joey was a detached eye. He couldn't win this fight, this fight was lost before it started. Knew too that Bug'd lick him but the Bug wouldn't be the winner.

Joey swung his right, his left, his right, and the Bug chopped him down. Down he went, down and down....

Joey taking on the Bug in a fair fight made a story and a half. Up at the Young Democrats they batted it around. It traveled on the good old tin-ear express out to the Spotter's speaks, and from there all over the West Side. He wasn't popular, the Bug, and his K.O. of Joey was just what could be expected. But what couldn't be figured was Joey's nerve.

"Joey, he says, 'Put down that gat and fight like a white man!'" the insiders with the inside dope gave it out. And in their enthusiasm they built the Bug up to Jack Dempsey's size, and sliced Joey down to a flyweight.

"That Joey don't weigh a hunerd ten pounds soakin' wet!" And if Joey did scale a hundred and fifty, what the hell was a lousy forty pounds when nobody could deny that Bughead Moore was big as a house, besides being a pain in the neck.

"The Bug's a prize bastid, but I don't want this to go no further," the Spotter said to Joey in his office at the club.

"Better tell that to the Bug, Spotter."

"I told'm! I told'm twice!" the Spotter had emphasized. "I told'm if he even looks cockeyed at you he's through. And that goes for you." And he had looked with those pale eyes of his that rarely saw cockeyed at the quiet kid. "You didn't have a gun on you up there in the sticks, did you, Joey?"

"I don't own no gun, Spotter."

"You're gonna get one now," the Spotter had guessed; and when the kid didn't answer that one, the Spotter said, "I don't blame you, but keep on bein' smart like you were up there in the sticks. You're aces high with everybody so don't spoil it. You come see me out my hotel, Joey. Around eight. Thursday. And don't buy no gun. Let me treat you for Christmas, Joey."

Thursday! Joey walked on air all that week. He couldn't believe his luck. A guy had to be somebody to rate an invite to the Spotter's hotel. And his own gun! When he climbed up the subway stairs to Times Square Thursday night, he almost laughed out loud. The Broadway lights whirled in his sight, a pinwheel of glitter, with himself the center of all brightness. He hurried four blocks north to Forty-Sixth Street, turned up to the Spotter's hotel.

The Hotel Berkeley was another narrow-fronted off-Broadway stone box like a dozen others in the sidestreets between Broadway and Sixth Avenue. Two pillars flanked the entrance, the name of the hotel carved above the door and looking as if it had been borrowed from some mausoleum: BERKELEY. Through the dingy lobby, forgotten schemers and dreamers had flitted on their way to the rooms upstairs; vaudevillians hoping to make the Palace around the corner, actresses seeing their names in lights, gamblers and con-men, and now a kid from a furnished room on Twenty-Fourth Street. On his way, up. Up into the cloudland floating above Broadway.

"This is doctor's prescription whiskey," the Spotter said upstairs in his room, setting the bottle down on the table. "It's been cut, not much, but it's been cut. You haffta go to Montreal for a straight drink. Or gay Paree," the Spotter added, who not so long ago had seen days when he couldn't have raised the fare between New York and Brooklyn. He patted the bottle, a Broadway princeling in his black silk robe, his feet in black slippers. "Help yourself, Joey. I don't drink, you know. God damn doctor's orders."

Joey poured himself a couple of inches, swallowed it in one shot.

"Help yourself!" the Spotter said, studying the kid in the chair before him. He recalled how he'd first brought Joey into the Badgers and how Clip Haley'd beefed. Now Clip was dead and buried, and a lucky break that was, for otherwise the Spotter might've been hiring somebody to get rid of Clip. The Spotter refilled Joey's glass and on the impulse he lifted it to his own lips. He tasted the whiskey, just tasted it, and then passed the glass to Joey. "Don't squeal on me to the doctor," he smiled, but felt a pang like some dark hand pressing down against his heart.

"Joey, I been thinkin' how you handled the Bug," the Spotter said when he was seated in an easy chair. "You done what I would've done. Joey, I gotta gun for you here like I said. And you're gonna be good with it! Remember what you told me—how you fired at that guy over the East Side? Sure, he had a table in front of him, but a good shot would've got him. I gotta phone number for you, Joey. It's a cop, a Jersey cop who's on the payroll of a beer-maker I know in Jersey. This cop, he got his own pistol range in the cellar of his house. He rents it to guys, see?"

Joey nodded and the Spotter continued, "Remember this, Joey. Don't carry your gun 'cept on a job."

When Joey left the Spotter's room, walking under the carven legend BERKELEY, he felt as if he owned the whole damn town. In his jacket pocket, under the cloth of his overcoat he carried his deed of title—written in iron.

But only the Spotter, sleepless in his bed, knew that iron was like any other ink, with all inks fading in the wash of time.

The Spotter couldn't sleep that night for thinking of Joey and as he brooded, his left hand glided under his pajama top to his beating heart. Steady, it beat. Steady, steady. A fake, the Spotter thought: One punch from the Bughead'd be enough to finish me. An old bum like me, worse than an old bum, I'm only thirty-one. Thirty-one and made of paper, my heart bad, my stomach bad, while a kid like Joey goes around shaking off punches like Jack Dempsey himself. Smartest shellacking he ever took, that one from the Bug, he proves to the gang he's game. He's got 'em all behind him. Smart, smart, like me, only I'm smarter than any Jew who ever lived. Okay, he's packing a gun now, just like Al Capone. I give it to him myself and I'll bury him myself if I have to. That Al Capone was nothing 'til Johnny Torrio give him his chance, another tough wop over the East Side, the Five Points gang, and now Al Capone's one of the biggest guys in Chicago, with Johnny Torrio playing second fiddle....

The man in the bed stared into the darkness, this sleepless midnight into which he sank night after night as if in a breathing coffin. Then, the long thin fleshless body under the blanket shook with the silent, the almost silent, laughter of those who cannot sleep nights. The Spotter thought: the trouble with Johnny Torrio, he didn't know how to handle Al Capone, or how to bury Al Capone.

Maybe it was the holiday air, the green fragrance of the Christmas trees for sale on the sidewalks, maybe it was the soft snow blanketing the streets, maybe she was sorry to see Joey's bruised face—"Some gangsters beat me up," he'd told her cunningly. "They tried to rob the warehouse where I work."— maybe it was the lonely winter nights, the white stars glittering lonely too, and yet splendid like the most wonderful of all snowflakes, never-melting, but whatever it was, Sadie Madofsky finally agreed to go to a movie with Joey.

He was waiting for her in front of Cavanagh's steak house on Twenty-Third Street, watching the trollies jangling down Eighth Avenue, the people buying tickets at the Grand Opera House. He whistled joyously, certain he was in the home stretch with that redhead now. So she didn't pet and didn't smoke and ten to one her worst drink was a cup of hot chocolate. And tonight she had to be home by ten from the girl friend she was supposed to be visiting.

For her kind the Spotter's boys had a sure-fire treatment. Rape, the coppers described it in their books. And yet, as Joey waited for her, the store windows yellow and cheerful like street bonfires in the cold night, he was thinking that anyway she didn't stay awake nights figuring out how to be a golddigger. She was just a dumb cherry, the dew was on her a foot thick, but she must like him for real to be meeting him tonight....

Once a week, all through January, he met her in front of Cavanagh's. He began to feel that maybe a golddigger wasn't so bad after all. For he hadn't had as much as one willing good night kiss out of Sadie Madofsky. "I'm no hundred yard runner," he protested that night as they hurried down the dark street to her father's store. At the door, she searched in her bag for her key while he stared at her, frustrated, his breath freezing before him. In a minute she'd be gone. What the hell was he breaking his neck for over this God damn girl? This God damn jewgirl, he thought venomously peering at the lettering on the dark plateglass. To his burning eye those letters spelled out JEW TAILOR. And suddenly out of nowhere, as if their faces were somehow reflected on that same plateglass, he thought of his family. Pack of Jews, he cursed to himself. He heard Sadie's key grating in the lock. Christ, if he had the guts he'd push her inside. He could keep her from yelling for help all right, all right.

He seized the girl, kissing her on the lips, kissing a mouth of ice. Disgusted, he let her go.

"Joey—" she said angrily, but whispering her anger.

"We won't wake the neighborhood, don't worry! Beat it!"

"Joey—"

"Why I keep seein' you I dunno."

"You don't have to."

"Damn right! You're just a freak inna circus. Like all them Jews! God damn jewgirls! 'Don't kiss me,'" he mimicked hatefully.

She slapped him. He caught her wrist, released it almost instantly. "Aw what're we fightin' for. The hell with it!"

They were both silent and then she said. "You're Jewish yourself—"

"Yeh, yeh, don't remind me."

"Joey, what's wrong—"

"G'night," he muttered and walked off. He felt dead beat, as if another hand twice as heavy, a hundred times as heavy as Sadie's—a hand big as a tenement on an arm as long as the street—had hit him.

"Joey," she called to him softly.

He ignored her, walking down sidewalks where hate and fear and lust could run like mad dogs, but not pity. Never pity.

He would've given odds he was finished with Sadie Madofsky. What a guy wanted from a dame was one thing. One thing only. That had been his code, straight out of the gutter and clinched to a fare-thee-well in coal cellar and backyard shed. But as he sat with Georgie in some night owl of a coffee pot, among the stags of the city, clerks out of furnished rooms and taxi drivers, stray college kids with empty gin flasks having themselves a snack and a yawning look at the headlines, he would see Sadie's reddish-brown eyes, twice as large as life and yet ghostly as his cigarette smoke. Sadie Madofsky, and what did she have? Nothing. A dumb redhead who when she finished high school'd get herself a secretary job and one of these days marry some jewboy. He was touched in the head chasing after her. The hell with her! He was through. And he would stir his coffee and wonder if he'd gone after her so long only because she was Jewish.

All winter long Joey felt a stirring in his mind: a springtime of questionings and speculations. Some thoughts he could see the sense of; others were just a swift pain and he wished he didn't have them. The last snow flurries of March blew in like January, to melt under noontime suns that belonged in May, and Joey was certain that at last he was growing up. Once, all he'd wanted was to be tough. Lucky the Spotter'd put him wise. The Spotter was right, the Spotter was always right—the guy who was both tough and smart was one jump ahead of the toughest guy in the world. The catch was that there were all kinds of smart. A guy like the Spotter was tops because the Spotter knew how to make things work like clockwork. The Spotter pressed all the buttons, one bunch of guys protecting his speaks and another bunch bringing the booze in. With Tom Quinn fixing the politicians, and Farber, the lawyer, fixing the law. He was one lucky guy to have the Spotter behind him.

When Joey and Georgie stepped into the clubroom that spring night, Mike, who was playing barkeep, yelled. "Hey, Joey, how about a bock beer?"

"What about me!" Georgie asked, but Mike didn't see him, none of the guys clustered like swilling flies around the beer keg could see Georgie. Georgie was now hitting six feet and wearing a brand-new spring suit, his black hair parted in the middle like Rudolph Valentino's. But they couldn't see Georgie because all their eyes were on the guy the Spotter'd given the nod to, the guy who'd stood up to the Bug. True, the Bug went around whispering about jewboys. And so what!

Jewboy?... To Mike, Joey was more a comer than a jewboy. Jewboy? Maybe to Bughead Moore, but not to Mike O'Reilley who wore a holy medal around his neck, or to Harry Halsey the best driver of a stolen car you could find, or to Ted Griffin the ex-pug who only had to show his face in a speak where they were fooling around with somebody's else's booze for the fooler-arounders to get white in the gills, or to Sarge Killigan trusted by all the guys, or to Cockeye Smith trusted by nobody, who carried his knockout punch in his pocket, a roll made up of two bucks in nickels. To all of them, beer drinkers and beer hustlers, Joey was a comer.

Jewboy, wop, or mick, a comer was a comer, with a nationality all his own, with an old man out of the land of good breaks, and an old lady from the special little church around the corner of all their dreams—where the stained glass was green as the green on a century note.

Joey drank the heady bock, the eyes of the gang intoxicating as another beer. They wanted to get next to him, he thought, the dark brown beer swelling his gut and his head.

Round after round they drank, gabbing of women, clothes, cars, of Babe Ruth coming up for another season, and Jack Dempsey the Manassa Mauler. Cockeye Smith asked everybody if they'd read what the *News* said about Al Capone having seven hundred strong-arms on his payroll. "That guy!" Cockeye declared with a true religious fervor in his voice. "He's got the mayor of Cicero on his payroll!"

Sarge Killigan blew a smoke ring into the blue cloud hanging over their heads. "Al Capone's done pretty good for a wop," the ex-doughboy said with a sly blue humorous twinkle in his eye.

"Done pretty good for anybody!" Cockeye shouted.

"If Torrio hadn't brought him out to Chicago," Sarge Killigan baited Cockeye, "where'd the wop be? Still down the East Side and lucky to have a pot to piss in."

"And a window to throw it out," Joey chimed in, laughing.

"You guys wisht you were half as good as Al Capone out there in Chicago," Cockeye said spitefully.

Joey recited:

> "Chicken in the car, the car won't go
> Thas how you spell Sha-gago"

It was a bit of Hell's Kitchen doggerel they all knew.

"Balls McCarty, Balls McCarty!" Cockeye said to Joey while Mike yelled for all of them to pipe down, waving his arms over his head. His shirtsleeves were rolled up and the tattooed mermaid on his left forearm swam and glided through the thick bluish smoke. Georgie, silent as a clam, now announced that he and Joey'd been to Chicago. All their eyes shifted to the man Who Had Been There, and Georgie, with an audience dropped into his lap, kept on talking. "New York's better for my dough!" the eye-witness wanted them all to know.

"Which is better?" Cockeye asked Joey. Georgie, his audience lost, gulped down his beer while Joey answered slowly as if he'd spent a solid year thinking it over.

"I'll take New York."

New York or Chicago. It jiggled inside Joey's head when with a belly full of the Spotter's dark brown bock he and Georgie and Cockeye and Mike climbed up the stairs of Mother Mary's place on Forty-Ninth. *New York or Chicago,* the stairs creaked and Joey remembered how he and Georgie'd blown into Chicago with not a buck between them. Two hoboes, fleas on the jump. Had Al Capone ever been that broke? Cockeye goosed Mike who giggled, the giggle coming out *New York or Chicago,* and when the door at the end of the landing opened, it too squeaked out *New York or Chicago.*

The four of them entered Mother Mary's sitting room, and in that whorehouse parlor with the furniture fat and stuffed and green, Mother Mary gave them all a smile made of genuine tin. She was a small fat woman in an expensive dress, her hair snow white, and a face underneath that would've gone better if it had been green like the sofa pillows. A face, fat and thin at the same time, fat-cheeked from the rich foods she liked, and thin from the bodies of the girls she'd consumed in her career. "New York or Chicago?" Joey asked her the riddle, laughing, while his beery pals roared and advised Mother Mary she shouldn't mind Joey, the best guy there ever was, and she should fix him with the best because he only deserved the best.

"If he don't stop yelling he deserves to get kicked down the stairs," the Madame replied in the scolding voice of a school marm.

"I'll take you," Joey said. He circled her corseted waist and whirled her around.

"Leggo!" she screeched. "No tough guys here! You'll get out you don't behave!"

He released her, thumbing his nose at his pals who were trying to quiet him, sing songing, "New York or Chicago, New York or Chicago."

"He's the Mayor of Chicago," Cockeye said, egging Joey on. "Ain't you Joey? Tell Mother Mary who you are!"

"I don't give a damn if he's Al Capone!" Mother Mary retorted. "If he don't behave—"

"Al Capone, this me," Joey laughed at her.

"Lissen, Al Capone, you wanta girl or don't you," Mother Mary asked. "You behave you want a girl—"

"Sure, I want a girl."

"What kind of girl, big-shot?"

"Jus' a lil redheaded girl."

Sadie Madofsky's red hair glowed darkly as the doubledecker bus rolled under the street lamp and Joey followed her down the bus aisle. She slid into an empty seat, he sat down next to her. All winter long he hadn't been out with her, but now it was spring, and he was sure he couldn't miss. Not if he worked her right. So she was a good girl. So what!

The good girls, the good girls.... A guy could get them drunk, slip Spanish fly into their drink, promise to marry them, promise the moon on a silver platter. The moon tonight was white as spilled milk on the flanks of the stone library lions at Forty-Second and Fifth. Tonight, the broad avenue was a spring lane, the great shining store windows cages of electric fireflies.

Bus rides, he thought. He'd give her bus rides, walks in the park, and a free look at the dumb stars.

"I missed you, Sadie," he said reaching for her hand. She pulled it away and he murmured plaintively. "Can't a feller even hold your hand? You let me in the movies." Without glancing at him, her eyes downcast, she lifted her hand from her lap, a hand stiff, as if carved out of wood. He took it between his own warm moist palms; he peered at her still face and wondered what she was thinking. As if he didn't know. Thinking she shouldn't be with him, thinking she should be going out with some nice little jewboy, thinking of getting married some day. Sure thing Mike, Joey told himself mockingly; let her get married, but first he'd get her primed.

Primed. Like that real estate guy Browning'd gotten Peaches primed, like Fatty Arbuckle'd gotten that Hollywood dame primed.

The bus traveled north with its lovers and its old married couples who kept a narrow space of indifference and even of hatred between their bodies, while Joey Kasow edged closer to the silent girl beside him. Their shoulders touched, she moved away, he grinned his private little grin and let go of her hand. He was in no rush. Some of the guys, and he'd been one of them last winter, would've pushed in on her. "Pet 'em enough and they stop hollerin'," the guys said. And if that didn't work, a guy could always trick a dame. There were always ways.

"Sadie, did you miss me? I missed you. Some nights I couldn't even sleep thinkin' about you."

"I don't believe that," she said and laughed nervously.

"Don't believe me but I know what happened." His voice buzzed persistently and he only became silent when the bus passed Fifty-Ninth Street. He blinked at the trees and meadows of Central Park. He chewed on his lip a second. Behind the low park wall he had glimpsed the winter pastures and woodlands of upstate New York, the roaring truck, with himself sweating in the sideroad, a haunted landscape to chill the heart. His smooth-shaven, talcum-powdered jaws clenched and he wondered what the hell was the matter with him. No sense thinking of that, no sense thinking of the Bug stewing around. Christ, let the Bug start something and he'd fill the bastid full of lead.

He averted his head from the park, stared at the east side of Fifth Avenue, at the rows of apartment buildings. The unwanted memories blew away like old newspapers in a street-corner wind. "I missed you all winter," he said. He could smell the soapiness of her clean washed hair, and he thought of the redhead at Mother Mary's a couple of nights ago. His blood lit like gasoline into which a match has been thrown and the Bug burned, flamed, was gone, and all that remained was a triumphant consciousness.

All through the month of May he kept seeing Sadie regularly on Wednesday nights. The leaves budded in the little parks of the city and they would sit on a bench in Madison Square or walk down paths winding like the tunnels of love in an amusement park. The little leaves under the park lamps looked like metal cut out with a shining shears, the windows of the Flatiron Building on Twenty-Third Street and Fifth gleamed yellow, and he felt as if he were playing kid games. This walking around in parks, this holding hands! This stealing a kiss when he brought her home at ten o'clock! A joke but he'd made up his mind to work her slow. Besides, he could work off steam at Mother Mary's. But the easy breasts of Mother Mary's girls didn't bring him any closer to the slow rise and fall of Sadie's small breasts fingered by his greedy eye in the passing light of a car. One of these days, he would promise himself as he sat alone in a coffee pot, one of these days....

May mornings, he would awake, the color of the sun on the drawn window shades reminding him of the deep red of her heavy coiled hair. He thought she was about the only girl in town who hadn't bobbed it, she didn't use lipstick, she didn't smoke, she didn't drink. A prize cherry.

Oh, the good girls, the good girls....

Days, he was busy as all the Spotter's boys were busy. The Spotter seemed to have a speak on every block in the Thirties and Forties. Across Eighth Avenue the Spotter couldn't go, for that was Big Bill Dwyer's territory. And Ownie Madden and Larry Fay couldn't be sneezed at neither. But just the same the Spotter with Quinn for a partner, had a good territory and he kept his boys on the hop. Supplying speaks and protecting speaks, running in the booze with now and then a hijacking, with Joey Kasow or Bughead Moore in charge. Joey and Bughead and a couple others were the guys picked to settle an argument where a bullet was the last word, but so far Joey didn't even have a single notch on that new gun of his. And the latest of the Spotter's bullet boys, truth to tell, was kind of glad. If he got the order to kill some no-good sonuvabitch, okay, but if not, that was okay, too.

The sunny days stretched before him like a shining yellow diving-board from which he plunged every Wednesday into the moist and murmuring night, the special night when he was out with Sadie, when the nighttime city rose and fell like a great swelling wave, rose and fell with her breasts tantalizing him under her thin dress, a wave of light and shadow in whose dark depth faceless men and women drifted by and where the red and green traffic lights had the magic of phosphorescence.

"Look how big and white the moon is! It looks different!" she exclaimed one night, and although he answered, "What's so different about it? It's the same old moon," he knew that it was different because he was with her.

"When I graduate from high school next year," she confided to him on another night as they sat in an ice cream parlor, "I'll get a job. I can type and take shorthand." He had glanced at her, a straw between her pink soft lips, thinking: what a dumbbell! She was full to the ears with all the junk they taught in the schools. Work hard and you'll get ahead, save your pennies and some day you'll be somebody. Joey Kasow knew better: the world was for sale, with cops and feds and even judges on the bargain counter.

Walking her home, he wondered where she kept her eyes. For sitting in front of the tenements with their husbands sat all the penny-savers. He remembered his mother sitting on her soapbox in the hot summer nights and how she'd carried it upstairs when it was time to go to sleep. Her special little extra-special soapbox. Oh, the dumb penny-savers.

At the corner of Twenty-Third and Eighth, he always let her go on home by herself. That was the way she wanted it. These God damn jewgirls, he'd think as if he were a bona fide Irishman himself. And dream of the night when there'd be no going home for her, when he'd be kissing her silly.

"Do you ever write to your family?" she asked him the next time they met. Always she was asking him about his God damn family. So when he lay abed in his room thinking of Sadie, sometimes he'd think of them. Her face—that Irishlooking face of hers that could look Jewish when her eyes had a sad look in them—would flip their faces into his memory: a family of faces like the related faces of cards with Sadie Madofsky the red queen of all Jewish hearts.

Did his dumb family still live on Thirty-Seventh? Was his brother Danny and sister Sarah going to school like Sadie Madofsky? The Jews loved school all right. The Jews acted like school was another kind of Holy Moses synagogue. And here he was all fouled up with a God damn jewgirl schoolgirl. "You ought to write to your family," she had scolded him gently when he'd said he wasn't much for writing letters. And on the bus—they were always on that God damn Fifth Avenue bus—he'd laughed and said, "I'll write you a letter."

"We live on the same block, Joey."

"I'll write you anyway. I'll write love and kisses, how about it?"

One of these days, he promised himself, she wouldn't pester him about his damn family. One of these days he'd have her in a bed and she'd forget about his family and her family, about her old man the Jew tailor and her dead mother and all the rest of that God damn family stuff.

Slowly, patiently, as warm May changed into hot June, his hands like the spreading green leaves in the city parks moved like shadows on her body. Retreating at her protests, moving again, touching again, always touching.

They walked along quiet Seventh Avenue, the lofts of the furriers dead in the night, the skins of mink and silver fox locked in safes, and only the unseen nightwatchmen pounding their beats inside the dark-glassed walls. "I never thought I'd be out with a girl who didn't pet—"

"Joey, don't start in again—"

"Don't you believe in no fun? Know what? I'm goin' call you Sweetie from now on because I love you." It was too dark to be sure but he knew she was blushing. He slipped his arm around her waist and laughed at her half-hearted protest: "Who'll see us? Anyway I'll marry you one of these days, Sweetie!" laughing at his joke and waiting for her to speak, but she was silent. Only their heels sounding on the pavement, only a bum shuffled north to Times Square. It gleamed ahead of them, a lovers' square, a lovers' rainbow of colored lights in the pulsing and fleshly darkness.

Through the windows of the kitchen behind her father's store, Sadie Madofsky watched the summer singing in the backyard. The windows were protected with iron bars against sneak thieves, the backyard fenced in on three sides, the row of sheds like a fourth fence. Scattered blades of grass had sprouted between the cracks of the slate slabs—and the summer sang.

She would glance up from her book or the dishes she was washing and gaze out at the faded fences painted bright with mid-morning, the washlines wav-

ing many-colored flags, the blue sky deeper than any sea. And invisible, yet
real as youth, sweet as first love, the summer sang like a little golden bird.

But when she turned her head away from the windows, she felt the silent
rebuke of this kitchen where she kept house for her father and brother, and
studied every night during the school year. The black castiron stove that
wouldn't be used again until another winter, stared at her like a hard-working
housewife; the linoleum on the floor gleamed with cleanliness; the round
kitchen table with its wooden lion paws spoke of the plain bread and meat of
life, while the blue-covered couch against the wall opposite the sink where her
father slept at night, his Jewish newspaper perhaps on the blue-covered pillow, reminded her of the father presence.

Goodness, narrow and strict as that kitchen, moved in a straight line to the
two tiny bedrooms of her brother and herself, and then down a long dark corridor to the curtain that divided the flat from the store. There, up front, in the
light of the street, her father worked, bending over his steam iron or seated at
his sewing machine. Her heart ached thinking of her father. At night when
she was in bed she would pray silently for forgiveness: Oh God, I'm being bad,
please keep me good. Please God.

But when she looked through the barred kitchen windows, the kitchen was
gone, her father and brother were gone, and even the all-seeing eye of God was
blinded by the golden singing in the backyard.

Had Joey tried to put his hand on her breasts as they rode on the bus through
the June nights? Tried to squeeze her knees as they sat in the movies dark?
Had he only two nights ago, while walking home, pulled her into a darkened
doorway, hugging and kissing and pressing himself so close and tight she had
felt the night changing into day, with all the people in the world watching?

Out there in the backyard the summer was singing.

Was she lying to her father? So many lies.... "Papa," she had said last Christmas, "I want to see my friend Judy Feiner once in a while, I'll be back early...."

Singing, singing.

Nights, she dreamed. Of running in dark woods, of drowning, of bleeding.
Of a jack-in-the-box like one she had owned years ago, but when she pressed
the lever, the dream jack jumped up huge and frightening with a red face and
a red fool's cap. The spiderwebs of her nightmares clung to her during the day.
She had conceived the notion that her dead mother knew about Joey. And
often she would go into her bedroom to the large framed photograph of her
mother which hung above a little bamboo table. "Mama," she would whisper
and gaze at the face in the photograph, a solemn face despite the forced smile
hastily assumed at the photographer's command. "Mama," the girl would
whisper her lips barely moving. "I don't want to be bad, but Joey loves me and
I love Joey, Mama...."

The solemn face was pretty, dimpled in one cheek, the eyes large and bright
and that little watch-the-birdy smile on its lips. It didn't look like a dead face,

and yet her mother had died in two weeks during the wartime influenza epidemic and her father and her brother and she had gone to the funeral with little camphor bags tied around their necks. "Mama," her lips would shape the word: the holy word of childhood, the magic word against all dangers. "Mama...."

While out in the backyard the summer sang.

On the night of Sarge Killigan's party to celebrate the speakeasy the Spotter had put Sarge in charge of, Bughead Moore decided that a certain jewboy needed a good lesson. "Sarge was gonna ask you, Bug," Cockeye Smith'd whispered in the Bug's ear, "but the jewboy let out a stink. Said if you'd be there he wouldn't, so Sarge, he give in." Still, if the Bug hadn't gotten plastered on the night of the celebration party, maybe he would've let things ride.

He sat with his girl Agnes in Dinty's speak on Forty-Third Street, his elbows on the whiskey-splashed table, his pink face in his hands, chewing on his wrongs. The cigarette smoke hung in clouds about him, the booze poured in rivers, and the Bug explored the winding whiskey trails known only to heavy drinkers in the land of Might-Have-Been. If that jewboy'd only stayed a hobo. If the Spotter'd only seen through the jewboy's tricks. If only Joey'd got himself croaked or broke a leg. If, if....

"Needs a good lesson," the Bug mumbled, hitting the table with the flat of his meaty hand. "Sarge, he usta be my buddy. Alla them usta be my buddy."

The girl tried to calm him. She was a full-bodied long-legged brunette who had been passed from one beer runner to another like an umbrella—a bootlegger's girl, living with the Bug now these five, six months. "We could go home," she tried to tempt him, smiling.

"Naah!"

"Let's go home," she said anxiously.

"Sarge, he usta be my buddy. Some buddy, the louse! 'Hey, jewboy,'" the Bug improvised, his voice rising. "'Should I ast my ole buddy Bughead?' 'Naah!' the jewboy says."

"This Cockeye, I wouldn't believe a word he says—"

"Who believes that rat? But did Sarge ast me or didn't he ast me?"

"Let's go home, big boy."

"Whose side you on?" the Bug shouted. The girl felt chilled although nobody at the nearby tables seemed to hear the barrelchested Bug with his voice like a megaphone. At Dinty's somebody or other was always yelling anyway, with no listeners anywhere. At Dinty's they fixed drinks strong enough to plug up the ears of a blind man. Dinty invented them all by himself. There was the Snorter which was mostly gin; the Three Cheers which was supposed to be real rye from Canada and maybe had an eyedropper of Canadian to every pint; the Volstead, named after the man who as Dinty explained, "Without him where'd we all be?" and which was something between a Manhattan and a can of Sterno.

"Jinxed from the minnit he showed his mug," the Bug was mumbling again. "Gives me a box-a candy. For your mother—"

"A box of candy?"

Old grievances and new grievances, they came alive in the Bug's liquor glass. "I'm gonna crash that party an' break that jewboy in half!" the Bug shouted and then laughed with pleasure, imagining himself giving the boot to Joey Kasow.

The girl stared into his happy eyes. Her head twisted as if looking for help. At the tables, downtown was rubbing elbows with uptown, mobsters and their girls near businessmen and their girls; a plainclothes dick on the Spotter's payroll was exchanging a friendly word with the great Dinty himself, the inventor of drinks, who sometimes used to wish he could invent himself a scheme to get out of buying the Spotter's booze. Between the tables, waiters in short black coats hustled through smoke thick enough to stuff a pillow with. There was no help out there and the girl knew it. But knocking around on bootleg row hadn't gotten her used to hearing a man talking about killing another man.

When they cabbed over to the Hotel Drexler—Cockeye hadn't left out a single detail about the Killigan celebration party—Bughead was no longer laughing or even talkative. He had crawled into the little black box of hate he carried in his heart.

The hotel was in a sidestreet in the Eighties near the Museum of Natural History, new when the museum had been new, in a day when the skirts of the women had swished the sidewalks. The elevator was an old-fashioned one with metal basketweave sides, the corridor up on Killigan's floor smelled musty, but when the door of Killigan's room opened to the Bug's knock— "Honey, don't start anything!" Agnes had begged him again as his fist crashed on the wood—they walked straight into what could have been a honky-tonk. The phonograph was playing *Smiles,* three or four couples foxtrotting, while over at the little bar set up on the table, the Spotter's whiskey and gin were being drunk by the Spotter's boys and their girl friends.

"The Bug hisself!" Sarge Killigan welcomed the bruiser like a long-lost brother. The Bug elbowed him aside, plunging through the dancers toward the face that had haunted him at Dinty's.

Agnes cried out, "Honey, don't start anything!" and all the dancers stopped dancing, the girls like stupid dolls in their short sleeveless dresses and flesh-colored stockings rolled below their knees, the men staring for a stunned second before they rushed between the Bug and Joey. "Take it easy!" three or four voices banged. "Take it easy!"

Sarge Killigan, Mike, Lefty and Georgie had the Bug surrounded, but no one put a hand on Joey.

Joey looked at the Bug wrestling the peacemakers and he felt himself tightening, every nerve, every muscle, even his eyes in their sockets, so that staring at his enemy, the lines of sight between them seemed to become fixed in space,

holding him and the Bug in a furious kind of balance that would only change
when a gun was pulled. But he didn't have his gun on him—wasn't he following the Spotter's advice to cache it unless he was on a job? A thousand to
one the Bug did. There was gun pointing out of the Bug's eyes. Gun pointing
out of the Bug's cursing mouth:

"Lemme at that jewboy!"

How many times'd he heard that word of hate? This night? Other nights?

"A celebration party!" Sarge Killigan was shouting indignantly, his arms
wrapped about the Bug. "You start anything, you get your head broke!"

"Take it easy, Bug!" his assistants shouted, their hands on the cursing Bug,
too. Like a drunk about to get the heave-ho, the Bug struggled a little before
giving in. "Okay," he said.

Joey said to the Bug. "Don't spoil the party. Let's bury the axe, Bug." For a second they confronted each other, the Bug in the grip of a dozen hands, Joey
standing free, a living monument that could have been called The Good Sport
and the Bad Sport.

Everywhere, voices were urging the Bug. "This is a party!"

"Kiss and make up, you guys!"

The Bug scowled, "Okay, okay." A girl in a green dress began to titter.

The Bug said. "Okay, take your dirty hands offa me—"

"Foist, I want your gun," Sarge Killigan said. "Nobody's carryin' guns at my
party. Hold onto him, youse guys!" They pinned the Bug's arms. Sarge unbuttoned the Bug's jacket and pulled the Bug's gun out of its holster. The Bug's girl
Agnes whispered a prayer of gratitude. Somebody put a record on the victrola
and the music, happy and idiotic, reminded them all they should be dancing.
As the Bug, followed by Agnes, beelined it for the bar, a blonde in a black knee-
length dress danced towards Joey, humming to the sax. She pushed her round
black-silked belly and black-silked breasts against him and they danced out
onto the middle of the room.

"You won't be mad at me, Joey?" the blonde smiled.

"Why should I be mad?"

"That big guy before, what he said—"

He glared at her smiling lollipop of a face.

"Oh, it don't make no diff'rence to me, Joey," the blonde assured him. "Just, I
never thought—You don't look—You never said you were or nothing."

His hand on her back tightened. "Go fly a kite!" His eyes shifted to the Bug,
seeing the Bug drinking at the bar, Sarge Killigan and Georgie with him. My
bodyguard, he thought bitterly.

"Joey, don't be mad at me."

He hardly heard her. *Jewboy, jewboy, jewboy...* the sax on the spinning record
blared for his inner ear alone. Each time he turned and glimpsed Bughead at
the bar, the *jewboy* blowing in his skull exploded like a sax gone mad, into
demented but controlled sound: jewboy, jewboy, JEWBOY....

And all was clear as light. He knew now that sooner or later the Bug'd come for him. Spotter or no Spotter. Staring at the Bug hoisting himself another drink, Joey looked, with the clairvoyance of fear, into a future that could be forecast—the Bug drinking on another night, the Bug working himself into a lather again, coming for him again. All because the Bug was the Bug and he was the jewboy. *Jewboy, jewboy JEWBOY....* What should he do? Wait? Wait, and get another pat on the head from the Spotter? Wait, a fall guy, dumb guy, until the Bughead put a bullet in his back? He couldn't wait any more. Tonight'd proved it double. He couldn't wait. He had to be smart. Yeh, smart. And the smartest kind of smart was to do the bastard in first. Spotter or no Spotter.

The dance ended—had he been dancing?—he slapped the blonde on her black-silked hips, but felt neither flesh or desire. "See you later," he said and joined the drinkers at the bar, with one smile for the Bug and another for Georgie and Sarge Killigan and the others, and only himself knowing which was the smile with the poison in it. He drank, they all drank, and after another shot, he said, smiling, "Bug, you and me oughta be friends, Bug. I'm willin' if you are." Smiling, even though he could feel the Bug's hate like a living thing, huge, spiky-eyed, a giant bigger even than the two hundred and twenty pound two-legged horse towering over all of them. "You beat me once in a fair fight, Bug," he said and that smile of his, for a second of revealed hypocrisy, hung false on his lips. But Bughead was too drunk to see—or was he? "Les call it quits, Bug, whatta you say?"

Mike the volunteer barkeep applauded, Sarge Killigan approved, Georgie ditto, Agnes, the Bug's girl nodded, while various other miscellaneous barflies nodded at this testimonial to the code of John L. Sullivan and Jack Dempsey, the fighting Irish champs. It was an act Joey was putting on, of course, good enough for tonight. And he was an actor who sensed that his audience really didn't give a damn about him. If tomorrow the Bug were to put a bullet in his back, they'd all send flowers, and be God damn glad it wasn't their funeral. Even Georgie. He could only depend on himself. "Whatta you say, Bug?"

In the hubbub of voices urging the Bug to be a sport, that bully and killer reluctantly, hypocritically, too, nodded his head. Mike filled up all their glasses to celebrate sportsmanship. They drank, and Joey's mind raced with fantasies of murder. He could challenge Bughead to a gun fight and with the bastard drunk as a pig, he'd be easy as pie, but there were too damn many witnesses tonight. Or tail the Bug some night and blow his head off, get somebody else to do the job, Georgie maybe....

The blonde in black came searching for him. Smiling, Joey said to Bughead, "Show you how I feel—you can dance with my girl, Bug."

Mike the barkeep said, "Yeh, we're all friends here."

Sarge Killigan, the new speakeasy prop, said, "What's a piece among friends?"

Georgie leered drunkenly at both girls and gave them each a hand on their rear-ends. Agnes slapped at him, the blonde laughed and the miscellaneous barflies snorted and smirked their lust.

"How about a dance," the blonde asked Bughead.

"Nah," the Bug said, but she danced up to him, pressed against him, and with a helping shove from the barflies, the Bug was launched.

Joey danced off with the Bug's girl. "How's tricks?" he asked her.

"No complaints from Buffalo."

He'd seen her around; she'd never interested him. But tonight, keyed-up with thoughts of killing the Bug, she seemed different, this woman of his enemy. She was tall, her face level with his own, smooth-cheeked, white of brow, her eyebrows jet black, a face suddenly as exciting to him as a woman's exposed breast; a third breast with the bright red mouth its nipple. "How do you stand a mug like him, Agnes?" he asked and his hand on her back moved, stroking.

"Joey, you looking for trouble now?" she said quietly.

"You mean this?" he said, his hand stroking. "He's blind drunk, baby."

If Bughead was blind drunk, Joey, with the Bug's woman in his arms, felt as if he had a hundred eyes, like the hawks over the Jersey Palisades, all hawk eyes himself, seeing how things were for the first time in his life. Seeing that the smart guy was the guy who made things work out his way. *His way...* the sax sang out loud as a fiend in hell, so loud he could hardly hear *jewboy* any more.

Seeing also what could be seen at Killigan's party. The heavy loaders at the bar, the dumb drunks, all the dumb bennies who never used their heads like Georgie. But not like Lefty who was trying to get the little wop girl he'd brought to the party to take another drink. A cherry, that wop girl, like Sadie. That Lefty knew how, all right, all right. For a flash, Joey forgot Agnes, his eyes on Lefty's girl, wondering if he could ever push a slug of whiskey into Sadie? Hell, she wouldn't go to a speak, he couldn't get her up to a party like this in a million years, for even if she came, one look'd be enough for her to run. Let her run, he vowed fiercely, she'll be mine anyway. Seeing, feeling, knowing the truth of the ages, that for the smart guy the dumb were always bait. Wop girl and jewgirl, dumb guy and tough guy. Yeah! Even the Bug was bait!

His way.... And smiling at what he knew, he tightened his dancer's hold on Agnes. She tried to edge away from him and he laughed "How about it, baby? How about it one of these days?" And with shining gray eyes he saw himself doing what he wanted with her, this woman of the Bug's and he saw the Bug dead....

But in the light of morning his will to murder drained away like dream blood in a nightmare. Yet leaving a bloody spot in his mind, a red root that grew wild in a second to be slashed down in the next, but never completely dug out or destroyed. Murder walked with him in the daytime, casting no shadow on the summer sidewalks, whispering in his ear. What you waiting for, Joey, murder whispered. For the Bug to make the next move? Is that smart? You make the first move. The guy who wins the fight's the guy who gets in the first punch, you know.

Every day he awoke, shaved, dressed, joked with Georgie as they ate their late breakfasts while the clock-punching city sat down to lunch. He reported to the Spotter at the Young Democrats, and if there wasn't a job for him, chewed the fat with the guys, played cards, took in an afternoon movie to kill a little time, or visited rooms smelling of powder, perfume and disinfectant, with the dame stretched out on the bed for him like a Coming Attraction in a darkened movie house. And always the whispers: Here you're having yourself a good time but what about the Bug? He'll knock you off one of these days. He'll get stinko, come for you and there'll be no crowd to take his gat away like at Killigan's party.

When he was on a job for the Spotter, calling on the speaks falling behind on their whiskey quotas, or kicking around some slob trying to pull a fast one, murder whispered even more persistently, almost with the outcry of nightmare: The Bug's got a hate on you that'll never stop, Joey. Bigger you get in the gang, bigger his hate. He hates you, always has, hates you for a jewboy and you are a jewboy, too yellow to show some guts. Knock the Bug off for Christ sake, what the hell you waiting for.

He would stare superstitiously at that gun of his, given to him by the Spotter, and still unused. The Spotter still had no gun jobs for him. That God damn gun of his was going to rust to pieces, he was thinking. He would lay in bed thinking, always thinking, listening to Georgie snoring like a judge; but what there was to think about, God only knew. All the God damn thinking'd been done long ago. Up in the sticks after the hijacking. Up at Killigan's party. Done, done in spades, and here he was still waiting for the Bug to make the next move. Don't wait, murder whispered. Work it your way! Take the Bug, take his girl, murder whispered slyly in the hot summer nights.

Murder will out—the saying goes. True. The wish to murder, suppressed, will out, also. The murder Joey Kasow couldn't quite make up his mind to consummate drove him hard and rough with the whores he visited. And when he was with Sadie, Wednesday nights, murder's twin—rape—whispered constantly in his ear. "I can borrow a car," he said. "How about a lil joy-ride, Sweetie?"

"No, no, Joey."

So he called on a druggist the Spotter was supplying with whiskey and told him what he wished. Then he rented a room in a cheap dive of a furnished rooming house. He was ready. Wednesday night, when he and Sadie were seated in the booth of an ice cream parlor, he sent her up front to buy him some cigarettes. She asked why he couldn't go himself and he pleaded he was dead tired, to please do him a favor. She left the booth and he dropped the pill he had from the druggist into her soda. A minute later, smoking one of the cigarettes she'd bought him, his heart violent in his chest, he watched her drink her soda. He watched her eyelids droop, she said she was sleepy. She was almost asleep on her feet leaning heavily on his arm when they hit the night air. He had to support her when he whistled for a cab, explaining to the cabbie his girl'd had too much. At the furnished rooming house, he tipped the cabbie a buck to help him carry her up. The door closed. He looked down at the girl in the bed, her red hair on the pillow, her breasts rising and falling. "Sweetie," he called softly, but there was no answer. For a long minute he hesitated—it was a dirty thing to do. Some girls deserved what they got, but she was no teaser. She'd always played it straight, he thought. She was dumb maybe but she was on the level. He stared about the room, the floor lamp shining, the end table burned in scores of places by the cigarettes of forgotten transients, two-bit whores, perverts, gangsters on the lam, old bummers. He looked again at the girl. He leaned over her and touched her cheeks with the gentlest of fingers, as gently as her dead mother might have done. Christ, a dirty thing, he thought and then cursed himself for going soft. A slob! A dumb slob! And murder whispered: What're you waiting for? For the Bug to put a bullet in you? For her to come across? Act tough, you dumb fool, murder whispered. Don't be such a yellow Jew. *Tough, tough, tough,* murder screamed, no longer whispering.

THREE • *LEAD SOLDIER*

The Bug died in a hallway where his killer trailed him to put three bullets in his back. Later, the dicks clomped into that same hallway, climbed to the second floor, questioned the Bug's girl, and climbed downstairs again. "Who killed Bughead Moore?" the boys with the badges were asking all over the West Side.

Nobody knew and everybody knew. Then one of the nobodies phoned the police with an anonymous tip. They hauled Joey Kasow in on an August afternoon. "You got nothin' on me," he repeated until the dicks who'd heard that song of innocence from a hundred other suspects in a hundred other homicides felt like knocking it off his lips. They didn't lay a finger on Joey Kasow though. He was one of Spotter Boyle's Young Democrats. He had an organization behind him, and the coppers respected organization.

The Spotter'd put Joey through the third degree himself, but all he got was a big no. "Not me, Spotter, not me. Sure, I'm glad he's dead, but it wasn't me. Not me when you said we shouldn't. Honest to God, Spotter, all I know's what I read inna papers." The Spotter's partner, Tom Quinn, had advised giving Joey his walking papers, but the Spotter saw no sense in that. If Joey was lying he had to get his ears pinned back, but he was too good a man to dump. The Spotter had grinned wryly: *Too good a man to dump.* Maybe that was what Johnny Torrio out in Chicago'd thought about Al Capone, too, in the beginning. The Spotter wondered if Joey had the makings of a second Al Capone. No, Joey was just snotty, with only his snottiness in his favor, the snottiness of a young guy feeling his muscle. A hell of a big favor that was, the Spotter had to admit to himself.

"He's got nerve, too much nerve, maybe," he had said to Quinn. "But we can use the bastid. Only we gotta put a crimp in his style."

But at night in his room, the clock ticking on the dresser, the Spotter was haunted by the ghosts of all the Al Capones who'd doublecrossed their Johnny Torrios. There was no denying that Joey was moving like a house afire for a stinking hobo hardly a year off the rods. He'd backtalked the Bug his first night in town, the Spotter remembered. And now the Bug was finished.

The Spotter, like the Bug before, began to look into the friendship of Joey Kasow and Georgie Connelly. Funny how a smart guy always teamed up with a lunk. If it isn't a lunk, it's a dame. The weak spot was Georgie....

He waited until Friday night, payday night, when Quinn passed out the pay envelopes. The Spotter left word that as soon as Georgie showed up he wanted to see him. "Sit down," he said when Georgie stepped inside his private office. Big Georgie lowered his hulk into a chair next to the Spotter's desk as if he were a heavy load on the end of a winch. The Spotter lit a cigarette, spoke of one thing and another. Then, smiling, he said: "Bug had it comin' to him. I'm the last guy inna world to blame Joey."

Georgie said not a word.

"What the hell's the big secret?" the Spotter asked him. "Everybody knows who got the Bug. So what's the big secret?"

But there was a big secret and the Spotter knew what it was as well as Georgie. Maybe half the West Side had the idea Joey'd shot the Bug. But with Joey swearing he had nothing to do with it, his pals had to believe him. Even if they didn't, they had to keep their traps shut. That was what a right guy had to do.

Georgie said not a word, his hands resting on his heavy thighs.

"Did you help Joey with the Bug?" the Spotter questioned, leaning back in his chair, completely relaxed although the office was suddenly alive with something like electricity. It leaped out of Georgie's silences, it shone from the sweat on his forehead. "I'm askin' you something, you big puke!" the Spotter said, but he wasn't the least bit angry.

Georgie's eyes like those of a dog were full of pleading.

"You're doin' the right thing, Georgie," the Spotter acknowledged. "Only you're forgettin' I'm not one of the guys out there. I'm the guy who give you and Joey your job. You can't pull no secrets on me. I'm not gonna sit here and have you playin' dumb, Georgie!"

"Spotter, I ain't doin' nothin' of the kind—"

"What the hell're you doin' then? Looka, Georgie, I don't need you and I don't need Joey. See how far you guys get without me. You two guys better hit the road," he suggested like a true blue friend trying to be helpful. "God damn wise guys!"

"I'm no wise guy!" Georgie protested in an anguished voice and almost the Spotter laughed.

"No? Then when I ask you somethin' you answer. Georgie, I'm gonna give you just one more chance!"

Big Georgie sat there as if strapped to his chair—the chance the Spotter was about to offer him like a knife at his throat. "Did you help Joey with the Bug?"

Silence.

"Answer, you big bum, or get the hell out!"

"No," said Georgie, sweating.

"Joey done it himself, huh?"

Again, Georgie was silent. As if the office had suddenly filled with witnesses urging him to be still. Witnesses from another time, 1-4-Alls in their knee pants and caps; the Badgers in the years before prohibition. The room shook with the most terrible of all their epithets: *Stool pigeon.* Hadn't Georgie himself gone around singing the old-time bit of doggerel?

"Dirty ol' stool pigeon, dirty ol' rat
Squealed on his mother, squealed on the cat
Squealed on his brother, squealed on the priest
Dirty ol' stool pigeon, cheese-it, cheese-it!"

"Georgie," the Spotter said. "Georgie—"

"I don't know no more'n you, Spotter!"

"He didn't tell you?"

"No."

"If Joey didn't get the Bug who did, Georgie?"

"Christ, I don't know nothin', Spotter!"

"Joey got the Bug! That's what you know, Georgie! That's what everybody knows so for Christ sake what's the big secret, Georgie? What's the harm when everybody knows Joey got the Bug? Georgie, ain't that what you think, too? Answer, Georgie!"

Georgie slowly nodded, his eyes moist in that second of shame, both betrayer and betrayed.

The Spotter ordered Georgie to stay in the office while he walked into the noisy clubroom. Half the guys already had their pay envelopes in their pockets—no shot in the arm can beat it!—laughing and horsing around and feeling good. They greeted the Spotter as if he were a tin god come down from his pedestal and he waved his pale immaculately manicured hand at them all, and in earshot of them all spoke to Joey, "You and me got a date, kiddo."

They cabbed over to the Hotel Berkeley and the Spotter, as with Georgie, again spoke of one thing and another. The Spotter closed the door of his room behind them. He smiled—the smile of a worn-out womanchaser alone with a new girl. Always the good host, the Spotter set down a bottle of whiskey and a glass on the table. Joey poured himself three inches of rye. The Spotter kept glancing at him. He saw a young, good-looking medium-built guy, not too husky or too slender, in a good brown suit and a two-dollar silk necktie. The Spotter got a real bang out of inspecting Joey's glad rags. It was as if he'd crossed the room and personally felt the cloth and rubbed that silky necktie between his fingers. The Spotter got a bigger bang out of Joey's easy pokerface.

"Here's luck," Joey said as if he began every evening with a cab ride to the Spotter's private stock of whiskey.

"Drink hearty! Want another?"

"No, that was a hooker!"

"The Bug could've put away two or three like that one," the Spotter remarked.

"He was a drinker," Joey agreed, nodding solemnly like any man speaking well of the dead. "He had hollow legs, the Bug."

"And all you know's what you read inna papers?"

"'Bout the Bug? Sure, like I told you, Spotter—"

"You sure of that?" The Spotter smiled like some racketeer playing with a bought-and-paid-for-dame whom he could strip any second he wanted, flesh and dress, smile and girdle.

"Sure."

The Spotter laughed. "You *sure* got a nerve. That's what I like about you." As he spoke, he realized he sort of meant it. Who'd fought for the kid against Clip Haley? Who'd watched over the kid like a good uncle, giving him every break? Nobody but the Old Spotter. "One thing you ain't never learned, Joey," the Spotter said like a good uncle a little on the sad side now. "This holdin' out on me's no good. This playin' under the table's n.g. twice over."

"I don't get you, Spotter."

"There you go again. Crappin' me again. But I can't help likin' you, Joey. You're just like I usta be before I got such a sick bastid. Joey, you're smart. Why does everybody think they can put one over on a sick bastid?"

"I don't know what you're gettin' at, Spotter."

"The Bug gets plastered. He comes for you at Sarge Killigan's party. What's to stop him from gettin' plastered again, comin' for you again? I would've done the same in your boots, Joey. Why didn't you come and tell the Ol' Spotter how it was?"

"'Cause there was nothin' to tell, Spotter."

The Spotter stared at that innocent face. It was the phoniest of phonies but in his heart the Spotter couldn't help handing it to the kid for trying. "You're just a lil too snotty," the Spotter said meditatively. "Okay, you lyin' sonofabitch!" he snapped. "So there's nothin' to tell! Some other guy killed the Bug, right?"

"Yeh—"

"Yeh, and I'm just a station house flatfoot to crap up! 'Scuse me, Mister Kasow, for botherin' you and don't slam the door on the way out! Wait!" he cried as if the hotel were a detectives' backroom after all. "I almost forgot— your pal Georgie, tonight over the club, he said you killed the Bug. That's what he said. And shut up! I'm not finished yet! T'night, your pal Georgie said you killed the Bug—"

"I didn't—"

"Okay, you didn't, and Georgie's just a damn liar, only shut up, I'm not finished!"

They were both silent. A silence that spread until it reached the hallway where the Bug'd died, his fingers clutching frantically at the floor. Joey couldn't have spoken now even if he'd wanted to. He was in that hallway again, listening to the Bug moaning, "Mama, mama..." in a world where all the ears were stuffed with cotton and the only listener himself, with a gun in his fist. As he was the only listener in this room to hear the lost voice in his own throat begging for help. And who was there to help him? No one, not even Georgie....

"That's what Georgie said or is he a liar?"

"A liar," Joey mumbled tonelessly.

"Joey," the Spotter stated. "You're not gonna hold out on a damn thing any more. Get that into your head and you'll be okay. I got big things in mind for you but you're gonna follow orders from now on, Joey. Look alive, Joey!" His eyes flitted at the kid's lost and betrayed face. "Makin' a big secret out of the Bug! Okay, we'll forget it! Only I wanna hear you say it. I want it right off your lil ruby lips. C'mon, Joey," he coaxed. "Speak up! You can speak up now. What's the big secret when Georgie's give'd you away. You killed the Bug and I wanna hear you say it! Cmon!"

"I killed'm. You satisfied, you bastid?"

He had never called the Spotter bastard to his face—nobody in the gang ever had—but the Spotter only smiled. The Spotter was completely satisfied, his sunken eyes bright, victorious. At last, he'd broken the kid, broken into a part of him that nobody had ever touched. And the Spotter knew he wouldn't have made it if not for Georgie—Georgie whom the kid'd trusted like a brother.

Every man had his weak spot: you could have sworn to that one on all the Bibles in the world.

Downstairs, Joey plunged like a blinded man into the river of light that was Broadway, he moved with the shirtsleeved sweaty crowds under the huge electric name of DOUGLAS FAIRBANKS. At the corner newsstand, an old man with a face like a gray rag was shouting hoarsely, "Lates' extry on Hall-Mills sex moider. Lates' extry...." Out in the gutter the cars honked, and the laughter of the joyriders shrilled wild like the saxes in the upstairs dance halls. Joey climbed a floor to an upstairs speak, he drank five straight whiskies in a row, but even here the Spotter'd followed him, a bony ghost mocking at him from behind all the red perspiring and arguing faces.

"Babe Ruth hit fifty-nine homers las' season—"

"That ain't the pernt."

"What's the pernt then?"

"What Babe did was save the game see? When Rothstein fixt the World Series he killt the game, but the Babe and his bat, he saved the game...."

It was the Spotter, nobody else but the Spotter, only the Spotter, and who else could it be but the Spotter.

"Saved the game from what!" Joey shouted furiously at the red faces staring at him, to recognize the Spotter. And although there were other drunkards roaring their heads off, the bouncer had Joey by the neck and the seat of his pants and before he knew what was happening, he was outside the speak door, while downstairs, the crowds waiting for him, packed him up and carried him to the nowhere he'd glimpsed at the bottom of one whiskey glass too many.

"You're drunk," he heard her saying when he walked into their furnished room, "Joey—"

"No, Sweetie, no Sweetie," he protested vaguely.

"You're drunk, Joey."

"Who's drunk?" He teetered around the narrow room where they'd been living almost two weeks now, marvelling at this dumb body of his that could get itself so God damn stinko. He paused, he shook his finger at her, grinning, because he alone knew the big secret. What big secret? "Think I'm drunk, doncha?" he asked, a foxy grandpa, tapping the tip of his forefinger against his temple. "Ol' head ain't drunk, Sweetie. Not on your life, Sweetie. Not the ol' head." And wistfully he thought that if only he could put his hands inside his head and take out what he knew, to take it out and hold it in his hands.... Hold what?

He remembered. Oh, Georgie, why'd you do it, he thought heartbrokenly, and mourned for himself too. Georgie wasn't the only rat that night by a longshot. He'd doublecrossed himself, too. Eaten dirt....

Joey lurched across the room to the double bed. The spring squealed at his dropped body. He covered his face with his hands.

"Joey, Joey," she cried, running to him. "What's the matter, Joey. Joey!"

"Who's drunk?" he challenged her.

"Not you," she humored him. She loosened his collar, unknotted his necktie. There was whiskey spilled on the tie. She took it off, wet the corner of a towel at the sink in the room, scrubbed the bright silk. She kept glancing at him as she worked. He seemed to be asleep, but when she tried to help him out of his suit, he muttered, "Who's drunk? Who's drunk—"

"Joey—"

"You're drunk yourself! You're alla you drunk...."

Sadie Madofsky winced. She sensed a truth in what he had said. For wasn't she drunk to be living with Joey? And her father? Wasn't he drunk, worse than drunk? She lay down on the bed without undressing, tried not to think, for it was no use thinking of her father, of Joey, of anyone.

Her father had refused to listen to her, calling her *kurva* and driving her out of the house. *Kurva*, whore. Oh, so she had been seeing him before, her father had hammered at her. And once a week! And lying! Visiting her girl friend, indeed! A liar, no daughter of his, a whore! It was all crystal clear to Tailor Madofsky. A girl was either good or bad: a judgment like a bolt of lightning to be borrowed out of the fist of the Tenement God whose obscure delegate the tailor was. Implacable and righteous and all-powerful, that God. His bolts lit, not only the Sabbath candles of the Jewish storekeepers, but the candles in the churches. Black was black and white was white; the heart's different colors unseen in a world of bedazzled and slitted eyes. And so she had returned to Joey like a thousand other 'bad girls' fleeing the railroad flats where judgment had destroyed love, seeking love's shattered doll wherever it could be found—even in the arms of lovers and seducers, even in the arms of seducers and pimps.

When Sadie had opened her eyes in her seducer's room, she had stared, confused at Joey, a cigarette between his lips, his white shirt open at the collar.

Where was she? Where? In a bed! What bed? The recognition of herself on his bed had plunged into her last innocence like a driving hot bolt. Herself—no one else was under this sheet! Herself—her dress above her hips. Herself, oh God.

Sadie had suddenly glimpsed herself as something shameful, obscene like a penciled drawing on a subway poster. Something no longer quite a person, but the hidden parts of a person. Herself, the raw meat, the spots of blood on the bedsheet. That couldn't be she, she had thought in shock; and yet second by second the Sadie Madofsky who had attended school and helped her father in the store and kept his house like a little mother seemed to be hurrying away from the Sadie Madofsky half-naked in this bed.

"Sweetie," the white shirt had said to her, smiling. "We had ourself some fun. How you feel? You better wash up and we'll get some breakfast."

So far, she hadn't cried or screamed. She had watched White Shirt pick up a towel and bring it over to her. Recognized her underthings and stockings on the chair near the bed on which White Shirt had placed the towel. In front of the chair, she saw her shoes as if she had put them there herself, as if in her own house. She had stared at her things and they had stared back at her, inanimate but animate with memory, their betrayal the more awful because it was so casual.

"What's a-matter?" she had heard his voice or with it White Shirt's voice or the voice of her shoes. Her mind see-sawing between hysteria and the truth of this room, this bed, herself in this bed, her shoes on this floor. "Papa," she had screamed, beginning to weep.

"Sweetie—"

"You—" she had screamed.

"I didn' do nothin', Sweetie, you didn' wanna do—"

"You, you, you—"

"We had a coupla sodas and when we left you let me pet you and when I said we should come here...."

White Shirt was talking. The shoes were talking. In a fit of hysteria, she had flung the sheet from her, for she was going somewhere—Yes! to the police, somewhere, somewhere!—but the sight of her naked legs made her gasp. She had reached down with trembling fingers to cover her thighs, and then pulled the sheet over herself again. "Papa, papa!" she had screamed. "I'll kill myself!"

"Sweetie," he had said. "You gotta use your head on this—Your old man gets the wrong idea, we'll both be in dutch. He'll go to the cops and you'll go to reform school. Don't be crazy, Sweetie! For Christ sake, you don't want the reform school. l love you, honest! I love you, Sadie. When I'm legal age, twenny-one, we can get married—I love you so don't start actin' crazy. For God's sake, don't start actin' crazy. For God's sake—"

God! The huge and holy word she had heard all her life, that she had seen spelled out in the mystic Hebrew letters of her father's prayer book, had blazed like the first star of evening in this room of spotted sheets and spotted souls. Blazed and vanished as if lost in the vast white glittering sand of a multitude of evening stars.

In their clothes, they slept as if the furnished room were out on the street— the tailor's daughter and Joey Kasow home from his talk with the Spotter.

He slept and wandered down the long corridors of broken dreams. He was with his mother. He was alone, walking down an endless sidewalk, carefully and deliberately treading on the dirtfilled spaces between the slabs. "Jesus Christ stay in hell!" he was saying, for if he stepped off, even for a second, Jesus Christ might get out.... He and Georgie walked into a church. They were the only ones there and when he looked up to see the ceiling, he was frightened, it was so high, so high. He wanted to leave but the stone saints shook their heads, No. The head on the cross shook Its head, No. He began to cry. His mother appeared but she shook her head, No. The Spotter sat like a stone saint in a long flowing robe. No....

"No!" he cried, awaking out of childhood. Years ago, he had chanted "Jesus Christ stay in hell!" and once on a dare from Georgie had walked into Holy Cross Church on Forty-Second Street. Dreams of childhood, dreams of fear.

"Joey!" the girl whispered, her fingers touching his cheek. "Joey—"

He tried to rise. His elbow caved in; he tried again. He stumbled out of the room into the corridor where small yellow bulbs in the ceiling lighted his way to the bathroom. He went inside, groped for the light-chain, found it, pulled it. Before him were the brown walls of the bathroom. Brown gurgled in his throat. He rushed to the white bowl and nothing would stay down any more. Nothing. He puked the night's whiskey and the night's betrayals; the pride he had eaten and the broken splinters of his dreams. Croak! he cursed heaving up his guts. Croak! he cursed the whiskey. Croak! he cursed the Spotter and Georgie. Croak! he cursed himself and when the spasm ended, drenched with sweat, he looked down the hole and had a vision of his grave.

He staggered to the sink, washed, soaking his head. A face emerged in the mirror. "Croak!" he muttered.

When he returned to their room, she was sitting on the edge of the bed, crying quietly. She had learned in her two weeks with him that the walls of furnished rooms aren't walls so much as ears. She glanced at Joey. "Are you all right?"

He looked at her with the heavy eyes of exhaustion. She was a regular crybaby, he thought. Served him right for tying up with her. Should've slammed the door in her face when she'd come around that night. So instead like a damn fool he'd chased Georgie out and here they were in their own God damn room. Served him right. What'd he expected?

Yes, what had he expected? From her, from the Spotter, from Georgie, from himself?

He walked to the closet, reached in for a quart of rye cached there. "Joey, don't drink any more," she whimpered.

"Here," he said wearily bringing the bottle and glass over to her. "Here! Have a drink. Stop that God damn snivelin' for once!"

"I don't want any, Joey—" she cried.

"It'll make you feel better. Gwan, have a drink!"

"Joey, let's go away," she said brokenly, rubbing at her wet eyes.

"Yeh, but take a drink first." He poured whiskey into the glass, pushed it into her hand. "Gwan, drink it down!"

The girl swallowed the whiskey, coughing.

A second they looked at each other. The hour was late, the furnished rooming house quiet, all its doors locked.

All hearts locked up for the night, too. Behind his store on Twenty-Fourth Street, Tailor Madofsky couldn't sleep for thinking of his daughter. And over on Thirty-Seventh Street, Carpenter Kasow slept with his wife who maybe was dreaming of her lost son. Georgie Connelly slept in the furnished room where he was living by himself these days. And even Spotter Boyle dozed in his room at the Hotel Berkeley on Forty-Sixth Street. Only the street didn't sleep, its thousand eyes dark with the shades drawn in the windows, its ten thousand shades dark but here and there, a shining golden eye, the golden unwinking eye of the stone that never slept, its jaws the night and the darkness.

The next day, at the Young Democrats, Big Georgie led Joey aside. Later, in a Tenth Avenue speak, Georgie put what was between them out in the open. When he was finished, he wanted to know, his eyes anxious, "Joey, you tell me what else could I've done?"

"Nothin'. Spotter says jump off the roof, we gotta jump."

"I'm just a rat, Joey."

"Spotter's boss, ain't he?"

After nine or ten needle beers, they had their arms around each other's shoulders, with Georgie shouting for the whole world and his cousin to hear, "I let yuh down, Joey! Gonna carry that cross 'til I die!" Tearily, he cracked a hardboiled egg, pulled off the shell with clumsy fingers and offered Joey the mangled meat. "Take it!" Georgie pleaded. "Holy Mary, we know each other our whole life and looka what I done."

Joey accepted the egg, its yellow center exposed like a heart. He ate Georgie's peace offering but he knew things couldn't be the same again. Georgie could cry in his beer all night. Georgie could roll on the floor a week, but it was too late. Georgie'd ratted on him! And they'd been pals all their lives, Joey mourned beerily. Through golden-brown colored glasses he peered through the speakeasy smoke at the good old days....

The good old days when they had sat around in a backyard, sailed on their black ship, the 1-4-All, the candle on the shelf glowing like a sun on a far horizon. Ship-mates on the 1-4-All, in the days when they had played fair in the gang and foul with everybody else, when teachers' pets and snitchers, rats and stool-pigeons, were somebody to mobilize.

A rat was a rat, a doublecross was a doublecross. The Spotter'd made a rat out of Georgie. And what about himself? The guy who thought he was so hot? The Spotter'd made him backtrack. Made him spit in his own face.

In the lonely nights when all friends are gone, Joey poured out a little of what was burning him up. Responding like other tough guys before him to the beating heart behind a woman's naked breast. But only a little. Hell, he was no sap to spill the beans. If you couldn't trust a guy you'd known your whole life, how the hell could you trust a dame. Especially a crybaby of a dame. "Remember how I said I worked in a warehouse? Well, it's a brewery, a closed-down brewery." And because she was such a weeper, he'd dosed up the truth with a little brand-new bull. "This is no cheap bootlegger brewery, Sweetie. A judge's one of the owners besides the Spotter. It's high class. Like a bank." Grinning when she had timidly suggested he get another job. "I will," he'd said with another off-the-lip promise and yet touched despite himself. Most dames didn't give a damn what the guy did as long as he produced the cash or the good times. She did. She liked him, she loved him even. And if he cynically remembered that she had no choice, since her old man'd booted her out into the street, that was okay, too. You had to expect everybody to look out for themself, he thought. Whether it was a guy he'd known his whole life or this dumb cherry. "Sweetie, it's a good job I have. Only this Spotter Boyle—he's what you call a boss! I usta think, Sweetie, he was for me. Whatta sap! The Spotter's the kind what wants to own you like the pencil in his vest pocket."

As he owned the beaten and dispirited girl whom without conscious irony, he called Sweetie.

The owners and the owned: in a world where all the rooms, furnished or unfurnished, were narrow.

Sadie, when Joey was working in the 'closed-down brewery,' had gotten into the habit of going on long aimless walks.

One day she noticed the stained blue glass windows of an upstairs synagogue. It was above a haberdashery on Seventh Avenue below Forty-Second Street. She looked at the Hebrew words on the blue glass and thought this was some place to have a *schul*. Right in the middle of the crowds!

The fast-walking Seventh Avenue crowds seemed to have no need for synagogues or churches whether upstairs or downstairs. The men all seemed to have important engagements, the corsetless women skipped along, their flesh-colored stockings rolled below the knees. But everybody with a minute to spare at the deep excavations where foundations were being prepared for the cloak and suit lofts, to gawk at raw earth and uncovered rock: the pits of a new time without devils.

Sadie Madofsky had paused near the haberdashery. Above was the synagogue. Her heart was beating fast, she was tempted to go up and pray. She did-
n't care. How could she who was living with a bootlegger? A *kurva!* Still, with
the holy Hebrew words above her, she surrendered to her mood. She felt somehow as if under God's roof. Her eyelids flickered, her reddish-brown eyes mois-
tened, and she prayed for forgiveness, facing the haberdashery window, elegant with the scrolls of fashion. The crowds shuffled by, the traffic rolled, the
rivet guns dinned of iron tomorrows.

She began coming here often on her walks, the haberdashery a wailing wall,
and God shining in blue glass over her head. But her prayers became briefer.
She was wondering instead if she shouldn't go upstairs and talk to the rabbi.
Why not? Yes, why not? She memorized exactly what she'd tell him. She even
imagined what he looked like—he would have dark sad eyes and a kind face
and he would understand it wasn't her fault. Something'd happened to her
that first time, something....

But when she did climb the flight to the synagogue and was admitted to the
rabbi's office, her set speech never reached her lips. "Please help me," was all
she could say, faltering and tearful.

"Who are you?" the rabbi asked quietly. His eyes weren't dark and sad as
Sadie had imagined, but blue behind their gold-rimmed glasses. "Who are you,
young woman?"

Kurva, a voice shouted inside her head. She wept.

"I will help you if I can," she heard the rabbi saying but she was already edg-
ing towards the door. He lifted his hands to stay her, "My daughter—"She
gasped, hearing her father calling her, but it was not her father. She stared at
the rabbi's hands and fled the peace voice and hands were holding out to her.
Like the peace of the Sabbath when all was white and gold, the table cloth a
spotless white, the dead hands of her mother white, the candlelight and the
twisted yellowish bread of the Sabbath, the *chalah,* golden.

Downstairs, the crowd directed a quick look at her reddened eyes and just as
quickly lost interest. She walked alone among the thousands, she prayed
silently:

Dear God, blessed Lord, please forgive me. Dear God, forgive Joey, too. Please
forgive his sin, forgive my sin. He'll marry me, dear God, when he's twenty-
one. He promised, he loves me, please forgive him, forgive us, dear God in
heaven. Forgive us.

FORGIVE....

Like a bell the mighty word clanged in her consciousness. She trembled. She
moved with the crowd to Times Square. The trollies on Forty-Second Street
clattered north and south, shoeleather scraped, voices argued. And shouts of
news-hawkers selling still another bootlegger killing for a couple of pennies.

"I'm givin' you the Bug's spot," the Spotter had said to Joey with Bughead

Moore still on a slab at the morgue. "I like you, Joey, I always have. You got no police record," he'd congratulated the kid slyly. "Keep on bein' smart. One of these days you'll be as smart as the Ol' Spotter."

Joey had shown the Spotter the cold and obedient face of a lead soldier while he vowed he'd be smart all right. Let the Spotter think he owned him. His break'd come. Christ, he could wait. He was young, wasn't he?

Joey Kasow was only nineteen, but just the same he was no longer as young as he believed. The Spotter'd put a crimp in him, all right—the crimp of caution.

Four, five weeks later, in late September, the Spotter sent Joey up-state on his first gun job. There were three of them: Joey, Ted Griffin, the ex-pug, and black-haired Lefty. They picked up the mark, a guy by name of Longo, in the house of one of the Spotter's boys by name of Zelucci. It was, Joey thought, a ginzo party. In Zelucci's house, Longo was ready for delivery, tied hand and foot, a gag in his mouth. How Zelucci'd managed it the three from New York would never know. They asked no questions. The hell with it! They had their job. Zelucci had his. They carried Longo into their car, drove as per instructions on a country backroad until a deserted barn lifted into their headlights. Lefty, the driver switched the lights off. The night was cloudy, real dark. They picked up Longo and moved towards the barn. Inside, they dropped Longo to the floor. Ted Griffin clicked on a flashlight. The white beam steadied on Longo's face, shifted to empty stalls, a stoved-in milk pail, a rusted axe, to Lefty, to Joey with his hands in his pants pockets.

Joey said. "Why the hell you playin' with the light?"

"Okay, Joey...."

Joey was glad the damn flash was off him. He was feeling sick inside at what he had to do. "Keep the light on his face, will ya!" He stared down at the mark on the haystrewn dusty planks.

The light shone steady. It glinted on the gun in Joey's fist. The bound man on the floor saw the gun. He began to thrash about. He was gagged but his frantic movement was like one prolonged scream.

Joey blinked, he pressed the trigger. God! The sound of the shot! Joey lowered his gun arm. Springing huge out of the light, then shrinking to a silent still shape, the corpse confronted him, the hole in it forehead a third eye: the eye of death itself.

The light lifted to Joey's face as sweaty now as the dead man's face'd been. "Get that outa here!" he snarled at Ted. Like a living thing the light slid silently down to the dead man.

Mutely, accusingly, the three eyes peered up at Joey. The killer began to tremble. He couldn't control himself. The trembles became the shakes. His arms hit his side like two pieces of wood, his forehead ridged with stiff wrinkles, his mouth crooked, all his face inhuman. The mask sobbed, and all that was left of the killer was a distorted and silent shadow on the barn floor.

"He's cryin'!" Lefty exclaimed. "Fer Chris' sake!"

"Whatta you know!" Ted Griffin murmured.

The Spotter's understanding went deeper. "You got a case of buck fever, that's all. Forget it, kiddo. That Longo was just a crumb. What happened with the Bug? You have a cryin' jag on with him?"

"No, Spotter."

"You got the Bug in hot blood," was the Spotter's reasonable guess.

A few more gun jobs and Joey Kasow managed the calm that comes with the mastery of any trade, the face of a lead soldier matched by a leadening heart.

In the winter he had his first important job, a guy by name of Fallon. Fallon was a sandy-haired knife-scarred gangster come up lately like a house afire in the Spotter's territory. Not the first nor the last. A mad dog, that Fallon bitten by the mad dog dream of flashy cars and flashy dames, who figured he could start a chain of speaks if Spotter Boyle could. What the hell was so great about Spotter Boyle and Fat Quinn anyway? That was what Fallon was preaching to honest speakeasy owners who wished to God they could be left alone two months running. Joey had no sooner done a little scouting, when he realized that knocking off Fallon wouldn't be enough. With Fallon there were two guys just as tough, a squint-eyed Dutchman by name of Hemmler and an ex-con by name of McGuire. It had to be a clean sweep or else the guns'd be firing both ways. "It gotta be three-in-one," he had explained to the Spotter.

"You're right," the Spotter had agreed and patted Joey on the back. For a second the Spotter had let his light hand linger. "That's usin' the 'ol head, Joey."

Joey had split up the job, keeping Fallon for himself. Big Georgie, a cap low over his eyes and looking like another truckdriver, shot down Hemmler as he walked out of his girl friend's house. But Ted Griffin missed McGuire when his gun jammed. As for Fallon, the luck was just as bad. Fallon was nowhere. Like he'd dropped into a great big hole. Every big town has them. He was out of sight but not out of mind. Twenty-four hours later, Fallon's boys smashed up a bunch of the Spotter's speaks and that wasn't all. The Spotter, leaving the lobby of the Berkeley, was scratched by two bullets from a Fallon gunman outside in a cab. "Their aim's punk," the Spotter had commented in complete agreement with a sardonic-minded reporter who'd written up the story for his paper, praising the superior marksmanship of Chicago. Accompanied by Quinn, the Spotter in a sedan full of bodyguards, pulled out of town. The shooting improved. Sarge Killigan whom everybody liked, was killed when he resisted the Fallons who came to wreck the speak he was managing for the Spotter. Two more Fallons were shot down by Joey's gunmen, and on the tenth day of the war, Ted Griffin and a helper caught McGuire on a sneak visit to his brother. Fallon, the invisible man, they never caught up with. Had he lost his nerve? Hotfooted out of the Spotter's territory? For all anybody knew, he was still on the lam. Anyway, he was gone for keeps, a name to be batted around over a glass of beer.

"That Fallon, he was a mad dog! Wonder what happened to him?"

The coppers had wondered, too. "What about Fallon?" they had questioned the Spotter's boys down the station house. "What about Hemmler... McGuire...." With the Spotter's demon lawyer, Farber, fighting legal tooth and illegal nail for his clients. It seemed nobody knew a damn thing about Fallon. Certainly not Joey Kasow.

And as one year after another skipped down the West Side gutters like kids playing jump rope in a hurry, Fallon and his crowd became just another memory. Mad dogs, they all had their day.

"What about this stabbing of Micky Carroll?" the coppers asked Joey six months later.

Down the West Side, it seemed that every time a gangster was taken for a ride in a car—the new closed models supplied speedy rooms for murder—or found in a hallway, or dragged out of the river, the first thing that popped inside the ironplated copper head was to haul Joey Kasow to the station house.

"Angelo Petrucci...."

"Charley Kobleson?... And while we got you here what about that other Charley? Charley the Chicken Butcher...."

They would question him for an hour or two, keep him overnight in cold storage while he singsonged, "I wanna see my lawyer, Mister Farber. I don't know why you're pickin' on me. My record's clean. I got no felony on me! Not even a lousy misdemeanor! There's nothin' on me!"

Which was true. The gold ring on Joey's finger was the heaviest weapon they'd ever found on him. They had to let him go since they couldn't book him on the general charge that he was another Hell's Kitchen rat come up out of the sewer. Or because a stool pigeon was phoning a true friend (who paid cash) at the station house that the guy to question was Joey Kasow. More cash was pouring through the other end of the funnel. The Spotter had his own true friends behind the twin green lamps of the station houses.

They had to let him go while, behind him, the plainclothes dicks who didn't go in for plain living any more decided like the well-heeled philosophers they had become: "That Joey'll get his one of these days."

"You said it, Mike. Let them racketeers knock each other off I say. But to tell you the truth, that sheeny gets me a lil sore. Him and his damn clean record. Where does he hide his gun?"

Clean-Record Joey, the dicks nicknamed him. No-Gun Joey.

And in the furnished rooms where the punks kept their guns in five-and-dime toy holsters, they also talked his name up, his name and his nicknames. In the furnished rooms, in the speaks, in the floating crap games. Punks and bootleggers and tinhorn gamblers—all had their two cents to say:

"Try and prove a thing on Joey! Hell, he's got the Spotter behind him!"

"He's a tough bastid, wunna toughest in the whole West Side."

"No-Gun Joey—ain't that a laugh for a guy like him?"

No-Gun Joey.... "Don't believe all the stuff you read," Joey had said to Sadie when she'd first read a story about him in the newspapers. "You ever see a gun on me? The cops hate my guts just because I'm clean. I've told you a hundred times—I'm practically legit, Sweetie. I work for a closed-down brewery. We got a *judge*, one of the owners! We're legit! We don't haffta go in for no rough stuff. Never have. Aw, it ain't worth talkin' about. Les have a drink and then les grab a T-bone steak somewhere." With a glass of sherry in her hand—the lonely redhead was no whiskey drinker—she could almost believe him. And when she refilled her glass in the long evenings when she sat alone, the lonely evenings of the winos, she did believe him. To awake in the mornings, without belief or disbelief, a woman in a furnished room.

Whose face did she see in the mirror? A woman's mirror in the first hour of a new day is like a crystal ball in which the remembered past is sometimes more mysterious than the unknown future. Where was the girl Sadie Madofsky? Another face was hanging on a hook next to the day's dress. Another face, another life. When she rubbed her lipstick on, whose lips? The lips of the girl who had worked in her father's store, or the lips of the *kurva*, the whore? She would stare at her face in the mirror and remember kisses that seemed to burn her lips away, leaving lips of teeth. Kisses of the furnished room evenings.

Mirror after mirror remembered the girl Sadie Madofsky. They were her true calendars to be consulted in the waking hour of every new day. Sometimes she would move her face close, closer, closer to the mirror, as if it were a door through which she could pass and catch up with her lost self. Her face would touch the cold glass and she would know again that there was no return.

Sadie Madofsky? There was only the girl he called Sweetie: The girl with the bobbed red hair who sat of an afternoon in the darkened movie houses, who waited for him to come home, with a glass of sherry in her hand. Between one sip and the next, all the phantoms of respectability came and went without agitating her, without heartbreak. Her dead mother, her kid brother, her father, the teachers at Washington Irving, a constant coming and going without meaning like the footsteps of other roomers on the stairs. A glass of sherry in her hand, and she would sometimes even feel the Phantom Presence of God, not the God of the synagogues and churches, but the All-Seeing One of the furnished rooms. The Lonely One who understood the bottle of sherry in her closet as He understood the little dog who lived with the widow down the hall. Sometimes, whinily, she would pray. "Dear God, please let Joey marry me some day. I love Joey, dear God, and he loves me a little. Dear God, forgive us...."

The Lonely One always listened to her and then He would vanish in noiseless slippers as if He, too, were another Roomer.

As the girl with the bobbed red hair reached for the bottle of sherry.

No-Gun Joey.... The Spotter had to laugh when he read that nickname for the first time in the papers. He even cut the story out, and from that time on, he began clipping each new item about Joey Kasow. He kept the clippings in a big manila envelope in his room at the Hotel Berkeley. After a while, the Spotter's scissors were cutting out the stories and pictures of other West Side racketeers. Including his own. It was a strange and seemingly indiscriminate hobby for he tossed all the clips into the same manila envelope. Of an evening, he would pull out his paper jungle, and sort through them, glancing idly at the photos. With their felt hats pulled low over their pokerfaces—still remaining poker-faces even when they gave the cameraman a great big publicity smile—there was a resemblance among all the boys in the racket. Between the big-shots and the little shots, the bootleg millionaires and bootleg's ten-buck-a-day men. Then, the Spotter would return all the photos, except Joey's and his own, into the manila envelope, and with narrowed eyelids study the fresh young face of No-Gun Joey Kasow and the peaked sunken face of Spotter Boyle.

There was one other compulsive move in this new and strange hobby of his. Whenever some West Side racketeer was murdered (or given a long stretch up the river) the Spotter would patiently gather together all the dead man's stories and photos, reach for his scissors and slowly cut the clippings into pieces.

Two years after the Bug killing, Joey was averaging a hundred and a quarter a week for policing the Spotter's territory. He was the Spotter's number one gun, with fifteen guys under him, strongarms and weakheads mostly, good at smashing a rib or breaking an arm. Old-time blackjack boys and brassknuck bruisers who'd taken to guns like kids to a giant size lollipop. Of the whole kaboodle, Joey only used four or five for the rub-out jobs. Not that the others weren't okay. But he favored the guys with some brains. Like Ted Griffin who went out on a killing as if climbing into another kind of ring. Or his old pal Big Georgie who, although you couldn't exactly call him smart, still wasn't dumb, a butcherboy who liked his work. Two or three others.

He was in the dough, but he hadn't forgotten that the Spotter owned him like he owned his pearl-handled .38. (Between jobs, he had it cached in the flat of Ted Griffin's sister, a respectable widow who worked for the cloak and suiters. She never looked inside the suitcase her brother'd take once in a while from the top of the closet in her kitchen.) Even that pearl-handled .38 of his was a present from the Spotter. Often Joey had thought of buying his own iron. But, superstitious like most gunmen, he was afraid his luck might change with a new gun. For it was the Spotter's luck he was traveling on.

When the Spotter quit his private office at the Young Democrats, he turned it over to Joey. The Spotter had rented new offices over on Broadway near Columbus Circle. Slick offices for insiders in the racket, for the Spotter and Tom Quinn who operated the brewery that was making most of their beer, and two or three other guys come out of nowhere the last year or so who'd never been Badgers or even Young Democrats. Over on Broadway the letters out front were: ELWOOD REALTY COMPANY. To Joey they spelled: THE BIG SHOTS. Hell, he'd wonder with his feet up on the Spotter's old desk. Was that skinny bastard going to keep him on the gun his whole life? When the hell would a guy by name of Joey Kasow get a real break anyway?

"A guy has to go up, down's for the bums," Joey began sounding off to his redhead especially when he was lit. With the whiskey warm as a woman's hand on his belly, he'd feel himself floating up, up. Why shouldn't he become a bigshot? "All I need's a break, Sweetie. I got the brains, and that God damn Spotter knows it. That's why he's keepin' me down. What he don't know is I can wait." And in their room, they would drink together and time would stop, flowing neither backward or forward. "You stick with me, Sweetie. You'll see, Sweetie. I'll get my break wunna these days. I can afforda wait, I'm young, God damn it!"

In that boom year, the town was full of self-made men and if Joey dreamed too, a self-made gun, who could blame him? Didn't he have the brains and the nerve? Hadn't he made good on every job he'd ever tackled? Even the Spotter said so.

Once in a blue moon, the Spotter showed his face at the old club, dropping into his old office for a private little talk with Joey. "I hear you moved into the Hotel Delmore on Forty-Fourth," the Spotter had grinned one day.

"How'd you hear that?" Joey was surprised, but not too much. There was nothing he'd put past the Spotter.

"Never mind, kiddo. I got my ears out all over town," and still grinning, "Bet you'd like to move to the new office?"

"Whoever told you that Spotter's a damn liar!"

"Nobody told me. Keep your shirt on!" His eyes fixed on Joey. So sharp and so intense Joey Kasow felt them like two pressing and probing fingers almost. "Don't you want to?" Those eyes were probing Joey's silence now.

"It's up to you, Spotter. You're the boss."

"Ted Griffin could handle your job, even Georgie."

"It's up to you, Spotter."

"Sweet, ain't you? Don't kid the Ol' Spotter, Joey. I know you inside out. You're just like me. I wouldn' be satisfied down here. You're too smart to be runnin' around with the gorillas down here. Only thing is, I got nothin' for you on Broadway. Soon as there's something I'll let you know. That okay with you, Joey?"

"Sure, Spotter."

That night, the Spotter lay sleeplessly in his dark hotel room, his mind roving across the night to the Hotel Delmore like a peeping tom: A regular sweet one, that Joey, he thought. Must come from sleeping with a redhead, I wouldn't mind myself, only who the hell are you kidding, Spotter? You're all done, done in.... Funny how she gets me, a dame I never seen even once. Funny, yeh, funny, and not so funny. She could be a blondie or a blackhair wop and I'd want her. She could be cockeye, with a shape like a sack and I'd want her. What's good enough for Joey's good enough for you, right Spotter? Right! That's better, Spotter. Don't kid yourself. You can kid the whole world but not yourself. Funny, how just because she's Joey's private piece you get a lil tickle. You must love that Joey something awful. Love, love, I'll give him a shove, that's poetry. I'll bury him like I buried Clip Haley, me with the Bum Ticker. Aw, cripes, Spotter, you ought to give yourself up to the undertaker, what good are you. Old Fat Quinn's a better man. He can eat, drink, and even take care of lady Quinn. So he says, anyway. Least he could, with a son and three daughters to prove it. That's a crowd to have at a funeral. Who'll you have, Spotter? Nobody but the devil. Who'll get your dough? The devil and his brother. Worked like a nigger, all work and no fun, to build up a racket. Suppose you conk out. Suppose the Bum Ticker gets you? Who'll run the racket? Old fat Quinn, with Manny Farber the shyster. More likely Big Bill Dwyer or Ownie Madden. Or Larry Fay. Or Dutch Schultz. Old Fat's talking of retiring to that place of his out at Tom's River, that mick Heaven-on-the-Sea. Manny Farber wants to be a magistrate. Those two'd sell out to the first big guy who makes a fist. That's how it goes. Jesus Christ, Son of God, that's how it goes. Aw, I'll ride to a million funerals, to Old Fat's, Manny Farber's, all of them. Joey's a better man any day, why don't I give him a break? He's learned his lesson. I knocked the Al Capone out of him, long ago. Him and me, we could be a pair. He's a jewboy and I'm a mick, damn queer jewboy, damn queer mick. Who the hell knows what we really are, any of us, deep down. I ought to give him a break, I like the kid, always have. That's the trouble, he's too much like me. Not a wrinkle on his mug, all the wrinkles inside. Young and raring to go, the worst kind. The hell with him, I'll bury him first, him and his redhead. Funny how she gets me. Georgie says she's pretty, with a shape. Only one in the gang who's ever seen her is Georgie. And that was years before Joey started laying her. Funny, how he keeps her under cover. Because she's Jewish I'll bet. He's been fighting the kosher-kosher all his life. Aw, the hell with them both. You got a date with the lawyer tomorrow....

It was a good year for the lawyers, and it would be good the years after, as it had been good the year before. Coolidge was in the White House, the boom years seemed endless, strutting out one after another like drum majors, each more beautiful than the one before, whirling the dollar-batons of prosperity while behind them the whole nation marched, a flask on its hip, and the Favorite Bootlegger's phone number in its address book.

Booze was still the Racket. In New York, it was the East Siders who were branching out of the Racket into the rackets. Some of the big West Side bootleggers had begun to invest a little money in gambling and whores, but mostly they only knew the Racket. Not the East Siders. "No wop eats an artichoke widout payin' a cut to Terranova," they said over on the East Side as if talking about an act of God. And Salvatore Lucania, who lately was calling himself Lucky Luciano, was beginning to wonder whether whorehouses couldn't be organized into chains like speakeasies. While another pioneer by name of

Bugsy Siegel was preaching, usually with a glass of imported whiskey in his hand, "Gambling's the racket that'll last! Prohibition can only last if the Republicans keep electin' guys like Coolidge. Gambling's, that's the racket with a future! So what're we doing about it? Only Al Capone out there in Chi with his dog tracks." True. Although another East Sider by name of Frank Costello was already knee-deep in slot machines. Of Frank Costello, the East Siders in the know were saying, "Frank won't be happy 'til he has every one-arm bandit in the whole city and the whole damn country workin' for him."

The garment industry began moving wholesale into the West Side, bringing among others, Lepke and Gurrah, two East Side labor racketeers, old friends of both the garment workers and the bosses. Lepke and Gurrah, when a strike situation was cooking, would call union and management and announce, "This is L. and G. How can we get together on this?"

"Garments always been our racket," L. and G. passed the word along to the West Side big-shots. "But this is your territory. How can we get together on this? We don't want no trouble."

"We been asleep at the switch," the Spotter said to his partner Quinn. "That L. and G.'ll be down the waterfront next and from there they'll muscle into our racket."

"Who gave yuh a shot in the arm!" old Quinn exclaimed. But he couldn't quiet down the Spotter. A meeting was called at the Elwood Realty. Invited were Tom Quinn, Manny Farber, the Spotter's lawer, John Terry, a politician on the Spotter's payroll (the Spotter suspected his Honest John of being in on two or three other tinboxes) and Hooker Alfiero, a hiring boss down the waterfront. They sat in a semi-circle inside the Spotter's private office, the Spotter their pivot: Tom Quinn with a mug on him like Paddy Pig, Manny Farber, sharp and smiling, a dark thin needle of a man, John Terry and his beer belly, and don't forget the steak belly, Hooker Alfiero with a grin on him as if he had an ace up his sleeve. The Spotter looked at all their faces and then swiftly evaluated the face inside. Quinn wanted to retire to Tom's River, New Jersey, and live on the fat of the land. Farber was conniving to be a magistrate. Those two had the itch to be respectable. Not the two other crooks, the Spotter thought. John Terry was already trying to land himself on the L. and G. payroll. Only Hooker Alfiero had nothing inside, just an honest crook.

The Spotter nodded at Hooker. "He's hiring boss down the Cunard piers and he's gonna work with us. I been lookin' into the waterfront. We can do ourself some good there. If we wait much longer L. and G. or some other bastid'll be gettin' idears. There's a local down there, Local 23, we can control. They got two guys fightin' to be top dog. A mick by name of Fitzpatrick. A wop by name of Luzzi. They're both on the level. Both wanna be president. Luzzi, we leave alone. He's a religious nut and works with the priests. We'll work on the mick. John Terry here'll handle the political end. Those dock wallopers're votes, they might squawk. Manny Farber, we'll all pitch in. Okay, any questions?"

Later, when the Spotter explained the picture to Joey, he said, "It's your chance, kiddo. I told you I'd let you know when I had somethin' for you. This is your chance to get into the labor racket. No reason why you can't run that Local 23 for me. Ted Griffin, he can take over your 'ol job."

They had talked it over at the Spotter's hotel. Leaving the Berkeley, Joey had intended going home; the Hotel Delmore was only two blocks away. But he knew he wouldn't be able to sleep tonight. He'd have to knock himself out first, and Sweetie was no good tonight. Every month these dames had to be sent back to the clock factory, Joey thought. What about Annabelle? He hopped a cab, gave the driver her address. He'd been keeping her in partnership with Big Georgie and Ted Griffin. It wasn't his night but Ted and Georgie were up in Albany on a job. Joey grinned, he started to whistle:

"'I'm sitting on top of the world just rolling along, just rolling along...'" Oh, that Local 23! His lucky number from now on! 23! That big 23, and he'd give it to Annabelle 23 times. Joey laughed. Thoughts of Annabelle and thoughts of Local 23 interlaced like two clasped hands. A date with Annabelle and who had a date with the Spotter at the Elwood Realty tomorrow? Nobody but himself! A date, a date, a date, she had the whitest legs he'd ever seen on a dame, the break he'd been waiting for....

The cab curved around Columbus Circle and north up Central Park West. Joey thought, about time he got himself a car, one of them Niagara blue roadsters, he liked them conservative, none of those canary yellows or firehouse reds, and he'd have his initials put on the door: J.K. Yesirree, J.K., the big-shot.

Uptown, he unlocked the door of Annabelle's apartment, stumbled in the darkness before he managed to find the switch. "Hey, you asleep?" he shouted. He was in a living room furnished like the miniature of a movie lobby, an ornate mirror on the wall, two marble-topped tables flanking the couch. He sailed his straw hat to the couch. He walked into the bedroom. "Hey, Annabelle, if you're out—" he shouted, fearing she was making a little hay on his partners.

Annabelle awoke. From her bed, she reached for the light. It shone at Joey through a big blue lampshade. "That's where I got that Niagara blue!" he said, smiling with joy.

"Don't you say hello or nothing?" she asked. He flopped down on the bed, his hands going for her.

He pointed with his chin at the lampshade, "Niagara blue!" Joey chuckled. The blue light was on her bobbed yellow hair, on her full sulky lips. He kissed her, she pushed him away.

"This ain't your night," she reminded Joey. "This is Tuesday. You're Wednesday and Sat'days. Ted's Tuesdays."

"It's okay with Ted, Sweetie. He sent a telegram. 'Go see Annabelle,'" Joey laughed, unknotting his necktie.

"You're a riot," the blonde sneered.

"Sweetie, if I get enough dough, I'll keep you all by myself."

The blonde was sitting upright now, her shoulders against the backboard—she seemed immovable, a white spread of solid curved flesh. "Dough? What's that? Where would *you* get enough dough?"

"I been thinkin' of another racket."

"What?"

"I never talk to dames *what*," he said, winking as he undressed.

"What about the wife when you strike it rich?"

"Hey," he peered up at her as he unlaced his shoes. "Why do you keep callin' her the wife? I'm not married to her."

"No?" Annabelle shrugged a milky shoulder. "You said yourself you been with that wino four years. That makes you married in my book—"

"You been with me close to a year. You my wife, too?"

"On third shares," the blonde said. She stretched her arms. "I work too hard."

"Aw, quit gripin'!"

"This isn't your night! Go to that wino—"

"Stop callin' her 'that wino'!"

"You call her that—"

"Will you shut up, you God damn arguin' hoor!"

"Okay, you whore-keeper," she retorted maliciously. "Tuesdays are Ted's! Wait'll I tell him."

He stared at her and all the fun was gone out of the night. It wasn't only her, he thought. It was the Spotter who a guy could trust like he could trust a whore. "Okay, Tuesday're Ted's," he yelled. "I'll slap you silly!"

"If you stay, you treat me nice, Joey," she said fearfully.

Joey... he heard her and heard the voices in the speaks and the pool parlors: Joey, he's the toughest bastard in town. By God he was, he thought. Tough and smart and Local 23 was just a beginning. He'd waited a long time for his break. Too God damn long. "I'll treat you nice," he said and slapped her face, seeing the thin bony face of the Spotter under his hard hand. And even when their argument was forgotten, he felt the Spotter in the shadows of consciousness, the Spotter, always the Spotter. As he plunged down long black streets, and whether he was in pursuit or being pursued, he didn't know....

Sunday morning Joey and Georgie climbed up the three flights of stairs to Fitzpatrick's flat. A radio was playing, "Mr. Gallagher and Mr. Sheean," a woman with a foghorn voice shouted at her children and the smells of late Sunday breakfasts still frying in the pan floated down the tenement stairs. "How high up's the guy?" Georgie wanted to know.

"Want me to carry you piggy back?"

Big Georgie laughed out loud like a little kid and Joey thought: he's a kid, that guy. How could a guy like that stand up against the Spotter? Joey frowned. The teaser he had asked himself over the years again flashed into his mind. Would he've double-crossed Georgie if he'd been in Georgie's spot? Maybe yes, maybe no. Anyway, he could half-trust Georgie, he decided. Who'd he picked to come along on Fitzpatrick? Nobody but Georgie, like Georgie was a lucky dollar bill or something.

On the fourth floor, Joey called, "Hey Fitzpatrick!" A big woman, her brown hair in curlers, poked her face out of a door, eyeing them as if they were two rent collectors.

"Who yuh want?" she asked suspiciously.

"Fitzpatrick. You the wife?"

"Who'd like to know?"

"We're from the union," he softsoaped her. "It's union business."

The woman led them into her kitchen. "I'll get Fitzpatrick," she said and walked into the next room. Georgie pulled off his straw hat. He fanned his hot face and winked at Joey.

He likes working for me, Joey thought, glancing about this kitchen that could have been his mother's or Georgie's mother's. The castiron stove unused now in the summer; the table covered with oil cloth; the sun threading the cracks in the windowshades. The old days stirred in his heart a second and he wished that things hadn't changed between himself and Georgie.

When Fitzpatrick stepped into the kitchen, the sleep was still heavy on him. He yawned, his big tattooed arms hung as if weighted out of their sockets. He wore a sleeveless undershirt, gray pants, his yawny red brick Irish face like a hundred others down the West Side. Then suddenly he was fully awake. His sleepy face seemed to have grown a heavy jaw. There were a pair of sharp gray eyes on either side of his short twisted nose. "You guys ain't from the union!" he said harshly.

The three men seemed to be meeting on a street corner, Joey and Georgie with their straw hats on their heads, tightening up, too, at the dock walloper's anger.

"Not exactly," said Joey. "We could help you against Luzzi."

"Who the hell's askin' for help! Who are yuh guys?"

"Friends. We can be your friends or Luzzi's—"

"An' you can git the hell outa here!"

The straw hats didn't move an inch. Fitzpatrick shouted, "Git the hell outa here!" His wife rushed into the kitchen.

"You got her worried," Joey remarked, smiling.

"Who's askin' you! Git out!" Jabbing his stiffened forefinger at the kitchen door. "Git out! Git out!"

"We're goin'," Joey said. "You're okay, Fitzpatrick. You're an hones' union man! Trouble is you're in my territory." His eye brightened as he said *my territory* and by God it was his territory. *His* territory, *his* break, *his* Local 23....

Three days later, as Fitzpatrick was leaving his house for work, a parked car rolled down the street, Joey at the wheel. Big Georgie, Lefty and Billy Muhlen jumped out, blackjacks in their fists. They left Fitzpatrick on the sidewalk. He lay there like a fly glued in its own blood as the housewives screamed for the cops out of the windows.

"The cops," the Spotter informed Joey, "they t'rowed his complaint into the terlet. Betcha three to one he comes around." But Fitzpatrick was stubborn. He wouldn't talk with John Terry who went to see him. John Terry, who described himself as, "A peepul's politician, for the peepul first and last," couldn't do a thing with the dock walloper.

It was up to Joey again. He used finesse this time. He waited until Fitzpatrick was strong enough to go back to work. He let the union leader earn close to a week's pay and even to fortify himself with a visit, after work, to a waterfront speak. When Fitzpatrick stepped out into the street, they kicked the whiskey out of him. They broke his twisted nose with the end of a blackjack. When they had him down, Georgie banged his fist into Fitzpatrick's right eye, and then as deliberately into the left one.

Mrs. Fitzpatrick had to lead her husband like a blind man to the station house. "Them gangsters hit him in the eyes extra on purpose," she wept. The desk sergeant listened to her and expressed his opinion it was Luzzi's boys slugging Fitzpatrick. "You better get yourself some pertection," the copper advised the union leader.

"What they payin' you for pertection?" Fitzpatrick bellowed.

"You're blind as a bat, man," the desk sergeant replied calmly. "Don't be dumb too."

At the Hotel Delmore, it was a chipper Joey these days. "Sweetie," he said one morning, a day or so after the second beating of Fitzpatrick. "Things're comin' along fine." Freshly shaved, his dark blonde hair slicked down, he looked at her on the bed. She lay there as unmade as he was made up for the summer morning blowing through the windows. Her red hair uncombed, her face pale, two tiny clots in the inside corners of her eyes. "Yep, I'm the early bird!" he laughed.

"Joey—I still don't understand it," she said as he walked to the dresser to knot his necktie.

"What doncha understand, Sweetie?"

"Why should the longshoremen union—"

"Let me run things?" he interrupted her. "Well, I skipped most-a the details so no wonder you don't understand. But take it from me, it's like everything else. A racket. It's the pull what counts." He patted his brown and blue necktie, walked to the closet for his jacket. "I'll tell you somethin' else I been thinkin'. This is a mick union and they don't love the Jews. I been thinkin' I oughta call myself Case. Spelled with a C, not a K. An American name, more like. How you like it? Pretty classy?"

"Joey, you know how I think," she began timidly. "If it was up to me—"

"You don't know what class is! These're a bunch of micks—but what the hell do I haffta explain it?" He slid into his summer jacket graceful as a dancer. "You're in America only you still don't know it."

"Joey, I don't want to fight with you—"

"Shut up then! Those foreign yid names're okay for tailor stores but that's all!"

Her lips twisted as if he'd slapped her. She was silent. Her head lowered meekly on her neck, reminded him of his mother. The thought infuriated him. All she needed was a shawl. "Lay off the *vino!* And wouldn't you be the one for the *vino!* The Jews and the ginzos! *Vino!*"

He was gone and after a while she got up and showered. After a while, she sat at the mirror.

That was she, Sadie Madofsky—or maybe he'd call her Sally now. Sally or Susie, to go with Case. C, A, S, E, with a C. Mrs. Sally Case. A real American.

She smiled bitterly at the face in the mirror. "Hello Mrs. Case," she in a flat tinny voice like a perfumer in a vaudeville skit at the Palace. And wept a second later.

She lit a cigarette. She smoked two in a row and then shrugging, poured herself breakfast: a glass of sherry.

The phone rang—a woman who lived at the hotel, Mabel Sears by name, with whom she'd become friendly.

"What are you doing, Sadie, on this gorgeous day?" Mabel asked in plush la-de-da voice.

"Nothing."

"Ditto! And am I sick of the papers! Did you read— They ask Rhinelander, 'When you slept with Alice didn't you see she was colored?' That nigger had her nerve saying she was Spanish. Why can't we meet millionaires like Rhinelander, or do you have to be a nigger, I ask you. Let's have lunch, all right? I know a place where we could meet us some nice men—"

"No."

"Still the pure in heart. Oh, you dope. What does he do with his spare time? Go to the library?"

"Mabel, I'll hang up!"

"Your Joe's just like my Bill—"

"I'll hang up on you!"

"I'm only trying to get some sense in you."

"Never mind, never mind!"

"Why all the excitement? Oh, you redheads! Why don't you do what I do when I'm excited, Sadie? I sit me down in a chair and I tell myself 'Day by day in every way you're getting better and better.'"

"That's Dr. Coué's—"

"What do you care whose it is? It's good for hangovers, too. I hate to see a girl drink before six P.M."

"Whose drinking?"

"Who said you were? I'll meet you in the lobby about one. All right?"

"All right."

Everything was all right. Dr. Coué said so, and Dr. Coué ought to know.

The Local 23 election was held on a Thursday night in August, with twenty of Joey's strongarms lined up against the walls outside the meeting room. At the table in the entrance, Joey sat, the membership lists typed in alphabetical order, before him. "What's your name?" he said to the first dock wallopers coming up from the street. They glanced uneasily at the delegates from the poolrooms leaning against the walls. "What's your name?" Joey repeated. "Only members in good standin' vote tonight," he stated. "No damn ringers tonight!" That night, members in good standing were limited to Fitzpatrick's supporters. Fitzpatrick'd come around—two beatings were enough plus the fact that the authorities were completely uninterested in his complaints. Fitzpatrick's supporters, their names checked off on the membership lists, were admitted; Luzzi's supporters kept out. The Luzzi votes milled around, waiting for Luzzi; for Luzzi's righthand men, Brennan and Pellicane.

Luzzi'd been knocked for a loop in the hallway of his own house; Brennan was in a hospital, his face smashed in; as for Pellicane, he'd listened to John Terry, "the peepul's politician." Fitzpatrick was elected president of Local 23. Unanimous.

During the next few months, the local was made into a juicy little racket. There was a cut to the Spotter and Quinn on the monthly membership dues. With Hooker Alfiero's help, pilferage was organized solidly—with cuts to Hooker, the Spotter, Quinn and John Terry—the steamship lines footing this bill. "I know I promised the local to you," the Spotter had said to Joey. "But John Terry, he gotta claim for what he done, and he got a coupla relatives to take care of. They'll be in the local with Fitz. Joey, it just can't be helped."

"I was counting on that Local 23," Joey'd said. For once he hadn't been able to manage the pokerface of a good soldier.

"Aw, I'll find you somethin' better," the Spotter'd promised him. "To cheer you up, here's half a G for the good job. Honest, I'll find you somethin', Joey. Remember, they don't call me the Spotter for nothin', and added a sly digging thrust. "I spotted you when you was nothin', remember, kiddo?"

As if either of them would ever forget that little fact again this side of the grave.

The first thing the Spotter did on awaking that May morning was to reach for his heart with the stealthy pickpocket hand of a man with a coronary. He picked its slow and even beat and looked with the palest of eyes at the light buff ceiling of his room at the Hotel Berkeley. The second thing the Spotter did was to turn on his bedside radio. From the square brown box an invisible songbird, female sex, fluttered: "'Barney Google with those googly googly eyes....'"

He turned up the volume, draped his black silk robe over his shoulders and to the tune of "googly googly" walked into the bathroom. Shaved to "It Ain't Gonna Rain No More." Dried his bony jaws and chin to "Yes, We Have No Bananas."

An excited announcer broke in with a news bulletin: "Lindy's on his way!

History is in the making! Lindy's on his way, God bless him! At 7:52 on this 20th day of May, 1927, Lindy, the man of destiny climbed up into his plane the Spirit of St. Louis...."

At ten o'clock, he sat with his partner Quinn in his lawyer's booklined office, the brown and red legal tomes backdropping Emanuel Farber, counsellor at law to the lawless. On the lawyer's mahogany desk lay a newspaper with a banner headline: LINDY TAKES OFF.

They figger he'll make it in thirty hours," Quinn remarked after the first hellos. He sat overflowing his chair, a fleshy and aging Irishman with a head on him like the end of a beam that had been sheathed with fat, his little eyes set in puffs of fat.

"Did you know Lindy's father was a lawyer and a Congressman for quite a few years?" Farber said with enthusiasm.

"Okay, Manny, you'll be a magistrate next year! A congressman, too!" the Spotter said. "Wanna know something? I'm sick and tired hearin' about this Lindy. Maybe I oughta call off my meetin' with Dutch Schultz account of Lindbergh? The hell with the Swede!"

"You ain't human," the old Quinn scolded him.

"Yeh, the only other guy that don't 'preciate Lindbergh today is John Terry an' he happens to be dead." The Spotter spoke with a definite relish like a man who has just put away a good meal.

The lawyer and the ex-saloonkeeper stared at him. The Spotter's lips split into a little grin. "Maybe John should've been allowed to stick around for all the Lindbergh excitement?"

For a second all three thought of John Terry. He had been their man, another West Side politician with a regular route like a milkman between the desks of the police sergeants, the roll-tops of the big politicians, and the Spotter's pay-off desk at the Elwood Realty. An under-the-table man, John Terry, shot down six days ago in the vestibule of a brownstone house in the Twenties bought on the proceeds of one under-the-table deal too many.

The lawyer was the first to speak—officially. "Spotter, I wouldn't advise that kind of loose talk if I were you!" Pointedly, he added. "John Terry left quite a few friends."

"Yeh, don't talk ill of the dead!" the Spotter mocked, and lowering his head he crossed himself with a mocking hand.

"You oughta be ashamed!" Quinn said angrily.

The Spotter jeered. "Honest John Terry! He would've been alive today connivin' and chiselin' like he done his whole life if you hadn't got so damn lazy. His blood's on your hands, Quinn."

"That's an awful thing to say!" the fat old man said in a trembling voice.

"We'll put it up to Manny here. Who was the one who got sick and tired supervisin' the brewery—"

"Spotter!" Quinn shouted. "What's that got to do with Terry?"

"Lemme finish. Supervisin' the brewery was your job. Okay, you squawked so much about retirin' and one damn thing and another, we sold it and began buyin' beer from Dutch Schultz. The worst thing we could've done—"

"We didn't know it then," Quinn protested.

"No? We knew he was the prize mad dog of all time. Dutch Schultz the guy never satisfied. We know'd he was the kind always lookin' to squeeze a guy out. And that goes for us."

"We didn't know he'd be turnin' Terry into a Judas!"

The lawyer lifted the hands of a well-paid peacemaker and said, "We've got enough headaches without arguing among ourselves." He smiled, "If these arguments continue, I'll be flying to Paris myself—"

The Spotter reached for the newspaper on the mahogany desk and flung it across the office. The front page, with its huge black headline and full-length picture of the pilot standing at his plane, pulled loose, flying with paper wings an instant before sailing down into the thick carpet.

"May I ask the purpose of that?" Manny Farber demanded.

"I'm seein' Schultz twelve o'clock on that hoss piss he calls beer!"

"All right," the lawyer placated him.

"I don't wanna hear no more Lindbergh! We're in a bad position. There's a limit to what we can make our speaks buy and Schultz's beer is that limit! Joey givin' 'em the muscle is no answer. They're right and we're wrong. They're the ones losin' the customers. We gotta improve the beer and that's all there is to it. So I see the Dutchman and he promises better beer. With John Terry out, he'll give us better beer awhile, but his promise you can wipe your feet on! The way I see it, we'll have to make our own beer again."

For more than an hour they argued it, the Spotter against both Quinn and Farber. This was no time to buy a brewery, Quinn kept repeating. Not when everything was skyhigh. A good brewery would come to three or four hundred thousand dollars. Besides, the presidential elections were one year off. If Al Smith got the Democratic nomination, prohibition would be on the way out. The Spotter retorted that dealing with the Dutchman wasn't the cheaper proposition, not even if prohibition were to end in 1928. Weary and exhausted, he rose to his feet at eleven-thirty. "I'll see Dutch Schultz. But I still say we got no choice. We'll haffta buy a brewery, make our own beer again."

Quinn's eyes were moist with excitement. "Not me, not me, Spotter! If you buy a brewery, you buy me out! You can buy me out—"

The Spotter blinked. He thought, it never rained, but it poured. "How much you want?"

"I ain't figgered it out in dollars and cents. You name a figger."

"How about five bucks cold cash?"

"You sonuvabitch, I don't like that kinda joke—"

Again the lawyer lifted his soft hands like a legal benediction—hands almost as white as the framed parchments on the walls—and as Quinn cursed, the Spotter faded out of the booklined office. When the door closed, Manny Farber scurried out of his chair and picked up the scattered pages of the newspaper from the carpet, glancing at the headline as if he hadn't seen it before: LINDY TAKES OFF.

"Where do you think he is by now?" the cabbie asked his new fare.

"Who?"

"Say, who you kiddin' mister? Who!"

The Spotter remembered. The propellers of the Spirit of St. Louis blew away the thoughts clouding his brain. Thoughts of Quinn.

"He started at seven fifty-two," the cabbie was saying. "Soon be four hours. His plane can do three hundred twenty miles an hour easy...."

The Spotter's mind picked up the phrase, converted it to his own problems: *three hundred twenty miles an hour easy*—three hundred for a brewery, maybe four, it's a boom market. That bastid Quinn! Buy him out! What'll I buy him out with if I have to dig up three hundred....

"In four hours," the cabbie was saying, "Lindy'll be more'n a thousand miles out. It's a big pond, mister. I remember when I crossed it in a troop ship, a big pond, and a thousand's just the beginning...."

And a thousand's just the beginning—beginning of what, I'd like to know? Dutch Schultz, end of prohibition maybe. No wonder Quinn wants to retire, leave me holding the bag. He's skimmed the cream. Twenty grand he put up when he came in with me. A lousy twenty grand. He's made a fortune. Made his lousy twenty back the first six months of prohibition. Averaged close to a hundred thousand a year the last five years. And I have to buy him out so he can sit on his fat butt the rest of his life out in Tom's River bragging what a big man he is to the fat ass cops retired out there. Buy him out, buy a brewery.

"That's a helluva big pond," the cabbie was saying, on the gloomy side now. "It's a big pond, Mister."

"What?"

"It's a big pond, I said."

The Spotter stared at the cabbie's red ears. "If he falls in who'll find him?"

The red ears became one red ear attached to the side of a horrified red face. "Mister, don't talk like that for Chris'-sake."

"We all fall in, don't we?" the Spotter said, shrugging.

"I getcha. Yeh, but not him, Mister!"

The first thing Dutch Schultz said when the Spotter came into his hotel room was, "Damn lucky Lindy pushed John Terry outa the papers, Spotter."

The Spotter removed his light gray hat and looked at the grinning face in front of him. A face with a neatly mended broken nose and a rocky jaw. It could have been a boxer's mug.

"Lucky?" the Spotter inquired politely.

"Lucky for you," the Dutchman grinned as he tossed this one, wild and reckless as a haymaker. That was the Dutchman all over, a guy like a haymaker.

The Spotter said, "I wouldn't go around makin' talk like that, Dutch."

The Dutchman laughed. "John Terry, he had half a dozen speaks, they say, in your territory, Spotter."

"They were safe by me, Dutch. It ain't the old days no more when you broke a blood vessel over every mad dog."

"That how you feel, Spotter?"

"That's how I feel."

"You're full of..." the Dutchman grinned. "How about a drink?"

"Not if it's your beer, Dutch."

"Always complainin' about my beer. Anyway, you don't drink, do you Spotter?"

"Your beer made me a tee-totaller, Dutch."

"You're gonna get first-class beer," Dutch Schultz assured him, grinning. "You're not gonna have no more complaints, no more, Spotter." He made these promises or rather he seemed to throw them: verbal uppercuts dissolving in thin air. The Spotter left within ten minutes of his arrival. He had been wasting his time.

Downstairs, the Spotter thought: there's nothing for it but to buy a brewery. He went into a phone booth and called Arnold Rothstein. The man who had fixed the World Series in 1919, parlaying a hundred grand into a million, was a banker now to every racketeer in town. Luck was with the Spotter. The big-shot had a late lunch date, but if the Spotter came right over they could talk.

The Spotter hopped a cab to Rothstein's hotel, the Park Central. Outside the radio stores, people were listening to the loudspeakers. Lindy hovered over the city as if in an airplane hanging on wires in the sky.

The Spotter went up to Rothstein's apartment. He shook hands with the dark-haired gambler. The Spotter was nervous, he couldn't forget for a minute that when he was still trying to squeeze three nickels out of a dime, Rothstein was rolling in money.

Like any other banker, Rothstein had to know exactly what his money was wanted for. The Spotter explained in detail why he might be needing three or four hundred thousand to buy himself a brewery.

"I'm not going to loan you that kind of money," Rothstein said finally. "Not that you're not good for it, Spotter. I don't want to get into the middle of a situation between you and the Dutchman."

"That your final word?"

"Next to final anyway, Spotter."

"What do you mean by next to final?"

Rothstein smiled. "You come to me when things're quiet down the West Side."

"If you mean this John Terry thing—"

"I'm not asking you anything, am I?" Rothstein said with honest indignation.

He had fixed the World Series, broken the hearts of a million kids mourning the White Sox become the Black Sox, but he drew the line somewhere and practiced what he preached. He would lay dying a year later, a bullet hole in his side, refusing to give the police any information.

The Spotter returned to his own hotel. He lay down on his bed and thought of three hundred thousand dollars. He had close to half million in a dozen banks but it was a principle with him not to use his own money. The three hundred G's could be raised. Every speak in his chain would chip into a war chest. But that'd take leg work, not to mention tonguework, especially if the word got around that Quinn wasn't in. Quinn.... The Spotter thought about Quinn. The Spotter left his bed, phoned the Young Democrats Club, asked for Joey. Joey wasn't around, he was told. The Spotter phoned the Hotel Delmore. Mr. Joe Case wasn't in his room, and neither was his wife, Mrs. Case. The Spotter phoned the Young Democrats again and instructed Ted Griffin there to hunt up Joey, that he was coming over right away.

He had forgotten about Lindbergh, but when he stepped into the clubroom, the radio was going heavy and fifteen or twenty of the guys were listening as if their lives depended upon it, like it was the last game of the World Series. Hats shoved back on their foreheads, cigarettes slanting out of their mouths, they helloed the Spotter and gave him the latest report. Although there was nothing really to report—Lindy was somewhere over the Atlantic, a single man in a flying speck of metal, out of all contact with his country and countrymen. Including this batch of strongarms listening now with one ear—the other ear cocked anxiously for the Spotter's opinion—as the radio voice stated: "... The expectation is that Lindy will fly for the Irish coast."

"He'll be in Paris tomorrow," the Spotter delivered his opinion, turning his back on the glad-handers. Their eager faces irritated him. "I'll be in my old office," he said. "Send Joey in when he gets here." He walked out of the clubroom, a narrow figure in his dark suit, his face almost as gray as the light gray felt tilted so jauntily on his head.

That sonfabitch Joey, the Spotter thought as he sat down wearily in the swivel chair at his old desk. Just when I want him, he's disappeared. The Spotter put his heels up on the desk. His head sank on his chest. His pale eyelids that somehow seemed as if they had been boiled in water a long time, closed. He dozed, and dozing, his face was oddly like a boy's—a middle-aged boy whose jaws and chin had become bonily fragile with the years, almost childlike.

His eyes opened but the footsteps that had awakened him weren't Joey's. Through the wall, faint but distinct, he heard the radio: "... the father of Lindy, Charles A. Lindbergh, might have been the Governor of Minnesota, but he failed to be elected..."

Governor of Minnesota, the Spotter thought bitterly. They all wanna be Governor of Minnesota, they're never satisfied. John Terry, Dutch Schultz, all of 'em. That Schultz! I'll bury him like I buried John Terry....

He glanced about this old office of his, the walls painted a fresh oyster white. He remembered when the office'd been painted green. That first year, back in 1920, and how when the paint was still fresh, some wise guy'd stuck a French picture postal into it. Cockeye Smith most likely, although Cockeye'd sworn himself black and blue it wasn't him. A lot of difference it made now. Cockeye was six feet under, killed in the trouble with Charley the Chicken-Butcher. Cockeye Smith and John Terry and all the other wise guy sonuvabitches who wanted to be Governor of Minnesota. One by one, he had taken their clippings out of his manila envelope and cut them to pieces. One by one, and now it was that greedy hog's turn, that fatass of a greedy hog, Quinn.

When Joey showed up, he found the Spotter asleep, his head pillowed on his arms on the desk. "Spotter," Joey said softly.

The Spotter awoke, he pushed a cigarette between his lips, inhaling the smoke as if it were blood. He was pale as a zombie after his nap.

"Where were you?" the Spotter asked.

"Seein' a guy who promised me a coupla tickets to the Maloney-Sharkey fight tonight."

"Didn't they call it off?"

"The fight? What for?"

"For Lindy."

The thinnest and coldest of smiles touched Joey's lips. The Spotter appraised that smile as he glanced into Joey's eyes, clear and bright and gray—and absolutely emotionless. The Spotter thought that ever since the Local 23 to-do a year ago, the heart was out of Joey. Which hadn't been a bad thing. It'd made Joey a perfect gunman. "You and Lindy must be about the same age," the Spotter said.

"Exactly the same. He was born in 1902 like me."

"That so."

"Yeh." Joey sat down alongside the desk.

Outside they heard the radio describing the Spirit of St. Louis: "... in this invention of man, as delicate as a fine watch, a heroic American defies the ocean and all the elements...."

"Real guts," Joey commented.

"Joey," the Spotter said in a low voice. "On this Terry job we had a deal. I promised to put you back into Local 23 and I did. Pull up your chair, Joey."

The chair scraped along the floor. The Spotter leaned towards Joey, their heads close, almost touching, the sunken-cheeked head of the Spotter and the smooth-cheeked head of Joey. "You oughta know, Joey. Quinn wants somebody else, kiddo, for the local."

Outside, the radio like a wound-up toy was beginning again: "At eight o'clock this morning, Charles A. Lindbergh electrified the nation by hopping off in his airplane, the Spirit of St. Louis...."

"Joey, this is 'tween you and me," the Spotter whispered. "Nobody else knows. And I'm gonna tell you somethin' else. Somethin' I learned today that can work out for you and me both. Nobody knows this, not even Manny Farber, only me and you. John Terry wasn't the only one on the Dutchman's payroll. Why do you think we sold the brewery? Why we buyin' the Dutchman's lousy beer? You know why? All this time, Quinn's been gettin' a cut from the Dutchman."

His whisper faded out but not before, sharp and spitting as a bullet, Joey had heard Quinn's death warrant.

"Nobody knows about this, Joey. Only you and me. You'll have to do the job yourself. And Joey. There won't be no other hitch on that local, not with me runnin' things. Okay, kiddo?"

"Okay."

Those gray eyes of Joey Kasow alias Joey Case could have been made of glass like the eyes a taxidermist puts into the heads of his stuffed hawks and owls.

For the first time the Spotter thought fearfully that maybe the kid ought to be dumped for keeps. No-Gun Joey was getting too damn perfect on the job. Another wise guy who wanted to be Governor of Minnesota! Waiting for his chance, always waiting.

FOUR • *THE OFFICE*

"The man didn't have an enemy," the Spotter told everybody. It was a big expensive funeral. The box in which Thomas Quinn was placed like a dollar cigar was worth five thousand dollars. It was a year of killings. Little Augie Orgen was killed in a doorway; Frankie Yale was shot down on a hot Sunday afternoon and buried in a silver coffin; the flowers cost thirty-seven thousand dollars. The flowers were beautiful in Kansas City, too, and in Philadelphia. In Chicago, at the funeral of Dion O'Bannion, there was a wreath from Al Capone with the simple and moving words, "From Al." While back in New York, Arnold Rothstein, with a hole the size of a saucer in his side, hung on for two days without naming his killers. Seemed there were no killers. Only funerals and flowers and headlines. 1928 was sensational but 1929 topped it. On St. Valentine's Day in Chicago, three Al Capone gunmen disguised as coppers walked into a garage where seven O'Bannions were waiting for a load of booze and mowed them down with machine guns. ST. VALENTINE'S MASSACRE the headlines screamed from coast to coast.

Too many killings, too much publicity. Everybody was shaking a head—the public, the law, and the lawless. Men like Lucky Luciano and Lepke (of L. and G.) decided something had to be done about the mad dogs who, as every sober underworld character agreed, "were plain lousing up the racket." Something had to be done about the publicity hounds who spat at public opinion. About Al Capone in Chicago, about Dutch Schultz, Jack 'Legs' Diamond and Spotter Boyle in New York. Guys like that were just plain bad for business. After all, the beer and whiskey business or the gambling or whorehouse business—take your choice, pal—we're no different from any other business. It was lawyers and accountants, supply and demand. The same customers, buying the new radios and the new cars, were also patronizing the speaks, the horse parlors, the whorehouses.

The sober men, the solid men, sent the word to practically every big-shot racketeer to come down to Atlantic City and talk things over. The beer barons came, and the hoss-thieves who ran the horse parlors, and the men who ran the dope dynasties, and the princely pimps who had organized chains of little pimps, and the fabulous friends of both Labor and Management.

From New York, Spotter Boyle accompanied by Emmanuel Farber, traveled down to Atlantic City and in the banquet room of a big hotel sat at a great big table whose shining surface reflected the faces of this first convention of big-time criminals. Al Capone was there, fat and dark and waving a hand when he talked as if expecting the newspaper photographers any minute, still behaving as if he owned Chicago. He was about to be dispossessed, but he didn't know it yet. He didn't know that the New York organizers of the convention had secretly scratched a bookkeeper's red line through his name. Opposite Al Capone at that shining table sat the big men of Chicago whom his gunmen had missed, Moran and Aiello. Mob war in Chicago had to stop, the New York organizers argued. Stop everywhere. The country was sick of it. There was a new president in the White House, Herbert Hoover. The federal agents were buzzing around in every town looking for a club. A new time was coming. "Prohibition wasn't going to last forever!"—this was a big slogan at the convention. And: "We've got to get ready for changes." And: "We've got to trust each other." And: "The public's dumb but we can't spit in their face forever."

And the first thing that had to be worked out was this Chicago thing. Now suppose Al Capone makes peace with Moran and Aiello and what's left of the O'Bannions. Yeh, peace, Al, the gangland diplomats argued; all this shooting has to stop. Wait a minute, Al, wait a minute everybody. You'll all get a chance to sound off. Wait a minute! Public opinion, ever hear of public opinion? Public opinion has to be satisfied. The suckers have to get something, so this is what we'll do. You, Al, you'll go to Philly and get yourself pulled in for carrying a gat. Wait a minute, Al! The public's in a lather about you, Al, it's the only way. You'll get six months in jail and the suckers'll quiet down, they'll be satisfied. Al Capone's in jail, see, and everything quiets down, Chicago quiets down. Your interests won't get hurt, Al. Johnny Torrio'll look after your interests. Torrio, the guy who brought you to Chicago in the first place. Torrio and Aiello and Moran here'll run Chicago 'til you get out and no more war.

Scarface Al Capone didn't want any part of it, but he was talked into the deal by the diplomats from New York. They had everything figured out—the future all cleaned up and ready for the oven like a twenty-pound Christmas turkey.

Take booze for instance. Yeh, booze. Ain't that a mess half the time? When we got too much booze in New York what do we do but dump it in Philly. And you guys out in the sticks are no better. In Detroit and Cleveland you get your booze from Canada. You war with Chicago where they depend on industrial alky. That's bad business. That's all wrong!

There were a lot of things all wrong and the convention organizers now revealed their pet project, the real reason for calling the convention: *A Central Office.*

A central office to milk the last whiskey millions out of the prohibition cow.

A central office to put gambling, prostitution, narcotics, the labor rackets on a solid business basis.

A central office to eliminate headaches, headlines and headline hunters.

A central office ticking like a thousand-dollar watch with everything and everybody, rackets and racketeers, moving like hour hands, minute hands, and second hands, all the way down the line.

The Spotter, cagey as ever, sought out the New York organizers, confessed he'd been off-base. Hell, he was no mad dog like Al Capone or Dutch Schultz. From now on, he'd let the central office handle his headaches. Privately he said to his lawyer, Farber, "If they can get Al to go to jail, who are we to buck 'em?"

"In The Office, there's gonna be one guy in charge of enforcement," the Spotter notified Joey when he returned to New York.

"What's that?" Joey asked.

"What you been doin', kiddo. This Charley Valinchi over in Brooklyn. You'll be with him, Joey. And your side-kick, Georgie, too. Now wait a minnit before you start askin' questions. This is a real break for you. It's workin' direct for The Office. A real break, kiddo!"

The Spotter was lying a mile a minute as Joey would discover in the months that followed. But even with the news piping hot off the Spotter's tongue he could see something was wrong. There was *wrong* in the Spotter's eyes. There was *wrong* in the little smile the Spotter gave him free of charge. It was all *wrong*.

Not that Charley Valinchi was a bad guy. The trouble with this enforcing was that instead of one boss, he now had a dozen, with Charley the only one with a face. The Office didn't have a face. Lucky Luciano, Lepke, the other big-shots—they were faceless. The Office! With Charley Valinchi their errand boy. And if Charley was only a high-class errand boy, what the hell was he, Joey kept asking himself. Where was he going now? What was ahead of him? When he'd been working for the Spotter, there was always the feeling he could get to be somebody. True, the Spotter'd kept him down, had him mobilize Local 23 only to double-cross him, but he'd played his cards close to his chest, and with the John Terry job, the local'd dropped into his lap, and after the Quinn job, he was in solid. Or thought he was. It was clear as a bell that the Spotter'd just been waiting for the chance to get rid of him. True, his dough came from Local 23—that was one of The Office's laws: its enforcers got their living from their own private rackets—but he no longer had much to do with Local 23. His new job was with The Office. Enforcing! And what was that? Nothing. A guy could be brainy or dopey, fox or dumb-ox, and it made no difference. I'm stuck, Joey was thinking, stuck for life....

Charley Valinchi summoned his enforcers when he wanted them to his restaurant out in Brooklyn. It was located in one of those run-down slums across the bridge from Manhattan where the red brick houses squat side by side like silent old folk on a park bench. The kind of neighborhood where the kids are always saying, "Nothin' ever happens here." Good times or bad, the worn red brick houses looked just the same. The collapse of the Wall Street boom in October 1929, the first cries of panic, the first waves of unemployment hadn't made much difference to the looks of this neighborhood or to

Charley Valinchi's restaurant, the Napoli. Like a dozen other 75c-for-an-eight-course-dinner Napolis, the walls had been decorated with murals of Italy, daubed on by an artist, half sign-painter and half hungry. There was Venice and the gondolas, Rome and the Coliseum, all done in ghastly bluish greens and funereal reds like the drawings for a wax museum.

Joey walked from the subway late that spring evening over toward the Napoli. He felt that he'd about worn a path from the subway to the restaurant this last year. The errand boy of an errand boy—that was what he'd come down to, he brooded. Christ, I better stop thinking of it or I'll go nuts. He hoped that tonight Charley wouldn't be sending him on another out-of-town job. From one month to the next, there was no telling. He'd been to Kansas City once, to Detroit twice, and lucky he'd missed out on L.A.

"Out there in the sticks they know who they gotta get rid of," Charley Valinchi had explained to Joey before his first trip. They could do the job them-self. Sure, but when we control it from New York, it's easier to keep it quiet." *Keep it quiet* was a favorite of Charley Valinchi's. More than once he had said, "Keep it quiet, boys. The soft pedal, boys. The soft pedal." Which meant sim-ply that the old way of plugging a mark full of holes and leaving the dead meat on the sidewalk was now n.g. New ways for a new time. The enforcers mixed the enforcees with cement. They soaked them in gasoline and burned them to a crisp in the stolen murder cars. It could be a rockhead of a gambler up in Boston moving into territory where he had no right, to be dumped into the river where he could argue territory with the eels. Or the kidnapping of some Baltimore junk peddler getting a little too cozy with the Narcotics Squad, who, when buried in a field out of the city, could be depended upon not to start up a big funeral. The office was against big funerals. Big funerals were headlines.

The Napoli was empty when Joey walked inside, with only its lone waiter Gregorio reading a newspaper at one of the red and white cloth-covered tables. "Hello," Joey said.

Gregorio smiled nervously. He was an old man and he'd never gotten used to the young men who came to see Charley Valinchi just before the Napoli closed for the night.

Joey turned into a doorway, into a narrow corridor. He passed the gaudy green-painted door of the Men's Room, the paintless door of a broom closet, and in the rear of the corridor paused at a fine mahogany door with an engraved copper plate lettered: PRIVATE.

There was a story behind that door which had hung once in a Brooklyn Heights mansion. There, in a neighborhood of elegant brownstones overlook-ing Brooklyn harbor, an old shipowning family had lived for three generations. When Charley Valinchi had bought the property in the lush prohibition time, he had occupied the office on the third floor: PRIVATE. On the floor beneath, Charley operated one of the classiest restaurant-speaks in all Brooklyn. He had sold the property in 1928 just before the crash and was sentimental enough to remove the mahogany door with its engraved copper plate. "My good luck," Charley would say.

Joey knocked, a voice said come in. He entered a room fitted up like an office. Charley Valinchi was sitting at a broad flat desk talking to two men. He had a yellow pencil behind one ear, in the lapel of his dark blue suit an almost fresh carnation—a habit continued from his years as a big-time speakeasy prop. His dark face was round and it had been handsome, but like the carnation, the bloom was gone. He looked like a floorwalker after a long hard day. With him, waiting for Joey's arrival, were Chuck Tillio and Walter Rozak. Chuck wore a conservative brown suit, but Walter Rozak was dressed as in the old prohibition days, in a light suit the color of cake icing and a necktie that could have lit up a dark room.

"Joey, you're always late," Charley said.

"How's the West Side Kid?" Tillio asked, while Rozak smiled, his fat pink face like a mean rabbit's.

"Sit down," Charley said briskly. "Let's get going here." He opened a folder on his desk. "This is a guy in our territory...."

The trial had begun. In the home territory of The Office, Charley was more than the chief enforcer. He was also the judge and he always had a trial, although the man on trial was never present. Always, too, there were witnesses, sometimes as many as eight or nine. But tonight in the case of Milty "The Poet" Finestein, there was only Tillio to defend Milty and Rozak to prosecute him. If the judge decided Milty was guilty, Joey would take it from there.

Charley Valinchi was consulting some scribbled notes in his folder. He lifted his head and said, "A couple months ago, in Febu'ry, to be exact, this Finestein comes knocking on the door and gets to see somebody in The Office. We can forget who, somebody big. He comes with a pitch how Dutch Schultz ain't satisfied muscling into Harlem and taking over the numbers racket from the dinges, but how Dutch got plans to take numbers all over the state. Oh, yeah!" the judge reminded himself, nodding at Joey. "This Finestein's one of Dutch's number runners. He still is. That's the trouble with Finestein. The story we get, he's reportin' on us to Dutch. The guy's working both sides of the street."

"He's a stool pigeon," the defense lawyer without a degree, Chuck Tillio, conceded right away. "What I say though is, The Office can use all the stool pigeons it can get with a guy like Dutch Schultz. There's a guy always been a nuisance. He was a nuisance when he was makin' beer. He's a bigger nuisance now. He gives everyone a bad name. What I'm tryin' to prove is we need stool pigeons in the Dutchman's mob even if they ain't a hundred percent reliable stool pigeons—"

The judge broke in sternly. "What's all this guff? A hundred percent reliable? You can either depend on a stool pigeon or you can't depend. Finestein's reporting to us on the Dutchman and the next day he turns around and reports to Schultz. Don't forget Schultz is smart. How do we know he didn't tell Finestein to come to us in the first place?"

"Where's the proof?" defense counsel demanded.

Walter Rozak said: "The proof's in the Dutchman's own big mouth and I'll prove it—"

"I'm not through yet," defense counsel said.

"You are so!" the judge overruled him.

Joey sat there, smoking, only half listening. The hell with them all, he was thinking. With Charley Valinchi the judge, and Chuck Tillio sweating to make a good case for a stool pigeon, and Walter Rozak sitting there like a tub of lard. The hell with this trial and the next trial. The hell with the God damn Office pulling all the strings and making them all jump. And the hell with himself. Why should he leave himself out? A God damn errand boy!

"When I say you're through, you're through," the judge was saying to defense counsel. His words to Joey seemed to be a sentence pronounced on himself.

Walter Rozak began the prosecution. "I said I'll prove it on the Dutchman and I will. Everybody knows how he's been soundin' off all over town. How he's always been an innapendent. How he's not taking orders from no mob." He dug into his pocket and produced a little notebook from which he read a name, "Maizie Willet. She dances in the show 'April Moon.' She gets around, this dame. She was at a party given by the Dutchman and Finestein was there too. She said the Dutchman got drunk and started in hollerin' how he was gonna run the numbers racket not only in the state, but all over the country—"

"What're we tryin' to prove anyway?" Chuck Tillio demanded. "We all know the kinda guy Dutch Schultz is, but he ain't on trial here. Finestein's the one on trial! What we wanna know is was he planted by the Dutchman on us? Or is he on the level with us?"

The judge stared at defense counsel. "You said before he wasn't a hundred percent reliable."

"That ain't what I said, Charley. I said that even if Finestein wasn't a hundred percent reliable, we needed him because we needed all the dope we could get on the Dutchman."

"He didn't let me finish," the prosecutor appealed to the judge who nodded at him to continue. "At this party where Maizie Willet was, the Dutchman said he wasn't taking orders from nobody."

Joey blinked at the phrase—*he wasn't taking orders from nobody*. That much could be said in the Dutchman's favor, Joey thought. He was no order-taker like a certain bastard by name of Joey Case. A conniver, yes. A chiseler. A liar. A phoney. A sell-out artist. The Dutchman was every damn thing in the dictionary but he wasn't an order-taker. Like every single bastard in this backroom was, from Charley Valinchi down. Order-takers one and all, not fit to wipe the Dutchman's shoes.

"What're we tryin' to prove?" Chuck Tillio sing-songed. "Who's on trial anyway?"

The judge waved at him to keep still. The prosecution went on. "At this party, the Dutchman said, 'They call themselves big names. The big mob, the big combination, the syndicate, the central office. But all they are is a bunch of fourflushers.'"

Again Chuck Tillio protested. He was one gangland D. A. who took his duties seriously. "Alla this is no proof on Finestein—"

"You want more proof!" Walter Rozak said viciously. "Okay, I'll give you more proof. We been tailin' the rat. He's suppose to be upstate organizin' for the Dutchman. So where is he? He's in New York half the time with the Dutchman! Don't that prove nothin'? The Dutchman's no fool. Finestein has to give out to be so damn popular! Why ain't he upstate where he should be?"

"Where's the proof he's sellin' us out? All that's no proof."

The judge frowned and then slowly, disgustedly, stated. "One hundred percent bottled-in-bond proof don't exist. This Finestein guy's spending dough like a drunken sailor. Where's that money coming from?"

"We're payin' him good money," defense counsel said doggedly.

"Who's paying you?" Charley Valinchi wanted to know and instantly smiled to demonstrate he was only kidding. "Enough crapping around on this Finestein guy! The Dutchman's paying him good dough and the Dutchman don't pay for nothing. So that leaves just one argument. Maybe this Finestein guy's stooling for the Dutchman and for us. Chuck, he's got a point there. But this is no easy time like prohibition where we can take chances. Not with this depression, and everybody hollering for action. Al Capone's in Alcatraz and although nobody's crying for him, who put him there? The Government. On income tax! It proves things're tightening up. The federals're looking for more convictions. What I'm driving at is that in a time like this we can't take chances on guys like Finestein."

The judge had passed the only sentence on his books: death. It was either death or acquittal.

Joey looked at Chuck Tillio, but the defense counsel was no longer in the defense business. Chuck's thin pointy face was as set as the judge's or the prosecution's. "Joey, I want to talk to you a second," Charley said when they all stood up to go. The door closed on Chuck and Walter. Charley Valinchi said, "What about Georgie Connelly?" Charley shook his head, answering himself. "He's getting in too many fights lately. He's drinking like a fish. You know what he done? He got drunk and went up to the Spotter's office."

"What for?"

"You tell me what for? You been with Georgie on enough jobs. Think he's softening up?"

"No."

"You sure, Joey?"

"Yeh."

"This is the second time he's gone up to the Spotter's office."

"First I ever hear. What's he do there?"

"What's a drunk do? Makes a pest of himself until they get him out. You better talk to Georgie, Joey."

"I will."

"I've seen it a dozen times," Charley remarked as if to himself. "They start drinking heavy or they start jabbing a needle or crying on the shoulder of some pott. They get punchy like a fighter, and before you know it go haywire. As he spoke, his eyes were dark and speculative. Joey felt a shiver across his shoulder blades like a finger dipped in ice. He thought, there was just too much black crepe hanging in this backroom.

The next day late in the afternoon, Joey and three other enforcers, Georgie Connelly, Pete Bowers and Tunafish Tunnetti, drove out of New York City across the marshes of New Jersey onto Route 17. Georgie was at the wheel, Joey next to him, Pete and Tunafish in the back seat. They climbed the first mountains at Wurtsboro, the little lakes of upstate New York glittered in the spring sun, the first frame and stucco hotels began to crowd the roadside. "It's called Sullivan County," Pete announced. "But when the hebes start comin' in the summer, it's called Solomon County." Only Joey didn't laugh. He sat staring through the windshield, thinking that Pete and Tunafish didn't know he was a hebe and Georgie wouldn't be giving him away. ("Georgie," he had said when he'd begun calling himself Joey Case a few years ago, "These Local 23 guys, Fitz and the others, they kiss our ass now, but they won't forget who gave 'em the lumps. That's why I'm Joey Case down here, savvy? It's bad enough without havin' em know I'm a Jew.") Well, he didn't look like a hebe, and maybe he wasn't a hebe anymore, he thought now.

Sometimes he just plain didn't know who he was. Joey Case or Joey Kasow? Sometimes he felt as if he were neither hebe or goy. Just one of Charley Valinchi's errand boys. Just a case of tough luck on two feet, an eight of spades to himself and everybody else, the little black jinx card dealt out by Charley Valinchi to so many guys it was getting hard to remember all their names. Or to remember his own, the name inside that a man slowly makes for himself over a lifetime out of the alphabet of his hopes and ambitions and dreams.

And as he lay in bed that night at the Monticello Inn, in the town of Monticello, the old question rolled out again inside his brain like the long curving highway itself: where was he going?

Sleeplessly he whirled down the speedway of all his doubts. Here he was again cursing out Charley Valinchi and the Spotter who'd gotten him into this enforcement racket. What was the percentage in that? He listened to Georgie snoring in the second bed. That Georgie took enforcing in his stride. Or did he? Maybe Charley was right and Georgie was beginning to soften up. He'd have to talk to Georgie. This going drunk to the Spotter's office was a dumb business. But no dumber than what he was doing, Joey thought. But how could he get out of it? Go up to the Spotter's office himself, beg on bended knees, "Hey, Spotter, have a heart, and take me back. I'm just nothing with Charley Valinchi."

Joey tried to sleep. Across his shuttered eyes the images of frustration slowly lost their blinding white edges, darkening. He thought of the eight of spades again, saw it as a real card moving as if from the fingers of a lightning dealer. But whether the card was for Milty "the Poet" Finestein or for himself, he wasn't too sure.

He awoke early, groaned when he squinted at his wristwatch. It was only 7:03. He glanced at Georgie sleeping in the second bed near the windows. That sonuvabitch slept like a baby, Joey thought, listening to the singing of the birds that had aroused him. Sonuvabitch birds, he cursed to himself and stared at Georgie's heavy face, the lips and cheeks bluish-black with stubble. "Georgie," he called. No answer. For a second Joey felt like a heel. Why wake up the guy? Then he reached for his pillow and tossed it at Georgie's head. Georgie grunted. Georgie slept. Joey studied the sleeping man. There was a happy boy, he thought bitterly. Give Georgie dough enough for dames and he wouldn't gripe in a thousand years. Just a happy lil sonuvabitch who maybe was beginning to soften up. Well, Georgie was no chicken no more, and neither was he. The pair of them'd be hitting thirty in another year or two. Thirty! For Christ sake! He'd be thirty and what'd he have in the sock. What was he? A God damn errand boy of Charley's. And even that couldn't last forever. One of these days when everything was running smooth, Dutch Schultz and all the other independents done for, there'd be a little meeting of the big-shots: "We don't need Charley Valinchi, we don't need Joey Case or any of those guys. What we oughta do is get rid of that whole Valinchi setup. They know too much. If one of them ever goes soft and runs to the D.A., the F.B.I., we'll be sunk."

I got too much imagination for my own good, Joey thought gloomily, glancing at his wristwatch. It was 7:05.

It was a long day. Their contact in town phoned at 9:20 and said, "Everything'll be ready tonight."

"We can have a second breakfast," Georgie said when Joey told of the delay.

They were all in Joey's and Georgie's room. Joey said, "No second breakfasts, no goin' for a walk. This is a hick town. We're gonna stay put."

Pete Bowers rubbed at his chin. "Yeh, Joey, but won't it look queer to the hotel hicks, us hangin' around all day?"

"They're in a fog," Joey said. "But even if they got a Gus-the-eagle-eye, we can't take no chance of Georgie or Tunafish gettin' tanked up."

Georgie snorted. "Who's gonna get tanked up?" Tunafish shrugged like a woman.

"Good news," sighed Pete dropping down on one of the unmade beds. He was short and dark with the appearance of a jockey gone to seed, his eyes pouchy, and only his clefted chin still hard in his face. Tunafish was also dark-haired, his nickname wished on him not only because of the Tunnetti but even more because of his fish-like mouth. Lazily now, stretching out each second to the breaking point, he reached into his pocket for a cigar. He stripped off the wrapper, studied the red and gold label and then in slow motion bit off the end. He didn't light up until another three or four seconds'd ticked off.

Georgie sat down on the second bed. "Wunna them hick whores," he remarked and stretched out his long heavy body.

"No dames 'til the job's done," Joey said.

"I know, I know, but can't a guy even dream." Georgie closed his eyes, a broad smile on his lips. "If I had me a lil dame now you know what I'd be doin'?" His left arm hugged an imaginary girl, his right hand began stroking her. His lips bunched up a kiss and he blew it off. Softly. Tunafish laughed, Pete shrugged.

Joey thought that Georgie'd sure changed. Here was a guy who once'd given out with the words like they each cost a quarter. A regular clam face. But lately Georgie was always up on a soapbox. It was the booze, the tons of booze, Georgie'd lapped up in his time. Joey's eyes darted to Pete and Tunafish who didn't seem to have a tongue between them. What he knew about them he could put inside his vest pocket, Joey reflected. Pete Bowers was a personal friend of Charley Valinchi's and once he'd owned a string of speaks in Greenwich Village, but he'd gotten into trouble, welched on money he owed, strictly a guy on the downgrade. Tunafish, with his long curly hair and fishmouth, from all Joey heard, had never been much of anything, a spooky kind of a cuss who did what he was told, and gambled in his free time. The rumble was that he'd grown up with Lucky Luciano himself and that Lucky'd sent him to Charley. Anyhow, Joey summed them up to himself: I wouldn't trust the pair of them with a nickel in cash. Or Georgie either when you got right down to it, not after that time.

He walked to the dresser, he fussed with his hair, straightened his necktie. He'd lost weight, his lips were thinner as if somebody had been filing them down to two sharp edges. He studied that mouth of his. The lips were shut but just the same he imagined, he knew, yes, he knew, what they were saying: You're one of Charley's enforcers. You're tough. Man, you're tough. You're the toughest guy in the West Side, in the whole damn country, in the whole damn world, and you're just a jerk.

Georgie had been watching Joey from the bed. "Hey, beyootiful!" he called. "Doncha wish you had a dame here?"

"Who's got cards?" Joey asked.

Tunafish fetched a pack from his room and they played four-handed pinochle until lunch. After lunch, they returned to their separate rooms. Georgie tugged off his shoes, announced to Joey he was taking a nap. Joey played solitaire. He smoked and time shook itself slowly like jello in a dish. He went downstairs to the lobby, bought two western magazines from the desk clerk. He thought that Pete was right. It must look queer, four guys from the city parking in their rooms all day. The hell with it! So it looked queer! So he was getting reckless. Maybe that was how he was softening up.... He returned to his room, lay down on his bed and read of cowboys and vigilantes and double-crossing sheriffs. The hoofbeats of their mustangs died away and he yawned at the printed words. Huger than any western prairie, his mind surrounded him, the dust of his thoughts rising from the galloping horses of his imagination. They carried their own sinister riders—Charley Valinchi with a carnation in his buttonhole; the bony Spotter. God, Joey thought, the Spotter's the only one who can get me out of this ratrace before it's too late.

Too late? It was already too late, or almost too late. Abruptly, he chucked the magazine and woke up Georgie. He felt he had to stop thinking or go nuts.

"Hell," Georgie mumbled sleepily.

"You're right one hundred percent," Joey said with a wry smile. "Georgie, what the hell's the idea botherin' the Spotter?"

Georgie grinned foolishly. "Who told yuh?"

"Charley. You better cut it out, Georgie. The Spotter don't like it, and lay off the bottle, Georgie. You don't want 'em yappin' you're a crazy lush. Cut it out!" he repeated in a voice so intense despite its low tone that Georgie forgot to inhale on the cigarette between his lips. "I'm warnin' you for your own good! Whatever the hell you do, stay away from the Spotter!"

"Yeh," Georgie agreed uneasily. "Yeh—"

"Don't *yeh* me like a muttonhead, Georgie. You're gonna get yourself in real dutch."

Georgie'd heard enough. "When do we get rid of this guy Finestein?"

Joey shrugged. "Who the hell cares?"

"Whatta you mean, Joey? We don't want to hang 'round here forever—"

"Don't worry. This Olsen'll deliver him all right."

"Who's this Olsen?"

"He runs the slot machines up here," Joey said and wondered why he was yapping now? It must be catchy.

"Finestein work for him?"

"Nope. "

"How's this Olsen fit in then?"

"He's got slot machines, the Dutchman's got numbers."

"I don't get it, Joey."

Joey thought he shouldn't be yapping to Loose Lips Georgie.

The hell with them! The hell with Charley and the Spotter and the whole damn Office! "The Office supplies the slot machines, Olsen pays 'em rent. See? There was no numbers up here 'til the Dutchman sent Finestein to organize. That Dutchman beat The Office to the gun, see? Aw, the hell with it! That Dutchman—him and Al Capone."

"What's Al Capone got to do with it, Joey?"

"Georgie," Joey said, shaking his head. "Sometimes I wonder if you breathe."

"Sure I breathe," Georgie retorted. "Only what's Al Capone got to do with the Dutchman?"

"Who got Al Capone to go to jail for a year? He comes out and where is he? Alcatraz!"

"Yeh, but the feds put'm in Alcatraz," Georgie yawned. "I don't see how the Dutchman or—"

"Skip it!"

"Joey, why don't you and me sneak down, t'hell with Pete and Tunafish, and cop us a lay?"

Joey had to grin. Al Capone didn't rate more than a minute's worth of talk to Georgie. Al Capone was finished business with Georgie and why he was putting on the crying towel Christ only knew. Still it showed you how that damn Office operated. They get Al Capone to give himself up to the coppers, and the guy does it, and comes out of the can to have the coppers smash his stills and the feds jump on his income tax returns. The guy runs to Florida and gets treated like a bum, gets arrested for vagrancy, gets a couple thousand tax evasion and bootlegging charges tossed at him, and ends up in Alcatraz. Christ, The Office must've celebrated with a champagne cocktail when they got the news. And now it was the Dutchman's turn coming up.

"Hey, you're not listenin' to me," Georgie complained.

"I'm listenin'. Dames."

"Yeh. These hick whores must be like pickin' daisies," Georgie grinned.

"You think so?"

"Yeh, not like that wisepott Annabelle, remember?"

They both thought of Annabelle whom they'd once kept in partnership with Ted Griffin.

"She was too wise," Georgie reminisced, scratching at himself. "Hey, Joey, you know what gets me?"

"What gets you?"

"You and that redhead of yours. You must like that redhead?" Georgie winked.

"Just a habit." Joey answered flippantly and knew he was lying. As he lied to Sadie Madofsky whenever he had to leave town. ("I'm just like a salesman," he had said before his first trips, his voice so beaten he could have been a bona fide salesman about to be let go by a bona fide manufacturer on the verge of jumping out of the window. "I see how much booze they want and I fill orders, that's me. It's gettin' real businesslike with prohibition about to blow up.") "A habit's funny," he now explained to Georgie.

"Yeh, but what's she got to keep you all these years?"

"What they all got. Who's your big flame now, Georgie?" As Georgie answered, he hardly listened, asking himself: What did that redhead have? Georgie was right. She'd been with him long enough to be his wife or something. Maybe that was it, his lil jewgirl of a wife. Something in the blood, something. And she was beginning to show it lately, getting a little fat. Yeah, but some of that was from the wine she was always drinking. Plenty sugar in wine and all those calory-vitamin things. *I trust her,* he thought suddenly with a hammering naked honesty that knocked down his superstitions and prejudices. That was it. He trusted her as he'd once trusted Georgie. And didn't trust the Spotter, Charley, The Office, the whole damn world where a guy always had to watch his step.

"City dames're no good," Georgie was saying, speaking of his newest girl. "These hick dames! They must be like pickin' daisies, Joey."

"You say that only because you're here in the sticks."

"Betcha they're like pickin' daisies or buttercups."

"Betcha a buck you don't know the name of a third flower."

"A what?"

"I bet you one buck cash you don't know the name of a third flower, Georgie."

"Wise guy!" Georgie's forehead wrinkled as he concentrated. "Les see now. Daisies, buttercups—roses!" he cried triumphantly.

"How about a fourth?"

"Pay the buck you lost first."

Joey tossed him a dollar bill. "Two bucks you don't name a fourth flower."

"You're easy," Georgie laughed. "Lemme see. Roses and daisies and buttercups and there's—I can see 'em with my eyes, but what the hell's their name? Violets!" he exclaimed.

Joey paid over two more bills and bet four bucks Georgie couldn't name a fifth flower. He kept doubling the bet and on the seventh flower Georgie lost. "You took me," Georgie said ruefully. "Double bets're sucker bets."

Joey smiled and then of a sudden he didn't feel so damn smart any more. Who the hell was he robbing? He returned Georgie his money. And felt as if somewhere, somehow, he had lost in a game that he'd been playing a lifetime....

It was nearly eleven that night before they checked out of the inn, driving up Main Street, the plateglass fronts of the stores bright under the dark spring sky, and then even as Joey was thinking: It must be awful lonely living in a one-horse town—they had left the lights and were out in the country. "Trees and fields that's all," Joey remarked to nobody in particular.

"My ole man usta talk of buyin' a lil farm some day," Tunafish contributed to the conversation.

"And make his own wine?" Georgie hooted. "All wops're the same." He was at the wheel. "All wops!"

"Hommade wine ain't so bad," Tunafish answered.

"To wash your feet with!" Georgie declared.

Joey thought, the big sonuvabitch's getting steam up already. He stared out at the countryside coming at them in dark sheets, the clumps of trees darker patches. Before the car's probing headlights, the moonless fields unwound.

"Joey, I keep on this road?" Georgie asked.

"Watch your mileage. At three point seven, we hit a crossroad where you make a left." Olsen had phoned again, a half hour ago, with exact instructions. "Three point seven!" But this was a driver with no head for figures. Joey had to direct him practically every inch of the way. They passed a huge stucco hotel whose name came out of the night printed on a signboard: HOTEL PARA-MOUNT and then vanished. It was deserted now before the summer season. "That's a Broadway name," Pete Bowers said. "The hebes call all their hotels with Broadway names."

Joey wondered if Pete Bowers knew he was a hebe. From Loose Lips Georgie maybe. Else why was the lil sonuvabitch always sounding off. Must be a sonuvabitch on hebes like the Bug... Bughead Moore, his old pal. He'd've been the prize enforcer of them all, so the sonuvabitch was enforcing the worms and served him right.

"Why they call him Milty the Poet?" Georgie asked again.

Even Pete couldn't answer that one. The headlights gleamed down a long straight stretch of asphalt, a lake shone on their left, and Joey thought: This whole show tonight's for a hebe and served him right for getting mixed up with The Office.

"Why they call him Milty the Poet—" Georgie asked again. "'Roses're red, violets're blue,'" Georgie chanted.

Joey remembered their betting back in the inn, and in his own head finished the rhyme: 'Milty's a hebe and so're you.' To Georgie, Joey said, "Should be there soon. Keep your eye peeled for Olsen's farmhouse."

"I start the job," Georgie said to Pete and Tunafish in the rear. "Okay?"

It was okay with Pete and Tunafish. The road narrowed. A few minutes later the farmhouse they wanted, like the last piece in a jigsaw puzzle, dropped out of the night. Their headlights shone on the canary-yellow side of a parked roadster.

It was Olsen's car and Olsen was waiting for them inside the farmhouse with Milty the Poet Finestein.

The farmhouse windows shone brighter than ever when Georgie switched off his lights. Georgie walked to the car trunk, unlocked it and pulled out a duffle bag. The three others had gone on ahead. Georgie heard the wooden stairs of the porch creaking under their feet. Georgie grinned, and his grip on the strings of the duffle bag tightened like a hunter's fist on his rifle. He left the bag on the porch and followed Joey, Pete and Tunafish into a Hollywood-style interior. The walls were knotty pine; a mounted deer's head hung over the huge fireplace.

Two men had gotten to their feet like a welcoming committee, a slender dark man in his forties wearing a sports shirt and corduroy pants, and a man who could only have been the owner of a yellow roadster. Olsen was fair and fat, wearing a fine gray sweater and plaid knickers cut so full and wide they looked like bloomers made out of tweed, his golf stockings patterned with red and green diamonds.

"Boys, we been expecting you," Olsen greeted them. "This is Milty Finestein, boys."

The slender man said, "Olsen here convinced me. He convinced me to tell what Dutch Schultz's doing here. I'll tell you and we'll get this whole thing straightened out." He had a long narrow face, his eyes large and dark, but he spoke quick and clipped like a businessman. Milty the Poet was all set to talk business. He had no idea the business'd been settled in Charley Valinchi's backroom. Chuck Tillio'd done his best but it hadn't been good enough.

"I'll be seeing you," Olsen said, and he waved a ringed hand at all of them.

"You said you'd stick around and put in a word," Milty the Poet reminded him quickly.

Christ! Joey thought. The poor sonofabitch still don't know he's a gunner. That Olsen should be a lawyer.

"Milty, it's okay," Olsen assured the slender man in the sports shirt. His red and green calves twinkled as he made for the door which he carefully shut behind him as if he wanted to avoid any unnecessary noise. As if a baby maybe were sleeping upstairs.

"Well," Milty the Poet began nervously. "I don't know what you guys know." He smiled. "Suppose we sit down—"

"I forgot somethin'," Georgie said. He filed through the door, picked up the duffle bag, blinked at the bright lights of the yellow roadster, watching it curve out on the road. Georgie came inside again, dumped the duffle bag to the floor. He winked at Milty the Poet. "Did I miss anything? I hate to miss anything," he rattled on while Joey listened with amazement. Talk of loose lips! Joey thought. But if big black-haired Georgie was making like a phonograph record, there wasn't a word now out of Milty the Poet. *He knew.* His eyes, like two lead weights he could never lift again, had fixed on the duffle bag. It was a dark blue bag, crumpled, sitting on the floor, a tongueless thing, yet shouting its secrets.

Joey couldn't stand the guy's eyes any more. Their centers, glittering like dark glasses, seemed to splinter, piercing his heart. His emotions frightened him for who the hell was Milty the Poet? Nothing but a lousy stool pigeon! A mark, a target, the night's job. Then why was he feeling sorry for the son-of-a-bitch, stalling around when Georgie, Pete, Tunafish were all waiting for the go-ahead?

The silence in the room had become enormous for Georgie's voice was no true voice. Pete and Tunafish had a mopey look on their faces like any workmen, eager but unable to get to work. And Milty the Poet *knew*—that blue duffle bag'd told him—what kind of work it was going to be. Joey lit a cigarette to ease his nerves. He sensed rather than understood this sudden and inexplicable sympathy for Milty the Poet. For he too was afraid whose own life'd gotten lost somehow in a blind alley.

"Nice place you got here."

It was Georgie, and who else could it be but Loose Lips Georgie breaking the ice.

"Yes, this is a nice place," Georgie was saying and he winked at Pete and Tunafish.

It had become a game like the time in Baltimore when Georgie and Pete'd taken pot shots at a wounded mark they'd pushed up against a hillside. Pete strolled around the living room. He stroked the antlers of the deer head over the fireplace. "A real one," he smirked.

"This is a place where with a dame and a coupla cases beer, huh, Milty?" Georgie winked at the silent man with the heavy staring eyes.

Joey watched, the go-ahead in his throat like a pit he'd swallowed and couldn't cough up. He was fascinated. It was as if enforcer and mark had swapped places and he were looking with Milty the Poet's eyes at the men who had come in the night. At Pete punching the soft red leather of an easy chair while the Tunafish chuckled softly and coyly, and Georgie, a wolfish grin on his lips asking which Milty liked better, "Beer or the hard stuff?"

"Olsen convinced me," Milty the Poet said in a strained voice. "That's why I'm here. This thing can be straightened out. I know all about what Dutch Schultz's up to."

Christ, Joey thought; he's not only talking he's smiling.

But Milty the Poet wasn't exactly smiling. The sound of his own voice was like a hypo, and the smile on his lips was as false as his courage was desperate. He didn't really believe he could save his skin, still how could he be sure? Abruptly, he became hysterically cheerful. "There's hard stuff here. Many a time Olsen and me—how about a drink, boys?"

"Sure," Georgie said. "Make mine a whiskey straight." And he kicked at the duffle bag. "I brought the sannawiches."

Tunafish laughed with appreciation. Pete over at an end table pocketed a silver cigarette lighter.

Joey saw him. "Put that back!" he ordered.

"Aw, Joey."

"Put that back!"

Milty the Poet faced the guy he now knew was in charge.

They looked at each other. "Give me a chance. I'll convince you, you'll see, you'll see!" His eyes had no glassy centers of fear now; his eyes were like two wet spots on the white face.

Joey turned his face away. "Get goin'. Christ, get goin'!"

The game was over. Pete came at Milty the Poet quick as a snapped knifeblade, the Tunafish glided over soft and feminine while Georgie rushed to the duffle bag, opened it.

Milty the Poet didn't try to run or fight. He dropped to his knees and gently, as if praying, he placed his hands on Joey's shoes. Joey shuddered, stepped backwards. Pete sneaked his fingers inside the collar of the man on the floor and Tunafish patted him all over searching for a weapon; he didn't expect to find any, but Tunafish always played it cozy.

"What do you want?" Milty the Poet screamed and then he tried to smile as if it were all a joke they would share with him in another second. In that magic second beyond life and death when they would all sit down and have a drink together, the killers and the killed.

That smile wavered on his lips, only he'd forgotten how to smile, his lips giving them all not a smile but its imitation. "You're choking me!" he wailed but still he smiled.

"Don't choke'm Pete!" Joey said sharply.

"I didn't do nothing," Milty the Poet shrilled. "Didn't Olsen explain to you?" he asked Joey in a fearful and yet hoping voice as if still deep down he knew that it was all a joke. Oh, God it had to be a joke. "Didn't Olsen explain? Olsen, Olsen," the man on the floor repeated as if the name, *Olsen,* were his salvation on this earth.

"Hurry it up, Georgie!" Joey yelled. "God damn you! It's your God damn job so get goin'."

Georgie got up from the duffle bag. He had taken out towels, several pairs of new cotton gloves and three ice picks, all of which he had arranged neatly like a surgeon.

Milty the Poet sobbed, he tried to crawl to Joey. Tunafish planted his foot down on Milty the Poet's left hand. Pete tightened his hold on the man's collar. Georgie approached. He stooped, he clipped Milty the Poet on the side of the jaw, a stunner rather than a k.o.

Milty the Poet groaned. "God, what'd I do. Didn't do nothing, didn't do nothing."

None of them had ever done a thing. Maybe a little case of an itchy finger on a trigger, or a little grabbing up of territory that wasn't to be grabbed, maybe a little trouble, a little stool pigeoning, but nothing really serious that couldn't be fixed. For when a man smells his death, he feels that nothing he has ever done is so big that it can't be fixed. For death alone can't be fixed. Everything else can or ought to be.

"I didn't do nothing. Honest to God, on my mother's grave, I swear I was with you boys all the time, not with the Dutchman. Ask Olsen, he'll tell you. Go get Olsen, you don't believe me. Get Ol—"

Georgie hit him hard behind the ear. He fell to the floor, he should've stayed there—it was a real wallop—but the death he smelled roused him like some potent smelling salt. "Olsen!" he screamed. "Olsen! Olsen, he can't do this to me!" he babbled as if it were all Olsen's fault. Double-crossing The Office in New York was Olsen's fault, the Dutchman was Olsen's fault, everything was Olsen's fault.

The man in the gray sweater and the plaid knickers carried all the faults in the world on his shoulders.

"Georgie you big bastid, quit foolin' around!" Joey cursed him.

Georgie stared reproachfully at Joey like a hunting dog bawled out for no good reason. Then he dashed over to the duffle bag as Milty the Poet tried to get to his hands and knees. The Tunafish raised one foot, pushed shoe leather against Milty the Poet's face, pushing rather than kicking him off balance. Milty the Poet tumbled, but his eyes swifter than his falling body seemed to tear upwards out of their sockets, focusing in a last agonized appeal on the man giving the orders.

"I didn't do nothing, God I didn't do nothing!" he screamed.

Joey wanted to say: Nobody's blaming you. And wasn't that a crazy idea! He couldn't stand the sight of the guy on the floor, turning to get him out of his eyes. To see Georgie pulling on a pair of clean cotton gloves, picking up one of the ice picks and two of the towels. Almost, Joey didn't recognize Georgie now, and then he recognized him all right. It was the Georgie of the jobs, his face smooth and his lips soft as if about to smile. Joey's heart gave a wild skip. Christ! Where was that other bastard? Pete Bowers? He searched the room for him, anything to forget the guy on the floor. Tunafish had to kick him this time, the tip of his shoe caught Milty the Poet in the ribs. Where was that Pete bastard? Then guessed Pete must be heisting everything loose in the other rooms, and thought wearily: Let him, let him, the hell with it.

Georgie walked to the half-conscious man. First he spread the two thick towels on the floor. Then he lifted him onto the towels, sitting down on his stomach and reaching for the ice pick nearby on the floor.

"Georgie!" Joey called. Georgie didn't hear him, his eyes almost as bright as the steel point of the ice pick in his white gloved hand.

What's eating me tonight, Joey wondered, exhausted. He felt dead beat as if his brain and his heart had been scooped out. For he hadn't given a damn one way or another on all the other nights. A mark was a mark, a job was a job.

"Georgie, finish him!" Joey shouted. Georgie didn't hear him. Joey ran to him, he seized Georgie's shoulder. "I said finish'm up!"

Georgie stared at him like a kid scolded by some adult for pulling the wings and legs off a fly. "Okay, okay," he muttered and studied the mouthing spitty face under him. "Why they call you Milty the Poet?" he asked. "Why they call you Milty the Poet?"

Joey stood there helplessly. Almost he felt like slugging Georgie, but he was aware that the Tunafish was watching him. The Tunafish who would be whispering in Charley Valinchi's ear: That Joey's not so tough. Know what he done up there up in Solomon County....

"Make rhymes if you're Milty the Poet. Lemme hear you make rhymes! Make rhymes!" And as Milty the Poet screamed the rhyme of his approaching death, the point of the ice pick plunged down into his heart.

Up in the Spotter's private office at the Elwood Realty, Joey felt the chilly sensation of dreaming the same dream over and over again. As if all his life he'd been asking the Spotter for one damn break after another. Not that he'd gotten around to himself as yet, for like the Salvation Army, he was first preaching Georgie. "Charley Valinchi, he had this talk with me how Georgie's makin' a pain outa himself, Spotter," Joey heard himself saying in the voice of a true blue pal. "So I says to myself, 'Joey, better see the Spotter yourself and get the story straight!'"

"The guy's softenin' up. That's all there is to it," the Spotter answered.

"That's just what Charley said, but it's not so. He boozes, yeh, and sometimes he goes off his nut a lil. I warned him good."

"You was always a boy scout about Georgie."

"Maybe, but when you get right down to it, how many of the old Badgers you got left?" Joey's eyes were downcast as he made this pitch at the Spotter's guarded heart. Yes, sir, a boy scout. But what he'd come up here for was to see if he could get the hell out of the enforcement racket. Georgie wasn't the only one softening up. There was a certain party by name of Joey Case. Something'd happened to him on that last job.... "Not many of the old Badgers left, Spotter. There's you and me and Georgie." He lifted his eyes and the chill deepened, for the man at the shiny desk didn't look like an oldtime Badger but more like a businessman in his dark gray suit, white shirt, and silver and black necktie. A businessman? Joey wasn't sure. More like a walking corpse. The Spotter's shrunken neck was swimming inside the white collar, the pale eyes like dulled metal, the skin so thin it seemed that a rub could break it and have the blood coming out. Joey despaired of making any kind of a dent when the Spotter replied.

"You're right, Joey. There's maybe eight or nine Badgers left all told."

It was true as gospel. Damn few of the old Badgers were kicking around. Some'd burned in the chair, some the coppers'd thrown into the can. Bootlegger wars'd put more than one good man on the marble slab. Like Sarge Killigan shot down in the war with the Fallons. And what'd ever become of Fallon? And Billy Gahagan? Or was it Billy Gavagan? "Was Billy before your time, Joey?" the Spotter asked. A lot of Billys had come and gone and the Spotter just couldn't keep track any more. "Good guys," the Spotter said. "They were all good guys. Remember Clip Haley? He had to get himself killed in a brawl."

But neither of them wasted a tear on Tom Quinn or John Terry and why should they? Quinn and Terry hadn't been Badgers. As for Bughead Moore, a Badger from way back, they both remembered him, and the Spotter was tempted to bring the Bug up, but good manners was on the menu this morning.

"How you gettin' along with Charley Valinchi?" the Spotter said at last as Joey had been praying he would.

"Swell, Spotter. He's a swell guy. But why should I kid you, Spotter. I'm nothin' there. It's close to two years I been with Charley and long enough. I remember when you first brought me to see Clip Haley."

"That's ten, twelve years ago."

"Closer to fourteen. I was fifteen then, Spotter, a kid and you was already a big man. Spotter, I'd like to be back with you."

Almost the Spotter weakened—Joey sensed it—but then the moment passed. The Spotter wasn't giving a thing away. All the Spotter had to spare, as one old-time Badger with another, was a smile and a promise, two commodities on the discount that skidding depression year.

That night, as the Spotter lay in his bed at the Hotel Berkeley, he counted up the old-time Badgers. Not many left, the Spotter thought. I shouldn't've given Joey the brush-off. No? Why not? Why feel sorry for him? Who's feeling sorry for me? The hell with him. He's getting soft. We all get soft. Me, it's the Bum Ticker. Two attacks the last year. Four weeks in bed, the last one. Soft, soft, all of us, one damn way or another. That Joey's smart, too smart, the way he dragged in the Badgers. He's worried and that's not so smart. He better stop worrying. It'll rot his brains out, rot his guts. You can be the toughest guy in town, but if you keep worrying, you'll go soft. I'll be cutting up all the clips I got on No-Gun Joey yet.... Must be that redhead of his softening him up. Why's he stick to her all these years? He don't love her. That kid's like me, he's got no real love in him. He never had time for real love, always on the make. But he sticks to her, that's the mystery....

The day after Joey went out of town again—"I have to go to Cleveland," he had said—Sadie Madofsky walked up Ninth Avenue, the El overhead a dusty blue color as the summer twilight deepened and the lights came on in the stores. Down here at this hour, in this neighborhood of broken slate sidewalks, the women in their any-old dresses, the men in sweaters that might once have been red or blue but now had a grayish look, the depression look, Sadie was sharply aware of her freshly dry-cleaned dress, her legs in silk stockings, her feet in lizardskin shoes.

About once a month, she would walk through the old neighborhood, playing a strange game with herself, a game in which she pretended to be visiting her father and brother. She would turn up Twenty-Fourth Street, her nerves stretched so tight she would almost sober, peering into her father's tailor store as she passed, never going inside or even thinking of doing so, flitting by, a plump redheaded ghost in good clothes.

She had bought her right to play this game of conscience. One afternoon about a year ago as she was returning to her hotel with one of her hotel girl friends, she had happened to see a dispossessed family crossing Broadway. A man, a woman, three children, all of them loaded down with goods, blankets, pots, satchels, the littlest girl carrying a doll. Maybe they were walking crosstown to move in with some relative beyond Third Avenue? Maybe they were going to the relief station? Sadie didn't know, but she had suddenly wondered about her father and brother and what the depression was doing to them. So taking a dollar from her bag, she gave it to the woman, and when she was in her own room, she had immediately sat down at the desk, still wearing her hat and coat, and written a letter to her father. He never replied. The weeks, the drinking weeks, floated by, and she would recall her unanswered letter as she sat in her room, a nice big glass of sherry in her hand, remember and forget as her thoughts climbed the fences of the years. All the fences were beginning to look alike to her. Like the fences in the backyards of Chelsea and Hells Kitchen, their paint long gone, but always with some freshly chalked message about some Billy who loved some Gracie. As she had once loved Joey.... With a glass of sherry in her hand, she could forget he was seeing women on the side, forget that she was unmarried, childless, separated from her family, forget, forget, forget.... Then she could smile gently to herself like a baby, and in a sense she had become her own baby: a baby to whom she faithfully fed the bottle. And nothing but the best, too. Wine smooth as a mother's milk.

But there were days when the wine hadn't helped or the movies or the long conversations with her girl friends, when the world had grinned at her through the windows of the Hotel Delmore like a hateful peeping Tom. She would remember there was such a thing as a depression and that millions of people were out of jobs. And who knew how her father and brother were getting along. She had written a second letter, this time to her brother Herman, omitting her name and return address from the outside flap:

Dear Herman,

How are you? I hope you and Papa are all right. I hope business isn't bad but if it is, let me know. Herman, I wrote Papa, but he didn't answer. Did he tell you? You must be in college. Are you? Write me here at the Hotel Delmore....

She had a reply in the return mail. Her brother was going to City College at night, working during the day, but the only job he had now was helping in the store, and business was bad. She had mailed him a money order for fifty dollars. Herman had thanked her, writing he would like to see her. They had met in the lobby of the Delmore, but their meeting was unhappy; their lives had separated, and he refused the money she had offered him. Still, before they parted, the brother had accepted ten dollars. "No more," he had said with the bitter pride of the poor: a pride full of holes like a bleeding heart. And every week when she mailed him a ten dollar money order, she would weep a little that she had to be the one helping the proud ones.

So she walked on Ninth Avenue now in the twilight, on another pretend visit to her family, the people on the streets staring at the pretty redhead going by, wondering where the hell she came from and what the hell she was doing here. She didn't belong. Not this dame in the fine feathers. She was from another part of town where maybe there were no apple sellers on the corners. She didn't belong on Ninth Avenue, that was a cinch.

There were soup lines on Time Square and when Franklin D. Roosevelt was elected president and prohibition repealed in 1933, the bars over on the West Side had to cut prices to get any trade. A guy about to be evicted couldn't be expected to pay more than fifteen cents for a shot of whiskey. And two shots for a quarter was a bargain to tempt any jobless scrounger sent by his missus to buy hamburger for supper. The butcher stores on Eighth and Ninth Avenues sold what they called *Dog Hamburger* at ten cents a pound. But many a tenement pooch had watched that very same *Dog Hamburger* being fried to a crisp brown and then dished out with nobody in the family asking him to sit down.

"Fifteen cents for real whiskey!" was the new battlecry of independence in the bars taking the place of the old speaks.

As for the big bootleggers, independents like the Dutchman waved good-bye to prohibition as casually as a quicky lover leaving a whorehouse. For several years now they been playing the field anyway: the numbers racket, the labor racket, narcotics, prostitution. That sweet little Bootleg Baby'd been getting a little worn around the edges anyway—the usual fate of a first sweetheart.

As for The Office, ever since the Atlantic meeting, they'd been organizing the whole works. Now with prohibition kissed off, they began to concentrate on organizing the remaining independents into the poorhouse. The biggest independent of them all, Al Capone, was safe in Alcatraz. In New York, though, the Dutchman was still operating. There'd been Jack Legs Diamond and Waxey Gordon also, but those two guys'd been taken care of with the help of Dewey, the racket buster.

"Dewey should be on our payroll," the big boys in The Office wisecracked back in 1931 when the newly appointed Dewey went after Jack Legs Diamond. Thomas E. Dewey was only twenty-eight years old when he was appointed Chief Assistant U.S. Attorney, the head man of the largest prosecuting office in the Government, with jurisdiction over a judicial district spreading from Manhattan to Albany. "The Demon Racket Buster," the big boys in The Office wisecracked. And: "Lil Buster Brown from Michigan." Predicting: "If he can be a hero the easy way why should he make it tough for himself. He'll go after the big noises. He'll play it smart."

For a while it seemed as if they'd known what they were talking about. Dewey, with sixty young lawyers under him, helped by the FBI, Treasury Intelligence, Narcotics Bureau and a staff of New York detectives had convicted Legs Diamond. Legs, appealing the conviction, was killed by what the newspapers called "unknown gunmen." But the big boys'd smiled and said. "Somebody's helpin' out the lil racket buster!" The smile was still on their faces when Dewey, after examining close to a thousand witnesses, had put Waxey Gordon away for ten years. "That Waxey cheated a bullet in his head," was how the rumble went. From the way they talked, the big boys sounded as if Dewey were a part of The Office. And when Dewey came after Dutch Schultz, their smiles were smeared on thick as jam. For if Waxey deserved a bullet, the Dutchman deserved all the bullets in the arsenal. Strictly poison—that was the Dutchman. Back in the bootlegging days, he'd gypped or double-crossed nearly everybody dealing with him. A lone wolf operator, he'd jumped the gun on the numbers racket, invading Harlem where his gunmen had gone around saying, "You dinges're through. The Dutchman's rennin' policy from now on." He'd spread upstate and was making deals across the river in New Jersey.

DUTCH SCHULTZ, the newspaper headlines headlined his jump to power. "It's a tossup who gets the Dutchman first," the big boys'd agreed. "Dewey or us." But Dewey, a Republican, lost his job when the new Democratic President hung his hat in the White House. The Dutchman dropped right back into the lap of The Office. He was the kind of hot potato they just couldn't get rid of right away. The Dutchman knew too much; he had smart lawyers, he was protected by the politicians, and all the time he was getting bigger and bigger in the numbers racket.

DUTCH SCHULTZ, NUMBERS KING, the headlines crowned him.

"Prohibition's dead," the organizers from The Office were preaching all over town. "But numbers, gambling's here to stay." They had organized the Spotter among others, giving him the okay to run the racket in his piece of the West Side. At a price of course. Natch. It was nothing for nothing with a depression on. The Spotter could still be number one man in his territory but The Office sent in a guy by name of Frank Fanelli to help with things. And Frank Fanelli had some guys to help him.

But what else could he do? That was a question a hundred and one other big shots were asking themselves who'd been given the same organizing treatment. It was knuckle down to The Office, take your slice of the pie, or fight like the Dutchman, a mad dog from the year one. The way Spotter saw it, there was no percentage fighting The Office. In the years since the Atlantic City meeting, The Office'd gotten too damn strong. Take Chicago, for instance. With Al Capone out, Aiello and Moran and Torrio'd been The Big Three. Those guys weren't independents exactly but neither were they rubber stamps. So where the hell were they? Aiello was dead, sixty-two machine gun bullets in him. Moran and Torrio were in hiding. Take right here in New York. Legs Diamond dead, Waxey Gordon in the can, with only Dutch Schultz still raising a stink.

"Let's go for a walk," Joey said, and even with the Dutchman on his mind, he had to smile at the way she was looking at him. As if he'd suggested jumping out of the hotel window. But he couldn't hang around here any longer. It must be the Dutchman, he thought. Who the hell else? Since when did Charley haul him out to Brooklyn in the middle of the afternoon and order him to stand by. There in the backroom behind the Napoli, Charley'd said: "Joey, you phone me every hour. Have your troop stay in their rooms where you can reach 'em if you have to reach 'em in a hurry." He'd wanted to ask Charley if it was the Dutchman, but he didn't have the nerve. Nobody asked Charley for information Charley wasn't giving. "Let's go for a walk, Sweetie," he repeated. He cracked his knuckles nervously. "It won't kill you—"

"Joey," she said mildly, the mildest drunk in town, smiling above her glass of sherry. "Why don't you have a drink?"

"Don't want any!" he snapped. A drink before a job was all he needed! A drink to foul him up, to gum the works! If his hunch was right and it was the Dutchman, he'd need all his damn brains. God, he hoped it wasn't the Dutchman. And suppose it was? What was the diff? Was the Dutchman his damn brother or something?...

For if there ever was a guy born without a brother, it was the lone-wolf mobster by the name of Dutch Schultz.

"A walk'll do you good," he heard himself saying.

"We used to do a lot of walking," she said sentimentally, and looked down into her sherry. There, and there only the memory of their courtship was preserved: the long summer walks, the summer bus rides on Fifth Avenue.

"Come on!" he urged her. "You're gettin' too fat anyway. Get a move on you! Hurry up!"

She smiled, a good-natured drunk full of love for the whole wide world, and for him in particular. While he watched her with eyes that were blazing *hurry up*. She was so tight, he knew she didn't really see him. She only heard him. If he wanted to do something crazy like going for a walk, that smile of hers was saying as plain as words, all right, all right. She got up from her chair and waving a fond hand at him, stepped into the bathroom.

She was gone, and he thought: God, the years I been living with that wino! His eyes shifted to the double bed and he glimpsed all the dames who'd come and gone with only the redhead lasting like the rock of the ages. He remembered when she'd been thin as one of those Italian breadsticks. Curving up now, becoming—what was the hebe word? *Zaftig!* Yeh, that was it. Yeh, that was it. *Zaftig! Juicy!* Fat, soft and juicy.

He glanced at his wristwatch. It was 9:18. At ten he'd phone Charley again. At ten, at eleven, at twelve. Orders were orders and he was standing by, a lousy no-good yellowbellied enforcer not fit to wipe the Dutchman's shoes. He lit a nervous man's cigarette and tried to forget how long an hour could be.

"Joey, I'm ready," she said, coming out of the bedroom, her round face freshly made up, her red hair glinting from the brush. She crossed to the closet and took out a lightweight green sport coat.

Joey looked at her steadily. He wondered what she'd say if he told her about Dutch Schultz. About Charley Valinchi. What did she know about him? Next to nothing. What did he know about her? The question pounded at him suddenly like an unexpected fist. Yes, what did he know? She'd gone to high school once upon a time, kept house for her old man once upon a time, and here she was a wino. She'd stuck by him all these years. Why? What was there in it for her? Clothes, a hotel room, all the sherry she could drink? Christ, dames were dumb. Dames must believe in this love racket, the dumb bitches. Yet as he looked at this redhead of his, buttoning her green sport coat from the bottom button up and not from the top button down—a habit of hers he had noticed over the years— his wound-up nerves relaxed and he felt glad she was around. And instantly killed the feeling. His lips curled with contempt. A dame! Just a dame. A sucker.

They went down in the elevator. Two bookies were arguing in the lobby about Mayor La Guardia. The desk clerk nodded a head smooth as a glass door-knob and in a glassy hotel voice said, "Good evening Mrs. Case, Mr. Case." The hell with you, Joey thought wearily. That Case name he'd wished on himself'd turned out a jinx. For hadn't the waterfront deal backfired, Mr. Case? He was Mr. Nobody working like everybody else for The Office.

That Office was like a department store. Some guys ran the gambling tables, other guys took care of the cocaine and heroin counter, and if you wanted a dame, please take the escalator to the next floor. The dames worked on a salary and so did the numbers men, the slot-machine men, the con-men. And the politicians and mouthpieces and accountants. Order-givers and order-takers and nothing in-between. There had to be Order. And that was where the enforcers came in.

Enforcer Joey Case and his steady girl friend walked over to Broadway. It was a spring night and guys with jobs were stepping out with their girl friends, the jobless kids snaking up and down through the crowds, joking and laughing as if they'd been promised jobs in the morning. Enforcer Joey Case, age thirty-three, glanced at them with the boiled-in-vinegar eye of a man who's had his share of disappointments. Peddlers barked their bargains as they watched out for the coppers. The huge signs glittered, forming brilliant arcades of light. Spring on Broadway.

"It's nice walking," she said and slid her arm through his, her eyes lifting almost shyly to his face.

"Yeh."

"Joey, why do you keep looking at your wristwatch?"

"Gotta call a guy at ten." He could see that the fresh air was sobering her up and wished to God he could buy himself a drink.

"We haven't walked like this in years," she said. He glanced at her smiling face, brightly seen as if in daylight, the yellow light from an auctioneer's reflected on her teeth.

"Like it, huh?"

"Yes, Joey." She pressed his arm with hers.

"You like me, don't you? He couldn't help asking, and before she could answer he laughed harshly. "If you think I'll break down one of these years and marry you—"

"I never think of that any more, Joey."

"Good for you. Marrying's for the crumbs. God damn rabbis—all these rabbis, priests! They got themselves a racket. Everything's a racket," he said with a bitter sigh as if he were the first mobster to coin the phrase.

"Joey, something's worrying you tonight—"

"Because I look at the damn wristwatch? I like lookin' at it," he jeered. "Cost me one fifty, didn't it?"

Three or four minutes before ten he said, "You wait outside. I'll be right out." He hurried into a drugstore lit up like a carnival. His head was rigid on his stiff neck, his eyes seeing a dancing meaningless weave of faces and objects. He stepped into a phone booth, closed the door behind him, and in the narrow coffin-like space dialed Charley Valinchi. "Hello," he said. The voice on the other end replied, a flat nasal voice like a thousand others, but unmistakably the voice of Charley Valinchi. Charley Valinchi, his God damn boss! Charley Valinchi, the God damn bastard of a killer-diller! Joey would've recognized it anywhere. It was the voice of judgment. "Joey," it was saying now. "Don't have to buzz me again, Joey. You're free."

Joey felt as if some huge and heavy cross had been lifted from his shoulders. A boyish smile wavered on his lips, he gulped, he wanted to shout out with a big voice. And heard the quiet level voice he always wore with Charley as if it were a necktie, the voice of an enforcer a man could depend on. "Okay, Charley."

"Joey, phone the boys, will you?"

"Sure. So long, Charley."

"So long, feller."

Joey hung up., He leaned against the wall of the booth. He smiled. "Thank God," he said. "Thank God." He searched in his pocket for nickels. Whatever they want, I don't want, he thought.

Joey Case, enforcer, was like any other man in a hated job, wishing he had the nerve to quit but knowing he never would, doing his job as well as he could and yet always hoping things would work out against the boss.

He phoned the boys in his troop; Georgie, Pete, Tunafish, and the two new guys, Ed Roscamino and Leo the Goneph. They were all on hand, waiting—except Georgie. Joey left the booth, smiling. Even that God damn Georgie falling down on the job, out drinking or whoring, couldn't get him down tonight. Not with the Dutchman still kicking around, a prize headache to the God damn Office.

He laughed when he saw the redhead in the green coat, and seizing her arm hurried to the curb where he whistled a cab.

"Where we going, Joey?" she asked.

"Where you wanna go, Sweetie?" he pulled her to him, kissed her on the mouth, the cab inching up Broadway, the bright lights whirling ahead of them like a swarm of purple and blue and green butterflies in a neon sunrise. He straightened up. He laughed, drunk without a shot. "How 'bout the Mocambo?"

"Joey, that place is expensive. When we were there the last time, you said—"

"What's money anyway?"

"What're you celebrating, Joey?"

That was a question for the monkeys, for when he considered what the hell he was celebrating, he couldn't hit on the answer right away. Sure, he was glad he was out of the Dutchman job, if it was the Dutchman. But why the three cheers? The Dutchman didn't know him from a hole in the ground, wouldn't give him a nickel for a cup of coffee. The Dutchman'd watch him bleed to death without lifting as much as the corner of his handkerchief. Still, he was celebrating the Dutchman, one guy with the nerve to go against The Office. He was celebrating what he himself didn't have the nerve to do. He'd had the nerve once.... Joey gritted his teeth at the memory. It was a million years ago now, that night when the Spotter'd made him eat dirt, made him say he'd killed the Bug. A little thing, but it was enough. He'd backtracked and once a guy backtracked, hell was the next stop. And that was no kidding. God, he should've spit in the Spotter's face that night! Taken his chances. And either the Spotter would've won or he'd've been somebody. Somebody! Like the Dutchman maybe.

On the strength of might-have-been, he tipped the cabbie a solid buck and slipped a quarter into the hand of the out-of-work opening the cab door.

The Mocambo was another spot in town where the depression was kept out like some plague and the medicine used was a simple one: money. Money popped with the corks drawn out of the champagne bottles, money poured into the glasses, money glittered on the ringed hands of the women, money laughed out of the throats of their escorts. Noisy and crowded, vulgar and frenzied, the Mocambo was all these and yet its patrons felt safe here. Three or four highballs later, Enforcer Joey Case, drunk to start with, was floating.

"Baby," he said as dance music played somewhere, reaching across the table for her hand, and blinking at her round face. In the dim Mocambo light, he saw the thin-faced tailor girl of long ago when he'd had his whole damn life before him and the sky the limit. "We been together a long time, baby, yuh know that?"

"A long time," she agreed.

"I'm thirty-three," he announced defiantly. "Yuh know that—thirty-three!" As if he half expected a sneer on her lips. But they were smiling rye-sherry fondly at him and he thought he had nobody else but her. Maybe he could even trust her.... He laughed bitterly, the enforcer laughed for who was kidding who? He could trust her only because he'd never told her a damn thing. Yep, he'd been smart, he'd used the old bean—Christ, let the Spotter croak! Smart, the one guy with the brains to keep his mouth shut with a dame. Smart, and ended up an errand boy anyway just like Georgie. He muttered. "What good's it done me? What's it all mean? The hell with it! You're better than any of these God damn dames here. So what'd it get you? Suppose I marry you even, what good's that? I'm gonna marry you one of these days," he said. "Why the hell not?"

All about them men were whispering to their mistresses, on the dance floor men were dancing with other men's wives, with only a down-beat enforcer promising marriage to the steady girl friend.

She was drunk, but not drunk enough to believe him, just drunk enough to remember hopes long since gone.

"You're not gonna cry, Sweetie?"

"Me, Joey?"

"You don't cry any more," he stated the fact. "You usta—aw!" he jerked his thumb at the laughing flushed women, "I could go out with one of 'em and you wouldn' cry, would you?"

"No, I wouldn't cry."

"No more cryin'!" he said as if it were a law he was decreeing in force from that minute on. "There's enuf misery. Now, looka, Sweetie. This, this cele-bratin'—You see, I hadda chance to be a big man down the waterfront. The Spotter, he killed it, see—"

"Joey, let's dance," she said. "We haven't danced a long time."

He stared at her smiling face and realized she didn't really care about his secrets. They'd been secrets too long. "Yeh, les dance," he said.

Out on the floor, he squeezed her close and they pushed out into the squeeze of other bodies while the music like hands made of sound nudged at his shoul-ders. He felt tired, he wondered what was happening to his castiron belly. Get-ting old, he mourned fleetingly while the drunks on the floor steadied him and the yellow and red and blue spotlights wove a basket of light holding him and all the dancers. He watched her yellow forehead change into purple, her face flickering in the colored lights like a face in a dream. "You're my girl," he said to reassure himself, and although she whispered "Yes" and pressed close to him, he still wasn't sure. A yammering drunk elbowed him and he muttered a curse and the jazz poured like the smoothest rye whiskey in the world as he danced with a stranger who didn't want to know his secrets. She just doesn't give a damn any more, he thought sadly.

"Yeh," he said. "Yeh, yeh—"

"What Joey?"

"Joey! Joey Case you mean. Classy huh?"

"It's a classy name—"

"What do you know! I'm jinxed—I could tell you but why should I?" he said and wished momentarily with all the fervor and innocence of a heartbroken drunk for a world where the best man could win with no Spotter calling the tune and no Office laying down the law....

When they left the Mocambo, cabbing back to their hotel, the newshawks were shouting the latest extra. This was another night when Hitler, the German Fuehrer had been squeezed out of the big black print by the Dutchman. That black print like funeral crepe was shaped into letters proclaiming the end of the Dutchman.

Enforcer Joey Case would read about it the next day.

"Why are you taking my picture?" The dying Dutchman yelled at the photographers crowded around the hospital bed. "You're going to kill me." And then he had stopped talking sense:

"Come on, open the soap duckets. The chimney sweeps. Talk to the sword: French Canadian bean soup. A boy has never wept or dashed a thousand krim...."

What did the dying Dutchman mean? The editorial writers wrote editorials, the psychoanalysts analyzed, the general public scratched its head over those crazy words. "A boy has never wept or dashed a thousand krim."

Language from worlds of dream—haunting Joey Case.

The Spotter opened his manila envelope and removed all the clippings and newspaper photos of Dutch Schultz. It was minutes before his scissors finished the job of destruction.

The death of Dutch Schultz, shot down with his two guards in a Newark saloon, was like a needle in the prosecuting arm of Thomas E. Dewey. He moved against Jimmy Hines, the Tammany politician whose name'd been linked not only with the Dutchman's but with the big boys in The Office. He moved against Lucky Luciano. Dewey wanted to get Lucky Luciano, not on an income tax charge, but on his rackets. And all over town, the word traveled: "The heat's on, Dewey's after Lucky!"

It was like saying, "It's the end of the world!" Here the protection had been gold-plated, with the cops taken care of, from the flatfoot pounding his beat right on up to the inspector in his cop-chauffeured car. The Office had helped the man in the blue uniform take care of his old age and the man in the magistrate's gown take care of the old-age problems of his grandchildren. Law and justice maybe had been blindfolded, but the bandages were made of folding money, guaranteed to soothe the most sensitive of eyes.

"The heat's on!" the word traveled. "Dewey's after Lucky Luciano!"

When the little mobsters spoke the name of a man like Lucky Luciano, they sounded exactly like government clerks speaking the names of cabinet members.

Lucky Luciano! He was one of the big men in The Office, he had organized prostitution into a million dollar racket. Now, with Dewey serving subpoenas all over town, casting a huge net into the underworld, the racket buster was certain to catch, among the fishy madames and pimpy eels and miscellaneous poolroom sharks, some singing stool pigeons.

"The heat's on!"

"The heat's on!"

Another word was being passed around too, a private word from Charley Valinchi to his troops of enforcers. "Anybody we think'll sing to Dewey we get rid of...."

Joey couldn't believe it, but after all there were plenty of guys who looked like the Bug. So he'd drawn a guy who could've been the Bug's twin brother.

Before him the street stretched, empty and dark as a tunnel, a street of warehouses and boarded-up tenements, the lights few and far between even in the tenements where people lived. Or were there people high up in the stone-like sheets hanging from that low and stony sky? Under his feet, he felt cobblestones like the cobblestoned streets of his boyhood. He realized he was walking in the middle of the gutter. Why? All because the guy was like the Bug and might jump out at him from one of those boarded-up doorways? The Bug? The Bug's double? Okay, call the bastard Bug Number Two. Tailed him once and he'd tail him twice, only where was the bastard and why did he have to come to this street? A now-you-see-him, a now-you-don't kind of a guy. Where was he hiding? He felt fear, its foul and filthy mouth sucking at him so that he was bone-dry, with not a drop of blood left in his body, not a drop of sweat. Fear forced him to pull his gun. And—"No-Gun Joey..." a voice called mockingly from a doorway. "No-Gun Joey, the enforcer..." it called safely from its doorway. He stood paralyzed in the middle of the gutter, listening to that mocking voice that yet sounded lonely, as lonely as the street. Run, his heart clapped, but he couldn't for the voice was talking again and almost he could believe the street was talking and not a human being. "What you enforcin' anyway?..." it hissed, mocking and lonely and sad. "What we wanna take pot shots at each other for? Why?"

Why?

Yeh, why? For what? For who?

Complete agreement was in his heart when the gun exploded. Not his gun, the other gun. He screamed inside of himself, hurled out of the gutter. Images of shooting gallery ducks floated along the grooves of consciousness. He flattened against a wall, trembling and grinning like a maniac at the shooting gallery ducks, the sitting ducks in his mind. He could feel that grin on his lips like a living thing, separate from himself: the grin of a lifetime. A grin of: *you got to be smart*. Oh, he was smart, so smart he'd almost gotten it that time. Took Bug Number Two to trick him. A now-you-see-him, now-you-don't. The bastard wasn't human. For a bastard like that you needed luck.

"Hey, Joey. No-Gun Joey..." the voice called while out of the high black walls, heads were calling too—had those heads always been there?—"what you enforcin' anyway?"

Another bullet exploded and, crouching, he rushed towards the doorway.

Luck, he prayed with tears in his eyes. Hesitating before plunging into the doorway of the gun. The shaking fingers of his left hand made the sign of luck, the cross, and he raced inside. Feeling as if he had dived down a chute head first, down a hole, a pit, and glimpsed, sensed, for it was too dark to see, a darkness running from him. He shot at it, controling himself to keep from emptying his gun. Missed! for the darkness still ran. A door opened, but it wasn't a door but another hole, a pit toward which he was sinking. Against it, Bug Number Two was silhouetted, a shape of the pit, inhuman, fleshless. He pulled his trigger a second time, frantically pursuing, frantically counting his expended bullets. Two of his, two of mine, two of his, two of mine, I'm gonna die this time.... Jingles of childhood lifted in a pandemonium of lost words and blurred rhymes.

And where was Bug Number Two? There was only the empty dark doorway, shining now, a square of darkness, steadily shining. Somewhere there was a moon, he thought with a sense of revelation, blinking at that shining doorway, a square moon leading where.... He peered out across the yard at the shadowy fire-escapes of a factory. White stars powdered the blackest sky he had ever seen and high in the sky, the moon. Its huge yellow-white eye winked at him in warning. He stayed inside the door, ready to wait all night, while behind him the hallway breathed with a black breath, black as the barrel of a gun, with himself the bullet, himself the trigger, himself the target.

Or was the target the now-you-see-him hopped up out of dark corners and legging it for the fire-escapes? He pulled his trigger, ran out into the backyard, up the fire-escapes, no longer sure who was chasing who. Why hadn't he stayed inside?

Why?

All he knew was that the standing still had changed into a wild and reckless climbing, the fire-escapes' iron ladders lifting into the sky. He fired again, cursed, sobbing at his own recklessness. One, two, three, four, one two three four, four of his bullets, against two from Bug Number Two....

Oh, God, he thought. Oh, God, he prayed and, hoarding the two bullets left, he climbed. Through the bars of the fire-escapes he saw him, through iron bars, and for all his chasing he felt himself locked inside some iron place he would never escape. For this wasn't Bug Number One, this was Bug Number Two, and he'd reach the top first with bullets galore to pour into him as he came over the edge. And he climbed and he climbed to the hole in the world the sky had become, a hole with a yellow-white eye staring at him. The eye of Bug Number Two.... Climbed to the top landing and the now-you-see-him, now-you-don't fired at him. Fired, missed, fired, missed. And he fired at it, and whatever it was, human being or ghost, it dropped. He laughed, he was so happy. He walked to it, turned it over, and it said: "No-Gun Joey..." And it said: "What you enforcin anyway?"

He answered. "Bug, I didn't wanna—"

And it said: "Mama, mama...." And it said: "A boy has never wept or dashed a thousand krim. Mama, mama...."

Joey choked as if he himself lay on that roof dying, and sobbing he woke up from the dream.

Georgie awoke with the alarm clock, calmly he reached out his hairy thick arm to shut it off. Nightmares let Georgie alone when he slept. The alarm clock'd been set for 2 A.M. because at 3 A.M. sharp he was meeting Joey and Pete Bowers for a little job. Georgie yawned and again that hairy arm of his coiled out in the darkness like a snake to the end table alongside the bed. He switched on the lamp. Light shone on Georgie and the woman in bed with him. She was sound asleep. A nice pott, thought Georgie. They were all potts to Georgie. Calling them potts gave him a good feeling. Just as he called real havana cigars, stinkerenos, steak dinners, grub, and sixty dollar new suits, glad-rags.

Maybe it was a depression on for the jerks, but for Georgie Connelly, in the enforcing business years now, the boom was still on. It was a pretty new business and he'd gotten in on the ground floor.

He patted the woman. She didn't stir. He reached for a strand of her hair, and gently at first with the gentlest of pressures, he began to pull.

A cry broke from the woman's throat, her eyes opened, and Georgie plunged his hand deep into her hair and tugged hard.

"Georgie!" she cried in pain and fright.

"Aw," he grinned foolishly and slowly, as if his fingers hated to let go, he released his hold. "Forget it, all I wanted was to say so long."

"Some way to say so long. You getting nuts or something," she mustered the courage to scold him.

"I'm not going to stand all your nutty stuff, Georgie. What'd you wake me up for anyway?"

Georgie laughed and put his hand down on her breast. He laughed louder....

He was only ten minutes late when he got to the meeting place, but Joey and Pete'd gone on without him. He cursed the two of them and walked to the nearest bar.

A few weeks later Georgie got himself so drunk he felt he just had to talk to the Spotter. And right away. Laughing like a loon, he blew into the front office of the Elwood Realty. "I wanna see the Spotter! Tell'm Georgie's here." The girl at the phone remembered him. "Mr. Boyle is tied up," she said. "What can I do for you?"

"Tell'm Georgie's here!" Georgie shouted. He had an unbuttoned look about him that autumn morning, top coat, jacket, vest, all open, the knot of his necktie slipped an inch from his collar.

"Mr. Boyle's tied up. What can I do for you?"

"What can you do for me, hahahahaha," Georgie laughed, and gave her the high high-sign, slapping his left hand down on the bicep of his right arm as he jerked his right forearm up.

She didn't flinch or blush and Georgie turned to the two men quietly waiting in the front office like a comedian to his audience. "What can a pott do for a guy? Should I tell her?" They stared through Georgie as if he were a sheet of glass and he realized he wasn't going to get much of a hand out of this crowd. "Whatsa matter?" he challenged them.

They were silent but their silence spoke for them. A drunk had no right barging into the Elwood Realty—in offices a guy had to behave himself. They knew how, so why the hell couldn't he. One of them, the one with the eyes out of an eye dropper, had a connection with the Cunard line; he supervised the importing of narcotics. The other was a numbers book with eyes like boiled onions.

"Shut up!" Georgie shouted at them. He pointed a bullying finger at the smaller of the two. "O.K., you!"

"That girl's only tryin' to do her duty," Eyedropper Eyes answered.

"Tryin' to do her doo-ty," Georgie repeated as if he'd worked hard memorizing this particular line. "She's a dope!"

"Mac, that's no kinda talk," was the reply. The girl had flushed and he glanced at her sympathetically. Nobody had a right saying things like that in an office.

Georgie shook that pointing finger of his at him. "Shut up, shrimp, or I'll mobilize yuh! Who the hell d'yuh think y'are. Me and Boyle—" He crossed his middle finger over the pointer finger. "We're like this, thas how we are. Hey, pott!" he said to the girl. "Tell Spotter I'm here."

"Mr. Boyle's tied up—"

Georgie rushed through the door of the front office, snapping his fingers at the girl protesting behind him.

The Spotter caught the breeze of the door of his private office as it opened and shut with a bang, but if it bothered him, he showed no sign, smiling at his visitor. Georgie jabbed his pointer finger behind him, in the general direction of the front office. "Tried to high-hat me, Spotter! Lousy pott. Tied up, she says, the pott—"

"Sit down, Georgie."

Georgie plunked himself into a chair, grinning foolishly and fondly at the man in the dark gray suit behind the shining desk. "Lousy pott," he complained.

"Been on a bat, Georgie?"

Georgie grinned like a school kid being scolded by a teacher and again recalled his grievances against the office girl. "Dumb pott! I says, 'You tell Spotter I'm here. Spotter and me're like this.'" He crossed his middle and pointer fingers, demonstrating.

"Georgie, I'm Mister Boyle here—"

"Yeh," Georgie agreed heartily. "Gotta remember that."

"It's all right with your pals to call me Spotter. Sure, why not? Sure. Why shouldn't you tell your pals all about me, how we come up together. It's no secret. We was in the Badgers together, wasn't we, Georgie? All through prohibition together."

Georgie smiled. The Spotter, glancing at the drunken lush, had a notion the office was crowded—with his own private collection of ghosts.

The ghost of his old partner, Tom Quinn, the ghost of John Terry, the living ghost of Dewey.... The ghost of Dutch Schultz squeezed inside, too. For The Office'd cut the Spotter and Frank Fannelli in for a slice of the Dutchman's numbers empire. The Dutchman, dead, was an asset of Elwood Realty as he'd never been alive. True, the name Dutch Schultz was not listed on the books of the corporation. And the corporation's attorney, Robert McKenzie of the law firm of McKenzie and Smith in which Magistrate Farber had an interest, would have testified under oath that there were no entries under the heading of murder.

There were only ghosts.

The Spotter wiped his sweaty palms on the cloth of his trousers. This Georgie was a headache. The son-of-a-bitch'd be breaking into Dewey's office next. Once they started going soft there was no limit. "Georgie, you have a drink on me, Georgie. That's what you do, and one of these days we'll get together and have a lil talk about the old days and what we done together, okay Georgie?"

"You said it, Spotter," Georgie smiled. So did Mr. Boyle.

The smile stayed on the Spotter's lips as Georgie lurched through the door. A smile as false as an artificial flower.

The Spotter phoned Charley Valinchi and Charley turned the job over to the one guy who could take care of it with the least noise: Georgie's pal, Joey Case.

That Georgie'd gotten just a little too soft and with Dewey hitting on all sixteen cylinders, there was no use taking chances. On nobody.

Georgie Connelly was no better than a mobster by name of Pretty Amberg who'd been burned to death in his own car because the feeling'd gotten around that Pretty couldn't be trusted a hundred percent any more. With the heat on, ninety-nine percent wasn't good enough. No better than a mobster by name of William Gage who'd been stabbed to death and dumped into Swan Lake in the Catskills, a slot machine pedestal anchored to his feet. No better than an honest Brooklyn clothing trucker by name of Joseph Rosen who'd been pumped full of bullets because he was about to be questioned by Dewey on Lepke's labor rackets and Lepke was a guy who happened to be Lucky Luciano's friend. Why should Georgie get special treatment?

Pete Bowers didn't look like an enforcer on a job. Rather he was wearing the face of a goodtime Charley as he suggested to Georgie they'd had enough to drink and how about a piece of tail? He led that happy drunk to a joint down near the river where Georgie cornered the knock-kneed pimp in the blue sweater and announced that he wanted the best pott in the place.

It was a four-room two-dame flat, and the girls waiting together in one of the bedrooms for sweet company's sake heard the racket in the kitchen and wished they didn't have to work on their day off. Yes, it was their day off and a fat lot of good it was doing them.

Georgie wheeled around to wave a drunken finger under Pete's nose. "Take it easy," Pete urged him, wondering when the hell Joey'd show up with the damn car. "Take it easy, Georgie, will you?" The big guy only laughed, he circled his heavy arm around Pete's shoulders, leaning hard on his whorehouse buddy, and hollered at the pimp. "What yuh hangin' 'round for, monkey? I want the best pott—"

"Yeh, yeh, but like your friend says, 'Take it easy.'"

"Pete, you gonna let this monkey...."

The girls in the bedroom had heard other riproaring boozehounds before. They'd heard about every kind of male animal there was, yipping and yacking and yelling, and they were deaf as the keepers in a zoo are deaf, and the only voice they really listened to was that of the man in the blue sweater: the chief keeper.

Pete winked at the pimp who said, "C'mon, big boy. See 'em yourself and take your pick." When he returned to the kitchen he said, "That big gorilla!"

Pete glanced at his wristwatch. It was 11:27. Joey was exactly twenty-seven minutes late. Pete lit a cigarette like a man waiting for a train. The pimp sighed and wished to God he could be left in peace without all this damn funny business thrown his way these last few months. And this was a Tuesday night, too, the night he wasn't open for customers. On a man's night off, he shouldn't be working.

Downstairs in the street, a car had just parked. "You need me?" the driver asked Joey.

"No." Joey hurried down the sidewalk. A lamppost cast its long shadow ahead of him and he felt as if he were on one of the streets of his dreams. How dark this street was, with its abandoned warehouses and boarded-up tenements, a November street, the air raw and cold in his lungs. He heard his lonely footsteps on the broken slate sidewalks. Heard the cars speeding by on the elevated West Side highway bordering the river: moving yellow beads on a string suspended against the sky. He had an impulse to turn around and look at those cars. God only knew why. There was no help there, no answer, no meaning. It was another world, on wheels, and he was on foot, on this street that could've been a dream street but wasn't—oh God, if he were only dreaming! He was late for this job. Job? Job, yes! he thought fiercely. That's all it was, a job, still another job. And if the job's name was Georgie Connelly, so what. It wasn't the old Georgie he'd known anyhow.

No, it wasn't the Georgie he'd hoboed with and it certainly wasn't the Georgie who'd been a 1-4-All. This was a Georgie drinking like a fish and if Dewey picked him up, a Georgie who might start singing. Like the time when Georgie'd squealed on him to the Spotter....

Still, the face of the old Georgie kept dropping out of his heart like old photos out of a forgotten box put away long ago, and really there shouldn't have been anything in it. He had emptied it over the years, nailed it shut and hung a padlock on it twice as heavy as those used by the feds in the prohibition days. Or so he would have guessed.

Georgie....

He turned into the doorway of the tenement where Pete and Georgie'd come before him and he thought: No ice picks for Georgie, no picture wire for Georgie, none of that for Georgie. They'd ride Georgie out of town and put a bullet in his head. They'd give him the fastest of fast shuffles.

But when Joey and Pete, with Georgie between them came down into the street again, Joey had to grit his jaws to keep himself under control. For Georgie, the happy drunk was now the happy lover, laughing as he described the girl he'd just had. "Joey, you shoulda see'd her. Okay and I mean okay! Anytime you say, you and me, we take her out, okay Joey?"

No, this was no street in a dream. And the Georgie hooking one arm around Joey's shoulders and the other around Pete's was no dream Georgie either. Then why did the street seem to be rushing at him on wheels like the cars up on the West Side highway? A street like some shadowy express pounding through the tunnels of memory, with all the streets he'd ever walked on with Georgie coupled up one behind the other like endless freights.... Why did he have to think of Thirty-Seventh Street? Twenty-Fourth Street? For Christ sake why'd he have to remember? For Christ sake, he was just an enforcer and who he enforced wasn't his God damn business. Just an errand boy jumping when Charley Valinchi said jump! For Christ sake, for Christ sake, for Christ sake.... He was no Dutch Schultz to buck The Office and what'd it got the Dutchman anyway? *A boy has never wept or dashed a thousand krim....* Those last mystical and terrible words of the dying Dutchman streaked across his consciousness and he heard himself saying when they came to the waiting car, his heart moving his lips—what there was left of his heart: "I'll take care-a Georgie myself— you guys beat it. Beat it!"

"Joey, what'll the boss say?" Pete whispered in his ear. "Joey—" the driver protested.

"Beat it!" he heard himself saying, his voice and their voices like voices in a dream. "Beat it I said!"

The next hour was no hour made of real minutes ticking off on his wristwatch, but like time in a dream. Timeless. He parked the car in a street that could've been in another city, marched Georgie into a Tenth Avenue coffee pot—and the avenue seemed no avenue he'd ever known, the coffee pot sliding into vision like another scene in a nightmare where the counterman maybe was an enemy and the few customers maybe hidden devils. He ordered black coffee, aspirins, for Georgie, his eyes constantly shifting to the door. Who'd expect to trail him here? Pete Bowers? The driver of the car? Charley Valinchi? The Spotter? Or maybe the dying Dutchman with a hole in his side, babbling of a thousand krim. Was Georgie talking? Or was he imagining that Georgie was talking? Maybe Georgie was dead and he was dead, only they didn't know it yet? Then why drag Georgie into the coffee pot toilet? Why open the faucets at the sink? A white sink once but now coated with the gray dirt of forgotten hands. "What's the big idear?" he heard Georgie saying and heard himself answering in a voice of fear and prayer and defiance. "You gotta sober up Georgie."

"What for?"

He leaned closer and said. "They were takin' you for a ride tonight's what for." And knew now it was no dream, for drunk as Georgie was, this bit of news hit home like the point of an ice pick. "The Spotter put the mark on you, Georgie! You dumb sonofabitch, I warned you not to keep pesterin' him."

Water poured in the sink, the walls were painted blue and scribbled with the pencils of idlers and drunks, and Joey, staring into Georgie's face, knew it was no dream. For Georgie's eyes seemed to be shouting: Me! *A mark on me!* Endless *Me's!* like soap bubbles from a pipe seemed to be bubbling up from Georgie's clenched lips. *Me! Me!...*

"Georgie," he heard himself saying and the sensation of dream closed in again like moving walls, all the walls painted blue. For what right did he have to be doing what he was doing? A job was a job, an order an order, and The Office was never wrong. He must be goofed-up to be doing what he was doing. Who the hell was he to fight Them. "Georgie, you gotta blow outa town! You're marked! Christ, George, *why'd* you have to pester the Spotter?"

Why? There was no answer to that. And if there was, it didn't mean a damn any more. "Soak your friggen head!" he ordered. "We can't stay here a whole friggen night!"

He watched Georgie lower his big head and splash his black hair and face. I'm nuts, Joey thought. Goofed-up. He pulled out his wallet, he counted forty-three bucks and shoved the wallet back into his top coat pocket. "Got any dough?" he asked Georgie.

"Dunno," Georgie spluttered and wet-handed he dug his wallet out of his rear pocket. Joey snatched it from him, counted twelve bucks.

"Cheap bastard!" Joey cursed like a madman for a second. Oh God, he mourned; I'm doing all this for what? For a no-good cheap bastard.... As if that were the final straw.

When they blew out of the coffee pot, Georgie had forty-two of Joey's bucks in his wallet plus his own twelve. And the transference of the money, like everything else tonight was out of a dream. For when Joey had returned

Georgie's wallet with the forty-two in new money, Georgie'd dropped it to the floor. Into a puddle of water under the sink. Had retrieved it, had dried it on a wad of toilet paper. And only then had Georgie come alive to what was going on tonight, his teeth chattering as if that wet wallet had plunged him into an icy shower. "I can't believe it, Joey," he'd mumbled. "I can't believe it."

"Better believe it! You're takin' the train to Philly, Georgie." Georgie had sobbed like a baby and Joey'd socked him on the shoulder with all his might, "Stop that, stop that! Philly! Get that! Don't show your face again! You stay in Philly! Get that! Don't show your face again! Stay there! You come back I'm good as dead. That Pete bastid was kinda suspicious before. Christ!"

Who had been talking so smart about Philly? Himself? Couldn't be. A smart guy wouldn't go around hiding in stinking toilets with a sonofabitch marked lousy.

Christ, Joey thought as they got into the car. Christ, he thought as he drove. Was Georgie sitting next to him? Or was the guy next to him Petey? Oh, Christ, what was he letting himself in for?

But like a dream-man magnetized to the wheel, he couldn't do anything but drive, the most perfect driver in the whole nighttime town—red light you stop! green light you go! Clutch and brake for a complete stop, first gear, second gear, third gear.... And the nighttime town, all of it, reddish sky, people on the sidewalks, lights, all of it, fitted snug and cozy inside the Pennsylvania Railroad Station where under a ceiling a mile above their heads, he led Georgie to the ticket windows, bought a one-way to Philly, hurried to the gates. There was a red and gold sign: *Newark, Princeton Junction, Trenton, Philadelphia* and there were people all around them but none of them were Petey, for Joey searched and the only guy to give him the creeps was a skinny guy in a black hat but it wasn't the Spotter, no it wasn't the Spotter, at least not yet, and the waiting people picked up their bags and Joey pushed at Georgie's shoulder. "You don't wanna miss your train," he heard himself saying. "Remember, Georgie, keep outa Noo Yawk, Georgie!" And in that moment of leaving and departure, dream-like as such moments always are, as if the surging crowd were rushing away from all that they'd ever known, towards some pearly gate, Georgie hugged Joey for a second and that renegade enforcer banged big Georgie on the back in farewell with a gladness he hadn't known in years. "Damn 'em, Georgie! Damn 'em!" Joey said.

Moving with the crowd smaller, smaller, Georgie changed into the old Georgie of their kid days.... And the gates closed.

What'd happened? It was hard to believe. Lead-footed he walked into the Waiting Room, sat down on one of the long endless dark brown benches. The waiting room was full of faces he'd never seen before and would never see again. Men and women waiting in a place where all leavings and departures seemed an illusion, waiting like prisoners for dreamlike trains that would never come....

What he was waiting for? Where was he going? He told himself he had to think. Think? That was a hot one. All the thinking'd been done when he'd put Georgie on the express to Philly. Joey sat there and the silence of waiting which is like the hush in the hours after midnight sounded in his ears. You better think, he advised himself humbly. Think what? Think of the car you parked. What for? Not a chance in a million Pete'd see it. Pete! Pete's phoned Charley Valinchi by now sure as fate, and Charley'd be phoning him, and if Charley didn't believe him he could kiss his life good-bye.

Christ! What'd he done tonight? What was to stop Georgie from getting soused in Philly and coming back on the next train. Nothing. Forty-two and twelve was only fifty-four bucks. Not much. Enough for a drunk, a dame. That sonofabitch might do anything, come back, run to the Spotter. Joey thought: I deserve it. I got it coming. They'll send Georgie after me....

And in that waiting room where people were dozing, sitting with drooping eyelids, Joey's eyelids stretched tautly open on an imaginary locked door. It swung wide and he saw Georgie with an ice pick in his hands.... And if not Georgie, Pete. Somebody. He lit a cigarette and the smoke he blew out into the stale dead smoke of the waiting room felt like the last breath of life in his lungs. No use kidding himself. He'd bucked The Office. His life wasn't worth a lead cent. He'd bucked The Office. Nobody could get away with that. Nobody. Not even the Dutchman with his mob and bodyguards and politicians and lawyers.

The loudspeakers announced a train. Some of the people in the waiting room picked up their valises and bundles, stumbling towards the gates like sleepwalkers. While in Joey's mind a private train dispatcher of his own began to bawl out private destinations: YOU OUGHTA GO TO PHILLY TOO.... IF GEORGIE COMES BACK YOU'RE DONE... PHILLY WHILE YOU GOT THE CHANCE... GO TO PHILLY... GO TO DEWEY....

He started as if some stool pigeon'd shouted his name out behind him. I'm getting soft in the brain, he thought frantically. I'm getting soft if I can think of that for a single second. Even here, alone, with myself.

He looked at his wrist watch. It was 1:19. As if the neat regular face of his watch with its twelve eyes, each exactly the same distance from the other, had calmed him, he thought: Joey, no sense working yourself up. Georgie's on his way to Philly. He won't come back. Not tonight anyway. So what you do is go back to the hotel and see if Charley's phoned. And if he did, you get your answer pat. You got rid of Georgie, you dumped him in the bushes.

Bushes?... He grinned wildly. What bushes? The bushes in Central Park, the bushes up near Albany, the bushes in Sullivan, no, Solomon County, phone Pete Bowers and ask him if it's okay to call it Sullivan. Sullivan, Solomon, Sullivan, Solomon, his head jingled off, Sullivan, Solomon....

He went into the Men's Room. The walls were tiled white, and he thought of the blue walls where he'd brought Georgie, and maybe he ought to soak his head in the sink too, only who'd put him on the train to Philly, who'd give him forty-two bucks in cash? The Spotter for old time's sake? The Spotter? Nah! Sooner get it from the Dutchman.... Joey washed his hands and there in the mirror, staring at him, was the blonde-haired gray-eyed mug of a guy he'd known pretty well. Joey Case, No-Gun Joey, the toughest guy in town, the toughest guy in the world. That was him all right, all right. Bucking The Office'd given him the title hands down. The Dutchman wasn't the only one, no, sir, not the only one. Both of them crazier than a bat. Ask Pete Bowers. "Pete Bowers," he said aloud, his lips barely moving, speaking as convicts do, under the eyes of their guards.

His head jerked around abruptly as if somebody'd come through the door to stand at his elbow, but there was no one. Still he felt eyes on him. Pete's eyes and the Spotter's who'd marked Georgie and by so doing marked him, and Charley Valinchi's eyes. The X-ray eyes of The Office that could see clear across the town, see through all the white walls and all the blue walls, see through the bone of his skull, see the creepy fears curling like worms inside his brain.

You bastard, he cursed himself. Stop your panic. You gotta think. Christ sake, you gotta think.

And he thought of Dewey.

Suddenly he was calm, calmed by the enormity of this idea. He walked up the flight of stairs—he had a sensation that all night long he'd been climbing one huge flight after another—and he pitied himself who was so ground-down that he could think, even for a second, of turning rat.

Time? There was no time. There was a cup of coffee on the counter of a railroad station restaurant. There were invisible tracks, criss-crossing, joining the late-hour coffee drinkers. There was himself, his mind filled with the lucidity of leavetaking as if soon he would be taking a train, destination unknown, and could look back at the township he'd built with the years of his life.

Call it Joey Case. A township different from the township of the next man's life, only as one fingerprint is different from the next.

This guy Joey Case'd sure got himself in a spot, he thought. Joey Case, Joey Kasow, No-Gun Joey, No-Jew Joey. Was he a Jew? More errand boy than Jew. A guy *was* what he was deep down. Suppose a guy was nothing deep down? Then what was he? Nothing! A nothing guy, neither hebe or mick. All his life he'd wanted to be one damn thing or another. Wanted to be tough, wanted to be smart, wanted to stand on his own two legs. Be independent. Had his chance with Local 23, but the Spotter, he killed it. The Spotter.... Who else but the Spotter, always the Spotter. Railroading him into The Office, putting him on the spot. Christ, God, he'd gotten Georgie off. How was he getting himself off? *Who* was he getting off though? That was the big question. Joey Case? Joey Kasow?

Joey's mind ran like a driverless car against the twin walls of his double self:

Joey Case versus Joey Kasow. And he thought as if he had all the time in the world, not of himself, but of Dutch Schultz whose name'd been Arthur Pflegenheimer when he'd been a boy. Dutch Schultz.... *A boy has never wept or dashed a thousand krim.* Who was the boy who'd never wept, Joey wondered. Where was that boy? Where was Arthur Pflegenheimer, where was Joey Kasow? He remembered how a few days after the Dutchman's death he'd picked up a dictionary and looked up the word, *krim*.... There was no word, *krim*. The nearest thing to it was kran—a Persian coin; kremlin—a Russian fortress; Kriemhild—the wife of Siegfried killed by his own brother, avenged by his wife; and kris—a Malay dagger. Funny, he had brooded how all the close words were money or forts or daggers or this Dutchie Kriemhild who'd gotten even for her husband's murder. Murder and money, daggers and forts—wasn't that what the whole God damn works was about, he asked himself now. With The Office always laying down the law to every poor sonofabitch who tried to buck it?

Joey finished his coffee. It was time to go. The train was coming in. It'd been long overdue. In fact it was God damn late.

He unlocked the door of his room at the Hotel Delmore, switched on the light and stared at Sadie sleeping in the bed. He'd wake her and find out if Charley'd called. But first he better calm down, he thought, put on that old pokerface. He closed his eyes, he pressed his two forefingers against his eyeballs. He opened his eyes again and thought as if it were a brand-new thought: she's got real red hair.

He rubbed at his jaws, he massaged his cheeks, and bit by bit worked control over every separate feature. He felt his jaws clinching hard, he was aware of his tight lips, their edges meeting like two strips of leather. No more cry-babying around, he thought with a profound and lonely pride in himself who'd gotten up the guts to buck Them.

He crossed the room to the bed, he shook her naked shoulder and when she was sleepily awake, he lit a cigarette and put it between her lips. "Take a big puff, Sweetie. Gotta talk to you."

Sleepily, she inhaled. "Now, Joey?"

"Now. Anyone phone me?"

"Yes."

"Who?"

"The one who always calls you, Joey."

"What'd he want?"

"Said you should see him tomorrow. Tomorrow at eleven, yes. Is something wrong?"

"Yeh, something's wrong."

She bolted upright and he glanced at her, but the face he saw was Charley Valinchi's.... Christ, here he was panicking himself again. If Charley really thought he'd let Georgie off the hook, they wouldn't be waiting until eleven the next morning. They'd be waiting downstairs in the lobby. "I gotta good record!" he said with a grim self-mockery. "They're givin' me the benefit of the doubt."

"Joey, I don't understand."

He sat down on a chair near the dresser.

"I'm blowin' out of town tomorrer," he said slowly. "I'm playin' it safe. Even I convince 'em, suppose Georgie shows up to queer me? I'm playin' it safe. No other way. Safe!" And a spasm of laughter broke from his lips.

Her eyes were staring with a clear and unmistakable fear. "What is it, Joey?" she cried. "Tell me." He looked at this redhead in the filmy nightgown, at her rounded plump arms, wondering how he was going to tell her he was blowing out for good. How? He looked at her and she was like a stranger. But she was all he had. And if he'd lost her, their life together a constant losing, losing her again and again with each kept woman, losing her when she started hitting the bottle, losing her in spades twice over and for keeps when she started hitting the bottle alone, she was still all he had.

A frightened hefty redhead sitting on a bed who liked her bottle. And a scared enforcer about to take a run-out powder. Christ, that was the end of it, he thought. Already she seemed far away from him. As if they were both looking at each other from the opposite ends of an endless corridor, rushing away as they looked, turning for a last look, rushing, turning, spinning faster and faster like trick dancers, all backs of heads, without true faces. Only the faces of loss.

"Remember Georgie?" he said. "The guy I lived with down on Twenny-Fourth? The big guy?"

She nodded and before he spoke again he thought why shouldn't she remember Georgie. She'd come to the room on Twenty-Fourth when her old man'd kicked her out....

"I was ordered to kill him tonight, I let'm go—"

"Kill?" she said dumbly as if the word were a harmless one.

"I'm a killer, that's my job," he said simply. "I'm tellin' you for your own pertection— Stop that!" he warned her. He jumped from the chair, grabbed her by the shoulders shaking her fiercely as if he'd knock the tears out of her eyes. "Stop! Christ, there's no time for that!"

He let her go. "You gotta know the truth, for your own pertection— See! I'm blowin' out and I can't take you with me and you can't stay here. They're liable to come for you. See—"

But her wet eyes saw nothing—only the jumping jack of a *killer* he'd released in the room out of its long hiding place in his heart.

He went to the dresser, but the sherry bottle there wasn't what he wanted. In the closet he picked up a half-empty quart of rye, poured five, six inches into a water glass. "Drink this!"

"No," she wept.

"Drink this, you God damn wino! You gotta lissen t'night like you never listened. Drink it! Drink it, I say!"

She obeyed him. He lit a cigarette and passed it to her. "Sweetie, you gotta lissen," he pleaded with her. "For your own good. Who the hell wants to be tough? Lissen, for God's sake," he pleaded. "All you know about me's a pack of lies," he said swiftly. "Remember the night we went to the Mocambo? I thought they were sendin' me after the Dutchman. Dutch Schultz! Remember how jittery I was? The phones I made? See—they got guys like me, the enforcers. They got their law like the coppers got their law, but I couldn't kill Georgie. Not Georgie. That's why I'm in trouble. See! You don't do what they order, and you're good as dead. That's why I gotta blow—you'll have to go somewhere, too. I haven't got it all clear in my head what's the best thing to do—Christ, I could use a drink myself. Aw, I'm half-shot without it! What was I sayin'? Oh, yeah! Anybody come see you, askin' questions, you don't know nothin'. Understand? You don't know nothin'! I never told you a damn thing and that's the God's own truth! Not 'til tonight and you can forget tonight. Tonight don't count. It's just between you and me. Forget it! See! What's one night when there's a million I never told you a damn thing!" He rubbed his forehead. Something was all screwed up in what he was telling her. What? And what difference did it make? He gazed longingly at the whiskey bottle on the dresser. "Nah!" he said despairingly. "That's all I need. I'm half-shot without it. Bad, it's bad. I know too much on all of 'em. Charley Valinchi, the Spotter, the whole damn Office. They'd make it hot for you." He had a notion he was repeating himself like a man in a dream going through the same parrot song motions. And was she crying? Always crying, he thought. Crying her whole life....

He went to her, he patted her shoulder gently. "Sweetie, better stop alla that. You hadda know, your own pertection. Yeh. You check out inna mornin'. Before eleven. Get me! Before eleven. Got any money saved?"

"Got any money saved?" he asked again. Had he asked her this question before? "You check out before eleven." He hurried to the dresser, but he didn't even glance at the bottles of liquor there. He yanked a drawer open, lifted a pile of shirts and waved a long white fat envelope at her. "How much you got saved?"

She sobbed, but he pounded the question at her like a billyclub until she answered. "Three, four hundred—"

He shouted. "Drunk it all up, huh?"

"Joey," she whimpered as if begging him to forgive her for her drinking.

He pressed his hand against his aching forehead muttered. "Who the hell am I to blame you? I can't think straight. You check out, Sweetie. Yeh! I got about two grand in this envelope—I'll give you five of it. Check out 'til all these damn Dewey investigations blow over."

"Take me with you, Joey."

"Can't. I'm too hot." He counted out five hundred bucks from the white envelope—he had a sensation he'd been counting money all night long like a regular bank teller—and put it in the dresser. "This is for you! With what you got saved you can go to California or something. Don't tell anybody where you're goin'."

She wept. He thought: She don't know the half of it, she's punch drunk.

He went to the closet for a suitcase, set it on a chair. He tossed in shirts, shorts, neckties, a pair of shoes.

"Joey," she groaned and rushed from the bed to him. He held her tight, he kissed her wet cheeks and wet eyes and then like a sick child, he led her back to bed. "I'll send for you," he promised. "I'll write you in a couple months, Sweetie." She clung to him. "Sit down, Sweetie doll, sit down." He half-pushed her onto the bed and straightening he glanced at his wristwatch.

2:58....

It was a lie, he felt. Time was a lie, for the only true hour was the eleventh hour that would come ticking in the morning. As the only true room was the backroom behind the Napoli, and the only true face the face of Charley Valinchi or was it the face of the Spotter? Sometimes a guy couldn't be too sure....

11:00.... Would They give him a trial if he didn't show up? Try him for dropping out of sight? Put the mark on him? The little old black spot?

He felt dizzy, crazy colors ran behind his eyeballs, ice-pick reds and the roary steely grays of railroad stations. He glimpsed the blue walls of the toilet where he'd given Georgie forty-two bucks and the creamy walls of this bedroom where he'd left five hundred on the dresser. "Yeh," he said. "I better blow."

He finished packing, he shut the suitcase. "Sweetie, I'll write you. Remember, check out! Check out before eleven!"

She flung herself over on her face, weeping. He wanted to kiss her again, to touch her good-bye at least, but he was afraid that if he did he'd be taking her with him and that'd be plain suicide. A guy with a redhead, a dame, was ten times easier to catch up with than a guy alone. No, she was staying. Christ, there was a limit to the times he could let his heart punch a hole in his brain tonight. A limit! He looked at her once more and then he walked to the dresser. He seized the sherry and whiskey bottles, emptied them in the bathroom. He searched in the closet where she kept her supply. There were two unopened bottles and he put them, one into each of his topcoat pockets. "Sweetie," he called to her. "I took all the licker—I don't want you drinkin' and forgettin' to check out. Check out early, baby, for your own pertection...."

Did she hear him? Face downwards, she wept, her red hair glinting. Christ, she was punch drunk, he thought.

He hurried to the desk. "I'm writin' what you should do." He sat down, grabbed a pencil and a sheet of the hotel stationery.

"Sweetie, check out before eleven. Don't forget. Before eleven. Don't tell nobody where your going. Don't tell them your checking out. Just go. Goodbye. I love you Sadie.

Joey

Sadie.... He stared at her old name. It had written itself. The name of a long-ago summer when they had both been kids. He got up from the desk and placed the note on top of the five hundred. "I wrote you what you should do, Sadie," he said. "Get outa town early! Forget you ever saw me! Find yourself another guy, Sadie," he said, with love.

She lifted her face toward him now, her eyes swollen.

"Joey—"

"That's the truth! That's the truth and I'm tellin' you it 'cause I'm afraid— Good-bye. Sadie...."

He presented the two bottles of sherry to the elevator operator. "From Missus Case," he said.

Downstairs, he whistled a cab. "Penn Station," he said. Through the window he looked at the dark West Side Streets and felt alone and afraid as when he'd been a kid. Had a lifetime passed? Or had the dark street never run in a straight line, curving back, a circle, to where Jack the Ripper and the Bogeyman were waiting, waiting with judge Charley Valinchi and The Office and the Spotter. Curve, circle, circle, trap. Yes, all of these. But *They* hadn't bargained for Georgie escaping and *They* wouldn't like it when he didn't show up like he was supposed to.... Joey's heart quickened like when he'd said good-bye to Georgie at the train gate. Quickened in triumph over death, over destiny, over all the forces that had made and unmade him, over curve, circle, trap as he too traveled to his gate.

Again the Spotter opened that manila envelope of his and sorted out the collected newspaper clippings and photos of No-Gun Joey. Again the Spotter reached for his scissors and quiet as death, went to work.

THE END